Alvar the Kingmaker

Annie Whitehead

Published in 2016 by FeedARead.com Publishing

Copyright © The author as named on the book cover.

The author or authors assert their moral right under the Copyright, Designs and Patents Act, 1988, to be identified as the author or authors of this work.

All Rights reserved. No part of this publication may be reproduced, copied, stored in a retrieval system, or transmitted, in any form or by any means, without the prior written consent of the copyright holder, nor be otherwise circulated in any form of binding or cover other than that in which it is published and without a similar condition being imposed on the subsequent purchaser.

A CIP catalogue record for this title is available from the British Library.

Acknowledgements

I must begin by expressing my gratitude to Ann Williams. It was in her lectures, many years ago, that I first heard the name Ælfhere. He was the earl described as the 'mad blast' from Mercia, such was his unleashed fury at the injustices he suffered and the hypocrisy he encountered. I began to wonder what drove him to that point and knew that one day I would write his story. This is it, although I have modernised his name to Alvar. Ann was always on hand to answer my queries and give me feedback on the early drafts. My thanks must also go to Kate Hebblethwaite, formerly of Trinity, Dublin, who looked at the first completed manuscript and, again, gave me constructive criticism. I would also like to express my appreciation for the time that Karen Cunningham spent, not only reading an early draft but also producing from it a detailed synopsis to guide me through subsequent edits. My thanks also go to Adam Brunn for helping me with my Old English verbs, to Julia Brannan for her help and support, and to Ian, for his patience and technical assistance.

Glossary

Atheling: a potential heir to the throne, almost always of royal blood.
Burh: a fortified town.
Fyrd: Anglo-Saxon fighting force.
Heriot: war gear, given by the lord to his man, returnable upon death.
Hide: a unit of land, varying in acreage.
Hundred: an administrative area of approximately 100 hides; a sub-division of a shire.
Moot: meeting.
Oxgang: a small unit of land; an eighth of a hide.
Pallium: white vestment, worn by archbishops, presented by the pope.
Reeve: an administrative official.
Scop: poet.
Ship-soke: land granted by the king where military service includes provision of ships.
Thegn: a landholder and fighting man; also the title of those with specific duties on the royal estates.
Wergild: man-price; payment for a killing, according to rank.
Witan: the king's council, made up of nobles, bishops and leading thegns.
Witenagemot: the meeting of the witan.

In the West

The Fairchild, king of England
Alvar, earl of Mercia
Brock, his brother, steward to the king
Swytha (short for Alswytha), Brock's wife

Helmstan, Alvar's friend *
The Greybeard of Chester, Helmstan's lord
Káta, Helmstan's wife
Gytha, her servant *

In the East

The Half-king, powerful earl of East Anglia
Elwood of Ramsey, his eldest son
Lord Thetford, his second son
Lord Brandon, the youngest son
Alfreda, Elwood's wife
Edgar, the Half-king's foster-son, brother of the Fairchild.

The Churchmen

Dunstan, abbot of Glastonbury
Athelwold, abbot of Abingdon
The bishop of Winchester, father of Goodwin
Oswald, a monk at Fleury, Frankia

* denotes fictional characters. For original Anglo-Saxon names of non-fictional characters, see author's notes

In AD937 the old kingdoms ~ Northumbria in the northeast, East Anglia in the southeast, Wessex in the southwest and Mercia in the midlands ~ were united under the name of England by King Athelstan. But he and his successors died young, childless, or both. Athelstan was succeeded by his half-brother, who sired two children: Edwy and Edgar. He died when these boys were infants and his brother, their uncle, became king before he, too, died prematurely. In AD955 the throne passed to the eldest of those two boys, Edwy, who was foolish, but handsome, and known as the Fairchild. His brother, Edgar, meanwhile, had been fostered by a noble family in East Anglia. They were brothers, but they were strangers. And they were young, with plenty of men jostling to win power and to influence them …

Part I – Sāwung (The Sowing)

Chapter One AD956

Cheddar, Somerset

Dunstan knocked shoulders with a reveller but did not apologise. He carried on, muttering, towards the sound of the laughter. For the first time in his life he thought to curse his monk's habit, as it wrap-slapped against his ankles and would not let him run. Irritated to be sent on a mission easily left to a novice monk, he, the abbot of Glastonbury, would now spend all night on his knees, atoning for his prideful thought that such a mission was beneath him. Wrestling thus with his wounded dignity, he hurried on, ignoring the rumblings in his stomach that told him that he should still be at the feast table. As should the king, since it was, after all, his coronation feast. Abbot Dunstan lifted his robe and stepped around the party-goers who vomited and urinated where they stood when they should have hastened instead to the latrines. He stopped in the centre of the royal enclosure and released his hem, listening again. He had tried the stables and the cook-house as well as the two private chambers at the back of the great hall. This would not do, for he had neither the time nor the wish to chase around the whole manor. He thought for a moment, head still cocked to listen for clues. Perhaps he should look for a boy, not a king. After all, the newly crowned youth had performed the earlier ceremonies with barely concealed boredom. Dunstan had watched the youngster fidgeting and yawning openly as the nobles stepped up greedily to receive land-gifts and titles in return for their continued support, and had thought him not a fit successor to the old king. But there was no-one else who was throne-worthy. The king was young, yes, and so beautiful that he was known universally as the Fairchild, but his brother was younger still and had not even been brought up at the court. He, Dunstan, must be as a father to this young king, watch over him and guide him, and admonish him only in the interests of bringing him back to the righteous path. With that thought, he checked himself. His anger was misplaced, for the lad had much to learn. So, where would a sixteen-year-old boy think to go?

Over by the gate, the newly arrived entertainers were laughing and joking with the guards. The harper was sitting cross-legged in the gateway, tuning his instrument. The tumblers, all clothed in yellow tunics, gave a preview warm-up performance, turning somersaults and coming upright to catch the knives and balls thrown by their partners. Some of the noblemen wandered over, and heckled the jugglers, hoping that by doing so they would witness a stumble or slip. A serving-girl came from the bake-house carrying a basket piled high with loaves. One of the tumblers danced over to her, kissed her cheek and snatched three of the flatbreads. He juggled with them before throwing them one by one to his partner, who turned and threw them in turn to land back in the girl's basket. She, flushed but smiling, tucked her chin down and braved the throng to get to the gate. She side-stepped the harper, who looked up and blew her a kiss. Behind the great hall, the door of the women's guest bower opened and the ladies of the royal court stepped out into the sunshine. Many had eschewed the wimple veil for a more elaborate head-cloth, the swathes of material wound round their heads and secured with pins. Their brightly coloured silk kirtles brought a rainbow swirl to the centre of the courtyard as they walked across the enclosure towards the hall.

But the sound of laughter that had drawn Abbot

Dunstan in this direction was still rising from the queen's bower. Now that the others had moved away, he recognised the sound that was left behind as the twinkling, affected cadence of the king's wife's girlish giggling and he detected another, older, feminine chuckle. The chortling was punctuated by a loud shriek, followed by more giggling, then another less distinguishable sound. Dunstan held his breath, for he could not be sure that he had heard properly over the noise of the air whistling through his nostrils. No, there it was again; the low rumble of a youth's teasing voice, the words indistinct but the meaning made manifest by the elicited responses from the females. Dunstan sucked in his breath, disapproval pulling him up tall, with his chest puffed out and his shoulders back, while he tried to make sense of what he was hearing. *Too many voices.* He was a pious man, chaste and celibate, but he knew what went on between men and women. And yet this assault on his ears made no sense. What kind of sin was this? He shook his head as the unwholesome sounds continued. There was only one possibility and he put his hand to the door latch, holding it there while he prepared his admonition. He would point first to the queen and denounce her as a fornicating whore. Then he would establish the identity of the man who dared to cuckold a boy-king in his own house. He lifted the latch. He would have to be quick; scan the room, pinpoint the queen's whereabouts so that he could go straight to her, brand her with the fire of his words. They would be chastened; the whore-queen and her lover who dared to geld the king.

But it was worse than he could have dreamed, even when he sat in the darkest part of the night and tortured his spirit by imagining the worst excesses of sinful flesh which must be rooted out and destroyed, forcing his mind to consider every possible depravity and linger on it, the better to learn how to defeat it. What manner of abomination was this that went against all the teachings of Holy Scripture and all laws of nature? The abbot stared, fish-gaping, his tidy speech forgotten.

Dunstan looked from person to person once more, in the same order as when he had first burst into the room, praying that this second scrutiny would prove the first one false.

But no; the king's wife did not even have the shame to cover her naked flesh and she remained reclining, one arm behind her head, her breasts exposed, the other hand somewhere under the covers, no doubt reaching to touch her lover in some unspeakable manner. He, meanwhile had his back to her, and lay on his side, locked in an embrace with the woman on the other side of bed. At the sound of the door crashing open, he had turned and met Dunstan's gaze and he continued to stare now, as Dunstan's eyes confirmed the scene. It was the king. The king was in bed with his wife. And her mother.

The older woman frowned as if annoyed to be interrupted, while her daughter insouciantly pulled the covers up to her chest, writhing with her legs as she slid away, but not far, from the king. The king, meanwhile, continued to stare at the abbot.

Dunstan's hand was stuck on the open door, while his feet remained poised for either advancement or retreat. As the younger woman began a struggle against laughter, his pretty sermonising skills flew away into the yard, along with all notions of protocol. "S-Satan's b-beasts! By the Christ and all his s-saints, you will all b-burn in hell."

The words were out, and his fire of bravery was suddenly quenched. The sound of the drunks in the enclosure pressed on his ears as it marched to fill the void of the frozen silence before him. In a minute, one would meet the other. More voices and now, footsteps, brought nearer by curiosity. They must not converge. He turned towards the open doorway. The noise must not collide with the silence of shame.

But now the jezebel had lost her battle and her laughter filled the room. His cheeks burned and his palms oozed moisture. A press of people barred his way. The onlookers began to laugh and their bared teeth and distorted faces melded into one grotesque tormentor. Behind him, the king and the other woman snorted and guffawed. *All. All of them are mocking me. Mocking God's servant. And God's laws.* Images conflated in his mind and he shuddered at visions of the inhabitants of Gomorrah constructing the tower of Babel. He put his head down and butted through them, catapulting into the enclosure and landing on his knees. He remained on the ground, feeling the press of the earth on his permanently bruised knees, feeling closer to his God down here, even while physically lower than those who came forward to gawp. Here came another one now, jeering, sneering.

The young man proffered a hand. "Need some help, Abbot?"

Dunstan stared up at him, into grey eyes that crinkled around the corners and were surrounded by locks of wavy, unkempt and somehow ungodly gold-brown hair. The youth's lean lips were stretched into a smile over straight teeth and his chin was stubbly. He was well past the age to shave, but didn't. *Another idle hell-spawn.* But Dunstan could at least see this face. He knew this one.

He ignored the outstretched hand and stood up, staring with what he hoped was obvious contempt at the young man. Alvar, newly made lord of lands in the province of Mercia, was one of those swaggering, easily bought young men who worshipped Bacchus and clung to the Fairchild's tunic to catch any scraps which the king might drop for them, whilst encouraging him to forget his duty. Surely it was not to any divine purpose that England, with its defiled monasteries only now beginning to revive learning and literacy after the Viking onslaught, should fall instead under the rule of such a king as the Fairchild was revealing himself to be.

He looked over his shoulder towards the bower of sin and shuddered to think what sort of children such a match would produce. Perhaps God would be merciful and refuse to grant them any issue. For was not Gomorrah destroyed, the tower of Babel collapsed? Then surely the kingship would pass to the Fairchild's younger brother, who, by all accounts, was a fine and pious boy who would never place power and authority into the hands of irreligious upstarts. For Dunstan was in no doubt that these men were as morally bereft as the Fairchild had shown himself to be. Oh yes, he knew this man, who stood before him, still smiling. This one, he would not forget.

Alvar's smile had been stuck on his face since he knelt and received his earldom, and he had allowed himself a certain amount of ridiculous pride at his investiture, patting the arm ring, newly placed there by his lord King. But now he paused to consider as he watched the abbot shuffling away and he shook his head. It would always be his instinct to reach out and help a humiliated man, but he was particularly perturbed that the victim in this instance was an abbot, a man of the Church who should be respected, not disregarded. He looked towards the royal bower and listened for a moment to the bawdy laughter. It was easy to guess the nature of the spectacle that Dunstan had witnessed and Alvar wondered what kind of king had been crowned that day, who thought nothing of shaming an abbot in such a manner. Now he fiddled with the arm ring, pondering the loyalty which it had supposedly rewarded. Any man who refused a title was a fool and Alvar was not foolish, yet he had experienced shivers of doubt when he knelt to receive such riches from the boy-king. The day was still young and already those misgivings were growing.

He sighed and looked up. Now that the carousers had gone inside, it was as if the incident had never happened. Folk on the royal estate went about their business as if today were the same as yesterday. On the other side of the enclosure, the huntsmen fed the Fairchild's hounds, whilst nearby in the mews, the fowler and his boy attended to the king's hunting birds. Outside the fowler's hut, the geese flapped and hissed at the dairyman walking to the cook-house with two buckets of milk. A monk, not yet tonsured, was sitting on the ground outside the writing-house, his lithe young legs crossed. Sitting beside him, with a small hand resting on the brother's knee, a village boy looked up as he listened to the monk's tale, his basket of freshly gathered strawberries temporarily forgotten. Another boy was guarding a cartload of casks of wine from the vineyard at nearby Panborough while an older youth and a man unloaded them into the cook-house.

In the corner of the courtyard, three men kept a regular beat as they threshed piles of wheat taken from the stores, winnowing it free of chaff as quickly as they could to keep the quern stones turning. Snorts and stamping emanated from the overcrowded stables as the groom arrived with another stallion, but the horse-thegns took the animal with orderly efficiency.

Alvar turned to greet the man who had come to stand next to him.

His brother, Brock, returned his smile and the two men stood side by side in comfortable silence, watching the scene as the players within it acted out the familiar daily routines.

After a few moments Alvar said, "Out here, at least, everything is as it should be and that is thanks to you as king's steward."

Brock laughed, running his hand through his hair and smoothing down the badger-stripe of premature grey that ran from his temple to his crown, the source of his nickname. "The business of running the kings' halls changes little, even if they do keep giving me new kings to train."

Alvar let out a sardonic laugh. "From what I saw earlier, you would be mad even to try with this one. And it was not a mess that could be swept away with a besom." Alvar shook his head and said, "I have taken an earldom from him and yet I cannot help but feel he is too shiftless to be a good king."

Brock said, "Then we must both teach him." He clasped

his younger brother by the shoulders and patted Alvar's arm ring. "To me, he is a whelp who will need to be taught, but to you he is a great gift-giver, eh my lord?" Brock emphasised the last word and gave a mock bow.

Alvar stroked the ring. He rubbed his finger over the smoothness of the inlaid garnets and traced the pattern of the gold filigree. Would his father's lands in the shires of Hereford, Worcester and Gloucester, and the title that went with them, have even passed to him if his elder brother were not already richly rewarded and occupied in the role of steward? He said, "I have much to live up to. You have worked so hard and served three kings now and I have yet to…"

"Make your mark?"

Alvar raised his eyebrows as Brock once again finished his thought for him. Sixteen when Alvar was born, Brock seemed sometimes to know him better than he knew himself.

Brock said, "Yes, I was the first to follow where our father trod and you think I have become rich and esteemed. You, on the other hand, never had to work for anything. One grin and our mother, God rest her soul, would look at your beseeching grey eyes and she would melt like butter in the sunshine."

Alvar laughed. It was true. Their mother often said that all he had to do was stare at her with eyes so like her own and she would believe his every tale. Brock, as the eldest, had to learn everything and all Alvar had to do was copy him. No wonder he felt that, even though he was now twenty years old, the earldom had come to him like a tame hound onto his lap. Their father was a man about whom hearth-tales were told, up and down the land. His boots were bigger than Alvar's feet and Alvar wondered how he would ever fill them.

Brock slapped him on the back. "Too much thinking addles the brain, little brother. You wield a sword better than any man I know. The Fairchild could not have picked a better man to protect the western marches and keep the Welsh away from our ale and women. Speaking of which, we should be away inside now."

Alvar squeezed the hilt of his new sword, reminded that now the ceremony was over, he would be obliged to hang the weapon up inside the hall. The hilt was decorated with the familiar threaded pattern that represented the winding and interwoven strands of life, unbroken between this world and the next. It was a trapping of his investiture that had quickly begun to hang heavily by his side, but its decoration represented continuity. Worthy or not, he should be prepared, as its new owner, to act accordingly and uphold the sovereignty of kingship, whoever the king might be.

In the dim light inside the hall it was still easy to spot his friend Helmstan, for even when he was sitting down his height ensured that his shoulders were level with the heads of his companions. Those shoulders were heaving up and down as the big Mercian showed his hearty appreciation of some lewd joke or riddle. On the tables below the hearth, where the servants did not go, the men from Gloucester and Herefordshire, now under Alvar's protection, laughed and talked as they passed the food and drink around the table. The Cheshire thegns sitting near them shared an aurochs drinking horn; unable to set it down, they had to pass it continuously or else spill the ale.

Alvar hung his sword on the nail nearest to where his shield lay propped against the wall. He walked over to the Mercian tables, patting Helmstan's shoulder before he swung his legs over the bench to sit down.

Helmstan turned at the touch and his smile stretched even wider. His dog-brown eyes peered out from under a shaggy fringe and then he pulled his features into a mock frown. "I had wondered if you were too good to sit with us plain folk, now that you have been made a great lord."

Alvar chuckled. "You will need someone to lean on when you can no longer walk straight. Besides," he nodded towards the thegns of southern Mercia, "They are my men now but I am not your lord, *Cheshire*-man."

The teasing insult induced the expected snort of contempt from Helmstan. "Cheshire? There was never a shire of Cheshire. It was a name made up by Wessex when their kings swallowed our land. My lands around Chester were part of the kingdom of Mercia in better days gone by." He slurped some more ale and wiped his mouth with the back of his hand. "Never mind though. Now that you are lord of your father's demesne…"

Alvar settled back, caught in his own trap and prepared to be snared for some time. Helmstan would not let the opportunity pass to voice his thoughts about the diminished ancient kingdom of Mercia, now governed not by its own kings but by earls appointed by Wessex. Alvar, looking up, wondered which was the greater: the oak beams holding up the roof, or the number of times that Helmstan had lamented the loss of Mercian autonomy.

"And now we can work together to get back all the land that was stolen from the old kingdom. The king has given you back your father's lands, but what of the fenland? That, too, once belonged to Mercia."

Alvar refrained from scoffing at the mention of the boggy marshland, but not with ease, for he could not imagine who in his right mind would wish for control of that wind-ravaged swamp. He laid a hand gently on his friend's arm. "Would that I had one tenth of your passion for the old kingdom of Mercia, but even though I grew up there, the truth is that I took the lands only because they were my father's. I wish merely to do my duty by keeping the Welsh out and the folk safe within." He squeezed Helmstan's arm and released it. "Put away your dreams for your homeland for a while. Here comes the food."

Helmstan's mouth hung open, an unspoken nationalist protest doubtless waiting to issue forth, but he hesitated and evidently thought better of it, grabbing the drinking horn instead.

Alvar smiled and waited, looking around the hall while

the servants knelt down with the spit-roasted lamb, and the diners took pieces of meat from the serving-plates.

Where once the wall-hangings shone with gold weaving, the embroidery was now snagged and faded. Alvar wrinkled his nose at the smell of tallow candles where beeswax should have burned. He looked down. The linen tablecloth was threadbare in places. There was bread, but it was ordinary barley bread and there seemed too much of it and now Alvar knew why, because the meat was meagre in portion and the serving-platters were soon empty. If the Fairchild did not care to show his wealth as a lord with plenty, he could not hope for men to love and follow him.

Alvar's plate was full and the servants melted away. He eschewed the dual purpose prong-handled spoon in favour of his own hand-knife. He stroked the silver decoration on the blunt side of his knife, winding his finger along the smith's engraving, '*Gosfrith made me*', and gazed without focus as he gathered his thoughts. As he felt again the constricting pressure of the ornate arm ring, Alvar knew exactly what the Fairchild was hoping. Never had so many men been made earls in such a short time. The Fairchild was too young to have proven himself politically and it was obviously his intention to buy the nobles and thereby bind them to him. Might this be the only reason that Alvar had been given his father's lands? It was possible; Helmstan was right when he said that under the previous kings, Mercia and Mercian lords had not done well out of the expansion of Wessex, so there must be a reason if their fortunes were suddenly to rise. Well, Alvar might have taken the bait, but it didn't mean that he had to be caught in the net. The king needed guidance, but Mercia needed a worthy lord, and that meant an opportunity for Alvar to prove himself to a dead father.

The hall door opened and the Fairchild sauntered to his seat, but took care to settle his young wife in her chair before sitting down himself. The noise levels rose again as those already seated resumed their meal. The Fairchild took a pitcher of wine from the servant hovering by his chair and served his consort, a gesture at odds with tradition, where the lady of the house personally served the guests. She smiled and held his gaze while he poured, leaning her head towards his chest and stroking his free arm. As Alvar watched the newlyweds it occurred to him that despite their callowness and taste for scandal, they were in love.

Alvar became aware of movement further along the head table as a figure rose unsteadily to his feet. Abbot Dunstan's lower lip hinged up and down as he prepared to speak. "M-m-my lord King, I would be doing less than my d-duty to God and Church if I did not sp-speak out."

Alvar looked down at his fingernails. Dunstan had clearly not put the earlier incident behind him; his stammer was worse than usual and Alvar felt unable to continue being eyewitness to his discomfort.

The abbot continued. "Today I have seen much land gifted away. Yet the late king bequeathed lands to certain abbeys and they have not received them." Stumbling on, he said, "Furthermore, the late king's widow has also b-been deprived of lands which were willed to her by the king." Snatching a breath too short to allow the Fairchild to speak in the pause, he said, "And the king's b-burial itself was unlawful…"

Alvar looked up.

The Fairchild did not move, but sat with arms loosely by his sides. A slight twitch of his shoulder suggested that the king still had one hand on his wife's knee. The Fairchild's expression gave nothing away, unless it was boredom. Indeed, as he opened his mouth to speak, his jaw dropped as if he were stifling a yawn. "So, Abbot… On my crowning-day, you begin by threatening me with hell and now you call me a thief. Yes, the late king bequeathed many lands and treasures, some of which seem to have found their way into your hands when they should have come to me. I say that it is you, Dunstan, lowly abbot, who is the thief."

There was a pause, and then Dunstan spoke, his voice

shrill. "I am steadfast and true. I was a faithful servant to the late king."

"I am not he. And you have stolen from me."

Dunstan stood his ground, but his eyebrows drew together in a frown, his brave anger giving way to dismay. "N-not true. Those lands belong to the Church."

The Fairchild placed his hands on the table, pushed himself upright and stared at Dunstan. "You are a liar and you will give back all that you have stolen. As for my uncle the king's burial, it is better that he was laid to rest in Winchester, for I would not wish you to profit from him in death as you did in life. Do not pretend that your abbey would be the poorer for having a king buried there."

"B-but it was not lawful. The king wished to be buried at Glastonbury. That was not my whim, but the written will of the king. How could you believe that I would seek to b-benefit from such a burial?"

"Abbot, I know that you will not, for I am sending you from these lands. No, do not speak another word, for I have had my fill of your stammering sermons. First you dare to tell me that I have withheld lands from the abbeys. Then you dare to say that I have robbed a grieving widow. Then you seek to dig up the king's body, not yet cold, and take it to your own abbey. Get you gone, wretched abbot, before I tell all those who do not already know how you tried to shame me earlier this day. Get you gone from my hall and my lands."

Abbot Dunstan's face shone red and moist. Alvar uncrossed his legs and shifted further back into his chair, discomfited by the Fairchild's clumsy attempt to assert his authority. Dunstan had served the boy's predecessors wisely and loyally. It was a show of strength on the king's part that succeeded only in seeming vindictive. Even while Dunstan was leaving the room, the Fairchild raised his ale cup and demanded the toast. "Be hale!"

Alvar had no choice but to raise his own cup and his echo, "Be hale", rang out as Dunstan passed by the Mercian benches. The abbot stopped but briefly, and stared in Alvar's direction, eyes narrowed and nostrils flared, before gliding from the room with his head held high, as if he were glad to be leaving the stench of the Fairchild's kingship behind him.

Ramsey, East Anglia

The afternoon shortened as the sun began to drop from the sky. The beams of reddened light forced their way through the window opening and illuminated a silk slipper, cast off and lying on its side on the floor. Its threads shone golden in the amber-coloured fading light. Outside, the peal of gentle teasing laughter told of dairy maids returning to the cook-house and tired-eyed women emerging from the weaving sheds, while a booming voice identified the reeve ordering the gate to be closed and the braziers lit. Alfreda lay on the bed, listening to the everyday sounds of folk reaching the end of their working day, as she gazed at the pretty slipper. She focused on the delicate threads of embroidery which wound around the opening of the richly adorned footwear, tracing with her gaze the trail of stitching from one side round to the other. She stared as long as she could, grateful for the distraction, then she closed her eyes and waited for the next blow, able to resist protecting with her arm, but unable to stop the instinctive curling into a ball. This time he managed only a glancing blow across the top of her thigh and, though she knew it would bruise, it would not have satisfied him. Finding sanctuary this time in her thoughts, she mused that were she a braver woman she would taunt him for his poor aim and tell him that even as a beater of women, he was a failure. For the most part, he only ever hit her body, because any marks on her face would be visible to the rest of the household, and Elwood of East

Anglia would not want his famous father to discover his secret. Not that there was a man in England who wouldn't sneer in disapproval, for it was not manly to hit a woman, but Alfreda knew that in particular her husband would hate for his father to find out.

She dared to glance up. Elwood wrinkled his nose as he looked down at her; his pinched nostrils were flecked with thread-veins which meandered towards his cheek bones. He lifted his chin and stared at the ceiling, as if engaged in some twisted act of invocation and, as his neck went back, his lank hair sat in untidy clumps upon the shoulders of his tunic. Pale lashes failed adequately to frame his equally pale, small eyes, so that his face was a melded mass of uneven skin tone which rendered it almost featureless. He stepped forward and she readied herself.

But not quickly enough. His frustration at missing his target last time added power to his arm and he thumped his fist into her belly, catching her by surprise and knocking the breath from her body. There was no pain in her stomach, but her chest felt tight and she tried and failed to snatch air into her mouth. Another blow to the same part of her abdomen robbed her of all ability to breathe and as he stood up, his still-clenched hand caught the side of her face and a burning sensation shot up her nose to a point of pain in the middle of her forehead. Gasping for air, she reached a hand to her face and her fingers immediately became sticky with blood. She sank back against the pillow, relieved. He would stop now.

Her husband stood over her, peering at her, and then he turned his back. He let out a sigh which set his shoulders shuddering, adjusted his tunic and left the bower. She waited, listening for the sound of his footsteps to diminish, and then she edged slowly off the bed and sank to her knees, holding the side of the bed until her breath came easily again. Letting go of the bed, she shuffled forward, still kneeling, and lifted the lid of her clothes chest, reaching around until she found one of the linens usually reserved for her monthly bleed. Folding it small, she held it to her nose, dabbing and inspecting until the flow ceased. Outside, the raised voices and increased footfall indicated that folk were moving along to the feast hall. Standing slowly she smoothed her kirtle and stepped carefully to the door. Squinting into the darkening gloom, her lower body still on the inner side of the door, she flapped a wave to one of her serving-women, and pointed to her veil, gesticulating that she needed help to tidy it. She shrank back around the door.

Her woman came to re-wrap her headdress but she worked in silence. Alfreda sat helpfully rigid while the woman rearranged the swathe of cloth, but did nothing to encourage any conversation. The servants on the estate were all deferential, but Alfreda was sure that this woman's quiet reverence was a result of pity. She needed no confirmation by drawing the woman into dialogue.

Dressed and no longer dishevelled, at least in appearance, she made her way to the hall, still unsure what had caused Elwood's latest bout of anger. Servants bobbed their heads, but she had no words for them either. At an age when most women of her standing would be running their own household, she was miserably aware that there were no keys hanging from her belt. The women were not hers to command, nor could they be her friends. Not that she needed any words, for as soon as they had nodded their obeisance, they turned away. The only armour she had was to deflect the hurt with the thought that, key-holder or not, she was of higher status than they were and she had no need of their pity. Lifting her kirtle hem with one hand, she quickened her pace and walked on, her chin raised and her free hand placed defensively across her chest.

Ahead of her, Elwood's two younger brothers were walking with Prince Edgar, their foster-brother. They strode in a relaxed manner, arms draped across shoulders, comfortable and familiar. Laughter rose up, in response, she assumed, to bawdy jokes. She slowed her pace, reluctant to catch up with them, but, as if she had not borne enough, the

Devil chose this moment to turn Edgar's head and he disengaged himself from the pack and hung back, allowing the brothers to walk on while he waited for her to draw level. He fell into step beside Alfreda and, even though she had nothing to say to him, he whistled softly, appearing not to mind the silence.

She remained mute, hoping to bore him away, but he stopped whistling and said, "I would never use you so ill. He should not do it."

She missed a step and stumbled as her heart began to thump against her chest. Shame then gave way to indignation. "How can you speak so, yet keep these brothers as your friends?"

He shrugged. "I am not answerable for the behaviour of others. All I am saying is that I would not do it." He lengthened his stride and caught up with the others.

Alfreda stared after him and embarrassment warmed her veins once more. But then she began to muse on his words. Could he put a stop to it, if he wanted to? He was certainly influential; he was the son of one king, the brother of another. When his father died, his uncle became king and Edgar, then a tiny infant, was sent here to East Anglia to be fostered in the household of the most powerful noble in the land. Now his uncle was dead, his elder brother was king and Edgar was heir to the throne. But he was still a child, a mere boy of thirteen. And what could a boy possibly do to help her?

Never in the twelve months she had been living on the Isle of Ramsey had she failed to be overwhelmed by the opulence of the mead-hall. She held her breath as she walked through the doorway, her gaze drawn to its great oak frame where carved wolf heads appeared to guard the entrance. Inside, the support pillars were decorated in a similarly ornate way, but instead of animal heads, the engravings took on the form of tendrils of ivy, symbols of protection, curling their way round the upright posts. Embroidered cloths, worked with golden threads, covered the lime plaster on three sides of the hall, and at the far end, behind the lord's chair, curtains embellished with chevrons hung from the beams to the floor, separating the lord's private chamber beyond. The lord's chair also boasted elaborate carvings, the high back covered in three-armed spirals and interweaving lines, the indentations coloured with gold. Along with all the other chairs for the high table, it sported cushions covered with the same sumptuous fabric that graced the walls. In this place, warm and yet not overly welcoming, Alfreda had sat every night amongst the guests of her father-in-law, the lord of East Anglia. He was a man so trusted by recent kings, and rewarded with so much land, either in outright gift or given temporarily into his custody, that he was known to all as the Half-king. She smiled, despite her sore body and wounded pride. Did the Half-king ever wonder, as he looked back on a life of power, success and influence, how he managed to beget such a spindle of an eldest son?

Most had gathered now and among them were the overseas visitors. The Half-king played frequent host to learned men and traders from the continent; the merchants from Frankia had arrived the previous evening, and sitting with them was the scholar from Germany who had been a guest for the past few months. Alfreda made her way to her seat. She was joined by the only man in the room who was not clothed in bright colours and who displayed no outward sign of wealth, having not even a sword to hang up. Abbot Athelwold sat down beside her and smiled. Despite his drab garb, the abbot's presence was the warmest attraction in the hall for Alfreda. His eyes, the colour of molten honey, his gentle smile and softly spoken words were always a fillip on evenings such as this. He was retained by the Half-king as tutor to the younger boys, but often he spoke to her of his dreams for reform of the monasteries, plans that he had begun with his friend Abbot Dunstan, but he was concerned to put the nunneries on an equal footing. His talk of holy women, pious ladies and gentle abbesses poured balm into her ears which had so often been burned with screamed insults, where the word *woman* was synonymous with *whore*.

But this evening he seemed not to want to expound his discourse on the development of the monastic houses. Instead, the kindly abbot leaned in close to her and said, "If there is one thing for which I am truly sorry, it is that when I was brought here as teacher to Edgar and the younger boys, it was too late to mete out any wisdom to your husband."

Alfreda's cheeks burned hotter than the hearth-fire. Was there no-one who was unaware of her shame?

But Abbot Athelwold continued. "It saddens me that at seventeen and wed for a year, you have no keys at your belt, nor have you been given your rightful place at the lords' bench to pour the drinks, as the lady of the house should do."

Surprise drained the heat from her face and she suppressed an impulse to let out a shrill laugh. Still, better that he should think her ill-treatment at Elwood's hands extended to no more than a slight to her position as highest-born woman in the widowed Half-king's household. Besides, there was a hidden blessing to her relegation at mealtimes; from her seat on a lower bench, she could hear the conversation at the head table, without feeling obliged, or being expected, to contribute.

The food was brought in; plates of eels, fresh cheeses and cereal brews flavoured with herbs and spring onions. The smells turned her already tender stomach and Alfreda glanced across at the foreign visitors and contemplated enquiring of them whether Frankish or German men ever beat their women, for she couldn't help but wonder where Elwood had acquired his notion of what constituted genteel behaviour.

The Half-king had taken his place at the head table and was sitting on the ornately carved chair, with Elwood on one side of him and Prince Edgar on the other. It took only a few mouthfuls of food before Alfreda discovered the source of Elwood's ire. As had become her habit, she pretended an interest in her food to discourage conversation, which enabled her to listen to those at the head table.

Elwood spat out gobbets of food as he spoke. "So, this brat of a king will not right the wrong he has done to us. You are the only lord who has not been given any new lands since the king-making. Worse, the lands in Mercia of which you were caretaker have been given to Alvar, when they should have formally been given over to you. We are poorer while these upstarts come from nowhere to wield power and strength."

The Half-king, who was grey-haired but sat with a straight back, finished his mouthful and wiped his lips on a linen napkin before he spoke. "The Fairchild is busy giving land in order to bind the lords to him. Since he does not wholly trust me or mine, and knows that in any case we cannot be bought, he does not try." He smiled ruefully at his son. "The raising up of the newcomers troubles me as much as it does you, but I will not stoop so low as to beg for more land."

It seemed that Elwood might choke before he managed to spit out more words and while he continued to splutter and fail to enunciate, Prince Edgar cleared his throat.

"I do not know my brother overly well, but I think he has misunderstood what it means to be king. You cannot buy men's loyalty, nor is it wise to think that you can earn their steadfastness. It is yours by right, but you must demand it without seeming to. And never show weakness."

Now it was Alfreda who struggled to swallow her food. She looked again at Edgar and shook her head slowly, trying to reconcile his sagacity with her awareness of his tender age.

Elwood's brow was creased. He took a swig of ale and said, "Yes, well, word-craft is all well and good, but how will that get me the land that is due to me?"

Edgar raised an eyebrow and shrugged.

"Hah! You see? You have no answer. For all your words, you do not know."

Alfreda thought that Elwood was wrong. It seemed to her rather that Edgar just didn't care.

Abbot Athelwold laid a hand on her arm to gain her attention and then whispered to her. "It is true that the Half-king held the Mercian lands after Alvar's father died. But the Mercians loved that man and they will welcome his son, Alvar, who, from what I have seen, is made from the same clay. He is not merely one of the Fairchild's creatures; he is a skilled swordsman and his brother, a man whom I have known a long time, tells me he has a sharp mind."

The Half-king was staring out far across the hall. Alfreda was moved again to think how imposing a figure he was. He was immense in stature and in reputation. He had been guardian not only of a future king, but of vast swathes of the country while kings came and went. If the new king did not require his services then however resigned he might appear, surely it must rankle? But he was naught if not pragmatic and after a few more moments of contemplation, he spoke again.

"I think we are allowing the chaff to blind us to the wheat." He lowered his head and Elwood leaned in to catch what he was saying. Whatever they were plotting, there would be no more eavesdropping; where Elwood shouted for all to hear, the shrewd Half-king kept his scheming secret. Alfreda would have to look elsewhere for distraction.

Her gaze shifted to Edgar and she was still staring at him when he looked up and smiled at her. Caught out, she looked away and found herself staring instead at Elwood's youngest brother. The lord of Brandon had the same pale features as the rest of the family, but his cheeks were less florid. He was of average height for his age and thus a little taller than Edgar, but he had yet to fill out and take on the shape of an adult. How could it be then, that he and his foster-brother were the same age? Edgar's poise and gravity belied his extreme youth. His widowed mother had entrusted him into the Half-king's care, where he would be nurtured and prepared for kingship when the time came. How soon would that time come? While she was still musing on the differences between Edgar and his foster-brothers, Brandon looked up and she averted her gaze. He liked her no more than did his brother, and she returned the loathing. The Half-king had three sons, but Alfreda thought that not one of them measured to a third of their father.

Laughter wafted now from the head table and Alfreda lifted her head. Several of the diners were engaged in ribald conversation. She heard, "It is said that she is a winsome woman" and the response, "But she is a whore, and everyone saw how she…" and it was clear that they were talking yet again about the scandal of the king's coronation feast.

Elwood said, "It is rare to find a woman who does not play the whore. It is in their blood, I think."

Alfreda's own blood flowed in warm pulses back to her face.

Prince Edgar said, "But at least my brother has a wife, which is something I do not have. He has a kingdom, too, which I also do not have. If you do not like women, Foster-brother, then maybe I'll have your wife off you."

Elwood's eyes flashed black. He looked first at his father, then back to Edgar. "Why not? It would not be the only thing you have had off me."

"I would not need your permission." Edgar smiled briefly and winked at Alfreda. "I take whatever I want."

Alfreda found reason to examine the food remaining on her plate and did not dare to look up again. *'I take whatever I want.'* It was a bold claim. And he mentioned kingdoms, as well as women. Edgar's confidence bordered on arrogance but there was no doubt that he was convinced of his destiny and his ability. There was, perhaps, quite a lot that a boy could do.

Chapter Two AD957

In the shadow of the Black Mountain, Wales/Herefordshire border

Sweat loosened Alvar's grip and the sword hilt shifted in his hand. The skirmish had brought little glory with it, for either side, but neither had it brought any riches for the handful of Welshmen who had launched the raid. He planted his sword in the ground and wiped his palm on his tunic while he counted the dead. None of his men, four of theirs, and three wounded. The corpses lay bent and ugly; one man with his legs folded under his body, one on his front with a Mercian axe protruding from his back. Next to him lay a young lad whose shield was pinned to his body by the spear that had penetrated both shield and stomach, and the last lay slumped by the wall of a shepherd's hut, his guts spilt.

It had been over quickly and had not resembled a pitched battle. In a way, Alvar preferred this method of fighting, for he was light on his feet and accurate with his weapons, sparingly effective with his moves, and he felt constrained at times by the formulaic fighting of the shield wall. He looked again at the corpse against the wall and thought about how, as a lad, he used to practise on the slaughter-man's carcasses; not for him the dull, unsatisfying thud of the wooden practice swords. His father wanted him to know what it felt like to thrust a metal weapon into flesh. The tactic had helped his preparation, but there was naught that truly felt the same as the pushing of iron into a living body.

A shout went up and the last Welshman ran from behind the hut, spear held high. Alvar freed his sword from the ground, immediately at a disadvantage with his shorter weapon. As his opponent ran towards him, Alvar had to raise his shield to deflect the first spear thrust and was momentarily robbed of his sight while he held the shield aloft. A counter-thrust was of little use as the spearman would simply step back, keeping the longer length of his weapon between them. Armed with only his shorter sword, Alvar would not be able to get close. When the Welshman hefted his spear back, ready to thrust again, Alvar dropped to one knee, rolled over one shoulder and brought his sword up into his adversary's belly before the man was able to lower his shield. The man sank to his knees, the spear crashed to the ground, the shield dropped, and Alvar thrust again with his sword, higher up this time, through the heart.

He was cleaning his sword when Helmstan, muddy and bloody, sauntered over. "That was done swiftly and well."

Alvar grunted. "He should have known when to give thanks for his life and walk away. Now he has made me cross and learned the hard way."

Helmstan whistled. "If that is how you fight when mildly irked, then the world had better look out if ever you truly lose your temper."

Alvar's laughter exceeded normal noise levels, as he released the tension after the recent utilisation of his warrior reflexes. "The greater worry is whether you will be keen to fight any more, with your bride waiting in Cheshire."

"Hah! If you saw her, you would find reasons aplenty to bide in Cheshire yourself. But what would you know about settling with one woman when you seem to find yourself a new one each night?"

Alvar lunged forward and aimed a mock punch at Helmstan's belly. Helmstan pretended to parry and then they stood, arms about each other's shoulders. Alvar was about to order the burial of the dead, when he looked back towards the border. "Before you go to your wife, it looks as though the lord of Mercia needs you one last time. That is a great many horses for a host not bent on fighting."

Helmstan turned and put his hand up to shield his eyes from the sun. "Who is it?"

Riding from the direction of the garrison at Hereford, a group of twenty or more horse made its way towards the skirmish site and Alvar could not identify the banners. He shook his head. "I do not know. Gather the others."

But as the entourage came nearer Alvar recognised the colours of the Half-king of East Anglia. Riding under that protection and surrounded by thegns was a youth who looked similar to the king; it was not a huge leap to assume that this was his younger brother, Prince Edgar. The boy sat not very high in the saddle, but he had a man's jaw and his shoulders were broad. The colour of the downy moustache indicated that the hair concealed by his helmet was as fair as his brother's.

The company of thegns dismounted, but Edgar remained in the saddle. Alvar made formal greetings, but said no more than was necessary. These men had gone to a great deal of trouble to find him when they could have awaited his return at Hereford and he would say nothing that would delay an explanation.

Edgar said, "It looks as though we are here too late. I was keen to see the fight."

Alvar frowned. "Why?"

Edgar stared at him, unblinking. "When a would-be king comes to ask a man for help, it is a good thing if he can witness how well he fights."

Alvar's heart speeded up. Which should he contemplate first; the call for help, or the professed ambition to be king?

The surprise must have been writ large on his face, for Edgar said, "I have come to ask you to help me win a kingdom and in return, I will see Mercia rich beyond dreams." He leaned forward in his saddle. "You are well known as a slayer of the Welsh. I am fourteen now, old enough for a kingdom and I believe you are the best man to help me get it."

Alvar shook his head. Help to overthrow the king? He

was no rebel. And why would this boy, whose foster-kin were the most formidable family in the land, need the aid of a newly appointed earl of Mercia?

Edgar straightened up. "Lord Alvar, may I be forthright?"

"I wish you would."

"My brother's only interests are his wife and his riches, and he believes that Wessex is where the wealth is."

Alvar nodded, recalling how the Fairchild had argued with Dunstan over the redistribution of the late king's bequests.

Prince Edgar continued. "The lords tire of his ways. My foster-father put it to him that he should share his kingdom with me, and my brother barely looked up from his ale. Wessex is enough for him, it seems. So here I am, asking for your help to set me upon a throne that will see me king in Mercia and the north."

So, not a rebellion; but if his brother had already agreed to a partition, why was Edgar here in Mercia asking for help? Alvar opened his mouth to speak, but Helmstan tugged at his sleeve and dragged him aside. "My lord, you must say yes." He shifted from foot to foot, as if he would jump in joy. "Think how well this could turn out for Mercia. Your father was…"

"I know who my father was."

Alvar walked back to where Edgar remained patiently on his horse, displaying no signs of agitation but sitting with shoulders relaxed, hands loosely on the reins. He was going to be a small adult, but he showed none of the attitude which oft-times afflicted small men, exuding instead nothing less than supreme confidence. But self-belief could still be misdirected. Alvar needed to know more. He reached up and patted the horse's neck. Looking up at the young prince, he said, "Lord Edgar, will you tell me why you think you need my help?"

Edgar lowered his head briefly as if nodding assent. He dismounted and touched Alvar's elbow, indicating a wish to withdraw from the others before speaking further.

"All my life, I have seen my foster-father forging bonds with men from other lands and I've learned that we must look outward, not inward as my brother does. I understand that there is an England beyond Wessex." He stared at Alvar and nodded. "And it is my belief that you do, too. Unlike the other earls who sit on their arses and flatter my brother, you have come back to Mercia, and serve the folk." He leaned in closer. "The other erstwhile kingdoms have no love for my brother, but nor do they have any love for each other. So, first I must get them all on the same side: mine. Then, and only then, will we take our fight into Wessex. From there I can make a vast kingdom, and who knows how far it will one day reach? And, to speak plainly, since there is no love lost between the East Anglians and the Mercians, it would be foolhardy of me to try to take Mercia by force. I have their oaths of loyalty; now I need yours." He stood up straight and took a step back.

Alvar sighed and scratched his chin. Oath-breakers were anathema; he had pledged loyalty to the king and, like all men, his word was his bond. But Edgar's brother had merely bought the nobility and it was a strategy which, if this boy could be believed, was not working. Thus was the two-way contract already broken? He said, "Even if I say yes, I am only one man. I cannot speak even for Mercia, much less the other former kingdoms."

Edgar held his hand up. "But, you are not saying no?"

"I am saying that I think there is little that I could do for you. My men and I are sword wielders, yes, and if it comes to pass that one day you move to overthrow your brother, then we could, if willing, help you. But we do not speak for every man in Mercia and I do not see an easy way to ask them all. In days gone by you could have called the old Mercian council. Maybe that is what you should do now."

"Yes!" The shout came from Helmstan, and Alvar turned to see his friend punching the air.

Alvar was still unsure, but perhaps it could not harm to

hear what the other Mercian lords had to say. He knew that the significance would be lost on none of them; the council had been defunct since the day Mercia lost its regal status and became subjugate to Wessex. He nodded. "Well then, my lord. Let us make our way back to Hereford and we will talk some more."

He stepped back as Edgar remounted and turned his horse around. The young man surveyed the battle scene. "It was a godsend that you were here when the Welsh came."

Helmstan snorted and stepped forward. "God had naught to do with it. Lord Alvar makes good use of the fort in Hereford. Every day he sends men out to look for any trouble that might be brewing."

Edgar nodded with satisfaction. "I knew I was right to come," he said.

Alvar looked around the hall and considered that perhaps in the Mercian heyday, the council at the royal seat of Tamworth might have been a more sophisticated affair. Here in Hereford, a permanently manned garrison, there were plenty of women, but they were not the sort of ladies who graced the benches of the great hall when the nobility met. He also doubted that this rough wooden hall had anything to offer as a rival to the renowned grandeur of the Half-king's houses. Nevertheless, all the men summoned had appeared; representatives of all corners of Mercia and all the ancient tribes who still cleaved to their own centuries-old identity, and it was clear from the good-natured chatter that they were happy to be there.

Alvar stood up and repeated the proposition as it had been put to him on the windy hillside only a few days before. He waited until the first wave of surprise had subsided. He would not say any more until questions were raised.

The first was simple, and perhaps the most expected. "What does the king think about this? Surely he will not sit idly by whilst he loses half his kingdom?"

Helmstan's overlord, Edelman the Greybeard, lord of Chester, stood up and said, "The way I see it is this: it is the same as thirty years ago when King Edward died. He left Wessex to his legitimate son and gave Mercia to his firstborn, Athelstan. No-one spoke against this and it worked well."

Alvar shifted on his seat, for he recalled that it had worked a little too well. According to Alvar's father, less than four weeks later that same legitimate son died in a manner which no man could fully explain and Athelstan had become king of the whole land. As he listened to increasing shouts of enthusiasm for the resurrection of the old days and the old ways, he could not help but feel uneasy that the nationalist Mercian lords were misinterpreting Edgar's intentions. But anyone could see that the result was a foregone conclusion, for the men in this hall had already embraced Edgar as their new king and no urging of caution would be heeded.

He was required to ask if all were in agreement that Edgar be declared king of the Mercians, but had not finished speaking when every man in the room began thumping his fists on the table, the booming noise rivalling the clatter of shields on the battlefield. It was done, and Alvar knew he was being carried along on a wave whose current was too strong for him to swim against.

Edgar's first act as king was symbolic. Gifting land at Staunton-on-Arrow to a Herefordshire thegn, Edgar stepped forward and gave a square of turf from the said land. The grant would need to be written in the form of a charter, but for now the gesture was enough.

Alvar sat back. Edgar had come of age and now he was king alongside his brother. Alvar could take no praise for thinking to call the council, for that was a snatching of an idea, not the result of reasoned political thought; he knew his value to Edgar was his military skill and the large numbers of men at his disposal. He thought that perhaps he should cease his agonising over the morality of the unfolding events and be content to know that, come what may, he could continue to wield his sword with satisfying regularity.

He had eaten his fill and enjoyed the spectacle of the knife-jugglers. Too drunk to solve the scop's riddles, he sat back and allowed his eyes to close. The orange glow of candlelight penetrating his shut lids darkened, and he opened his eyes and sat up.

Edgar was standing at the end of the table. "I wish to speak to you."

Alvar sat up and shuffled along the bench. "Sit, then."

Edgar remained standing. "Not here."

Alvar stood up. If Edgar's words could not be spoken in the hall then they must be weighing heavy.

The new king of Mercia said nothing more and Alvar shook his head and tried to snap himself awake as he followed him out of the hall and across the courtyard. Braziers kept the dark night at bay, and the clanging of the smithy well past evensong was enough to tell any traveller that the garrison was overflowing with wealthy guests that night. Edgar stopped outside the little limestone chapel. A guard stepped away from the door and Alvar stumbled into the gloom. The oak door swung shut behind them and closed with a heavier thud than in daylight.

Edgar genuflected and then sat down on one of the little pews. He gestured for Alvar to do the same. Older by seven years and taller by nearly a foot, when Alvar sat beside the king his shoulder was level with Edgar's chin.

Edgar said, "I would have your thoughts on how I win over the rest of the north, Lord Alvar."

So, Edgar had a use for him beyond the securing of Mercia. He perhaps should have felt flattered, but he thought that the compliment was misplaced. He said, "Why do you seek my thoughts? I am but a Mercian lord with a reasonably good sword arm."

"Indeed. Yet you are the man who thought to revive the

council that has today named me king of the Mercians. It seems to me that your mind might be at least as sharp as your blade."

Sharper than the boy's mind apparently, if Edgar could not grasp that the Mercians would probably have elected a milch cow if they thought it would bring them back their independence. "What do you wish to know?" Edgar already had the East Anglians' loyalty. But perhaps his education had not been as comprehensive as Alvar's own; in which case he might not know that of the other former kingdoms, Northumbria was once not one, but two realms. It had only very recently come under the control of Wessex and it was still culturally cleft in two; the southern half, centred on Danish York, spoke the language of its erstwhile Viking rulers while the north, incorporating the ancient seat of Bamburgh, spoke English. He said, "Northumbria has no kings, only high-reeves, and some would say that is a fall from a great height..." Alvar spread his hands out, palms up. He had no need to point out the similarities with Mercia. But maybe he needed to remind Edgar that the Danes who dwelt in the southern reaches of Northumbria and the north-eastern part of Mercia were used to their own autonomy, and would guard jealously the specially written law codes which had given rise to the naming of the area as *Danelaw*. "And the Danes will listen to no man who will not swear to let them keep their own laws."

"So, if I am to win over the hearts and minds of the Northumbrians and the Danes, I will need to be mindful of the things that make them what they are." Edgar flashed one of his rare smiles. "And also keep a great number of weapon-men at my beck and call."

This boy had indeed a sharp mind. There was no way of knowing what kind of king he would eventually become, but the beginning was promising. This self-assured youngster had demonstrated the understanding that he must at least acknowledge the discrete concerns of all the disparate parties whom he sought to rule, and this showed a maturity beyond his tender years. He was also aware of the need for military strength, to serve as a deterrent against dissent. But even if he had not, for Alvar, there was no turning back; after wrestling with his conscience he must honour his decision and he resolved never to break his oath again, come what may.

Edgar was still smiling.

Alvar wondered what it was that pleased him so. "My lord?"

Edgar shook his head. "I was merely thinking that I owe you many thanks. I foresee that I will oft-times need to call on you, not merely for your sword arm but also for your knowledge of my kingdom. Our bond gives strength to us both."

After the intense concentration of the past few days, Alvar welcomed the levity. He laughed and tried a joke. "Let us hope that neither one of us ever feels fettered by a bond tied too tight."

Edgar's smile fell away. "Hmm. Indeed."

Just for a moment, Alvar felt as he had when the last marauding Welshman had come at him and he had been caught with the wrong weapon, still stuck in the ground.

Ramsey, East Anglia

Alfreda sang quietly while she worked with the batches of wool. The rhythmic movement of the carding-combs moving back and forth in her hands was familiar from childhood and now, as then, she was soothed by the pulsing regularity of the action. She sat slightly apart from the other women. She was still unsure how much they knew or guessed and she wished neither to insult them by pretending, nor to reveal the truth if they were not already aware. Thus rendered dumb, she worked alone, speaking only when she needed some more wool to work on. She had almost finished the latest lot when she heard the shouting. She was always frightened by the yelling, but now her hand went quickly to her belly in an instinctively protective gesture. How tempting it was to stay here in the carding shed, to hide, let the storm pass. But Elwood liked her always to know what it was that had caused his anger so that she would know why she was being beaten for it. She knew she must go and the fear and urgency caused her to bark an order to one of the girls to take on her work as well as her own. "Here, take this. I must be with the lord Elwood." As she hurried to the hall, she wondered briefly if her words had carried a haughty tone, but she had no space in her heart to take on more worries. As she ran, she wondered how it would be this time. Would he harm the unborn babe?

In the hall, her husband strode from mead-bench to side table and back again, shouting and jabbing his finger in the air. The Half-king was sitting in his great carved chair, nodding when the pauses in the rant required it, but saying nothing. Alfreda cast about for sanctuary, spotted Abbot Athelwold and went to stand beside him.

The abbot turned to acknowledge her presence, and answered her unspoken question. "Young Edgar has been named king of the Mercians and of the North and East. His brother holds only Wessex now."

Alfreda was stupid. She knew this because Elwood told her it was so, but she struggled particularly with this information. "But how can that be a bad thing?" If the Fairchild's kingdom had been thus reduced, then surely all those whom he'd advanced would be put back down and the likes of the Half-king would be restored to power and influence.

Athelwold smiled and patted her arm. "Since he became king, Edgar has not sent for his foster-brothers but is leaning instead on Alvar of Mercia."

"Is he the one who was given the lands once held by the Half-king?"

"The same."

And, if she understood it correctly, her husband considered those lands to be part of his birthright.

Elwood picked up an ale flagon and hurled it across the room. "How was this thing done? Edgar should have spoken to me about it, yet he said naught. How did he know where to go?"

The Half-king waited until a serving-boy had cleared the shards from the floor. "It was I who gave him the war gear. It was I who armed him. I thought his intention was to ride to Wessex."

Elwood halted in mid-step and whirled around to face his father. "And you are proud of his treachery?"

The Half-king stood up and placed his hands upon the table. "I am, in that I have still helped Edgar safely to his kingship and thus fulfilled my oath to his mother. Now, I am going to acknowledge the creaking in my bones. It is my wish to leave this world and live out my days at Glastonbury Abbey."

Elwood's face throbbed scarlet. "You are going to do what?"

The Half-king stepped down from the dais and walked over to his son. "When you have done with your spluttering, you will understand that my leaving means that you are now earl of East Anglia. I spoke to Edgar on your behalf, and you will be the new lord. I have done this much for you, now I will do something else. I will ask you to think." He gestured for his son to sit down and Elwood, still flushed, but now muted, obeyed.

The Half-king sat down next to him and said, "Edgar will not settle for half a kingdom. When he makes his move, do not let there be an uprising. If you do, you will allow Alvar and his ilk to hold sway. Do not let your wrath put you beyond reach of Edgar. He has been brought up to be pious and he has already recalled Abbot Dunstan from his banishment. He will need many good men about him, men whose strengths lie in other areas. Think hard about how you can be of use to him. There is more than one way to tan a hide."

Elwood stuck out his bottom lip as if he were still a sulky child, but Alfreda thought that his father had been less blunt than he could have been. Elwood was no warrior, and would need to find some other way of becoming indispensable to Edgar.

Abbot Athelwold cleared his throat. "How many men does Edgar now have with him, my lord?"

The Half-king held up his cup and waited while the serving-boy filled it with ale. "Alvar has brought many weapon-men from Mercia, and Edgar has summoned yet more from over the sea."

In a soothing voice obviously adopted to placate Elwood, who bent his neck as if his head were being stroked, the abbot said, "Well then, what is wrong with that? Is not the hall here at Ramsey often filled with great men of learning and traders who bring us wealth?"

The Half-king shook his head. "No, these are not the same. These are men from beyond the northern sea and they have been hired to steer ships. Edgar will have so many speaking into his ear that the trick will be to find the best way of being heard." He shook his head, clearly still shocked by Edgar's seeming ingratitude for all he owed this illustrious family. He clasped Elwood's shoulder. "Come, lad, now you are calmer, let us finish this game that we started." He led Elwood away to the gaming table, but Alfreda thought that the Half-king had been alluding to a game played on a much wider surface, one that covered the whole of England.

She lost her fight with the shudder that had been threatening her composure. The situation was also of great significance to her, though none would think of it. Edgar was gone and the Half-king had announced his plans to retire to a monastery. Who would protect her and her unborn child from its father's petulant violence? She blinked quickly to prevent the newly formed tear from growing large enough to fall. Her husband and his kin were proud to consider themselves less the soldiers, more the statesmen. And yet these same men who set themselves above those they thought of as mere weapon-men were capable of immense cruelty. She sat back and wondered about this Alvar, falling into a reverie about the fearsome soldier who was portrayed as a throwback to a less sophisticated age and yet who had the whole of Mercia at his command and held the young king in thrall. In her mind-picture this supposedly uncultured oaf would never lay a hand upon his lady, being only attentive and kind, siring children who would be every inch as handsome as their father.

Athelwold touched her arm. "My dear, is all well?"

She turned to stare at him. "What?"

"You gave a great sigh. Naught is wrong with the bairn, is it?"

"No." She raised her hand to shield the tell-tale redness

of embarrassment. "I was brooding on what has been said. Could there be an uprising, do you think?"

Athelwold said, "It might come to that, yes."

"Why do you say that?"

"The Fairchild is older than Edgar and already wed. If he and his wife have children, they will be more throne-worthy than Edgar. She is from a royal line; her forefathers were of Alfred's kin and so their offspring would have higher atheling status than Edgar. He is too young yet to wed, so..." He held his palms up, his point made.

Alfreda remembered how Edgar had mentioned his need for a wife and his threats to steal her away from Elwood. *I take whatever I want.* "Somehow I do not think Edgar will let something like that stand in his way, Abbot." Elwood was still at the gaming table, so Alfreda decided that she was not needed after all. She took her leave of Athelwold and stepped outside into the warm sunshine.

On days like this she could almost make herself believe that life here was not so bad. The cloudless sky stretched out above her and she wondered where it ended. It had not rained for some weeks and the ground felt comparatively firm under her feet. Looking out through the gateway, she saw that the causeway was sitting clear of the marsh, a sign of how low the water levels had sunk. Even the biting eastern wind had abated. Alfreda took pleasure where she could and decided not to return to the confines of the carding shed. It would still be there on the next rainy day.

Over by the enclosure boundary, Elwood's youngest brother Brandon was standing with his back against the fence. His hands were tucked into his tunic belt and he was scuffing the ground with his boot, moving his leg from side to side, kicking up showers of dust. Alfreda watched him for a while, puzzled, for Brandon was not normally to be found alone and without a purpose. But then she mouthed a silent, "Ah, I see." Little Brandon was now a shadow with no solid shape to mimic; he was lost without Edgar. A flicker of pity crossed her heart, but soon dissipated. None of them would be any the better for Edgar's departure.

Strong fingers gripped her shoulder and she turned to face her husband. "You left the hall. I did not say you could."

She dropped her gaze and stared at the ground. "I am sorry, my lord. I had thought that you were busy at the gaming board and had no need of me."

He gripped her arm. "Come, woman, and I will show you what my needs are."

A butterfly movement in her belly awakened a brave defiance. "The bairn is kicking, my lord, so I would beg you…"

He reached with his free hand to jerk her chin up. "You would do better to beg the Almighty that this child is fair like me. If it should have the Devil's dark eyes like yours I shall not bear to look upon it, much less name it as my own."

She had seen many a bitch hound snarl and bite any who came close enough to pet her whelps and now she understood, for she would suffer no threats or insults to be cast at her child. She stared into his eyes, tried hard not to blink and said, "My son will not be throne-worthy but he will be high-born and he will be loved."

He released her and fanned his fingers up and down in a gesture she recognised as an attempt to fight the urge to make a fist. He made as if to move away, but then he took a step back. "Why did you say that?"

"I said that my child…"

"No, no. About being throne-worthy, what made you say those words?"

She shrugged. "The abbot told me that the Fairchild's wife can trace her line back to Alfred, so her children will be higher than Edgar in rank. He might have to take Wessex by force or lose it to his brother's children."

He closed his mouth, leaving the tip of his tongue visible between his lips. It remained there for a moment as his thought took shape. Then he said, "But what if someone could get Wessex for him, with no blood spilt? What if there were never any children born?" Elwood's lips pulled back into an alarming snarling smile. "My father was right. It seems that there might, after all, be more than one way to tan a hide."

Edgar's Court, London

The woman, Eva, lay propped up on one elbow. Her milk-white hair fell across her face and she peered up at him with only one eye fully visible. "My lord, will you not lie back down? It is cold in here without you." She parted her lips to smile and ran her tongue across the tips of her upper teeth.

Alvar leaned towards her and put his hand on her cheek. Her skin was as soft as Persian silk and the hair, swept back by his touch, released the gentle fragrance of rosemary. "Your offer is hard to ignore…" He took a deep breath, swung his legs over the side of the bed and picked up his breeches from the floor. "But I am needed at the witan meeting." He gestured to the window. "Here is the sun, though, so you will soon be warm."

She pushed her bottom lip forward and settled back on the pillows. As the light from the window penetrated the room she swam her fingers in front of her face and said, "Pretty motes, but not hard enough to hold. It was not a shaft of sunlight I wanted."

Alvar snorted a laugh, stood up and adjusted his tunic. He blew a kiss over his shoulder, left the bedchamber and took the stairs two at a time.

Elwood of Ramsey turned his head at the thumping descent and his cheeks flushed red.

Alvar placed his hand on the newel-post and leaped over the last three steps, landing close to Elwood. He sought to assure the East Anglian that he was not the subject of the joke. "I was laughing at something Eva said." Alvar put his hands on his lower back and stretched up, grinning.

Elwood's mouth shrank into a creased round, drawing wrinkles from his cheeks until his face resembled the tightly pulled rumpled hide around the drawstring of an otter-skin bag. He took a step closer to Alvar and said, "That woman is a whore."

Alvar's smile dropped and he sniffed. Half empty ale jugs crowded the side tables, but the lord of Ramsey's breath smelled clean. The man was sober as a saint.

Elwood's mouth moved as if his tongue were reacting to some unseen poison. "Bad enough that Edgar should give you one of only two bedrooms, but I thought we had left lewdness behind at his brother's court?" Elwood stalked off, to pause and admire one of the new wall-hangings.

Helmstan wandered over. "What? Does Ramsey not wish to hear the words of a woman well laid?" He covered his mouth in mock concern and then laughed. "Or is it worse? Was she not well laid?" He slapped Alvar playfully on the shoulder.

But Alvar shook his head. Was it possible that another man could envy him so much simply because he had been given a separate chamber? "I feel as if I am in the shield wall and have stepped forward with the left leg."

"He has you on the wrong foot? He is a man who rarely smiles, so do not take it to your heart. It may be that he does not care for Eva and her ilk."

Alvar nodded. "I think that the lord of Ramsey cares for few women." He turned to face his friend. "Not like you, then, still warm from your wedding bed and grinning. And yet you do not bring your lovely wife to court to meet us. Is she too shy?"

Helmstan nodded. "As it happens, she is indeed shy. She would come if I asked her, but I do not ask. I love her too much to have her suffer your crude manners."

Alvar feigned indignation. "What do you mean? I know

how to speak to a pretty woman."

"Yes, but only to ask them into the nearest bed. My lady would be hard pressed then, knowing how to say no."

Alvar grinned. "Most of them struggle to say no, so strongly are they drawn to me."

Helmstan adopted an expression of mock pity and laid his hand gently on Alvar's arm. "No, my friend. She would struggle because she knows it is rude to tell an earl to stick his ugly head in a water butt."

Alvar laughed and thumped Helmstan on the shoulder. He waved his arm in a wide arc. "But, she is missing a treat; look at this wonderful new building."

Away from the stairwell, only a few men remained in the hall, most of the nobles having moved along to the meeting chamber at the far end of the building. Beyond the open doorway, the tree-wrights in the yard were sawing the freshly coppiced wood, and inside, a carpenter ambled by with an armful of planks. A ladder lay propped against a wall where a small section of daub plaster remained bare, even though several embroidered cloths had already been hung. The carpenter sniffed his disapproval that the lime-wash had not been finished, although he seemed in no hurry to reach his own area of incomplete floorboards. A plump-faced bishop walked through the doorway, his arms folded in front of him, hands hidden in his sleeves. He took short steps so that although he moved forward his robes did not touch his legs, giving him the appearance of floating. Alvar smiled. Dunstan, reinstated not as abbot but elevated to bishop of Worcester, carried himself as if born to the role. "My lord Dunstan, do you fare well this bright morning?" He waited as the newly appointed bishop moved his mouth in preparation.

As he walked, Bishop Dunstan dropped his lower jaw, resting it on the cushioning fold of flesh beneath his chin. His head bobbed forward and his large ears began to redden from the exertion. "It is c-c-colder than I would like…" He worked his mouth again in silence.

Alvar fingered one of the wall-hangings, feeling along the stitching as if keen to know how the thing had been fashioned.

Dunstan drew level with Elwood. "B-but now that I am back I must make do, for I will not g-go over the sea again." He flashed a glare at Alvar over his shoulder.

Helmstan shook his head. "The stammer gets worse. He had reached Elwood by the time he was able to speak."

Alvar disagreed. "No, I think he never meant to speak to me. All the time I have been in London, the bishop has snubbed me at every turn, but I do not know why. Come, we should go into the meeting."

Alvar slid his thumbs through his belt and Helmstan hummed softly as they followed Dunstan and Elwood into the meeting chamber.

Elwood had his hand on the bishop's shoulder. He glanced back at Alvar and smiled as if he had just made the winning move on the gaming table.

Alvar could not understand the animosity; he did not recall ever challenging Elwood at the gaming board, even symbolically. Elwood raised a hand to wave to his brothers in the chamber, threw one last scowl at Alvar and went to join them. Dunstan turned his head and held Alvar's gaze for a moment before he glided to his seat next to Edgar.

Helmstan stopped humming and let out a low whistle. "Look at all these fine folk."

Alvar followed the direction of his stare to the ladies who had flocked with their newly ennobled husbands, and now found places to stand near the windows where the sunlight lit up their rich silk kirtles.

Helmstan said, "My wife would no more feel at home here than if a cow were to be lowered into a snake pit."

Alvar murmured a vague response, wondering why Helmstan would denigrate his wife by intimating that she would compare unfavourably with these beautiful ladies. Then he looked around the room, thought again about Helmstan's exact words and realised that it was meant as a compliment, that Helmstan's wife had better things to do than fawn and flutter and be seen in all the right places. And now, all jokes aside, Alvar's interest was ignited and he was keen to meet this intriguing woman.

But that would have to wait for another time, and he shifted his gaze from the women to look at the newest arrivals. Edgar had wasted no time in using his East Anglian contacts to good effect, but these Scandinavians were not merchants but mercenaries. The boy was taking his kingship seriously; these men had been imported to build and sail a new fleet, and Alvar could only hope that the new ships would be used in the national interest only, and that the young king had heeded his advice to treat the Northumbrians and Danes with respect.

As well as the elegant ladies and the foreigners, the churchmen also brought colour to the scene with their opulent clothing. The archbishop of Canterbury was an old man who looked as if he had cheated death for a decade or more, but his chasuble was of expensive silk, with gold bordering, and his shoulders were swathed in layers of the finest fur.

Alvar took his leave of Helmstan, who went to sit with his lord the Greybeard of Chester, and made his way to the top table, replying with hand gestures behind his back to the good-natured mocking from the Mercian contingent.

"He cannot remember to shave, but he can find his way to the king's bench."

"We are too dull and dreary for him now."

Alvar, laughing, took his seat next to Edgar and tried to adopt a more serious expression. "Lord King, you wanted to see me?"

The boy-king stared into the middle distance. His clear skin was contoured only where a thin beginning of a line traced its way vertically from his brow to the bridge of his nose. He gestured towards the document on the table in front of him and said, "Your thegns tell me that we must take great care with the wording in this land gift." He pushed the document towards Alvar. "I have already given this man the turf so I do not see why such care is needed with the writing of it."

Edgar's fingers drummed the table, but he kept his head tilted with his ear close to Alvar's mouth.

But if Edgar was keen to listen to anything that might increase his knowledge, Dunstan was impatient to get to other business. "Lord King, it is a small thing and is best left to the scribes to deal with."

Alvar felt a dull tarnish finally settle on the sheen of his good mood, so expertly buffed to gleaming by Eva's attentions. The bishop seemed determined to contradict his every word, but Alvar knew that Helmstan would never forgive him if he did not at least set the cleric straight on this one subject.

He said, "To men of Wessex, all other land is *the north*, a great swathe of land where kings have seldom ridden. But those beyond Wessex do not think themselves as one lump. The Danes, to name but one folk, are well settled but they are, even so, Danish. In Mercia, most men do not think themselves to be English, but dwellers in an old kingdom that in days gone by made its own laws and named its own kings."

Dunstan grunted and said in a quiet voice, "They would do better to help us in our aim to bring holiness back to this land."

Alvar ignored him and leaned forward, the better to direct his words to the young king. "The land in Herefordshire which you gifted to my thegn is in the land of an ancient tribe, a proud folk who have lived in this land since the Angles and Saxons first came over the sea. If you are seen to allow the ancient land-edges and the old-rights therein, then your folk will love you well." He handed the vellum back to the king.

Edgar said, "You are knowledgeable indeed, my lord Alvar. I am grateful."

Dunstan made a strange spluttering noise.

Edgar stared again at the writing and handed it back to his scribe. "That will do well; you may write the rest now."

The scribe bowed and backed away.

Alvar sat back and breathed in the clean smell of new timber. He was aware of Dunstan's glower, but kept him in his periphery and refused to turn his head to meet the hot stare.

Edgar said, "Wine, lord Bishop?" He clicked his fingers.

Now Alvar looked across and it was clear from the dismissive wave of the hands that Dunstan was keen to get started.

"We have pressing business."

The two exchanged glances. Alvar watched them, unsure how to read their expressions. He tried to remember the nature of the day's business and assumed that his memory of it had been washed away by the ale that Eva had served him all the previous evening. Again he wondered how he had got to this place, he who had never paid attention in witan meetings and was now expected to add his voice to weighty decisions. He still felt like a fraud. Even here in London, away from his brother Brock and wearing his own shoes, he was unsure of his footing. On the battlefield, he knew where to place each step, to keep his balance as he wielded his weapons, but this was new, requiring not a sharp spear point but a sharp mind, and it seemed a long journey from the training yard to the inner circle of government. Dunstan stood up and Alvar sat forward, ready to listen.

Bishop Dunstan cleared his throat and the chattering subsided. "My lords," he raised his sleeve to wipe away spittle, "It is the wish of our b-b-beloved archbishop of Canterbury that I speak for him about something which has lain heavy on our hearts and minds."

Alvar looked with all the others to the seat by the hearth. The archbishop gripped his fur cloak around his shrunken frame like a second skin. His head, bald except for the tufts of hair which grew seemingly from his ears, hung forward as if it really were too heavy for his neck to bear the weight.

His eyes gleamed vital, but cold.

Dunstan said, "It grieves us that the king in Wessex, the Fairchild, is living sinfully with a wife to whom his kinship is too near. Therefore we have sent to his Holiness, the pope, to have the match undone."

"What?" Alvar gripped the edge of the table and sat up straight. A cup tottered and he reached out to hold it, choked, round its stem. He addressed Edgar. "Lord King, you cannot. Theirs is a love match." Was this really the business of grown men who thought to rule a kingdom? "What good will be done by this heartlessness?"

Edgar's breathing was rapid and shallow but he kept his gaze fixed on the far wall. Alvar shook his head and stared at the bishop.

Dunstan prepared himself for speech once more. He dropped his jaw and puffed out shots of breath. "Lewdness cannot be sanctioned. We are all of one mind."

Alvar looked around the room for verification of this assertion, but only the East Anglians and the churchmen sat upright, alert and interested, while the rest of the witan members were sitting with heads bowed, or stared at the ceiling, or gazed out of the window, as if any sight were preferable to looking at Dunstan and being drawn into his scheme. *All of one mind?*

Alvar slammed his palms down on the table. "Are we? It seems that most men here think that for the Fairchild to lose half a kingdom was enough. I did not think the Church would needlessly seek to harm him further."

Elwood of Ramsey said, "You are new to the ways of the witan so I will tell you that we do not speak thus to our beloved bishops. You should take care, lest you earn yourself a bad name."

"For what; plain-speaking?" Alvar looked at Dunstan, hoping that the bishop would answer his earlier question.

Dunstan held his hands out as if there were nothing more to be said or done.

Alvar persisted. "But what will become of his young

wife; does she have land of her own? What has she to do with a fight between two brothers? She does not even have any children to bring her comfort in her loneliness."

Elwood let slip a small smile, as if victorious. "And that is the point…" He stopped and composed his features into a scowl. "That is a good thing. She is no better than a whore. And you are a whore-monger if you speak on her behalf."

"I take it you think that she will be better clothed in widow's weeds?" Alvar glared at Elwood's brothers, both of whom were nodding emphatically.

The second-eldest, the lord of Thetford, said, "The Fairchild must give her up."

Brandon, the youngest, said, "It must be as my brother says." His smooth cheeks glowed and he clenched his fists, but his gaze remained fixed downwards. His pale long lashes beat quickly below purplish lids.

Alvar ground his back teeth together and, under the table, out of sight, his hands clenched and unclenched while his foot tapped in quick beats upon the floor. This was not what he came for; this was not what was promised. At least on a battlefield there could be a fair fight, with each man knowing who the enemy was. He did not like the scheming of politics. He looked again at Dunstan. "Lord Bishop, you say that all the churchmen are as one on this, but what of our friend the bishop of Winchester?"

Dunstan wrinkled his nose. "I am glad that you asked me that. *Your* friend, the bishop of Winchester, stayed with the Fairchild and your elder brother in Wessex instead of coming here to stand with Edgar. But even had he come here, he could not speak on such matters. As a wedded man, he remains a shameful stain upon the Church." He frowned. "The good name of your kin is besmirched by this friendship. Take care that it does not d-drag you down."

"Is that a threat? I make my friends where I will, lord Bishop, and not at any man's behest."

"You should be…" Dunstan, alerted by a strange sound,

glanced over to the hearth. The archbishop's head bobbed up and down as a rattling cough faltered, unable to rise above his chest. Alvar watched Dunstan's face, wondering if in fact he was concerned for the frail old man, or merely waiting for the archbishop to hurry up and die.

King Edgar spoke in a low voice, assuring attention. "I think that we must wait for the pope's word on this and turn to other things now, my lords."

Alvar followed the king's lead and lowered his voice. "My lord, may I have one last word? This annulment might push the Fairchild too far; he agreed to the carving up of the kingdom but if he were to lose his wife might he not fight back?"

Edgar shrugged. "That's what I've got you for."

Elwood of Ramsey laughed shrilly and said, "It will not happen, my lord."

Alvar looked at the East Anglian. The man looked panic-stricken and it seemed to Alvar that his assurance to the king sounded more like a prayer of hope than an avowal of certain truth.

He was alone in the meeting chamber. Most folk were lying in the hall, to sleep or hold their over-indulged bellies, or else were playing at the gaming boards by the light of the hall's great hearth. Helmstan had ridden home to his lovely bride, unable to bear the separation any longer. Less than a twelve-month had passed since Alvar witnessed the same deep devotion shared by the Fairchild and his bride. Naught had been said of their close kinship before their wedding day. It was only when... Yes, it was only when Dunstan found the boy in bed with his bride and her mother. He'd threatened them with the wrath of the Almighty and the Fairchild banished him. Alvar sighed and sat forward to warm his hands by the fire. The early summer evenings were still cool and not all of the new shutters were a snug fit at the windows. He stared into the flames. So now Dunstan was back and wanted his revenge, and how better than to destroy the marriage? The strategy had been revealed as a means by which to ensure that Edgar remained sole heir to the whole kingdom, but nevertheless, delight was being taken in the shameful settling of old scores. He shook his head. There would be a great sorrow wreaked in the name of spite.

Alvar sat back in his chair. Dunstan had served three kings well and loyally, but the moment he had met resistance in the form of a lustful youth he had shown himself to be mettlesome. It was possible that he sought fame beyond his reformation of the abbeys; there had certainly been a covetous gleam in his eye when watching over the archbishop's failing body. He had declared his determination never to be banished again and was doing all he could to ingratiate himself with Edgar. Alvar's first day in the witan had shown him that Edgar would favour whoever could give him what he wanted. Everyone was elbowing for power and Alvar would have to do it too, or be swept aside. He was thrashing in water too deep for his liking but had no choice but to start swimming, for if not he would bring shame upon his father's memory. In the meeting, raw and untried, he had perhaps spoken too much and too harshly, and it was probably not a good idea to antagonise the churchmen, but he must step in and make sure that Edgar was not influenced too much by the Church's self-interest. Although he was still feeling light-headed, Alvar knew that there was no more time for wondering how it was that he had been picked up, spun round and placed in this absurd situation. He had sworn loyalty to Edgar, his king had asked for his service, and now Alvar knew that he must use more than his sword arm in the giving of it. He raised his head as the bell from the chapel broke into the stillness as it called those in the hall to compline. Alvar sprang to his feet.

He paused in the doorway as Elwood of Ramsey and his youngest brother walked by in silence on their way to the chapel.

Alvar, affable mood restored, called out after them.

"Why so grim, my lords; have you so much to confess that you have forgotten how to smile?"

Elwood laid a hand on his brother's arm, turned and retraced his steps until he was level with the entrance to the chamber. He lifted his chin and stared at Alvar through eyes drawn into nearly shut lines. "Oh I can bare my teeth, my lord, as I think you witnessed in the meeting. You saw what we did this day and we have barely begun. You are a warrior in an age of peace, and it is we swift-witted men who are the strong ones now."

Alvar shrugged. "There will still be a need for warriors if the Vikings ever come back. Meanwhile, I'll do whatever England needs."

"You still do not understand, do you? This is not about England; this is about us and you."

The brightness of Alvar's mood dimmed once more. Ever since the coronation debacle at Cheddar and his speedy reassessment of the Fairchild, he had learned to value those who based their judgements on what they saw, not what they heard. "At least let me give you a reason to hate me," he said. But then he sniffed. "Although, having seen your choice of friends, I must say that I am beginning to be glad that you do not count me amongst them."

Elwood stepped closer, his breathing rapid and shallow. "I will make friends where I need to until I get back what you stole from me."

Alvar was puzzled by his comment, and the fact that even now the man's breath smelled oddly fresh. What had he been drinking all day if not the ale? And what kind of a man eschewed the king's ale at the king's table in the king's hall where every other man, including the king, was more than comfortable in his drunkenness?

Elwood stalked back down the corridor and his younger brother waited until he was back alongside him before he dared to scowl.

Abbot Athelwold, Edgar's former tutor, came quietly along the corridor and stopped in the doorway. Like Bishop

Dunstan he was nearing his fifties, but, as he lifted the corners of his mouth, the skin between his dark eyes and high cheekbones remained smooth and unwrinkled. His hair was only barely flecked with grey and still dominated by fine strands that shone golden brown in the hearth-light.

Athelwold smiled. "I take it that you are not now coming to night-song, my lord?" He shuffled past, turned and said, "I understand, but take care. You are not the only son of a great man with a place at the king's side, and you are not the only one with a yearning to keep it."

Alvar stood in the doorway after the abbot had departed, silently paying him the courtesy of considering what he had said, because as tutor to the East Anglian brood he must have based his statement on personal knowledge. But whilst he could acknowledge the warning, there was little Alvar could do to act upon it. What was it that Elwood thought had been stolen; the land which Alvar's father had held, or perhaps he perceived the theft of Edgar himself? Alvar was stacking up enemies without trying too hard and his briefly found optimism for his new role was now swiftly waning. He sighed. Perhaps Helmstan had had the right idea, going home to his wife as soon as the meeting had ended. So Alvar trotted off down the corridor, his nostrils twitching for the smell of Eva's scent and a clue as to where she might be.

Chapter Three AD958

Helmstan's house, near Chester

Káta pulled down a green-shoot branch and held it while she stepped out of the woods and onto the path. She let it swish back into place and stood with her face turned skyward, eyes closed against the sun. Switching her weight from one foot to the other she listened for the squelch as each shoe sucked away from its mould in the mud. A mistle-thrush sang its agreement that spring had arrived and she opened her eyes to look up into the trees. Unable to spot the bird, she turned and waved as Hild of Oakhurst sauntered up the path, leaning, as always, on her stout blackthorn walking stick. Some said that an Irish monk gave it to her, some that she kept it to beat her numerous children. Some even suggested that she used it to fend off her husband, but Káta was sure that they were teasing.

"My lady," Hild said, pointing her stick skyward, "I see that you, too, are thankful for the sunshine."

"I am as glad as that throstle," Káta said. "With this sunshine, the roads will dry out and firm up, and my husband will soon come home."

Hild tapped the ground with the blackthorn. "Aye, God willing. Lord Helmstan has been away more days than not in these last twelve months." She took a step forward and laid her free hand on Káta's arm. "Not so lonely that you yearn for your old hall and a warmer hearth?"

Káta shook her head. "No. I'm glad this is my home now. And there is so much to be done when Lord Helmstan is away, I have no time to think of my old life."

Hild smiled. "Not as busy as we could be, eh?" She winked.

Káta knew what she meant and would accept no more gratitude. There had been three bad harvests in a row, and the first thing she had done as Helmstan's lady was lift the obligation for feasts to be cooked on saints' days.

"My little ones are running round with fat on their bones now, thanks to you."

Káta waved her hand. "You owe me no thanks for that. We were blessed that there was no fever. Oats and barley might not have grown well, but there is always fish to be had from the Dee and I would have been a dull-wit if I had not learned swiftly to send to Chester for our needs." She leaned forward and touched Hild's arm. "You know, it was no great hardship to leave Northampton. If you had met my mother…" She pulled her veil lower on her forehead and squinted until her cheeks lifted. She hunched over and wagged a finger, imitating her mother's harsh tones. "*I had to cross the sea from Denmark when I was wed but you, daughter, have only to take the road west.*"

Hild laughed at the impersonation. "Your mother must be a fire-breather indeed, my lady."

"Oh, you ask Gytha about my mother; she would brook no thought of being left with her, and came here to live with me. Before we left, Gytha told her that the dragon heads on the Viking long ships were carved in her likeness."

Káta bent over again and teased Hild with the wagging finger. "My mother said, '*Take the idle bag of bones, then, for she is too slack for my house.*'"

Hild held up her stick as if to ward off evil spirits and set off backwards down the path. "Not to be rude, but I would hate to meet the woman who frightens even your Gytha." Laughing, she turned and ran a few steps, slowed to a walk, and waved without looking back.

Káta chuckled. Turning her back on the line of trees which marked the edge of the forest, she climbed the fence where the path crossed the mill-track. Burgred the herdsman had been milking when she passed him earlier, but now he was holding a lamb, one of the first of the new stock, grown fat and almost as big as the adult ewes. He waved a temporarily free arm at his lady before he grappled once more with the headstrong beast. Káta laughed as the lamb sheep-smiled at him. All the lambs and kids born this year were healthy. If they remained blessed, the hungry winters were behind them.

She slowed her pace to climb the upward slope on the far side of the field. As she came down the other side her toes pressed against the soft leather of her shoes, and she turned her feet sideways until she reached the path which linked the field with her home, the settlement of Ashleigh. Káta pushed open the gate and stepped into the enclosure.

Outside the bake-house Siflæd, wife of Wyne the miller, was sitting with her back against the wall. Her cheeks were flushed and, beneath the edge of her headscarf, wisps of damp hair clung to her face. She used a scarf which was Norse in style; a silk cap fitted closely to the head and tied at the nape.

Káta smiled and said, "I see Gytha has lent you another hat. Is it hot work today?"

Siflæd scrambled to her feet. "It is, my lady. But the first loaves are cooling and the next batch is baking. I stepped out only to get away from the heat of the oven for a while."

Káta gestured with her open hand towards the ground. "No, no, all is well; you sit. It is cooler here in the yard. I was thinking, though, that the roads from the south might be hard enough to ride now, which means that Lord Helmstan might be home soon. Can we bake a few more loaves? Would it help to knead the dough outside?"

"It would, my lady, thank you. There is enough flatbread, but if my idle daughters hurry with the grinding, I can bake with yeast and the finest ground meal to make risen loaves for the lord. With your leave, I will go now and get my man Wyne to lift me down another bag of meal."

On her way to the main hall, Káta stopped outside the cook-house. Amongst the sacks of dried beans and mushrooms stacked against the open doorway, a bag of peas was flapping open. She reached down and let a scoop of the hard pellets run through her fingers before she caught the corners of the sack and tied them. She turned sideways to peer through the doorway but stepped back as two flustered chickens squawked through the doorway in a flurry of feathers and outraged dignity, followed by Leofsige the cook, brandishing a knife with a blade that shone sharp enough for any meat, dead or still living. Káta took a step back and slipped. Leofsige lifted the knife and pulled himself to a halt before he bowled into her.

"My lady, forgive me." He offered her his hand to help her back onto her feet, his giant strength pulling her almost beyond upright. "I had some oats ready to boil up when those hens came in and began pecking at them."

Káta lifted her kirtle with one hand and twisted round to look at the back of her skirt. "It will dry and brush off, do not worry. I am not bruised, only startled." She righted the sack of peas. "A good thing I had tied it up. And see, you always get cross when the cats come up from the mill, but they are on your side today."

He looked behind him. The cats had stretched out low, front paws forward, as the chickens settled to peck outside the bake-house, unaware.

Leofsige clapped his hands and the cats melted away. "They should be warding off the rats from the corn and meal, but I will forgive them this time," he said.

Káta left him to his muttering and brushed again at her skirt when she entered the weaving shed. Looking down to check that Gytha had replaced the straw rushes, she saw that she had been followed. "Away, cat," she said. She let go of her kirtle and glanced up at the loom, propped up against the wall with the red and green cloth still awaiting completion. The cat slid round her legs and as she bent down, it opened its mouth in a silent meow. She tickled its chin. "Well," she said, "It takes two to shift the loom. You are not strong enough, and as we do not have Gytha's big hands to help, I can leave the weaving until another day, can I not?"

In the hall, she checked the floor and sniffed to ascertain the blend of dried herbs that Gytha had sprinkled around. She walked the length of the room to the private chamber beyond the dais. Here, strewn across the bed, her sewing tasks also awaited completion. She selected a blue woollen tunic of Helmstan's, ripped during a recent hunt, and a linen undershirt whose stitching had come apart. She picked up her sewing box and collected a stool from the hall. Outside, she put the stool at the edge of the morning shadow, where she would not have to keep moving with the westward shifting sun.

When the rip was mended, she held up the tunic to inspect her stitching. The dogs began to bark at raised voices, borne on the wind from the Chester road. Káta leaned over to look through the open gateway and stood up. Burgred was running towards the enclosure and she thrust the mending onto the stool. Faster than Burgred could run from the fields, Helmstan's horse was galloping along the lane and Káta reached up to pat her veil tidy. Helmstan turned the horse across the corner of the field and brought the beast to a halt beyond the bell tower. Burgred came alongside him and leaned over, one hand on the fence and the other on his knee as he panted. Helmstan slipped from the horse and handed the reins to Burgred, who lifted his hand but not his head as he fought to find his breath. Helmstan shuffled towards the hall in an exaggerated walk as he eased his legs after the long ride. Káta stepped forward. He scooped her up in a bear's embrace, spinning her round before he set her down and stepped back.

"Let me look at you, woman. You seem well?" He looked down.

She laced her fingers together across her belly and gave a small shake of her head. She coughed and raised her chin. "I am well. And the better for seeing you home again." She touched his cheek, scared to do more, unsure of how much to show that she had missed him. "Come inside my lord, you are smeared with dirt from the road, and you must be thirsty after your ride."

In the hall he sat down, and she picked up a jug of ale from the table by the wall. The once pretty Stamford pottery she had brought from her old home was shabby, the glazed red lines of decoration faded and crackled. She ran her finger along the chipped edge of the cup and presented the good side to her lord. "Will you bide at home a little longer this time?" She fetched a footstool and set it in front of his chair.

He put his feet up, one crossed over the other, sat back, and wiped at his face with his sleeve. "I shall be home a while now, even until the harvest. The next meeting is that of the borough at Chester so I will be there and back in a day. Then the hundred-moot is at Twemlow, not even half a day's ride. After that the Michaelmas shire-moot is at Chester also, and by then we shall have Burgred's fat sheep to eat." He set the cup down on the table, put his feet flat to the floor again and patted his knees. "Come, do not be shy."

She hitched up her dress to loosen it from her hips and tried to balance on his lap. Shifting her weight first onto one thigh, she then tried to spread it over two, but only succeeded in wobbling over the dip between his thigh muscles. She put her arm round his neck to steady herself, but her cheek brushed his unshaven chin and she sat forward once more and reached with pointed toes onto the floor to anchor there instead.

"Tell me your tidings," he said.

She ticked off the items with her fingers. "Sigeberht over at Barwick has a new milch cow and Burgred's girl who went to Chester, she gave birth to a... Oh, you cannot wish to hear all our dull tales. Tell me what you have seen while you have been away."

He sat back in the chair, pulling her back with him and

allowing her to lay her head against his chest. "The Fairchild is still king of Wessex, but his grip even there is weak. I hear that he is bereft after the loss of his wife. We have been north into the heart of Northumbria, deep into the Daneland in the east and rotted our feet in the wetlands of East Anglia. Everywhere we went, men swore oaths to Edgar and pledged to send weapon-men whenever he might ask for them. Edgar's hold on the north, the east, and Mercia, is strong. Alvar thinks it cannot be long before Edgar moves to take Wessex from his brother." He wrapped his arms more tightly around her. "If there is a fight, I will be at Alvar's side."

She wriggled her head free. "Then I must hope that day does not come soon."

Helmstan kissed the top of her head. "All this is good for us too, my love."

Káta shook her head. "How? It will take you away."

He kissed her again, this time on the cheek. "It means that Mercia will grow strong again, as it was in the old days."

Káta rolled her eyes and slipped off his lap. She took a broom from the corner and swept a dead mouse towards the door. "Old dusty tales, oft-heard," she said, "Of folk who are all long dead. My father told me that the lady of the Mercians was dead and gone before the days of the great Athelstan who was king even before Edgar's father. Her daughter was shut away, and ever since there have been only West Saxon kings." She had said too much. It was not her place. She propped the broom against the wall and moved away, her back still to him. She kept her head low, but dared a glance over her shoulder to gauge the depth of his anger.

But Helmstan slapped his hand down on his thigh and laughed. "Dearling," he said, "Do not ever be frightened to speak your mind to me. When I wed a maiden with Danish blood I did not think to get a shy mouse for a bride."

She smiled and let her shoulders drop. "Forgive me all the same; I should try not to let my tongue become as sharp as my mother's." Before he could make another joke on the subject, she said, "Now, will you eat?"

Helmstan looked around. "Where are all the women?"

"They are about their work." Emboldened, she attempted to tease him. Head bowed, but glancing up, she said, "We are not like the ladies of the kings' houses, that we can sit about the whole day long."

"Once more, you are right." He stood up. "No, indeed, you should not be sitting. Leave your besom where it is, for I left my men at Chester and they will not be here for some time." He nodded towards the bedchamber. "Why sit about all day when you can lie down?"

She wafted her sleeve in front of her face. In what she hoped was a sufficiently coy tone, she said, "But my lord, I was always taught that it was wrong to lie. Have you more to teach me?"

She was gratified when he grinned. "Oh yes," he said, taking her hand. "And I hope that you will not learn too swiftly, for I would not wish to stop until you are sure that lying is a good thing…"

Now she was brave enough to speak her mind. "For you, my love, I will gladly be a slow learner." Giggling, she allowed him to lead her to the bedchamber.

The leaves in the summer canopy fluttered in the breeze and the sunlight mottled her hands. After a precautionary prayer full of apology, Káta took the cheese and bread from their cloth wrapping and laid them on the ground, pulled her kirtle and under-dress over her head and slipped her feet out of her shoes. She knelt down, leaned forward and scooped the water from the well-spring onto her upper body. Standing up, she wobbled as she dipped one foot then the other into the water. Her plea was silent; the food was a gift and the price of a promise that any child born after this day would never go hungry.

Despite the heat of the day, she shivered and rolled her clothes into a ring to slip them over her head. With no Gytha to help her, she struggled to replace her veil and she held the material in her hands, lifted it halfway to her head again, and sighed. "I cannot be a true lady without a child to show my worth, so why do I have need to look like one?" She stuffed the veil into her basket. As she walked down the slope away from the well she pulled her back up straight, linked her arms in front of her and rocked the basket as if a child lay there. The old gods would decide and she would accept the decision, and hope that the true God would not be angry for her betrayal, but how could any heavenly being deny her on such a beautiful day?

On the edge of the lane, the white-flowered ramsons thickened the air with their aroma of wild garlic. Káta put up a hand to shield her eyes against the afternoon sun. Moisture had formed on her top lip again, even so soon after bathing, and she brushed her sleeve over her face.

She climbed into the field and stopped to press her feet into the grass. It sprang back straight away, growing strong in mud which was no longer waterlogged, and the confirmation of the arrival of summer made her smile.

On the other side of the field, the breeze carried shouts and laughter from the river and Káta quickened her pace. On the riverbank, small children splashed their feet in the water by the edge and ran back to their mothers. Little boats bobbed in the deeper water, the occupants fishing for eels. The two young boys who lived in the little dwelling beyond the mill were standing in the shallows, scooping for minnows with crudely fashioned nets, and an older youth waited further down to stab at passing aquatic life with a sharpened stick. Mothers shouted warnings to children who swam near the far bank and Burgred, who had sheep in the field on the other side, leaned on his crook and kept a shepherd's eye on those who strayed beyond shouting distance.

Gytha, knee-deep in the water, was standing with her skirt hitched into her belt. She held a linen undershirt behind her head and she brought it forward, laughing as it smacked into the water and bubbled into a ball before it sank. Her blonde hair hung loose in wet ringlets and her cheeks glowed like ripening apples in the warming sun. She shouted up to Káta. "Will you come in with us, my lady? But you must swear not to throw water all over us this time."

Káta's hot tired toes wiggled inside her shoes. She stepped forward. "I might help you to wring those…" She shook her head. "No, I cannot," she said. "I am looking for my lord husband; I saw his horse in the paddock so I know that he is home. Have you seen him?"

"Yes, my lady. The lords are further down, on the far bank, beyond the bro."

"Thank you, but you must say the *bridge*." Káta walked on, stopped and backed up two steps. "Did you say *lords*? I must tell Leofsige that the lord of Chester will be sitting on our bench tonight. But I think he was boiling some lamb today and I do not think there will be time to set up the spit…"

Gytha said, "No, my lady, it is not…"

"No, you are right. Boiled meat it will have to be." She walked on. More vegetables might make up for the lack of flavoursome meat. If she hurried back there would be time to soak some dried beans, or perhaps dig up some carrots. She crossed the wooden footbridge and her hips swung as she took longer strides along the west bank of the river. Would there be time to make a broth, or would Leofsige the cook have some already made that could be bulked out with pulses?

Two piles of clothes lay near the water's edge and she stopped. The garments had been discarded carelessly, but on top of them the swords and their belts had been placed with precision, to sit proud of the dirt and grass. Both scabbards were leather-covered but one, which she recognised as Helmstan's, was lined with wool, whilst the other had a fur lining, was finely decorated, and housed a sword with a jewelled hilt.

Helmstan's voice rose up from below the high bank.

"Ha! Lord or no lord, I nearly beat you that time."

Káta had no desire to discomfit the lord Greybeard of Chester, who was nearly fifty and apparently naked. She felt the embarrassment of the intruder and turned to go home the long way.

"Kat? Dearling? Is it you up there?"

Her foot in mid-step, she turned a circle and brought her hand up in greeting, but a flush rose to her face, reminding her that her head was bare, and she let her arm fall and snatched her veil from the basket. A hairpin jabbed her finger as she flung the cloth over her hair. The breeze caught her dress and she twisted to hold it with her elbow as she struggled with her veil. She straightened up and held her breath, as if that might stop the blood rising to her cheeks, for her husband was not swimming with the Greybeard, but with a man less than half that age.

The young man was grinning at her, evidently amused by her struggles with the swathes of material. His gaze remained steady upon her as Helmstan shouted his introduction.

"This is my friend, the lord Alvar."

At last, she was to meet her husband's oldest friend and it was not the most propitious setting in which to greet such a mighty lord. And, worse, Káta found herself staring like some low-born Chester whore at Alvar's upper body, at the fine down of chest hair visible above the water. Helmstan's black chest hair always lay like a hound's coat in the water, the muscles beneath it solid, moving as one. The contours of this man's skin changed with each lithe movement. The only similarity was the crisscross of scars on the arms and shoulders, but then he, too, must spend at least as many hours fighting, training and hunting. How could she be so bold, to take in so much with one look, when she had scarcely been brave enough to look upon her husband thus after over a year of being wed? She looked up, where it was safer to gaze, to notice that the earl's hair fell in light-brown waves, the wet ends touching the skin of his shoulders. She focused on his lips, which were not as full as Helmstan's, and then his face, which was less rounded. But still a wicked devil, one that she hadn't known even to be dwelling within her, wondered what remained hidden from her view, below the water line. Appalled at herself, Káta took a deep breath. Chicken broth, there was some broth left over from last night. If she ran back and told Leofsige, he could boil it up again with some barley and herbs. "My lords, forgive me. I will go back to the hall and I will see to it that food and drinks are on hand for you when you come back."

"No, Dearling, bide where you are. We are coming out now and can go with you back to the hall."

She looked about for somewhere to hide, deciding on the trunk of a willow a few feet away. But with great fuss and waves and splashes, they had already begun to haul themselves from the water.

She turned her back and her face burned, whilst behind her they squelched up onto the bank.

Helmstan rumbled out his friendly-bear laugh. "It looks to me that in some things, all men are the same, my lord."

"Ah, but tales can grow in the telling…" Alvar's voice rang higher, a wolf-call, sharper, leaner.

Grunts and stumbles told of their struggle to pull their clothing on over their wet bodies, where normally they would have lain naked in the sunshine to dry off.

She hummed, but could still hear the teasing.

"See how I have to stretch my breeches to make them fit over my…"

"Belly? Is that the word you are seeking?"

Káta took a step away from the bank, hummed louder and opened her mouth to sing.

"We are dressed and fit to be looked upon now," Helmstan said.

At last. She turned, but kept her head low. Alvar was lying on the grass, his upper body propped up on one elbow, one long leg bent and the other straight. He looked up with a hint of a smile that showed no trace of the humorous exchanges moments before. It was a smile which she found impossible to interpret and she wanted him to stop it.

She met his gaze and held it long enough to greet him properly. "Lord Alvar, I welcome you to Ashleigh."

He inclined his head, and, the moment his smile faded, she wanted it to come back again.

"Lady Káta, I must ask your forgiveness. I thought that the water would be cooling after a hard ride. Who could know that the thing would turn into a show of swimming strength?"

Helmstan patted the grass next to him. "Sit, my love, until we are dry. I would sooner not stride back with these wet breeches sticking to my legs."

She lowered herself to the ground, but her foot caught on her hem. She stood up and lifted her kirtle to her ankles. Sitting down once more, she wriggled to ease the folds of cloth under her until they formed a comfortable seat, shifting again when the grass tickled her leg.

Helmstan said, "Lord Alvar has been in Chester on King Edgar's behalf and craves a meal with us before he goes home to Gloucestershire."

Káta tried one last time to hook her dress round. "And will you sleep the night with us, my lord?"

"I would be glad to do so."

She forgot the struggle with her skirts. There was no trace left of his smile and she blushed at the thought that she had missed a hidden meaning. She found a blade of grass unlike any other and studied it until she felt sure that her cheeks were pale again.

Alvar said to Helmstan, "Tell me; how often have the Welsh come over into Cheshire lately? If you have one weapon-man for every five hides of land, could you spare more if they were needed? If we had to go and fight in the south…"

Forgotten, Káta stretched out her fingers and ran them through the grass. In amongst the pliant blades the tougher stems of the daisies offered resistance and she reached around for more. After threading them into a chain she looked for buttercups and clover to add to the necklace. She stared at the ground long after she had all she needed and when it was time to leave, she looked up. The men were already on their feet and Alvar offered her his hand.

He said, "That is a pretty thing." The smile was no more than a gentle curve, yet still it lit his eyes.

She thrust the flowers behind her back. "Oh, it was but child's play."

He kept his hand outstretched and beckoned with curled fingers. She had to reach out or offend him, so, with the habit of a lifetime, she kept her right hand hidden behind her back while she offered him her left and, as he pulled her upright with a hand no warmer, no stronger, no less calloused than her husband's, a tingle travelled along her arm to arrive as a flutter in her belly.

At the river bank, with the sun behind her, he had not been able to determine the colour of her eyes. It had not mattered; her high cheekbones and delicate chin shaped a face that was so appealing that when she drew near enough, even though her eyes were downcast, he would have handed his heart to her like money to an armed thief for one kiss on her bow-shaped lips.

Tonight, in the firelight of their mead-hall, her eyes had shone cornflower-blue. Yet she had appeared only briefly at the feast table, fretting about the state of the pottery in a voice which remained little more than a whisper, like a breeze too scared to blow until the rain arrived to bolster its strength. Then she had disappeared to the bedchamber at the end of the hall. In response to Alvar's enquiry after her health, Helmstan had merely muttered that she might have found that she was once again lacking something she craved.

The great hearth in the centre of the hall burned with less enthusiasm now; sleeping men breathed in smoky air and blew it out stale. Helmstan's eyes closed and his head lolled forward and jerked up again.

Alvar nudged him. "Why do you not go and find your lovely wife?"

"No, I will sleep here with my men. She will wish to be on her own, if she is not with ch…" Helmstan's head went back and he sank a little in his chair. A snort came from the back of his throat and his hand slipped from the table.

So, that was the reason for the lady's sad demeanour. She craved a child. Alvar laid a hand on his sleeping friend's arm, squeezing it gently before patting and releasing it.

The servants began to tidy away the empty trestle tables and Alvar looked around to see if there was a spare length of bench along the walls where he could lie down. A small dog, too puny to be used for hunting, sniffed round the far side of the table for scraps. Alvar held out a lamb bone and the animal came to him and licked it.

"Well, hound, is that good?" He scratched behind its ears as he mused that Helmstan would still be better sleeping with his fair-looking wife than with his men. Comradeship, forged while men spent the day hunting and enjoyed nights at the mead-bench, formed the bonds that held communities together. A lord gained much respect by staying with his men; status within the group was everything, and worth dying for. Alvar had given up a lot in service to the king and in his role as a warrior, but he wondered if he would forgo the opportunity to share a bed with such a beguiling woman. He sighed. The dog looked up, its tongue hanging from the side of its mouth. Alvar bent nearer to its ear and whispered. "And she is fair-looking, you know." Helmstan had spoken the truth in calling her beautiful.

Standing in a state of agitation with her clothing in disarray, she had presented a vision of a woman utterly devoid of the preening habits of the ladies at court, and it was refreshing to see. She obviously eschewed such niceties when she was on her own manor, and was caught out looking vulnerable only because she knew that by going bare-headed she was flouting convention. Unlike many of the women of his acquaintance, she was embarrassed at the sight of him and he, likewise, was mortified to be seen naked. Such a thing would not normally have bothered him, any more than it worried his female companions, yet he had been uncomfortable to be found thus in Káta's presence. So much so that he made a complete goose of himself with his stupid remark about the flowers. Since when was he so tongue-tied around women? Somehow it mattered so terribly much that Helmstan's wife should think well of him.

The dog licked his outstretched fingers. Alvar recalled how a jagged scar traced a diagonal line across the back of Káta's right hand, from the heel of her thumb to the joint of her little finger. It had been visible while she fought with her veil, but as soon as she could, she had pulled her sleeve over it and lowered her arm by her side. It was so swiftly done that he was left in no doubt that she had done it many times before, a habit born of self-consciousness. He had wondered briefly how she had come to bear such a mark, but he would no more ask her, or indicate that he had noticed by asking Helmstan, than he would dream of taunting Dunstan about his stammer.

Alvar stretched and yawned. No man had held a sword to his back, or forced him to go with Edgar and, now that he knew it was the right thing to do, he had no reason to feel discontent, beyond an itch to get back to what he knew best and put his sword and spear to good use. But there was something… He knew his purpose, he knew his duty, but somehow he had lifted the cup of promise and found it to be empty. Where was the reward; what was it that he was fighting for? There was nothing to soothe his soul, to give him personal succour, beyond serving the king. And as a soldier, he'd always thought that would be sufficient. Around the hall even the remaining whispered conversations stalled as men drifted into slumber. He looked at Helmstan, snoring gently in his chair, felt his own arms and legs growing heavy, and a creeping desire to sink into the deepest slumber. Helmstan, so loyal to the men who served him, so bound up in his Mercian cause, yet with a welcoming hearth and a lovely woman, had less, but seemed to deserve and appreciate it more. Alvar recalled Helmstan's comment that Káta would not fit in at court, and now he had seen for himself that from here, London swirled like an adder's nest, while this hall brought to mind the stillness of a mill pond.

The dawn light spread round the edges of the shutters. Alvar side-stepped through the tumble of sleeping bodies and sniffed his way to the latrine. In the enclosure, the insistent cockerel agitated the hungry hounds with its breakfast call. Stiff from having dozed all night in the chair, Alvar shivered in the dewy dampness and lengthened his pace along the path which led away from the house. At the edge of the woods he stopped and looked about to decide the more interesting route.

The undergrowth crackled and the leaves shushed and hushed. Helmstan's wife stepped from between the trees, pulling small twigs from her gown, and put a hand up to smooth her veil. She straightened up, saw him, looked left and right and turned towards the field.

In two steps he was level with her. "Lady Káta?"

She stopped, but did not look up. "My lord, I beg you to forget that you have seen me here this morning. I have no right to ask this of you, but…"

Alvar looked behind him to the forest and both ways down the lane. "Lady, I have seen naught…"

She lifted her head. Her eyes were full of tears one blink from release. She seemed not to have heard him, for her confession tumbled out anyway. "I have left gifts this morning. In the woods, by the ash tree."

Alvar let out his held breath. "Is that all? Many folk worship trees, my lady. The Church looks the other way, for the old ways die hard. But I will not speak of it, if that is your wish." He rubbed his hand across his chin and laughed.

"What a sorry sight we make, you about the Devil's work and me looking like I have come fresh from a night in hell."

She raised her chin and gave a little shake of the head. "I must go home." She reached round to lift her skirts and walked off.

He caught up with ease and laid a hand on her shoulder. "I am sorry if you thought I was teasing."

"Please, my lord, do not." She was standing stiffly, looking at her shoulder.

He looked down and his hand snapped away as if from a hot cauldron. His apology was lost under the noise of a cry from further down the path.

"Lady Káta, Lady Káta!"

She turned and put her hand up to her brow. "It is Wulfric, son of Brunstan. They farm an oxgang of land beyond the church."

The boy juddered to a halt in front of them and bent to rest his hands on his knees until his breath came freely. "Lady, you must come. My father is wounded."

Alvar looked back towards the manor. "I will fetch my horse."

"No, the way is swifter by foot, over the stile." She set off at a brisk pace, turning to say to Wulfric, "Go to the hall and ask Leofsige for some bread and morning-meat," before her skip progressed to a run.

Alvar trotted alongside her, musing that he would not have paused to think about the youngling's empty belly; his initial reaction was merely to pat his belt to make sure his hand-saex was hanging there. Her breathing grew less rhythmic, but she did not slow her pace until they came to Brunstan's dwelling, so that although the sun had some distance yet to rise, her already prettily pink cheeks glowed red. He smiled at her and stepped back to allow her to enter the dwelling.

The house had one room, with a central hearth and a smoke hole above it in the roof. A rush-light was guttering and the fire was almost out. Alvar reached to close the door but Káta shook her head. "Leave it; I need the light."

On a cot at the far end of the room, Brunstan was lying with his left leg out straight. Blood was seeping through the tunic which had been wrapped round the wound. Káta knelt beside him and peeled back the makeshift bandage. With half-returned breath she said, "What happened?"

"One of my ewes got snared in thorns in a ditch on the far side of Lyfing's field, my lady. I thought I had her, but I fell, twisted withershins, and found myself at the bottom of the ditch with what felt like a bough stuck in my leg. It was really no more than a twig and Wulfric helped me pull it out but…" He winced as she pulled off the bloodstained tunic. "How does it look?"

She patted his good leg. "Not as bad as it feels. I will wash it for you now, then I will send Wulfric back with some vervain to put on it to stop it from festering and he can brew up a wort-drink for you; it will taste bitter but you must drink it all. Afterwards, drink watered ale if you are thirsty."

Alvar stayed by the door, redundant, as she bathed and dressed the wound, using her veil as a bandage. With her sleeves hitched up, her scar showed white on her warm hand. Her fingers moved with speed and yet the wounded man did not flinch at her touch. She stood up and tidied Brunstan's few possessions. She handed the bucket to Alvar.

"You can fill it up again from the stream outside."

Alvar chuckled softly, amused by her ability to dispense with all notion of rank as she assigned him his task. He ducked his head and stepped from the dwelling, dropping to one knee at the edge of the brook to scoop a mouthful of water for himself. He walked back in with the full bucket and placed it on the floor by the hearth, where Brunstan's meagre collection of pans and utensils lay.

Káta was on her feet. She said, "I will send food back with Wulfric, but before he leaves the hall I will show him how to shred and blend the herbs. Burgred will help him with the flock until you are on your feet again."

Out in the sunshine again, Alvar said, "In there, when you handed me the pail, it was as though you forgot that I am an earl."

She put her hands up to her face. "My lord, I am... How can you forgive me?"

"I liked it."

She lowered her scarred hand, but the other remained on her head, reaching for her veil. "I am sorry my lord, what did you say?" She twisted round to look behind.

Wondering whether to repeat his comment, he took a moment to stare at her uncovered head. It was like panning for gold as with each turn of her head the sun showed new lines of honeyed strands in her hair. "You left your veil on the man's leg. Do not worry," he said. Still in awe of a lady who did not slavishly adhere to the strict fashion codes at court, he sought once more to compliment her. "The ladies at the king's houses never throw off their headdresses."

To his surprise, she was not soothed. "No, I can believe that they do not. You must forgive our ways."

He retreated. "All I meant was that you will be cooler without it. Will you wander a while?"

Her answer was merely deferential. "If that is what my lord would like, although you might find me a little dull." She waved at the path beyond the bridge. "This road will bring us back to Ashleigh."

The track was busy with folk about their daily business. Káta greeted them all by name; the milkmaids on their way to churn the milk at the dairy, herdsmen moving their beasts along the tracks into different fields, Grim, whose smithy they passed, and Seaxferth the peddler.

"Seaxferth, is your wain still with the wheelwright? You must chide him, for it is too far for you to bring your wares from Chester without it."

Alvar wrinkled his nose as they walked past the tanning pit, but Káta smiled and nodded at the tanner.

"How goes your little one? Is she on her feet yet?"

Alvar listened to the brief conversation and his regard

grew for this lady who echoed his own inclinations, that duty was paramount. When they moved on, he said, "You look after your folk well."

As she walked, she held out her hand and brushed her fingers through the hedgerow, and now and then she kept hold of a leaf and pulled it free as she went past. She said, "How can there be any other way? I must be as the dock leaf to their nettle stings; they look to me as well as to Helmstan to watch over them."

"It is true," he said. "And the Greybeard of Chester speaks highly of your husband. You are truly blessed. It is a bare life which asks for little."

The smile fell from her face and she slowed down. "I... I had not thought of it like that."

He frowned. He had intended to flatter, but she had not appreciated his comment. He needed to explain his meaning, that he was envious of her simple life when his was of a sudden so vexatiously complicated. He waited for her to resume walking and then he made another attempt. "Once, I was but a soldier, and then lately became lord of my father's lands. But this year has taken me away from my brother and seen me swear to one king over another. Now I have to sit at every witenagemot and tell men what I think, for they say it matters."

She sniffed. "You live a much higher life than mine, my lord." She strode off ahead.

He cursed under his breath. All he wanted was to convey his admiration that she worked hard and was blessed in return with a blissful, peaceful life, whereas he had yet to feel deserving of the honours thrust upon him, so that his itinerant lifestyle remained a wearisome necessity. But, tongue-tied and blustering, he was succeeding only in convincing her of his arrogance.

He came alongside her once more. He knew he was falling some way short of eloquence, but he ploughed on. "You know but little of me..."

She interrupted. "You must have many houses?"

A piece of grit blew into his eye and he blinked and stopped to wipe it. "I do. But I am not oft-times at home, for I have to go to hundred-moots and am needed at all of Edgar's meetings, wherever they might be." This time, he was quicker to realise that whilst he was comparing his life unfavourably with her settled existence, he might still be mistaken for a braggart, so he followed it with a refutation. "But I am sworn to the king and must ride where he goes, whether or not I would rather bide at home."

"From what you say, your life is a world away from mine and Helmstan's."

He did not know the reason, but it was important that this married woman knew that he lived alone. "Oh, yes, for I do not have a woman at home."

"No, I can see that there would be no room in your wandering life for a wife," she said.

"In truth I think my household might be the better for a woman's ways, for today I have seen how well you…" His tongue had finally untied itself, but she had gone on ahead.

He followed her onto a tree-lined track. The path was rutted, churned in wetter weather by cart wheels and now baked hard by the summer sunshine. As he caught up to her, she stepped on a raised edge of mud and her foot slipped into the track carved out by the wheels. Alvar moved forward and grasped her elbow, supporting her weight while she found a firmer footing. This time she did not shrug him off, but smiled her thanks. She led the way again and he watched her as she walked, looking at the golden braid of hair swinging softly with each step. Oh yes, his household would certainly be better for the ways of a woman such as this one.

In the yard his retainers, apparently regretting the previous night's ale consumption, shielded their eyes from the daylight as they stumbled through their packing routine. Káta's cook moved among them with a tray of herby omelettes. One thegn reached out and held the omelette hovering at his lips, before he replaced it and ran to the latrine.

Káta asked the cook if the remains of the food from the previous night had been distributed.

"Yes, my lady, and I gave six eggs to young Wulfric. How goes Brunstan?"

"He will live. The wound was not too deep and it is clean, so it will heal swiftly enough." She jerked her head in the direction of the men. "It looks as though you will have fewer mouths to feed today."

Alvar stood by the tether-post and patted one of the horses there. He examined its bridle, making a show of inspecting the leather. She had forgotten him.

"Gytha, is the hall clean?"

"Yes my lady. You were gone a long time; what did you think of…"

He could not make out the rest of the woman's question and he scowled at the thegn who had dropped his saddle at that precise moment. But he got the gist of the question when the last part of the answer rang out clear across the yard.

"Is a rich man of the king's house and we are but dull folk in his eyes. Come, we must see if the hens have laid this morning. Is there rennet for the cheese? When I used boiled nettle it did not curdle the milk enough."

Alvar raised his head and stared out at the hills.

"My lord? Is it a good dream that you see?" The stable-boy who had spoken was holding Alvar's saddled horse for him.

"No, it was not. But I think it was one that I needed to see." Alvar took the reins and turned at a shout from the other side of the hall.

A runner pushed through the clusters of men. "Lord Alvar! Where is the lord Alvar?"

"Here."

The man stopped and panted. "My lord, I come with tidings. We sought you first at Chester. We had hoped to find you here; otherwise we were at a loss to know where to go…"

"Spit it out, then."

"My lord, the archbishop of Canterbury is dead."

Alvar sucked in his breath. So the old archbishop, who had tenaciously clung to life for years, had finally loosened his grip. His last act had been a vindictive connivance, depriving the Fairchild of his wife. Alvar could not pretend sadness. But how would they all fare under his successor, whoever he might be? If it was Edgar's favourite… "Will Dunstan now leave Worcester for Canterbury?"

The runner took a few more gulps of air. "No, my lord. The Fairchild of Wessex has given Canterbury to his friend the bishop of Winchester, who has gone to Rome to be given the pallium by the pope."

Alvar scratched his chin. His family had long been friends with the bishop of Winchester, but Winchester's marriage was a long-standing irritation to Dunstan. Now the Fairchild had reasserted his authority, promoted the bishop, thus denying Dunstan the archbishopric. Depriving the Fairchild of his wife had not had the desired sedating effect. Young Edgar had been under no illusion that force would one day be required in order to secure the whole kingdom for himself, but his devotion to the Church had led him to take ill-conceived advice in the first instance. Now; now was the time for the more honest approach of warfare. Alvar smacked his lips together and jumped onto his horse. "Let us go, my fellows. There is a storm brewing at the bishop of Worcester's house, and King Edgar will need us to take its lightning into Wessex."

Helmstan was sleeping on his back with his arm under her neck. Káta lay against his shoulder and listened to the quiet of the afternoon. Once the herbs and straw on the floor had been replaced each morning her duties carried her around the estate, rarely to return to the bedchamber until evening. She took the opportunity to look at the room in appraisal.

One of the shutters was loose at the hinge and the largest of the wooden chests would not shut. New boxes would be needed if Helmstan's clothes were to be stored as befitted his rank. The walls were bare; they should be brightened with wall-hangings. They did not yet have the money to put silverware, never mind gold, on the tables, but they needed new cups. Perhaps she could ride to Chester for new pottery, maybe a softer-worked fur for the bed, and while she was there she could buy gold thread for embroidery, to make her walls match those at the royal houses. She was surely not the only young wife who wanted her home to look pretty.

Helmstan stirred and she said, "At the new king's house; are they all rich men who dress well and dance with the pretty ladies?"

His shoulder twitched. "God, no."

She lifted her head and he slid his arm from underneath her neck. Turning onto his side, he opened his eyes and smiled.

He yawned and rubbed his face. "There are many rich folk there, but now that Dunstan is back, he and Edgar are keen to show that the court in London is more pious and godly than the old court in Wessex." He chuckled. "Alvar said to me once that he had seen more mirth at a burial... What is it my love; are you cold?"

"No, it is only that the name brought to mind..."

"Whose name; Alvar's?"

Pretending a cough, Káta moved onto her back and turned her head away so that Helmstan could not see her face. She found a mark on the corner of the blanket which she must rub off and she kept her head turned to the wall as she thought of the earl. Helmstan loved him beyond measure and therefore so should she, but she had found him haughty. She realised now that it was his arrogant remarks that had prodded her into thinking her home too shabby. But beyond the insult itself, why should she care what he thought of her? The only blessing was that he had been so busy thinking himself too good for the likes of her, that he had not even spotted the scar on her hand, so high was his nose in the air. No, it was to her shame that she could not warm to her husband's dearest friend.

And yet, she also had a memory of his face. He had been so excited, when he left, at the prospect of a fight, and perhaps being able to be of use to his king. She saw how his eyes lit up, those lovely grey eyes surrounded by squint lines where the sun had not reached, eyes that had teased her into believing that she wished him to look at her more often. She thought about his mouth, set in a permanent smile even when he was speaking, that flattered her into wishing he would talk to her more, even though her cheeks would set on fire. She lifted her head, breathed in, and stroked her hands down her stomach. She wriggled her buttocks and moved closer to Helmstan, disturbed by the way her body felt. How aberrant, to have such thoughts about a man who was firstly her husband's greatest friend, and furthermore a man whom she found it impossible to like.

She exaggerated a shiver and hoped her feigned distaste would distract him from the rise of her body temperature. "Dunstan; I meant Dunstan. I have heard what happens when he witnesses sinful acts."

Helmstan tunnelled one arm underneath her body and wrapped the other around her. He tickled her ribs. "Have you been worshipping at the well-spring today?"

Her diversion had worked and, the danger passed, she exhaled deeply and laughed. "I did as the old women bade me. I left gifts in the hope that I would get with child. Your wife is naught but another wretched sinner."

He pulled her closer still. With his mouth against her hair he said, "Ah love, the priest sees you every day in his church, so he would not guess." He lowered his voice and stroked her arm. "Besides, no man would bear you ill-will for craving a child. Churchmen give no thought to the words of the wise women, and the best way to beget a…" He coughed, following it with a laugh that was just a little too loud. "As for Dunstan, he wants to alter the Church, yes, but not little churches like ours, nor their flock. When he is not playing his harp and writing sermons he is telling all who will listen about the sorry plight of the monasteries."

She drew small circles on his chest with her fingertip. "What is wrong with them?"

"Many were left in ruins after the Vikings came and went. Dunstan and his friend, the abbot Athelwold, wish to bring all the monks under one law, that of Saint Benedict. They will be far too busy to worry about folk in the north who still cling to something of the old gods to see them through each weary day."

She barked a sharp laugh. "Good for them, for it would be like gathering water in a sieve. My mother is a heathen Dane and she is not alone. Many folk leave gifts by the oak tree for Thunor, many folk leave ox blood on an elf-hill thinking to heal their sick loved ones. If those men were to make laws against such things..."

"No, they would not." He kissed the top of her head, and spoke in no more than a murmur. "Although, if they could make a law to put a stop to your mother…"

Káta wriggled her head up away from his chest so that she could breathe more freely. "I will forget that you said that. And if you say that I will not be damned for what I did today, then I must believe you." She brought her right hand up from under the covers and scratched her scar.

"What ails it? Does it twinge?"

"No, merely an itch." She hid it away again. "It is not as useful as my mother's finger bones. She always swore that they ached when the wind was about to turn west-wise." Káta sighed. "I can still hear her screams when she saw my bloodied hand, wailing that she would never find me a husband."

Helmstan's belly vibrated against her as the laugh worked its way up his body. "Ha! How little she knew. I was smitten by love the first time I saw you."

"You say so and I thank you. But I know that most men

would not think the same way." Indeed, how much lower would his friend's opinion of her have sunk had he seen her disfigurement? She reached up and twisted a curl of Helmstan's hair round her finger as she stared at the scar, thinking back to the day when the tree-wright reached too high into the tree, seeking to lop one more branch, and lost his grip on the saw. As always when she saw it again from the distance of years, the blade fell to the ground where Káta the child was playing, but her mind came back to the present before it landed. She shivered and brought her thoughts to the strands wrapped around her finger; Helmstan's hair, coarse but strong. Káta smiled. Her mother always said that sadness did not cook the broth and she was right; life was for getting on with. Her hand was spoiled but not ruined, for mercifully no fingers were severed, and her husband loved her. She propped herself up on one elbow and leaned her head until it was above his. "So, now that I have snared you, I must be sure to be good, or you might call me *witch*, and then who knows what I might one day be asked to answer for?" She giggled, enjoying the newly found confidence to flirt.

He grinned and put his finger on her lips. "I can tell you that. In my house, it is my word that is law, so you will be found guilty of naught as long as you do as I say."

She kissed the finger before he slid it away. "What would you have me do?" Her cheeks were warm but she managed to hold his gaze.

The shutter began to clatter against the window frame. He kissed her mouth. "Hark at that. The wind is getting up. You should stay abed with me where it is warm."

"Well then, if you say so, my lord…" Still smiling, she closed her eyes. She could afford to linger; there was time enough before the storm came to worry about the task of mending a lame shutter tossed in the strengthening breeze.

Worcester

Dunstan's legs were stiff; he was too old, perhaps, to spend an entire night kneeling in prayer on the cold cathedral floor. But pray he must, if he were to discover God's plan for him. So far he had received no clear answer, save that it was not to serve Him from the throne at Canterbury. Taking respite now in the comfort of his hall, where the fire blazed in the hearth and the heavily embroidered wall-cloths kept the warmth in the room, he held his hands in front of the flames, flexing them in and out of fists to get the blood flowing back through his numbed fingers. He rubbed his right knee, attempting to massage some life back into it. A visitor came into the hall, and as Dunstan stood up to acknowledge him, he noticed that his newly arrived house-guest, younger than he, had a limp which was much more pronounced than when they had last met, during Dunstan's year of exile. Dunstan embraced the other man and gestured to the seats. As he sank back into his chair, he said, "I am sorry to meet you again in such times. God forgive me for my pride, but I had hoped that when next we met, I would be welcoming you to your new church here at Worcester whilst I packed my chests and rode to Canterbury."

His guest shuffled to a cushioned chair and spread his black robes out as he sat down. He said, "When I buried my kinsman the archbishop, I had hoped the bitter brew would be sweetened by knowing that you would succeed him. It seems that the Fairchild has thwarted you once more."

Dunstan smiled ruefully. "Indeed. First he sends me overseas and now he sends the bishop of Winchester, not in exile, but to receive the pope's blessing as the new archbishop." He shook his head, still puzzling. Had he not served, prayed, answered his calling? Was the Fairchild sent by God to test him?

"Edgar would have chosen you."

"Alas, the thing was done too swiftly. I think that the bishop has powerful friends who were standing by with an armed escort and a ship waiting in port."

"The Lord Alvar is a friend of this bishop of Winchester, is he not?"

Dunstan's arms tensed at the mention of the name, and a twinge pinched the top of his shoulders. "I had not heard that he was there when Winchester sailed."

His friend smiled. "Maybe he was. Maybe he was not. But your life would be simpler, would it not, if there was no Lord Alvar and no Fairchild?"

Dunstan chuckled, despite his despondency. "Ah, yes. But where is the man who can do what God so far has not seen fit to do? Now, dearest friend, let us put our heads to thinking how we might find you a church now that you are here to stay."

"Oh, yes. There is much to plan."

Ramsey, East Anglia

Alfreda looked at the house-guest and tried to suppress an involuntary shudder, hoping that her revulsion would not harm her unborn babe, a brother or sister for little Leofric. The visitor had surely sprung from some nightmare, made real by devilry. He was a tall man who leaned forward, exaggerating the curvature of his neck and shoulders. His pale blue eyes shot glances around the room that seemed as sharp as any arrow point. When he moved, it was with a limp, one leg dragging slightly behind the other. Her mother, making up fireside stories for her when she was a child, could not have conjured up so hideous a being to scare the children gathered around the hearth on a winter's evening. Alfreda hugged her arms across her body, wishing she could reach back into that childhood and snatch a moment of its warmth. In the Half-king's day, the house at Ramsey had been filled with faces that, if they were not friendly, were at least not openly hostile. Now the Half-king was cloistered at Glastonbury, Edgar had gone and his former tutor the kindly Abbot Athelwold with him, and all those around her were pinched-faced and sour-looking, with one exception. Brandon would only have to put his tongue out to look like the puppy he resembled, and perhaps his tongue should indeed go out, the better to lap up every word the newcomer uttered. For Brandon followed the tall man at every turn, little hand gestures suggesting that he would touch the stranger's garments if he would let him.

She knew that the man's name was Oswald, that he was a Dane, that he was studying reforms at a monastery in Frankia, and that he was related to the late archbishop of Canterbury and had come back to England when he heard of the archbishop's death. He had already been to York to try his luck for a position there, since he had family connections there too, and she stared at this strange and fearsome creature and wondered why such a well-connected person should be so interested in a backwater like the fenland. He was an odd choice to replace Edgar as an idol. Apparently Brandon had met Oswald at a funeral of a nobleman and brought him back to Ramsey, where Elwood had promptly appropriated him. She watched and listened, trying to understand exactly what she was witnessing.

Oswald said, "I hear what you say, Lord Elwood. But we need to hasten our work so that all religious houses follow the rules of St Benedict."

"Dunstan and Athelwold are doing what they can…" Elwood explained to Oswald how much the other churchmen had been influencing Edgar, persuading him of the benefits that the reforms would bring, to England, and to his place in heaven. Alfreda nodded, inwardly agreeing, for she had sat many a long hour and heard Athelwold's plans for a new Church. But this man Oswald was pushing for more. He got up and began to walk a few steps, first away from Elwood, then towards him.

"I need a church of my own. Better still, a bishopric. And then it will all be done more swiftly. Left to Athelwold and Dunstan, good men though they are, it will take forever."

"Winchester is free," Elwood said, wincing as if he knew the offer to be as welcome as a mouldy piece of flatbread on a feast night.

Oswald's blue eyes narrowed. "Yes, Winchester is free, because the bishop of that place has moved on. And yet he is still in the way, for in moving on, he blocks Dunstan's path to Canterbury. And who put him there?"

"The Fairchild."

"Yes. So everywhere we godly men turn, there is an ungodly one standing in our way. What we need is Edgar on the throne of both the English kingdoms, and Dunstan on the throne at Canterbury."

"We have begun work on that. Edgar will be king after his brother, now that his brother has no wife."

Oswald stopped pacing and put his head to one side, staring at Elwood. "There is a flaw in your work. We have seen that the annulment has not subdued the Fairchild; he could take it upon himself to wed again. This must not happen."

"No, we all hope that it does not, but without an uprising…"

Oswald held up a hand, demanding silence. "There must be no uprising. Better that Edgar is grateful to us than to the weapon-men, for then he will give us what we need. Once before, there were two kings, one of Wessex and one of Mercia, and did not one die soon after taking the king-helm? Who knows what can happen, without warning?" He looked up at the roof and cupped his chin between his thumb and forefinger. "So, we must think how best we can be of use to Edgar."

Elwood grunted. "I can answer that one straight away. Get rid of Alvar of Mercia."

The Dane raised an eyebrow. "He vexes you, too?"

Elwood's mouth was already open in reply and his wife knew that he had no need to rehearse this well-worn speech. "I grew up with Edgar and have always been loyal to him, even though I lost my father's love to him. It was my idea to wrest the Fairchild from his wife, but somehow it was Alvar who was rewarded. The Fairchild gave my father's lands to Alvar and yet Edgar has not returned them to me, not even as payment for getting rid of the Fairchild's wife. Every time I try to get nearer to Edgar, Alvar is standing in my way."

Oswald laid a calming hand on Elwood's shoulder. "This

upsets me. Lord Elwood, you have given me a home and shown me naught but kindness since I came to England, bereft at the death of my kin. I think that there is a way we can spear two boars with one thrust." He led the younger man to the mead-bench and bade him sit down. Alfreda leaned to her left and strained to listen.

Oswald continued. "If Dunstan left Worcester, his church there would be empty. And where is Worcester?"

Elwood shrugged. "In Mercia." He registered no interest, clicking his fingers for a servant to come forward and pour his guest a drink.

The Dane accepted a cup of wine, but Elwood put his hand over the rim of his own cup and Alfreda's heart began to hammer. She would pay for that abstinence later.

Oswald spoke again. "Worcester is in Mercia, yes. And if I were to become bishop there, I could be of great help; to Edgar, to the Church, and to you."

"Me?"

The Dane licked his lips. "Edgar loves Alvar. He thinks he needs a strong weapon-man by his side. Oh, but these warmongers have a blood-lust that can do more harm than good. If Edgar were to see…" He lowered his voice, presumably to plot the downfall of the lord of Mercia, and Alfreda could hear no more without picking up her chair and moving it nearer. She would not do it; her eavesdropping must remain unnoticed, or she would be forced to cease the practice.

Brandon had no such qualms. Having spent the duration of the previous conversation staring mournfully while his elder brother monopolised his new friend, he dragged a stool from the hearth, squeezing as close as he could to Oswald and staring at him, even when it was Elwood's turn to speak.

Alfreda rested her hands on her belly, hoping to feel another of the tiny flutters that proved the existence of the new life within. Her love for this babe, whom she had yet to meet, was natural and instinctive; could hatred be the same?

Oswald was newly arrived in England, but already his loathing for the lord Alvar was strong enough to drive him into dark corners where secrets were born. Her husband called her stupid, but she could foresee naught but strife ahead.

Chapter Four AD959

Gloucestershire

Wilfrid yawned, stretched, and scratched as he made his way to the bake-house. An earlier start than usual saw him stumble into the gloomy building before the sun was fully up, but his widely gaping mouth was not a result of the awakening but a consequence of barely having slept at all. Joyous with pride, yet earnest in his determination not to disappoint, he pushed up his sleeves and lit the fire under the bread oven and shut the door. Later, when it had burned out, he would clean the ashes out and put the bread in to bake. Meanwhile he began to gather what he needed for the new day's loaves, including the sour-dough reserved from the day before. An hour or so later, Herolf came in, rubbing his hands against the cool October dawn, and whistling. He stopped, his mouth still pursed in its circle, and stared at Wilfrid. Then he said, "Why are you here so early?"

Wilfrid stood back from the table and brushed his floury hands on his tunic. "I have made a start on all the extra loaves that will be needed today."

Herolf moved towards the bench to inspect the dough. "Why do we need more than usual today?"

"Because the king is coming."

"King Edgar is coming here?" Herolf began a dance of panic, poking the proving dough to make sure it was beginning to rise, and tidying the utensils on the table into unnecessarily neat groups.

"No, the Fairchild. He is coming from Wessex."

Herolf released his grip on a sack of flour and laughed. "The Fairchild? Have you gone daft? Why in God's holy name would he come here?"

Wilfrid pouted and muttered, "There you go, disbelieving me as usual." He shrugged. "Lord Alvar must've invited him. One of the Fairchild's men rode in last night and told me to make ready."

Despite Wilfrid's truculent insistence, Herolf said, "You must be mistaken. The steward said nothing to me. Come, let's make a start on the…"

The sound of hoof beats turned his attention to the door and he went to stand in the opening. Wilfrid stood behind him, peering over his shoulder. "What is it?"

Herolf folded his arms. "It's Lord Alvar. But see, you must be mistaken about the Fairchild coming because the lord is riding out."

Wilfrid craned to see. Sure enough, Lord Alvar was riding away from the manor with, it seemed, all his men at arms. One rider peeled away from the formation after they rode through the gate, presumably, Wilfrid thought, to rally more men from the surrounding villages.

The bakers returned to their work with grudging co-operation, one grumbling about the wasted dough, one stubbornly insisting that the additional loaves would be required. By mid-morning the heat had become oppressive and they stepped outside for a rest. Wilfrid went first and Herolf followed him through the doorway and handed him one of the two drinks he had brought with him. Wilfrid took a few gulps and then wiped his hand across his mouth. "You will owe me another of those. Look."

Emerging from a haze of kicked dust, a group of riders was approaching the gateway, the banner of the Fairchild of Wessex flapping, proclaiming their identity. The Fairchild himself rode at the front of the pack, his pale blond hair making him easily distinguishable. Just before he reached the gate, however, a rider appeared from the village road, blocking his path and causing the entourage to come to a halt. Words were exchanged and then, as Wilfrid and Herolf watched, the Fairchild turned his horse and followed the rider down the track away from the manor house.

Herolf patted Wilfrid on the shoulder. "Looks like you were right; Lord Alvar must've bidden him here, though I cannot think why. And why has he ridden off?" He drained his cup. "Ah well, best get back to our kneading."

Among the men who had stood in the church at Gloucester that morning, many were old enough to have witnessed four king-makings. Alvar doubted that they had ever seen one conducted so hurriedly. Even now, the bells were ringing softly. When a man was crowned king, there should be no hiding in shadows. The Fairchild of Wessex was dead and buried and only nineteen years of his life lived. Most folk said he should have cooled his grave a little more before Edgar took the king-helm to wear on his own head, and when Alvar had spoken to Edgar he was of the same mind. But between then and now, Edgar had been persuaded by persons as yet unknown, although Alvar had his suspicions, that a hasty coronation would remove any danger of civil unrest and Edgar had allowed Dunstan to place the crown on his head, but without ceremony. Dunstan, who was no longer bishop of Worcester, but was now the new archbishop of Canterbury, and had used his new powers to bar the Fairchild's grieving widow from his funeral.

Alvar tried to shift his weight without wriggling. Edgar's first act as king was to call him up before all others, to swear his oath as foremost earl of the realm and, standing to receive Edgar's kiss, Alvar saw Elwood's face, creased into such a frown it seemed his eyes might be lost forever. Alvar could not shake loose from his head two nagging thoughts: a seemingly fit and healthy nineteen-year-old king lay dead, and the bishop of Winchester, so recently appointed to Canterbury, was conveniently dead before he could receive his pallium from the pope. Elwood, an opponent of both the Fairchild and Winchester, should have been happy at the turn of events but he looked thwarted, as if his plans had gone awry.

As to what those plans might have been, Alvar could only guess, ruminating as he watched the other lords stepping forward to receive Edgar's gifts. Why had the Fairchild been in Gloucestershire at the time of his death? Alvar's baker was adamant that he had been ordered to prepare food for a royal visit, while his steward was unwavering in his assertion that no such directive had ever been received. The message had never reached Alvar, but someone had gone to the trouble of informing the baker so that Alvar's claim of ignorance would seem spurious. A rumour then swiftly followed that the Fairchild had come at Alvar's invitation. Many gave credence to this assertion, questioning why Edgar's sworn man would invite a king of Wessex into the heart of Mercia. It seemed that they had their answer when the Fairchild was found dead, having apparently fallen from his horse. But any fingers pointing suspicion at Alvar soon had to cease their wagging, because Alvar was not in Gloucestershire at the time. And those who maintained that he contrived to take himself from the scene of the crime and leave his men to do the foul deed were silenced by the facts: Alvar was clever, perhaps, but not so clever that he could have arranged for the Welsh to begin an attack on Shrewsbury at the very same moment. And, having ridden home with the smell of battle in his nostrils, he now had a foul taste in his mouth. Elwood might well have expected to become chief earl by contriving to have Alvar executed for murder, but he did not need to murder the bishop as well. No, this was a far deeper and murkier sea of intrigue, and the ambitions of more than one man had been set to sail upon it.

Moving from the chapel to the timber building alongside it, Alvar blew on his hands and stood aside to allow his brother Brock to enter the hall. Alvar stepped inside and stamped his feet. After the stone floor of the chapel he was grateful for the familiar springy luxury of the wooden floorboards. Looking around, he noted with satisfaction that the hall was bedecked in the finest manner. This hall was the king's, but it lay in the heart of Mercia, within Alvar's area of authority. Gold and silver plate had already been laid on the tables, the candles in the gold candlesticks were newly lit and the bread baskets were stacked full almost to overflowing. Alvar nodded at the steward and smiled his approval. He took a jug of wine from a serving-boy, waved him away and filled two cups on the table. He handed one of the drinks to Brock. "However it was done, I think we now have a king who is worthy of the name."

Brock murmured an agreement and then looked at Alvar as if hearing a second time. "However it was done? What? You cannot believe that the archbishop..."

Alvar looked behind him and set the jug down on a side table. "Ah yes, the new archbishop; what are we to think of him? How much did Dunstan mourn the poor bishop of Winchester before he made a nest for himself at Canterbury?"

"Now brother, be fair. None can be held answerable for Winchester's untimely death." Brock sipped his drink. A group of thegns passed by on their way to the mead-benches and he held his cup high to avoid spilling the contents. He said, "Who could have known that the weather would take the man's life like that as he rode to seek his blessing from the pope?"

Alvar moved the gaming pieces around in his mind. "If that is truly what happened. Many things could befall a man who is far from home and far from friends." He shook his head. He would move those pieces around again at a later stage. He smiled. "It was kind of you to take Winchester's child as your foster-son." Alvar picked up the wine and gestured with the jug, but Brock shook his head. Alvar refilled his own cup.

Brock shrugged the compliment off. "Any man would do this for a friend."

"I cannot see that I would ever find it within me to take

on another man's son." The diners began to take their seats and the noise subsided. Alvar straightened up. He waved the jug again. "Another? No?" He filled his own cup and said, "And you are not merely *any* man. The Fairchild's steward becomes earl of Hampshire and thus Edgar has mended the rift with Wessex."

"Indeed he has. And he has shown how much he values our kin." Brock chuckled; his head went back and the light from the fire showed flecks of yellow in his grey stripe. He touched his new arm ring, placed there as he knelt to receive the earldom of Hampshire. "Do you see who else Edgar keeps near to him?"

Alvar turned. He mouthed as he counted the men who surrounded the king. "I have never seen so many bishops, abbots, monks and priests outside a church. Who is the one sitting next to Dunstan who looks like a dried up old stick?"

Brock turned to the wall and Alvar leaned in to hear his words. "That is Oswald, a Dane from East Anglia and nephew to the old archbishop. He has been in Frankia for some years, where he took the monk's oath. When he sailed home to find that his uncle had died, he took himself off to the archbishop at York, another of his kinsmen."

Alvar sniffed. "So why is he here and not in York?"

Brock said, "He met Elwood's little brother, who took him back to Ramsey. From there he had a path straight to the king."

The Dane, alone among the gathering on the dais, looked straight ahead and did not converse with his neighbours. He was probably a tall man, but his back was hunched. His black garb hung off the narrow slope of his shoulders and his small blue eyes flashed rapid blinks as he stared out into the hall. Something caught his attention and he put his head to one side. The darting gaze stilled and he righted his head to blink at the middle distance.

Alvar wrinkled his nose. "And Edgar will have a straight path to heaven, with all those priests speaking to God on his behalf."

Brock nodded. "And, since churchmen are now forbidden to wed, they will not be like trees; they will not sow their seed. If you recall, it was the Fairchild who first allowed men to bequeath earldoms to their sons. Edgar looks as though he seeks to offset the strength of the earls by giving the churchmen as many seats on the bench."

Alvar cocked his head. "You might be right." Although with relatives scattered throughout the Church, it looked as if Oswald had his own deep-rooted kinship. Alvar's tongue moved slowly across his top lip as he surveyed the group huddled around Edgar. He smiled. If the lad had learned to keep a balance, then he was learning well. He would not take it to heart if Edgar sought to lean less heavily on the old kinships, for at least he was learning where the Fairchild had not. "I would rather have my place at Edgar's side through merit and not mere kinship. But, having won Mercia for him, I wonder why then does Edgar still keep me near?"

Edgar stood up and walked towards them. Brock patted his younger brother on the arm. "I think, humble youngster, that you are about to find out." He stepped aside, nodding to the king.

Edgar reached up to rest his hand on Alvar's shoulder, propelling him with minimal pressure to the far end of the hall, where shadows aided inconspicuousness.

"Lord Alvar, before we eat, I would like to hear your thoughts on something which has been troubling me. In a word: Northumbria. They did not oppose my kingship but how do I keep them loyal?" He jerked his head in a nod towards the dais. "My learned priests have no answer other than to build more churches. I will pay my foreign boatmen to ensure that the Northumbrians are not tempted to welcome any more Vikings to their remote shores. But I am not dim-witted enough to think that fear will keep them loyal. The fleet might be my eye in the north, but I need more."

Alvar scratched his ear. They would certainly need to

tread carefully. Many who lived in Northumbria had Danish blood in their veins; they spoke another language and did not think of themselves yet as English. He said, "It is only in living memory that the Viking king was driven from York and the two Northumbrian kingdoms were brought back together. If we could build upon this, if the two halves of Northumbria could be made to feel whole, and be made to feel English... Aside from sending a fleet to threaten, you must send a hand in friendship. What if I were to go there, make what friends I can amongst those who will matter, and speak on your behalf?"

The king nodded. "I should like that; leave as soon as you can."

Elwood of East Anglia had been watching them as they huddled in the shadows and now he made his way over to the end of the hall, his brows drawn together in an expression of indignant curiosity. Alvar's inner child rose up and he struggled to refrain from asking Edgar why he kept such a sour-lipped lump-head in his inner circle. Instead he said, "He is rich beyond reckoning, he is foster-brother to the king of the English and yet he scowls. What is it then; does his wife look like a shovel?"

"No, she does not." Edgar steered Alvar back towards the centre of the hall, so that they approached Elwood as he came towards them. The king lifted his lips in a rare smile. "Lady Alfreda is comely indeed." He saved his next comment until they reached Elwood. "And I have told my foster-brother many times that one day I shall have her off him."

The lord of Ramsey clenched his fists, but his arms hung impotently at his sides. His lip curled in a sneer. "I hear that you have not yet taken a wife, Alvar?"

Alvar hiccupped. "Never found a woman I wished to keep," he said. He looked down and made a study of the dried herbs and straw covering the floorboards. He felt a squeeze on his arm, announcing Edgar's departure. When he looked up, the East Anglian was smirking at him. The lie had not convinced.

Elwood said, "Those who make the loudest din oft-times shout louder than they need to. Some might say Lord Alvar wishes to hide the truth, which is that no woman will have him."

Alvar swept his arms wide and let them fall in an act of feigned indifference. "You have it, my lord. The truth is that I while away too many days drinking and whoring to find me a wife."

Elwood took a step nearer and his mouth stretched into a snarl. "You besmirch the good name of your kin. It is a wonder to me why Edgar keeps you so near to his side. You are a drunken halfwit."

Alvar said. "No, I am merely half drunk. So is almost every other man in this hall; what is wrong with that? At least I do not fear to be in my cups, for what kind of a lord will not share the drinking horn with his men? As to my being a halfwit…" He held the next words back, letting his anger rise up from his belly. For three years he had endured this man's disdain, nay odium, with never an explanation offered. If his crime was nothing more than his long ago severed connection to the Fairchild, well, had he not proved subsequently his loyalty to Edgar? And had Edgar not charged him with a diplomatic mission? Perhaps it was time to stop doubting his abilities. And to give credence to the growing suspicion that Elwood was driven purely by envy. "You can rest easy, knowing that Edgar is all yours for a time, for he has asked me to go to Northumbria on his behalf." He echoed Elwood's movement, and stepped closer. "You see, Edgar owes you, but he needs me."

Alvar was sitting next to his brother, with the Greybeard of Chester and a group of lesser thegns, who, when they were not pouring drinks for their lords, were firing playful punches at each other. Alvar hoisted his legs up on a bench, one foot crossed over the other. The air was thick with the smell of sweat and slopped ale and he laughed along with the others as an ale-soaked napkin flew across the table and landed on the head of a Worcester thegn. Alvar took a sip from his cup and put his free hand up to the back of his neck. He shivered and rubbed his fingers across the gap between his hair and the neckline of his tunic. He turned his head a little. Edgar and Dunstan, still seated on the dais, were staring at him. Edgar's head was tilted forward while Dunstan whispered with the side of his mouth. Edgar nodded once or twice, but more often cocked his head one way and then the other, as if unsure whether he agreed with what Dunstan said. Alvar held out his cup as a serving-girl walked by with a flask of wine. "I will have a drink before you take that to the ladies," he said. "No, better yet, leave us the flask." He filled Brock's cup and said, "Come, let us drink to the Fairchild, that he might lie still in his grave, and then to the memory of Winchester." Alvar chinked his cup against his brother's, they drank the toast to the Fairchild, and Alvar poured another drink for them both.

Brock said, "He was a good man. Winchester would have made a good archbishop."

Up on the dais, Edgar lifted a loaf and broke it in two. He tore a chunk off with his teeth, but the piece was too large and he chewed with it sticking out until there was room for him to swallow. Oswald the Dane picked up a small crust, nibbled a little from the outside and put the rest back on his plate. He lifted a lap-cloth and dabbed it unnecessarily around his dry lips. Dunstan batted his hand at a servant who tried to replenish his plate. Yes, Winchester would have made a fine archbishop and Dunstan had much to prove. But it made no sense. Alvar moved the pieces around his mind again but could not put Dunstan into the role of murderer. Once, he had played at the gaming board with his young nephew and neither of them had realised immediately that one of the pieces had fallen on the floor. There came a point when they noticed that the game was incomplete but could not straight away fathom why. Alvar had the same feeling now.

On the other side of the king-seat another two men were now looking at him, but in their case Alvar felt as if he should duck his head to avoid the looks of loathing being fired at him like elvish arrows. Oswald the Dane was talking and pointing as if he needed confirmation of an identity and Elwood of East Anglia scowled as he jerked his head in Alvar's direction and grumbled into the ear of the Dane.

Brock kicked Alvar's foot. "Brother, are you still with us, or has your mind wandered for good this time?"

Alvar did not turn, but raised his voice above the giggles of the others and said, "I was wondering who this Dane might really be, who is all at once such a friend to East Anglia."

Oswald stood up and left the dais.

Brock said, "Why not ask him then? He seems to be coming this way."

As Oswald walked towards the benches, one leg dragged where the other lifted, causing his head to bob up and down with each step.

Alvar said, "Should I feel like a worm that is about to be picked from the earth, do you think?"

Brock laughed. "I see what you mean; he does walk a little like a bird. But is he a harmless wren or a murderous crow?"

Alvar laughed, but there was something in Brock's words that made him wonder. There was no time to muse on it, though, because Oswald had arrived in front of them and was standing silently, presumably in expectation of a greeting.

Alvar shrugged, put his feet on the floor and sat up straight. He held his hand out and gestured towards the now vacant bench.

Oswald bowed his head and sat down. He arranged his black robes around him and lifted his sleeves clear of the sticky table-top. "It is time that godliness was brought back to this land." His voice was as tuneless as the dull strike of a blunt sword.

Alvar, annoyed by the lack of preamble, objected. "Who are you to speak to me thus? I do not know you."

Oswald blinked at him. "But I know you. You are the one who has been speaking lewdly to our lord of East Anglia."

Alvar drummed his fingers on the table. "So that is why Elwood was bleating in your ear." To Brock he said, "I do not know whether to be wroth, or to laugh." He turned back to the newcomer. "I spoke light-heartedly about whoring. It was not meant, and it was but one word. The only mystery is why he ran to you with his tale of woe."

Oswald ignored the slur on his social status. "Whispered words will always find an ear." He nodded back towards the direction of the dais. "The king listens well and wisely to the words of the archbishop of Canterbury."

Alvar yawned. "Dunstan can clatter on all day about the Church for all I care. Why should it trouble me?"

The Dane's staccato voice cut through the end of his sentence. "I will tell you. The Church can give Edgar what you cannot."

By the hearth, near the sleeping dogs, a drunken Northumbrian balanced a full wine cup on his head, only for a Gloucester thegn to knock it off and into his lap. The two jumped up and began a play-fight. Around them their friends took sides and spurred them on with yells and whoops. The hounds, woken by the commotion, joined in, yelping and leaping between the men and whimpering when they got too close.

The Dane spoke as if there had been no interruption. "You helped Edgar to the throne. But at any time you could leave your king for another. Is that not what you meant when you said that Edgar should need his lords and not owe them?"

"Oh for God's…" How could Elwood have been so stupid as to take his words and twist them so? Did he really think that Alvar was planning revolt?

The newcomer continued. "You will be wasting your

time and your horses riding to Northumbria. The only way to truly bind men to the kingdom is through a strong Church. Every day, I tell God what needs to be. When the Church owns land, all are true to king and God."

"You *tell* God?" Alvar rolled his eyes.

Oswald blinked and his eyes narrowed. "Kingship is naught without godliness. The Church needs more land to be strong, in order to make the king strong."

"And you are the man to do this? You nod your head at me but you are naught. What are you, aside from forgetting who I am and how you should speak to me?"

"I do not forget who you are. You are a proud man; too proud. As for who I am, let me ask you this. Dunstan is now at Canterbury and Worcester is free. Who do you think will be bishop there now?"

Oswald gave his little bob of a nod and stood up. He bowed, not low, and hobbled off.

Brock let out a low whistle. "Do you think, brother, that he was threatening you?"

Alvar took a long drink, wiped his mouth with the back of his hand and grunted. "He does not frighten me. He might become bishop of Worcester but those are my lands. I will look after my folk there and as long as he does not get in my way I will not tread on him. At least in a bishop's garb he will look less like a crow."

He reached for the ale and laughed at the continuing ribaldry, determined not to let the foreigner's ill-manners detract from his enjoyment of the evening. But when a severely inebriated thegn produced a gaming board, Alvar's thoughts began to wander once more. The diocese of Worcester, in the very heart of Mercia, was wealthy and well-endowed. And now, suddenly, it was vacant and a Danish newcomer was about to walk into the bishopric. Oswald had made his way back to the dais and resumed conversation with Elwood and now the pieces sat neatly on the board. A huge wave had been called forth to wash away all vestiges of the Fairchild's reign, and when it receded,

Dunstan was left sitting on the throne at Canterbury, while Oswald, great friend of East Anglia, was hobbling his way to Worcester and Elwood... Alvar thought back to the murderous looks he had received when Edgar had confirmed him leading earl. Elwood's ambition had not yet been realised. Little wonder then that the man's face looked as though he had been hit by the flat of a tree-wright's axe. He was the only one who had not profited from the deaths of two men; but Oswald had revealed himself as evil, and if Dunstan was not complicit, then at the very least he was a steaming hypocrite. And never again would Alvar apologise for doing his duty to his king.

Dunstan was keen to get back to civilisation and make a start at his archbishopric. The lord of Mercia was a relic of a barbarous age and had no sense that these would be years of peace, of laws and learning and religious reform. Reform, in particular. Dunstan was a besom, twitching to sweep into all the corners of the old regime at Canterbury. He still offered up daily thanks that God had seen fit to clear the path for him. He also felt guilty daily for the sin of pride he'd experienced when Winchester was appointed. He had been suffused with gratitude when Edgar overrode the decision and then he suffered guilt once more, for it felt as though he were profiting from Winchester's unfortunate accident. The urge to get to Canterbury and prove himself worthy was overwhelming, but Edgar had insisted on some hunting before he left the fertile Severn valley and Dunstan shivered astride his horse, and could for now only dream of his new church and all that his being there would allow him to achieve. He had long harboured an ambition that monks from his old abbey at Glastonbury would build and colonise new monasteries, *proper* monasteries; the religious communities clustered around the shrines and resting places of saints did not adhere to the rule of St Benedict and had never, in Dunstan's opinion, constituted monastic institutions. Monks trained in his new houses would provide a pool in which to fish for all future bishops, all known to him and eminently suitable for the posts. He shook his head. The more he thought about his plans, the more it irked him to be stuck in this freezing field.

If Dunstan felt uncomfortable, Oswald looked even worse. Black robes flapping out behind him did not mask the shivering. The October sky was cloudless and the sun shone brightly, but the overnight ground frost had lingered and it was a bitter wind that blew. Dunstan knew that he was a rarity; a lord who disliked hunting, but he was keen to leave Mercia as soon as he could. It was time to move on, not to stay where memories of the recently departed king still cast shadows. Why had the Fairchild even been here? It could not have been at Edgar's invitation, for Edgar had not mentioned it to Dunstan, who was, after all, supposed to be his foremost adviser. He looked across at Alvar, sitting upright with a hawk on his arm. Yes, he, Dunstan, *was* the foremost advisor, despite what others might think. Dunstan was aware of the rumours that were now circulating. The Fairchild died in Alvar's province. Dunstan had condemned Alvar many a long year ago as a reveller, fornicator and worse, but there the list of crimes ended. He was no murderer. So why had the Fairchild been lured to Mercia, and by whom; had the sole intention been to besmirch Alvar's name?

Edgar's hawk had caught a sparrow and brought it back. A thegn brought down yet another with his bow and arrow and, since his girdle now had six dead birds hanging from it, he added this latest to Edgar's stack. Dunstan experienced a bilious taste in his mouth and he turned his head from the pile of feathered corpses. He was relieved that what he saw as too large a pile of bodies was deemed to be just enough for the rest of the hunting party and when the shout went up that it was time to retire to the hut, he welcomed the chance to dismount and have a warming drink.

He settled himself by the fire and allowed the young thegns to fuss round him, as they laid a fur blanket over his lap and ensured that food and drink were left on a table close to where he was sitting. Edgar, slapping friends on the shoulder, sharing a joke with others, gradually made his way to join Dunstan by the hearth. After a few solicitous enquiries after the archbishop's health, the young man coughed and tried to settle his voice into its newly acquired lower register.

"There is a young woman who has caught my eye but I need your help."

Dunstan shifted in his seat. In what possible way could he be of assistance in the procuring of a woman? He lifted his cup to his lips.

Edgar continued. "You know of the lady Wulfreda?"

Dunstan forced the sip of liquid back into the cup, fearful that if he swallowed, he might choke. "That lady is given to the Church. She is not for you."

Oswald came to join them, carefully spreading out his robes before sitting, hands neatly placed in his lap. Edgar acknowledged him with a nod, but continued to press Dunstan. "She is high-born, though is she not?"

"Yes, my lord, she is. But..."

Oswald leaned forward. "Of whom do we speak?"

Dunstan explained that Edgar had taken a fancy to the lady Wulfreda, but that she was promised to the Church and might very soon take her vows.

Oswald nodded. "High-born, though, you say?"

"The highest. She is, indeed, throne-worthy. Her mother and father were..."

Oswald laid a hand on his arm and repeated the phrase. "Throne-worthy, you say? A waste, then, maybe, to give her life to the Church. Whilst we would always welcome those few chaste women who will give their lives to God, there might be a better way in which she could serve Him."

Dunstan opened his mouth to reply, but found he stumbled over the sound he wanted to make. Unable for now to formulate the words to tell Edgar to proceed with caution and subtlety, he merely nodded his assent.

Edgar squeezed him on the knee before he stood up, nodded to Oswald, and turned back to his younger friends.

Oswald smiled. "We must do whatever we can to free this lady from her vows. Edgar is the son of a king. If his wife were throne-worthy, too, then their children would be, hmm, what is the word?"

Undisputed? Legitimate? Sinfully begotten? Dunstan remained tight-lipped. Not just because the words wouldn't come but because the nasty taste was back.

Oswald seemed unperturbed by the archbishop's silence. He sat back and put his hands precisely in the centre of his lap. "Whilst we are speaking of giving boons, I would beg one of you. I would like a ship-soke in Mercia."

Of course he would. The land here was fertile and all the churches very rich. A ship-soke consisting of three hundred hides of land would yield a fortune. But it was not within Dunstan's power to grant such a request. He shook his head. "I-it is not for me to say. You would need to ask the king."

Oswald scratched his chin. "I had thought of this. I think that if the king were to get the lady whom he craves, then he might be grateful. The king must always be grateful for what is done in his name by those who love him."

Dunstan tilted his head to one side as he scrutinised his newly appointed bishop. "You have not lost sight of our aims, I hope? By which I m-mean, to reform the Church?"

The Dane stared back at him, unblinking. "Oh, I have not forgotten."

Dunstan sipped again from his cup. If he promised to shrive Edgar for any sin involved in removing Wulfreda from the Church, thus allowing Edgar to produce undisputed heirs, the youngster would undoubtedly be grateful and would not hesitate to grant the lands in Mercia to Oswald. But what about these other things *done in his name*? Oswald would not be in Worcester had Dunstan not vacated it... Nay, *been able unexpectedly* to vacate it. With a sideward glance at Oswald he wondered, for a moment, whether the price for his reforms might not be too high. A shout went up at the other end of the hut. Alvar was holding the drinking horn up for Edgar, who, under the earl's influence, seemed all too willing to indulge in drunkenness. The lord of Mercia was watching and smiling, with the same frivolous grin that Dunstan had seen on that shameful day when the Fairchild made mockery of the solemnity of his coronation day. Dunstan ground his teeth together. No; the truth might have dawned, but that dawn had beauty in it yet, and it lit the road to Canterbury.

Part II – Weaxung (The Waxing)

Chapter Five AD961

The Vale of York

As Alvar came away from York with his small band of retainers he looked briefly to the far north, thinking again about the bleak landscape of Stainmore. He wondered where exactly it was that the notorious Erik Blood-axe had lost his life after the earl of Bamburgh chased him there from Viking York and put an end to Danish rule in the city. Only seven years had passed since then, and Alvar had been relieved to find that commerce and stable governance had been so swiftly revived. His meetings with the nobles of the north had gone well. He had travelled to both parts of the old kingdom, from York eastward to the coast, and then up to the ancient fortress at Bamburgh, where he met the heads of all the leading families. Understandably wary at first, they had listened to his testimony. He told them that he had been sworn to the Fairchild but had been swayed by the personal strengths of Edgar. He showed them copies of detailed land charters which demonstrated that Edgar was prepared not only to reward loyalty, but to respect ancient land boundaries and tribal borders. They had welcomed him then; he smiled as he recalled in particular the hospitality of one northern lady. She was the sister of Oslac, a man so big and ursine of gait that he was known to all as the bear, or Beorn. He was a nobleman of the southern portion of the old kingdom who would one day make a fine earl. Alvar was on his way home to tell Edgar so. And, just as when he sang

Edgar's praises in the north, his personal recommendation would add weight to his words now to Edgar, for Alvar and Beorn had become great friends. Beorn kept his head shorn, but joked that even without the extra height of hair, he looked down upon the Mercian, which amused Alvar because few men were taller than he. Like all hearth-companions, he enjoyed a play on words, and Beorn's shaven head meant that he was a bare bear. Beorn's hall was in the heart of Deira, in the vale of York, which seemed permanently to be swathed in mist that swirled dank and cold and rivalled the fenland in the east for the honour of being named wettest and most miserable in all the old kingdoms. Yet Beorn's hearth always burned bright and homely, and whether his sister was there or not, Alvar had always felt at home.

They rode on through the fertile valley. The route would eventually take them down the old Foss Way, bearing south until Alvar could link up with another great road cut by the Romans, following Watling Street to the west to get back to his own house in Gloucestershire. He had been away for many months. He shifted in the saddle, weary and numb. Thoughts of a warm hearth and good company began to call out louder than those of his little-used home at Upper Slaughter. Edgar's bold but competent law-making heralded a belief that these times of peace were likely to last. Of course, such peace was further guaranteed by those who, unlike the fyrd, stood ready to fight at a moment's notice: mercenaries, the fleet, and agents like himself. But, in such times of peace, the fyrd was not called out and he reflected with self-reproach that because of that, he had not seen his friend Helmstan for some time. Signalling to the men, he urged his horse onward at speed to Nottingham, from where he knew there was a road to Chester.

Her husband leaped up when he saw Lord Alvar arrive. Káta, who, only moments before, had been happily absorbed in a conversation about her plans for planting a new herb garden, now found that her hand, held until that moment in Helmstan's palm, was cooling rapidly while her face was growing warmer and she was all of a sudden in a state of discomposure.

Helmstan could not hide his delight in seeing Alvar again. It was a source of happiness to her, but frustration to him that, as a local thegn, he was only required to attend witenagemots if they were held in the immediate area. As her husband and their visitor hugged, Helmstan joked that Alvar was now powerful enough to persuade the royal household to travel to Cheshire more often.

Alvar said, "Believe me, much as I treasure your friendship, I would welcome a break from riding up and down the land for a while."

A groom came to hover in the doorway and shuffled his weight from one foot to the other. "Lord Helmstan, the grey mare is lame again."

Helmstan turned and Káta knew by the slump of his shoulders that his loyalties were torn. "I have the lord Alvar in my hall," he said to the groom.

But Alvar said, "Go. Believe me when I say that little in this world matters more than a healthy horse. These last few months have taught me that much, at least. I seem to have been in the saddle since Pentecost and here we are now at Lammas-time."

Helmstan chuckled. "Then I will ask a boon; will you sit awhile with my wife and see to it that she rests?" He laid a hand on Káta's shoulder and squeezed it, before turning on his heel and following the groom out of the hall.

The unbounded echoes of Helmstan's huge voice took their time to fade away. Alvar pulled out his hand-saex and polished it with the hem of his tunic. Káta wiped imaginary dust from the table.

Alvar said, "I hope that you do not mind my coming here. I sought to prolong the feeling of stillness and warmth before going back to the bear's den that is the court. It is as if I can breathe freely here."

"Oh, but I thought you looked down on us, who are not so high-born…" Inexplicable relief had pushed her words out and now her hand went to her mouth, too late. She sprang up and stood in front of the wall-table. Keeping her back to him, she fingered the crockery that was stored there.

"Your husband said that you must not tire yourself."

Her cheeks grew hot. She moved the plates and bowls inside each other, took them out and restacked them. "He is fretting over-much. I am with child; that is all."

"Oh? Helmstan is right, you must sit down."

She fanned her cheeks before she turned and sat down. "Helmstan is over-chary I know, but in truth we are both a little worried." Her face cool again, she dared to look at the great lord, rich and influential, who had no interest in her little life. But she had begun, he was holding a polite expression of enquiry on his face, and the only way left to her was to blunder forward with her tale. She leaned forward and said, "I was with child once before, but the bairn died inside me. That is why we did not go to witness Edgar's king-making."

Such a fool, to speak to any man so, let alone this man. That she had spoken out of turn was obvious, for he lowered his voice and said, "I am sorry. But you are well now?"

She sat back. "Oh yes." She closed her eyes and offered a rushed but oft-spoken prayer that this time the pain would be worth more than a dead baby, born a season too soon. A coil of shivers twisted round her spine and she opened her eyes.

Alvar did not move, but stared at her. "All will be well," he said.

How wide was his world, where hers reached no further than Elfshill at the edge of their settlement. He would be a great earl and a father of many healthy children, easily begotten. She thought of him in his many-roomed houses, the jewelled swords hanging on the walls, and servants pouring the finest wine into smooth gold cups. The pottery would not be chipped or cracked, for his lady would… Her arms tensed, even though it was of no consequence to her what any future wife of his might or might not do. She sniffed in defiance of the tears that always came with memories of the miscarriage and she spoke stridently, compelled to declare her indifference to his charmed life.

"What it is to be a truly rich man and so assured of God's favour. Folk here have only their own hands, to use for both praying and digging." She waved her arm in a sweeping gesture that indicated the hall and the grounds beyond. "All will be well, you say. I cannot know, but I know that whatever comes to pass, I still have more to be thankful for than those who till the soil, their meagre hopes fulfilled merely if the sun rises and the harvest is good."

Silence hung heavy in the air and magnified his presence. She put her hand up to her stupid mouth to stop any more insults from tumbling out. Eyes wide, she dared not blink, and only drew breath because her body insisted upon it.

His hand went from his chin and he scratched his ear. He leaned towards her with his forearms laid flat to support his weight. "You might be right, lady. And it is something which I, and indeed, the churchmen, must always bear in mind if we are to be worthy of the name 'lord'."

Surprised at his humble response, she lowered her hand, tilted her upper body forward and laid her arms on the table. "I am sorry; I should not have spoken thus."

They remained in silence for a brief moment, their positions held in mirror image.

A shout went up from the far end of the hall. "Whitgar, you have spilled the lot."

Another thegn responded with a tease. "Do not worry; he is too mean to let it drip. Watch him lick it up."

Gytha came from the noisy end of the hall, bearing a jug of ale.

Káta sat almost motionless, her breathing shallow in the silence while Gytha poured Alvar's drink. His head was so close to Káta's that she could feel the warmth of his breath and the chill it left behind when he inhaled.

Alvar waited until the cup was full and Gytha had stepped back. He tasted the brew and nodded his approval before the Norsewoman wandered down to the far end of the hall. He said, "This is the Welsh-ale?"

Káta looked at her feet and made a gap in the straw with her shoe. "We like it, but cannot always get it." It was the best they had to offer; would he like it? She glanced up.

He lifted his chin and drank some more of the cloudy brew. His Adam's apple moved up and down as he swallowed. Her gaze followed the movement of his throat, and her finger traced a line on the table while she wondered how the taut skin on his neck would feel to the touch.

He wiped his mouth on the napkin provided and laughed.

Her hand jerked off the table. "My lord?"

He pointed and she turned to look at the doorway, where Helmstan was standing, covered in straw and horse dung. "A horse stall is not the best place to lose one's footing," he said, unnecessarily. "My love, will you fetch me my…"

"Fresh breeches. Yes." Welcoming the opportunity to leave the men to their drinking and roistering, she hurried away, sending Gytha to find Helmstan some clean clothes. Striding outside, she noticed that her steps proclaimed her anger. Well why shouldn't she be angry, having been so easily temporarily seduced, by his reasonable behaviour, into forgetting his more usual demeanour of arrogance? But although it seemed that she had identified the source of her discomfiture, the feeling persisted, even as her footsteps slowed, and by the time she reached the weaving shed she was still confounded; firstly by his indifference to the news of her pregnancy and secondly, that his muted reaction should have been of any consequence to her.

Worcestershire

Alvar was uncomfortable in the saddle, unusually so. This morning he had hung back, allowing the rest of his men to lead the way. He had no confidence in his ability to engage in any witty word-craft, not after his poor performance in Cheshire. To receive news of Helmstan's impending fatherhood with the dull utterance *'Oh'* was charmless enough, but he had neglected to offer any congratulations. He already knew Káta's opinion of him, and his actions would have done little to assuage her notion that he was haughty and over-proud. But, even if he were summoned by Saint Peter himself, he would not be able to answer for his deeds. A man would not reach out to grab the sun as it fell from the sky at night, yet Alvar felt like he had done exactly that and now sensed the loss of something that he had never owned. Four years ago he had pledged his life to Edgar, and had perhaps always understood that his duty would keep him at court or in the saddle and thus devoid of a personal life. Rarely had he acknowledged this pact, let alone questioned it. But now, like an old wound, it had begun to twinge a little. Given more time, would he have chosen a life like Helmstan's? With every visit, it was as if he stared into the reflective mill pond and saw another world, one which could have been his. On campaign, Alvar valued Helmstan as a loyal and beloved friend. But at his friend's home, the appeal lay in the way of life that Helmstan enjoyed, and it was more acute whenever Alvar was in Káta's presence, when he was confronted with the benefits brought by a happy marriage.

The high summer sun seemed to melt the skin on the back of his neck as droplets of sweat found their way down inside his tunic, and he was not surprised to see a family of churls sitting under the hedgerow by the side of the road. Tilling the soil in the midday heat would send the hardiest farmer to seek shade, and Alvar's men rode past the group of huddled figures without a downward glance. But as Alvar neared the group, he noticed the bundles of clothing, pots and pans, and bedding rolls. Tugging on the reins he brought his horse to a halt and dismounted. The man, apparently the head of this curiously displaced household, rose to his feet, placing one hand on his knee and then the other on the small of his back as he straightened up. He bowed his head. "My lord."

Alvar's gaze went from the man's bony hands, to the wife who lifted hollowed cheeks into a reverent smile, to the children whose shadows cast almost skeletal shapes. He addressed the man. "You farm the land here?"

"Not any more, my lord."

"Tell me."

"The new bishop of Worcester has turned us off our land and out of our house."

Alvar felt his blood warming as if to boil. The harvest looked set to be poor this year as there had been little rain in these parts. No need to have spent the summer here to see that; the parched fields told him all he needed to know. The rising anger clamped his jaw so that he almost snarled when he said, "So who is in your house now?"

"As I understand it, my lord, it is the kin of a monk who is himself able to claim some kinship to the bishop."

"And who is your lord? Why has he not spoken to the bishop on your behalf?"

The man stood up straight and his chin jutted forward. "My lord, I might not look it but I am no churl. I am a king's thegn. There are many of us, who once held land from the king but now find ourselves at the mercy of the bishopric. We were told that the bishop now holds jurisdiction over the land. Those who live on it were told to leave and given no redress. Many will starve."

"Well, you shall not. Go to my house at Worcester and speak to my steward there. You and yours will be well looked after."

Alvar rode away, all thoughts of returning to Upper Slaughter put aside once more. What in God's name was going on? Since when were leaseholds in Worcester subject to the bishop and not to the king or the earl? He grunted. No, not in God's name. This was not an act of God, but of His representative on earth.

Winchester

The sun was shining red and low when he reached Brock's manor. Alvar pressed a finger to the bridge of his nose and rubbed his thumb up and down his temple. He walked his horse into the yard and a young boy ran from the kennels and stood ready to take the lord's horse. A cook was dragging the roasting-spit away from the fire so that it could cool before being cleaned, and a kitchen-boy was walking towards the gate, his parcel of food suggesting that he was on his way to dole out sustenance to the shepherds staying overnight in their huts.

Brock ambled from his mews, calling out to the fowler who remained inside and whose answer was audible but indistinct. Brock smiled broadly at the sight of Alvar, but his expression sobered as he came nearer. "What is wrong, little brother? You look as though you have been riding with the Devil on your tail."

Alvar was weary and had tried to shy from his thoughts during the long ride. Under Brock's enquiring gaze he buckled and the words tumbled out. "I have been riding for days to rid myself of the smell rising from a heap of steaming shit. Its stench is fouler than a Welshman's fart. That dried up old windle-straw, Oswald... No, wait, I must call him by his rank... The snivelling louse-scabbed *bishop*, has sweetened the king into giving him three hundred hides of land around Worcester. And how did he do this? By vowing to turn it into a ship-soke and promising to provide seamen to serve in Edgar's new fleet. But this land is rich farming land so now, as if he has not already sucked enough of England into his greedy Danish mouth, he has begun to throw the folk off the land and give it to his kinfolk whom he has brought from East Anglia." He continued to curse as the young stable-lad took his horse from him.

Brock laid a hand on his shoulder and said, "Your steed is in need of a rub down and so, I think, are you. Stop spitting your oaths and go into the hall. I will be there as soon as I have made sure that your horse gets the best stall."

Alvar, spleen vented, sighed and smiled. The sun was a half ball of red fire. All men should be by the hearth at this hour and he turned towards the noise and warmth that beckoned from the hall.

Indoors, the fire was lively and welcoming, and folk had gathered round to begin an evening of story-telling and riddles. Overhead light flickered from cressets; the wicks sucked up oil, burning it to light up even the corners of the hall, where children yawned while they played with the dogs and tried to shrink into shadow when their mothers came close, looking to send them to bed. Alvar closed the door on the cooling dusk and, as the oak panel clattered, Brock's wife, Swytha, spotted him and darted forward.

"You are welcome, Brother."

He held her to his chest, kissed the top of her head and pushed a grey-blonde curl from her cheek. She stepped back, and mimed food and drink to a servant.

A little boy of about five years edged closer and disappeared behind Swytha's skirts. Alvar pretended he had not seen him.

The boy peeped from behind the dress.

"Oh, and who is this?"

Swytha reached round and placed her hand on the boy's back to bring him forward. "This is our fosterling, Goodwin."

"The bishop's son? Winchester's child?" Alvar squatted

down to bring his face level with the youngster's. "I am your Uncle Alvar," he told him.

The boy reached up and placed a small warm hand inside Alvar's.

The servant returned with bread, cheese, and ale. Alvar sat down at the long table and hoisted Goodwin onto his lap.

Swytha sat beside him. She waved her hand. "No, no, you must begin. I ate earlier with the rest of the household."

A shout went up from the men at the gaming board. "I win again. Your throw."

By the hearth, the harper slid his instrument from its beaver-skin bag and plucked a few notes to test the tuning against the piper's whistle.

The servant returned and poured ale into a cup, and Alvar broke a loaf of bread. Swytha watched him and smiled.

"What is it?"

"He barely knows you, yet he does not even wriggle in your lap. You have a way with the little ones," she said. "Is it not time you gave thought to having some of your own?"

He swallowed a mouthful of ale. "I think that if you knew which ladies of the king's house to ask, you might hear that the lack is not for want of trying." He laughed and sank his teeth into a chunk of cheese.

The piper began to play a lively tune and two young girls stood up to dance.

Swytha raised her voice and said, "Do not brush away my words, for that is not what I meant, as you well know. You need sons to leave your land to. Maybe your earldom, too."

He stopped chewing and turned to look at her. The face he had known for so many years was unchanged but for the handful of grey hairs around her temple. Alvar had been six when she wed Brock. He said, "When I first met you, you were taller than me. I am a grown man and it is a long time since you named me your 'little busy-bee', yet still you are like a mother to me. Do not look at me so..." Alvar pulled a chunk of bread from the loaf, gave it to the boy and set him down. "Off you go and find your foster-father." He wiped his mouth on the back of his hand and sighed. "I can see that you will not rest until you know my thoughts. It is true that when I look upon my brother I see how wedded life and children are good for the heart. But I cannot think of settling with a woman when the road oft-times takes me north, where I must keep the folk bound to Edgar. And now, where being away at least used to bring me some freedom to breathe, I will forever be worrying about what Oswald is doing in my lands." Anger rekindled, he returned to his curses. "Even in your sweet hall, I can still recall the din of his foul lies…"

"You dislike him." She smiled.

"Dislike? I loathe him. He stoops lower than a weevil crawling through dung…" He stopped and stared at her. "Ah, you were teasing. You understood me all along."

Brock appeared, with Goodwin on his shoulders. He said, "Here is my brother, staring like a halfwit. Does your fish-eyed look mean that you have been chided by my wife after your little show of self-pity?" He slid the boy from his perch and held him in his arms. "Well now, have you done with cursing the new bishop to the everlasting heat of hell?"

Swytha dabbed her eyes with her sleeve. "Your sweet-tongued brother has me in tears with his thoughts on Oswald."

Alvar looked from husband to wife. He said to Swytha, "Ah, yes, I nearly forgot. I must tell you what has arisen at Worcester."

"There is no need," Brock said. "If my lady wife has heard your thoughts on the new bishop then she does not need to learn all your new names for him."

Swytha looked up at her husband and back to her brother-in-law. "Well, one more would not harm."

Brock said, "If I have it right, one of the milder ones was 'soft-arsed worm-riddled son of a Danish whore,' but there were others."

Alvar crossed his arms. "It is true. He *is* Danish."

Brock gave the boy to Swytha. Swytha gathered him into her arms and stood up, and the little boy smiled at Alvar over her shoulder.

Alvar winked at the youngster. It was a wonder how any man could say that the boy's existence was a sin. Yet in this new world, that was how it would be; clergy could no longer be wed, nor their offspring acknowledged.

Swytha carried Goodwin towards the stairs and swayed as she picked her way through the dancers. Alvar smiled. He patted the empty chair next to him.

Brock squeezed onto the seat, wriggled, and coughed. "You missed the witenagemot."

"So I did. How was it?"

Brock chewed the inside of his cheek, giving his face a lopsided appearance. "It was odd. Dunstan spoke again about a second king-making. Edgar said that he had worn the king-helm long enough to be known as king, but Dunstan seemed to crave a more fulsome affair. He looked almost thwarted."

Alvar grunted. "I am glad I was not there. Dunstan would have blamed me. And…"

They looked up as Brock's eldest son Bridd walked over to the hearth, cradling a puppy. Brock smiled. "He will not leave that hound. As soon as it was weaned he would have it for his own. Still, it is a sweet thing."

Bridd lay down by the fire and let the puppy jump onto his stomach. The harper flicked the young dog's soft ears and two thegns leaned over from the table to pet it.

Brock's scop stood up and gathered the children to him. He sat in an armchair on the other side of the hearth and allowed the children to sit on his knee, weathering the stern looks from the mothers who stood with their arms folded and their feet tapping.

Brock laughed. "They will have a tale before bedtime, come what may. Now, what were you going to say?"

Alvar sighed. It was time to concede. "No, I will not say it, for it was about Oswald and I understand that I am forbidden now to speak his name in your hall." He winked at Bridd, slapped Brock on the thigh and stood up. He set off towards the door and thence to the latrine. Over his shoulder he said, "But he is still a turd."

Glastonbury

The abbey at Glastonbury welcomed benefactors, visitors, and weary travellers, and Alvar was known to the novice at the gate as all three. His horse was taken to be fed and watered and a messenger dispatched to find the abbot. In the church building, extended during Dunstan's tenure as abbot to include a tower and aisles, Alvar knelt, crossed himself, and said a short prayer before making his way to the rectangular cloister, another concept introduced by Dunstan from the continent.

He sat on a stone seat and, to loosen his muscles after the hard journey, he breathed in and stretched out his legs. He closed his eyes against the sun. In the quiet between nones and vespers, he heard only the low hum of a bee. He focused on the warmth on his eyelids and played for a few moments, opening his eyes just a fraction so that he could see only light. Without any defined images, his mind was free to give him a vision of a golden-haired woman. She smiled and his nose twitched to recall the soothing smell of lavender released with every shake of the head. He sat upright and opened his eyes fully. She had not been smiling when he left her hall. He leaned forward and scratched his side. She should be happy. *'I am with child; that is all.'* He recalled how his inner being had reeled as if from a powerful blow. He frowned and the images faded as he heard the shuffle of sandals across the courtyard. The abbot came forward in greeting and opened his arms wide to indicate that he had brought company. The Half-king came towards him, arms outstretched.

"You have been away from home for a while."

Alvar put a hand to his stubbly jaw and rubbed it. "I must be a sorry sight. I have been riding hard for some days now."

"If you seek the king you have missed him, for he left Cheddar last Friday."

"I wonder why I bother to keep a house of my own, so rarely do I see it. My fate is to ride the width and breadth of the land, chasing Edgar." Alvar paused, remembering that whilst the greeting might have been friendly, this man was the father of one of his sworn enemies. "But do not think me an ingrate. I often rest here on my way between my brother's house and my own lands."

The abbot bowed and moved off and the Half-king smiled. "To rest? Or to see where your gold might next be of some use to the abbot? Since I have been living here I have heard many tales of your generosity towards this abbey. Indeed, the only man whom they praise as much as you is Dunstan. If only you and he could have found a way to… Never mind; let me say merely that I might have been too hasty in my condemnation." He touched Alvar's arm. "You look full of woe, Lord Alvar. Walk with me in the gardens and tell me your tale. Once, I was a man who could mend many things. Perhaps I still have a small bit of thread to stitch with."

The Half-king took him through the herb garden by the monks' kitchens and listened with, "I see," and, "Yes, I had heard it was so."

The monks tending the plants remained on their knees and kept their heads down, making no apology for their presence, yet respecting the noblemen's privacy. The walled garden was small, but as they turned the last corner Alvar said, "And that is my tale; it does not take so long in the telling the second time."

The Half-king smiled. "I think the tale you have given

me might be tamer than the one that others have heard."

"The thing that irks is that all this was done while I was away doing the king's business in Northumbria."

"I do not envy you. And I am glad I came to this place before Oswald turned up at my hall at Ramsey. Tread lightly when you walk near the bishop; I think he is not to be trusted. But as Edgar's foster-father I had many years to learn how his mind works, and he will use Oswald if he can. Edgar will do whatever he feels he needs to, and make use of whomever he needs to. If a deed is done when your back is turned, it does not mean that Edgar thinks to betray you."

Alvar gave a wry laugh. He was already familiar with Edgar's lack of scruples. He pushed open the gate for the Half-king and followed him down the path to the pond.

The older man said, "Edgar grew up with my sons, but he is a stronger man than any of them. Elwood is a bitter man and that is my fault, but Brandon was the ivy to Edgar's tree, and he was lost when Edgar went to London. If he has wound himself onto Oswald's robes then it will take a keen blade to loosen him. They grew up with Edgar, but he favours you, and for that you have earned their hatred." He patted Alvar on the back. "But it is not all grim news. Last week a monk came from Abingdon with words of greeting to me and mine from our old friend Abbot Athelwold."

As they walked, the Half-king spoke at length, evidently glad for the company, and Alvar wondered how often any of his sons came to visit.

"And he sent me a gift of two books, Hucbald's *De Harmonica Institutione* and King Alfred's translation of Pope Gregory's *Cura Pastoralis*. I knew of Alfred's work, but not the other. Athelwold is keen that I should learn of this monk who wrote about music, but I confess it is not to my taste."

"At least Athelwold keeps his head in his books. A holy man's thoughts should not tilt too much towards earthly things. Dunstan wants to bring the kingdom together as one under God, but the English speak with more than one tongue, and put great faith in the old folk-ways." Alvar bent to scratch an itch and adjusted his leg-binding, and then stood up and stretched his back. "And as for Oswald, how does it please God to throw those who till the soil off their lands?" He was unaware of his clenched fist until the Half-king laid a hand on his arm.

"Come," the older man said, "I will show you the bees and the winery, though I think I know which one will better lift your mood."

Chapter Six AD962

Cheshire

"You should not even think of stepping out today; it is too cold. On days like this the flocks are in their pens and the shepherds bide in their huts. Learn from them."

Káta put down the loaf of bread. "Was it Leofsige who told you I was in here?" She turned and leaned her bottom against the cook-house table. "I am not ill; I am with child."

Helmstan stepped forward and covered her shoulders with his hands. He bent his head so that his gaze could meet hers. "You must take care. After the last time…"

"And you must not worry. The women have told me that all the spewing was a good thing, for it means that the bairn is set fast. I often feel him kicking when I am on my errands…" She clamped her mouth shut, but too late. She looked down at the floor and wriggled away from his grip.

"My love," he ducked from the herbs hanging from the roof and followed her round the table, "I already knew that you have been out every day in this bad weather."

Káta looked at Gytha, standing by the wall. The older woman stared at the floor. "Hmm," Káta said, "I wonder who told you." She turned back to her husband. "It has not been that bad."

"No? Let me see…" Helmstan put his finger to his chin in an exaggerated gesture. "The Yuletide snow was still lying thick on the ground at lambing time, and Burgred told me that the lambs born overnight were freezing to death. Now the worry is that the seeds might not grow up through the frozen ground. Yet still you go on your rounds?"

Káta folded her arms. "You are wrong. There have been sunny days." She cast her mind back. One bright day, she and Gytha had scrambled up the slope past the church but yes, they had been caught in a shower and the ground froze again straight afterwards. The following day brought a cloudless sky, but even in the late afternoon with the sun at their backs, it had shone on blue-white frost which clung to the slopes, and the ground under their feet remained rutted and frozen. February had brought rain, with a wind so strong that it made their eyes water and the paths, saturated by all the sudden water, became all but unusable. She smiled and clapped her hands. "There was one time when I sent Gytha out by herself and it must have been sunny, because I remember that the gate was steaming as the sun dried the rain off the wood and there was a rainbow…" But then the snow had come again. It had begun as a few flurries, but as the day progressed the flakes grew larger, until by noon the fields were devoid of all contours as the flat light reflected off the blanket of snow and levelled the landscape. He was right; it had been a harsh, prolonged winter, but that only meant that there was a greater need to distribute what little food they had.

He folded his arms. "So, if Gytha can be sent alone, then you do not need to go out yourself?"

She opened her mouth and shut it again. He looked so triumphant that it put her in mind of the cats who licked their lips with satisfaction when the dairy maids left the lids off the milk buckets and inadvertently left them a treat to steal. She pointed a finger at him. "Do not smirk. It makes you look old."

He lifted her hand to his mouth and brushed a kiss across her fingers. "I might be older than you, my love, but I am right. Now, will you heed my words and stay at home?"

"Oh, if it will soothe your mind." She shrugged off her cloak. "Gytha, come take the bread and fetch the salted meat and cheese. You must take enough for all those who have none left." She turned to examine her store of dried herbs, ticking them off on her fingers. "Chervil, dill, feverfew, oh and have we peppercorns and garlic?"

Gytha put the last of the bread into the baskets and scanned the table near the door. "Yes, Lady," she said, and left for the dairy.

Helmstan moved up behind Káta and put his arms around her waist as far as they would reach. He nestled his mouth near her hair and said, "Thank you, my love. I would not rest for worrying about you."

She turned round and moved in as close as her belly would allow. She reached up to kiss him.

"I spoke only out of love for you." He patted her stomach. "Both of you."

With her arms around his neck, she rested her heaviness against his body. He put his hand to her cheek. Someone out in the yard walked across the doorway and as the shadow passed across her face she found herself wondering, as she occasionally did, about the feel on her skin of another, more slender-fingered hand. She kissed Helmstan, hard and quickly. "I have work to do, Husband."

It was not until the middle of March that the rains came in earnest to melt the snows, but it remained cold, so that walking became a struggle over slippery ice. Káta, already confined within the boundary fence of the manor, was forced to stay indoors for a week, waiting for the thaw proper. She watched Gytha go out and welcomed her back as she stamped the slush off her shoes.

"Gytha, I have been penned in for seven days. I need to walk; I cannot say why, but I know I must not keep still today."

Gytha nodded. "Some say it is like this when the bairn is ready to come. Where is Lord Helmstan?"

Káta stopped pacing. "He is with the shoe-smith in the horse stalls. I do not want him to think that I have gone against his wishes but…"

"Come then, Lady. It is not so bad; the sne, sorry, *snow*, has nearly melted away. And young Haward is sick again. Maybe you can make him feel better?"

Káta stepped outside and stood in front of the doorway. She lifted her cheeks and breathed in the sweet, odourless air until her nostrils tingled from the cold and she was forced to breathe through her mouth. "I feel a little better now."

But she found little springtime cheer. Three lambs, born overnight, lay dead in the fields, and on the path in front of the woods a chaffinch was pecking at a lump on the ground. When they got closer, it flew away. Káta put her hands up and sucked in a breath. "Oh, Gytha, it was eating another of its own kind."

Gytha shrugged. "It has been cold. It is not only the folk who feel it."

Káta blew on her hands. "It was sad to see his passing, but I thank God that we buried only old Seaxferth last month and none of the children. I see they have been busy, though, for all that they are near starving." In the far end of Burgred's field, the youngsters' snow sculptures were standing, still upright, but less defined. On the ground the remains of the decoration, sticks for limbs and an old cap, were lying where they had fallen after the thaw released them from the statues. Káta clapped her hands. "These are wonderful. Did you give them that?"

Gytha giggled, picked up the cap and stuffed it into her basket. "Yes, Lady, I helped to build them." She stopped laughing when her mistress gasped. "You should not bend over like that, Lady; what are you doing? Oh, I see. Is it broken?"

Káta's brooch had fallen onto the path, and now she rubbed the mud from it and turned it over to examine the clasp. "No, I think not. Bad enough that it should unfasten, but worse yet that I then trod on it." She inhaled sharply. "Oh, now I have pricked my finger."

Gytha pulled her cloak tighter around her shoulders. "Or

is it elf-shot, Lady?"

Káta squeezed the blood and sucked her finger. "What? Oh Gytha, you must not tease. Young Haward was earnest in his belief that the elves had pricked him with their little arrows."

"So will you leave meat on Elfshill as payment for them to take away his aches?"

Káta smiled. "No. Why would the elves have any reason to be wroth with one as small as Haward? The brew I gave him should be enough to ease his bellyache."

Gytha counted them off on her fingers and grimaced. "Wormwood, henbane, bishop's wort; a good thing you put fennel in to make it sweeter. I think I would retch on it."

Káta gave the smile that Gytha was expecting, but she continued to rub at the scratches on the brooch, visible now that the mud had been cleaned. It could have been worse; the ground was slushy enough to swallow it forever. A gift from Helmstan, brought back from a recent visit to London, it was the only one she had which was made in such a way. She stroked the enamel. "I will see if Grim can shine it for me. We could go past the smithy on our way home. I... Oh."

"Lady?"

Káta stared at the ground, where a small patch of snow was dissolving in the warm liquid trickling down her legs. "Gytha, should there be blood in the waters?"

Gytha put down her basket and linked her arm through Káta's. She steered her back along the path to Ashleigh. As Káta stepped through the gateway into the yard her womb tightened and she gasped and put a hand to her belly. Gytha put her free arm around her lady's back and guided her towards the hall. She shouted to Siflæd in the bake-house. "Siflæd, look lively. Lady Káta needs our help."

London

The last time Alfreda had packed her chests for travelling was when she left her father's estates in Devon to journey to East Anglia, a bride at sixteen. Since then, she had been no further than the various houses of her husband and his kin, the most frequent of the visits being to Huntingdon, Ipswich, and Bedford. It was her husband who told her that she may accompany him, but surely the trip to London was a gift from God. And as she had whirled about her bower, selecting clothes suitable for appearances at the king's court, she knew that God gave naught for free, and her giddy thrill was sobered by the knowledge that her sons must remain at home with their nurse.

The separation had been fretful, but the mounting sensation of freedom had increased with every mile of the journey as they left behind the dank wet swamps of the fenland and progressed into the land of the old East Saxons and finally to London. The big skies of the flatlands shrank behind the buildings of the town, but Alfreda had never felt so unfettered.

But it was her first and last glimpse of cosmopolitan life. For five weeks she had been cooped in the house that her husband used when in London, a grand building with a whole upper floor, to which he returned at the end of the day's business, and from which he left her every morning.

And here, as elsewhere, she learned to turn a haughty cheek from the stares of pity from the household servants who learned very quickly the nature of the lord's temper. With no estate lands to wander and no weaving sheds to offer occupation and distraction, she had nothing to do but sew. Now, the incarceration was all the more bitter, for Elwood had fallen prey to the plague which, she was told by a lucky serving-girl who was allowed outside, was sweeping through London faster than a Viking fleet could sail up the Thames. Instead of spending the day alone with her thoughts and nursing her bruises, she was forced to minister to her abuser, who, whilst he could no longer use his strength against her, was still a challenging patient. In his lucid moments he threw plenty of insults and when gripped by the fever, he gave her no choice but to stay by his side, pressing cool cloths to his head and stripping or covering him, depending on whether he was sweating or shivering. In rare moments of quiet, she would apologise to God for wishing herself ill, that she might die and make her escape to a better place.

Now, as if to punish her further, He sent an unnaturally warm evening and while her husband lay shivering in his bed, she lay on her cot and flung the covers down to her ankles. Lifting her linen shift, she wafted it in an attempt to fan some cool air onto her body. The shutter was open and the sound from the street teased her, carrying the laughter of those who had been whiling away their evening in the drinking hall. London folk were not tied to the land but to the tides and could often afford to stay out of their beds long after sundown. Some of the shrieks wafting up gave the impression that many were destined for a bed other than their own and Alfreda tried not to listen, knowing that envy would send her even further from sleep.

The laughter stopped abruptly though, and the chatter turned into enquiries, with the conversation no longer contained within the small groups, but exchanged with others across the street. Detecting consternation in the raised voices, Alfreda left her sweat-soaked mattress and went to the window. Out on the street, folk had huddled into groups and many were pointing at the high ground towards the church of St Paul. Did she hear the word before she sensed the heat; did she detect the thick stench before she saw the flames? Or did her senses receive all the information at the same time as a drunk came running past the window shouting "Fire!"?

Now the only sound to be heard was that of panic. Bundles were thrown out of windows, hastily clad servants ran from the houses, and horses, mules and cows all emitted the same bestial scream of terror. Alfreda was aware only that she was oddly calm and was able to think for a while about which gown she should put on. She turned back into the room, trying to remember which chest contained her green silk kirtle. She walked over to the corner and lifted the lid of the largest chest. Slipping the dress over her head she turned to the rasping sound emanating from somewhere under the bedclothes.

"Wh… What is it?" Elwood, still shivering, tried to raise himself up on one elbow, but fell back.

Alfreda crossed the room once more, pulled the shutter tight against the window space and said, "It is naught. Some drunks, that is all."

She made her unhurried way down the stairs and walked through the ground floor. Every bench was empty, there were no hounds left by the fire. The servants had needed no prompting to get out before the flames came licking at the walls. She stepped out into the street. She stood for a moment, wondering where she should go, before deciding merely to follow the crowd, away from the conflagration and, she presumed, towards the river. A man approached her and pointed up at the first floor of her house.

"Lady, the fire is nearly upon us. Is anyone still in the house?"

Alfreda cast a perfunctory glance back towards her recent prison and then looked at the man. In a voice that sounded very far away, as if it were not her own, she said, "No", before she picked up her skirts and walked up the street, hurrying until she caught up and became just another one of the crowd.

Winchester

Death always stalked nearby. Though it was many years since any Englishman had died at the hands of the Vikings, famine and sickness were ever present. Churchmen, with food rents still paid to them, even in times of hardship, fared well during periods of pestilence, safe from elf-shot behind their monastery and minster walls. Noblemen, too, usually remained well-nourished enough to fight off the diseases which carried off the old, the weak and the very young. The news that the latest outbreak had claimed a victim in Elwood of Ramsey had set tongues clacking throughout Edgar's court. Rumours abounded, but the predominant one was that his servants had abandoned him and, left alone, weak from the plague, he was unable to escape the fire. But if the lord of Mercia's face was sombre-set, it was not because of grief. Edgar had explained his reasons for choosing Ramsey's successor but, whilst Alvar understood the thought process, he saw no reason to pretend happiness. To his complaint that there should be a much less suggestive man in charge of such a large area as East Anglia, Edgar had merely shrugged. *'I owe them.'*

And then there was the baby. Despite Dunstan's initial protestations, Edgar had helped himself to the lady Wulfreda, removing her from the nunnery before she managed to dedicate herself to Christ, and then ruining her prospects of returning to the convent by promptly impregnating her. Dunstan, who had so publicly denounced the Fairchild for debauchery, had sanctioned this union and declared the child to be throne-worthy. Alvar had been right to suspect the archbishop of harbouring political ambitions; Dunstan had served two martial kings before Edgar and his brother, and every day he appeared to be less the naïve cleric and more the shrewd statesman. Indeed, he had already shown that he would use murder to get his own way if necessary. The sordid murder plot had not produced the desired outcomes, so to push on with their reforms the churchmen now had no recourse but to retain Edgar's favour. Thus Edgar was forgiven and allowed to keep his nun, and Alvar could only shake his head at the hypocrisy of men who made a pastime of denigrating men such as himself. He smiled mirthlessly, for Edgar, meanwhile, was never one to dissemble, recognising the value of a mutually beneficial contract and acknowledging that a fee must be paid. Alvar marched across the enclosure, Edgar's words ringing still in his ears. *'My brother upset the Church and look where it got him. I cannot risk their ire. Dunstan is my confessor; he has blessed my child and is content. He might even forget past hurts if he is not upset again. I cannot call off his hound, so I have thrown Oswald a bone. We must all do with this what we can.'*

Alvar barged up to the great doors. *'I owe them.'* Indeed. And here, proof of that portion of the debt having been settled, was the new earl of East Anglia, smoothing his feathers. Oh yes, Edgar always paid his dues. But he was too clever to leave himself vulnerable, and perhaps only Alvar really understood this. It might prove diverting to watch as the new lord of East Anglia learned at first hand the genius of Edgar's gamesmanship. *'We must all do with this what we can.'*

Waiting to go into the king's hall, Brandon, the youngest brother of Elwood, was standing against the antechamber wall. He ran his hand over his blond hair and adjusted his tunic belt. The neck of his tunic was edged with gold embroidery and beneath it he wore a delicately embroidered white linen undershirt. His belt buckle was richly jewelled, with inlaid garnets and gold filigree. As he wriggled it into a comfortable position, his rings flashed their gemstones. All around him, the earls and leading thegns wore expensive, brightly coloured silk and they, too, were laden with gold and jewels. Yet in the crowded room, Brandon alone looked self-conscious and uncomfortable, his pale face even more wan than usual. Oswald was standing beside him, his head still but his eyes blinking quickly as he glanced round the room. He moved only to step back when necessary to allow the press of people to move on.

Alvar stepped away from the doorway and moved with the tide of thirsty men.

When Brandon hitched up his belt for the second time, Oswald said, "Do not worry, my lord, you look well-clothed. As you did when you swore your oath as an earl."

"Did I? Did I? I hoped to. It is a hard thing, to dress well enough but without outshining our king. I think I have it right."

Alvar, arriving next to them, stopped alongside Oswald and steadied himself against the flow.

Oswald met his gaze, staring at him with his blue pin-hole eyes, but spoke to Brandon. "The king raised you up to be earl above your elder brother. He sees your worth." Oswald smiled his worm-thin smile.

"Horse dung." Alvar was gratified to see Oswald's sneering smile slip away.

The bishop's mouth shrank into a wrinkled pout. "You speak crudely. You are rude."

Alvar snorted a laugh. "Am I? I wonder why? Could it be that if a hound is poked often enough with a sharp stick, it will rise up and bite its tormentor?" He stepped forward. "And rude or not, I speak the truth. Brandon is earl because of his shared childhood with Edgar, and because you spoke on his behalf and promised to pray away Edgar's sins. Look at the youngling; even he does not believe he can do this unaided."

The tip of Oswald's nose twitched, and even in the confined space he managed to draw up to his full height to look Alvar in the eye. "But he will do it well. And he will do what he has to without having ale in one hand and a whore in the other. I throw your words back at you and say that only friendship binds you to Edgar. Why else would he keep such an uncouth man by his side?"

"My lords, it is not becoming…"

They looked at Brandon.

"I thought you had forgotten I was here," he said.

"You are right," Oswald said. "We must not make a show of ourselves. It is time to be in the hall. Lord Alvar, I cannot move forward; you are in my way."

Alvar leaned nearer the bishop and met his gaze, unblinking. "Never did I hear a truer word. But have a care, for one more step and you will be on my toes. And then…"

The corridor cleared and a line of monks made their way past, cowls on and heads bowed. They were followed by the archbishop of Canterbury. Dunstan smiled as he approached the lords and they followed him into the hall.

Up on the dais, Edgar's lady companion was seated in the queen-seat, holding her newborn son. Alvar shook his head. "And I, branded whore-monger, am the only one who sees anything wrong in this."

Oswald turned to face Alvar. His thin skin stretched over his cheeks like that over a ripe plum. "This land has been rocked too many times by the deaths of young, childless kings. Edgar has a good woman and a healthy child. Lord Brandon has a high-born wife and more than one son." His lean lips curled upwards. "Where is your lady? Where are your children? You have only whores, but you dare to tell others that they live shameful lives? A hound with fleas will not tell a great man how to wash, my lord." Vitriol expelled, Oswald's face faded to its usual grey. He said, "A new son born to the house of Wessex is a good thing and we must thank God for it."

Alvar glared at him. "So, if I understand you: bishops,

like poor old Winchester, may not wed. Monks, unless they are your kin, may not hold land. And you, the bishop of Worcester, now hold a ship-soke in return for absolving Edgar of the small matter of his not being wed to the mother of his child. I bow to your learned wisdom."

A crackle gurgled in Oswald's throat.

Brandon said, "Again, the two of you speak athwart me as if I am not here."

Oswald pointedly turned his back on Alvar before he answered Brandon. "You are right. We should be speaking instead about how, through the use of land, we can make East Anglia stronger. We will show the godless lords how mighty the Church can become, and where better to do it than Mercia?"

Alvar clenched his fists and breathed in until his nostrils stretched. In the lowest, growling tone his voice could project, he said, "You can try. Mercia has never yet bent to the rule of a Dane, be he Viking or churchman."

He sought out his brother. Brock was sitting near the hearth with the abbot Athelwold and a young woman who remained in the shadows. Alvar approached them, still muttering under his breath, vowing to minimise the East Anglian religious influence on Edgar, denouncing their ingratiating attempts to indulge his every whim, and bemoaning the foul smell of hypocrisy.

Brock looked up. "Are you behaving yourself?"

"I should have felled him where he stood. Rotting crow-body…" Alvar sat down and shoved his legs out straight in front of him. "I reminded him that he is not one of us, but I only spoke the truth."

The abbot chuckled. "I think he owns enough land in East Anglia to call himself an Englishman. And, some might say, enough kin in the Church to call himself archbishop whenever he thinks the time is right. But you would not hear that from me."

Athelwold sat forward and the young woman looked up. A few strands of her Celt-dark hair hung free from her headdress and the deep beauty of her sloe-eyes erased all thoughts of churchmen and holy pastimes.

The abbot spoke on. "But... Oswald's sorrow... Sad shape of our monasteries... Heartfelt..."

Alvar's pretence at listening enabled him to pick out a few words, but he was not looking at the abbot. "I believe we have not met, my lady."

The young woman bestowed a smile on Alvar that was warm enough to melt glass.

Brock knocked him from his catatonic state. "This is Lady Alfreda, widow of Elwood of Ramsey. The lady widow is under the abbot's care."

Now Alvar had another reason for disliking the late lord of East Anglia; why had this exquisite creature been hidden so long from view? He continued to stare, feeling the rising heat from the fire and aware, but unashamed, that he was behaving like an unsophisticated stable-boy. The lady held his gaze for longer than was seemly and then slowly looked down, her long lashes dropping delicate shadows on her cheeks.

Brock's wife Swytha came to join them, and Alvar heard snatches of her whispered words of assurance to Brock that their young foster-son, Goodwin, was settled and happy with Swytha's serving-woman.

Swytha said to Alfreda, "The shapes on your kirtle are pretty."

Alfreda smoothed her patterned skirt. When she spoke, Alvar thought of honey, dripping from a spoon. "I have my cloth sent from York. It is the best. Where is yours from?"

Swytha shrugged. "We weave our own cloth, my lady." She looked at Alvar as if requiring help, but Alvar was cognisant enough of his own shortcomings to know that his was not the best advice to seek on how to speak to high-born ladies without causing offence.

Swytha tried again. "The child Edward has wind griping in his belly. I told Lady Wulfreda that she should put him high on her shoulder to bring it forth, but she will not heed me and sticks to rubbing his belly with her hand. Which do you think is best?"

Alfreda looked round the little group and smiled. "My firstborn was trouble-free. He was never full of wind and slept long hours. Oh, but with my next…"

Alvar was content to listen to the mellow voice whatever the topic of conversation, but even as an uncouth man, he detected the change in the tenor of that voice when she began to speak of her children. Swytha was smiling, evidently relieved to have hit upon a subject which drew the widow to speak out, and the two women continued to exchange stories of child-rearing.

One of the king's thegns came to stand next to their bench. "Alvar, Brock, Abbot, it is good to see you. Lady Alfreda, the king asks that he might renew your friendship." He held out his hand and she stood up.

The thegn led her to the dais and Alvar watched them go.

Brock nudged Alvar. "Your mouth is hanging open, Brother."

Alvar turned to his brother and grinned. "Well, it is not often I lay eyes on one who is so…" He glanced up at the group on the dais. "Ah, but look up there. What heartbreak does that foretell; Edgar's eyes open with lust, and Wulfreda's narrowed with sourness?" He shook his head. Perhaps Elwood had been right to keep his wife away from Edgar.

Abbot Athelwold said, "It is a shame that young Edgar has not learned to quench his fires with worship, or if not that, then a grope of a seamstress or some such. Lady Alfreda has had a hard life thus far, and she might not have the necessary strength to become one of the king's playthings."

Alvar raised an eyebrow. "How is that so?"

His brother said, "You spoke once of how Elwood never brought her to the king's house. Yes, Edgar lusted after her, but the truth is more that Elwood did not want the world to see his fist marks on her cheeks and eyes."

"Truly? How could any man…"

"I am sad to say that it is true," the abbot said. "Even as a child, Elwood had a temper, but his fear of his father meant that he kept it fettered. After the Half-king went to Glastonbury it was not the same tale, but one of strong drink not held well."

Alvar said, "So that is why he would not drink in the mead-hall. He feared that he would lose his grip on his wrath in front of witnesses?"

Athelwold nodded. "She has two little boys but I hardly need say that her sons were not begotten through love." He looked again at the dais. "It is no small thing to be loved by a king. Stronger women than she have been broken by it." He sighed. Wulfreda was continuing to serve Edgar his drinks but her smile was painted and her eyes were dull as she followed the king's gaze to the end of the table, where the young widow sat with her chin up, eyes focused on some distant point at the far end of the hall.

Swytha said, "She has her nose in the air. I hope that it is only to mask her shyness and hide her suffering, and not because she believes herself better than the rest of us."

The piper dropped his flute and it rolled along the floor, coming to rest by their feet. He scrabbled after it and said, "I am sorry, my lords, it is not the beckoning to the board that you are wont to hear, but I hope it will do." He snatched up his instrument and returned to the other musicians in the corner behind the king's table. The song of the harp, whistle, and pipe rose with the smoke to the high ceiling and the glee-men turned somersaults and took up their positions in front of the dais.

Alvar said, "They make me giddy. And I have lost my will to eat. I will come back later, to help you wipe pig grease from your fat chin."

He ducked a playful punch and wandered to the far end of the hall, where the grey-bearded lord of Chester was nursing a cup of ale and looked content to sleep in his seat.

Chester opened one eye as Alvar approached. "Well youngling, I thought you were keeping away from your fellow northerners tonight?"

Alvar laughed and clutched a make-believe chest wound. "Stinging words, from one so dear to me. But you forget that I hold lands in the south, too."

The Greybeard grinned. "I, forget? How can I, when you tell me every time I see you?" He sat up and shuffled along the bench. "Sit. I would hear your thoughts on the new earl."

Alvar grunted. "He is a mouse where his brother was a fox, and he has lived his life in the shadow of the barn while his brother was in the hen-house. You know it and the others in the witan know it. But he has land and he has Oswald…" He held his hands out, as if the point were well enough made. "Now, I wish to speak instead of a man who roars like a boar and is never frightened to say what he thinks. Where is your thegn, my old friend Helmstan?"

"I told him not to ride all this way, but to bide at home. He is now a father, for his wife bore a child not long back. He told me a dreadful tale of how she fell into a swoon from which she would not wake and the child was weakened, for her womb had… My lord, where are you going?"

The girl had a name, but he had not asked to hear it. She had stilled her tongue, crying out but twice, the second time when he dropped the silver pennies in her lap afterwards. He dozed on the hay, with no desire other than to listen to the snorts of the horses, but she stroked his chest and moved her hands lower.

"I can feel that the night is not yet fully over, my lord. Shall I slide under you again, if you have nowhere else that you need to be?"

He reached to move her hand away. "Where is it that you think I should be? Wooing a high-born lady to earn her love? Begetting some high-born sons to leave my lands to?"

"I am sorry, my lord. I did not mean to make you wroth." She sat up and straightened her clothes.

"No, bide where you are, for then I can bring you no nearer to the ground." He pulled her back down and rolled towards her. "God curse that wizened old Dane, for he is right. This is where I belong."

Chapter Seven AD963

South Yorkshire

With little wind to carry the rain clouds forward, it was easy enough to outrun them, and in moments the group was riding on firmer ground, and the men had the warmth of the early summer sunshine once more on their backs. On either side of the lane the hawthorn blossom showed the way, flanking the road with pillows of delicate white. Even though there was always a warm welcome waiting for him in Yorkshire, Alvar was glad to be travelling south where, usually, the weather was better and the air less damp. On this occasion, his leaving had been made easier, because he had not ridden away alone.

He turned and smiled at his friend Beorn riding alongside him, ahead of their small company made up of men from both Mercia and Northumbria. "We should reach Dinnington soon. I rested here last year on my way south; Thegn Brihtric is a good man and a better host. We will be made to feel welcome."

Beorn nodded, but his smile faded. He rubbed his smooth head. "It is not the welcome of the thegns hereabouts that worries me." His voice, deep and doleful at the best of times, rang unusually morose as he spoke the last two words.

Alvar leaned over as if to land a playful punch on his friend's arm. "Not this again. I have told you; Edgar is keen to meet you and to show you how grateful he is for the loyalty that you and yours have shown since he became king." He could see from Beorn's expression that he remained unconvinced. "You will believe me when you read the new law which is even now being drafted." Alvar was no scholar, nor an expert in legal matters, having come but lately to the world of politics. But even he couldn't fail to notice the difference between the old laws of the famous King Athelstan, who spent his whole reign fighting and whose charters were full of threats and curses, and Edgar's, which were written in the same tone as his speech, assured, confident. There was no pleading or coercing, merely the recognition of existing ways and customs, and a granting of rights and privileges commensurate with the support and loyalty which had already been forthcoming. "So it is that we are riding through the Danelaw. He will not alter the name, or the laws by which the folk here abide."

They slowed their pace to pass through a cluster of homesteads huddling beside a small chapel. It was an old building with timbers faded and weathered, and the roof was in need of new thatch. The parish priest was sitting on the grass outside the church doorway, with a small child perched on his lap. Reaching round the child's tiny form, he was whittling a wooden flute. Occasionally the child would reach out and touch the instrument and the priest took care to lift his knife well away from the tiny chubby fingers. Alvar said, "There is yet another thing that should be left well alone."

Beorn raised an eyebrow in enquiry.

"The Church might well be a rotting body, but it is the head and not the feet which needs lopping off." He chewed the inside of his lip. The dispossession of canons continued, the jurisdiction of the earls was gradually being eroded, and now a tithe tax had been introduced. Devotion to God and the rule of St Benedict was no doubt laudable, but the reforms seemed to overlook one fundamental role of the Church. Away from the cathedrals and monasteries, tending the flock was the most important function of the clergy, and the parish priests were doing a fine job. "Why sharpen a blade that is already keen?"

"Ah, you mean Oswald and the reformers. There is no such nonsense going on in the north, thank God. Tell me again why it is a good idea for me to come south?"

Alvar chuckled. "There are other newcomers apart from Oswald who are more pleasing to the eye."

"Oh yes? Is this why my sister looked elsewhere for a husband?"

"Hah! She would never have wed me, knowing as she does that she is far too good a woman for me." Even so, he was not about to insult Beorn by telling him any more about the beautiful widow from East Anglia, who had the delicious habit of tilting her head down before she looked up at a man through the darkest eyes, and stopped just short of giving him a full smile, so that the tiniest suggestion of amusement or even pleasure hovered as a hint around her carmine lips.

"Shall we turn west and go by way of Cheshire?"

He was shaken from his reverie as abruptly as when the cockerel shouted him from his slumber. "What? No, there is naught to be gained from going that way. We will keep to this road. South of Dinnington we will go west, into the Corringham wapentake, cross the river at East Ferry and then on to Lincoln. From there we have a straight ride down the old Ermine Street to London." Why had he been so quick to demur? And why was the notion of going to Cheshire the more repugnant for having broken into his thoughts about Alfreda? He fixed his gaze on the road ahead and contrived to turn his mind to more mundane matters.

They passed from the cleared land of the hamlet and lost the light of the sun when the path took them towards a wood, where the trees on the approach were taller and more closely spaced. Further into the wood, the temperature dropped. The path became less easy to follow and Alvar tried to remember from his last journey south roughly how long it would be before they emerged into the bright heat of the day once more. The track narrowed still further and the riders had no choice but to go forward in a single column. Alvar began to feel a sense of unease which had not troubled him when he first came this way. He leaned out first left and then right from his saddle, listening.

Behind him, Beorn said, "What is it?"

Alvar shook his head. "Naught. I thought that maybe…"

The distinctive song of the spear ended with a dull thud as the point penetrated a tree trunk six feet in front and to the right of him. On or off the battlefield, in or out of the shield wall, the spear throw always meant the same thing: *the fight is on*. Alvar leaped from the saddle, pulling his spear from its bindings and ducking down by the horse's flank. Crouching, he reached up with his free hand, twisted his shield from its resting place on the back of his shoulder, and brought it to a defensive position in front of his body. He craned his neck to see if Beorn and the others in their group were similarly prepared. Beorn had mirrored his every move and remained in a squat, his long legs folded beneath him, shield and spear ready.

While they waited for their assailants to show themselves, Alvar wondered what nature of foe they were about to face. Who could have known that he and Beorn were headed this way? Although they were obviously a party of lords and their retainers, they were nevertheless but a small band, with no baggage carts or visible sign of wealth, other than their personal gear. Had they been incorrectly targeted, either by English warring locally with Danes, or vice versa? A cry went up and a ball of sound rolled out from the trees, containing the scuffle of men's boots, the rustle of leaves, shouts of aggression, the clatter of spears, and axes thumping onto shields. Alvar slapped his stallion on the rump, sending the beast running further along the path; he would round him up later. If, indeed, 'later' came.

Beorn and the next handful of men behind him all followed suit, and they moved close to Alvar to form an impromptu shield wall. A baby-blond-haired man with ragged clothes and a battered shield ran towards him and Alvar held his spear up. He used gravity to bring the spear point to his opponent's face, taking a step forward as he thrust, and he felt from the flexible yet unyielding wall that Beorn was doing the same. Alvar's spear ripped through the flesh of the blond's cheek, slicing down and embedding into his shoulder. Alvar tugged hard to release the weapon and the baby-haired man fell back. Another, shorter, darker man took his place but Alvar could see in his peripheral vision that the line of attackers was, at any time, only one or two deep. They were not outnumbered and although they had been caught by surprise, this would be as fair a fight as any.

Despite the fact that, as a group, these men had never fought together, the shield wall held. He and Beorn worked in concert, protecting and deflecting blows for each other, thrusting with spear and pushing forward with shield, arms alternating in a pummelling action, and Alvar was grateful to have such a man by his side.

The smell was no longer the aroma of the forest; the sweetness of sap and foliage quickly became overpowered by the stench of warm bodies and the unmistakeable pungency of spilt blood. As the wall pushed a few steps forward with each onslaught, the ground underfoot became slippery, the woodland carpet greasy now with oozing blood.

But now there were more enemy dead than living, and the last handful backed away before turning to flee. The victors banged their shields with their spear hafts and sent a loud cry after them, shouts of triumph to ring in their ears as they ran.

Alvar and Beorn lowered their shields and Alvar held his hand out. Beorn grasped it, so that they held hand to forearm in a gesture of solidarity and friendship.

Beorn said, "We picked a bad day to ride this way."

"I thought the same. How could they have known that we were coming, and got fight-ready so swiftly?" Alvar walked to the nearest corpse and turned the slumped torso with his foot. The man's dress gave little away; it was perhaps Danish in style, but that told more about where he lived than his ethnicity. Any man living in or near the Danelaw would dress in a similar style, be he Englishman or Dane. One thing which was clear, however, was that he was not a rich man. His shield, lying useless by his side, was roughly made and simply decorated. He had a spear, but no sword, and his boots were fashioned from the most basic of tanned leather. He wore no jewellery and, if he possessed a cloak, he had lost it in the fighting. Yet there was a fat, lumpy otter-skin bag fastened to his belt. Alvar lowered onto one knee, took his hand-saex and cut the purse strings. Hefting the bag up and down in his palm he frowned and handed it to Beorn. "What do you think?"

"I think that a man like that would only own this many coins if he had stolen them." Beorn opened the bag and poured a few of the silver sceattas into his hand. "Enough here to give to our men, who fought well this day."

Alvar nodded, but placed a hand on Beorn's arm. "Let me see them?"

Beorn tipped a few of the coins into Alvar's hand, and he picked one up and examined it. "These were minted in Worcester."

"Really? Either he robbed a wayfarer, or he has been a long way to steal these."

"Or someone came a long way to give them to him."

As Alvar had hoped, they caught up with the king's household in London. Edgar, however, was not to be found with the rest of the court at his house at Greenwich, but had, they were informed, gone to the river. Alvar was used to the sights and smells down by the banks of the great river, where trading ships offloaded their goods and foreign sailors spent their profits on English ale before they piled their cargo high for their return journey to the near continent, or further afield to Rome, Byzantium, Baghdad or even Iceland. But the sight that greeted Alvar this day was different. Moored to the wharf were three newly built boats, and a further two were under construction. The workforce was English, but it was a Norse captain who barked out instructions as the carpenters planed the planks and nailed them, overlapping, onto the frames of the boats. These boats would be war ships, long enough for sixty crewmen but narrow, with a shallow keel to keep them sitting low in the water, and this shallow draft would allow them to navigate rivers. Alvar wondered what the folk of London thought about these ships, so Viking in appearance, emerging from the wharves. He could only hope that Edgar would order them painted in different colours than the blue, red and yellow that the invaders so often used.

Edgar, hair bleached by the sun, was not wearing a tunic and his linen undershirt billowed in the breeze blowing across from the water. He stood still to listen when the Norseman spoke to him about some element of design, and periodically he leaped from one vessel to the other, inspecting the detail of workmanship.

Sitting on cushions spread out over the grass above the wharf, Alfreda acknowledged Alvar's presence with her slow blink and a small smile. The breeze lifted her skirts a little and revealed the merest glimpse of expensive silk slippers and pale white ankles.

Beorn pursed his lips in a silent whistle. "This will be one of the prettier newcomers of whom you spoke?"

Alvar said nothing.

Beorn laughed. "And that man; is that Edgar?"

'*Man*'. The lad was not yet twenty-two and here he was overseeing the building of a fleet supplemented by mercenary ships and sailors. Alvar smiled his approval and beckoned Beorn to step forward to be introduced.

One of the men on the boat caught Edgar's attention and pointed to the new arrivals. Edgar, cheeks flushed, bounded over and clasped Alvar to him. "You are back. How are my friends in the north?"

"I have brought one to meet you, my lord. This is Oslac

'Beorn' of Deira, the man I told you about."

Edgar held out his hand and Beorn bent to kiss it. Edgar said, "Lord Alvar has told me how you have been speaking on my behalf in the north. I am grateful."

Alvar said, "There is yet more to tell. We were set upon on our way south, and Beorn here proved himself a fearless fighter. I was glad to have him at my side."

Edgar's smile faded and his face reddened to an angry glow. "You were set upon? In my lands?"

Beorn said, "Lord Alvar thought that it might have been men who…"

But Alvar saw the bishop of Worcester walking along the wharf and put out a hand to silence his friend.

He said, "It was naught, my lord, a skirmish, nothing more. And few of theirs left alive to speak of it." As he watched the Dane approaching, he was tempted to suggest that whoever set the assailants upon him had not known that Beorn was travelling with him.

Oswald had quickened his pace when he saw Alvar talking to Edgar and arrived slightly out of breath. "Lord Edgar, do not be hasty to anger. This is not lawlessness, and your kingship is not to blame. This is godlessness, and shows how much work is still to be done in the heathen north. And I see that the lord Alvar still lives." This last was loaded with venom, despite being delivered with the smile required by social convention.

Alvar, standing next to Beorn, felt his friend go tense and suspected that he had taken an instant dislike to the Crow of Worcester, while Alvar himself struggled against the temptation to ask Oswald how he knew what they were talking about, despite having missed most of the conversation.

"Nevertheless," Edgar said, "I would like to ride there and mete out some punishment."

The bishop paled. "Lord, there is no need."

Edgar would not be gainsaid. "I wish to be known as a peaceable king. But the folk who live in these lands need to know that every misdeed will be dealt with. And all men need to be made aware that I can, and will, fight." He draped an arm over Alvar's shoulder. "Come, my lords, let us make ready to go back and finish the fight."

As they walked back to the court, Edgar spoke to Beorn. "You live in Deira, but my thegns tell me that your grandfather was a Cambridgeshire man. Is this true?"

"It is, my lord." Beorn looked across at Alvar, raising his eyebrows in query.

Alvar chuckled. Edgar was indebted to Beorn and might well reward him. But before he chose to make Beorn his eyes in the north, he had ascertained that the man had southern credentials and, therefore, southern loyalties, too. Not yet twenty-two, only just a man, but very much a king.

Alfreda leaned back and turned her face to the sunshine. She opened her eyes when a shadow cooled her face. Edgar, Alvar, and Alvar's friend were walking past and, as they passed by, Edgar turned his head and gazed back at her. Unsmiling, he looked her up and down and she felt her belly leap. There was no mistaking his desire. Edgar was determined to have her, and she would be a fool to refuse the man who believed her to be beautiful. How could she do other than respond to the flattery by acceding to his request whenever it came?

She returned his stare and smiled in a way she had learned, a way that seemed to please most men. The three companions walked away and she noted the rip in the back of Alvar's tunic. She tried to imagine him in the thick of battle, but she had no experience of such things, and could only dream up an image of him nimbly dodging axe blows whilst dispatching his foes with lethal accuracy. He, too, had appraised her with his gaze when he first arrived at the wharf. Her interest in him had been fuelled long ago by tales of his adventures and she was not disappointed when she finally met him. How could any woman not love him on sight? Probably she loved him even before that, on the strength of his reputation, but his behaviour towards her did nothing to erode his appeal; he was always attentive and if, of late, his smile had been tempered by a lack of warmth in his eyes, as if his life had been touched by sadness, it only served to heighten her curiosity. How to choose between these two men: one, valiant and loyal, harsh on the battlefield, gentle and shy off it and the other, confident, arrogant, and insistent that she should have whatever she desired and that he should, too. She raised her face to the sun once more and wondered how she might contrive to have them both. Why not, if she was, as they seemed to think, so desirable? She was frequently aware, nowadays, that men were looking at her; it was so much more pleasant than the foreboding that had dogged her moods when she was still wed.

It had been some time since she had given any thought to Elwood. Whenever she thought back to the dark house in London, it was only to be grateful for the one moment of premeditation that found her arriving at the open air folk-moot on the high ground at St Paul's, being recognised as a noblewoman because of her choice of fine dress, and being directed to the court where she was immediately welcomed as a woman of quality. Abbot Athelwold became her champion, and, now that he had been promoted to the bishopric of Winchester, his heightened status elevated her own. Only he and Edgar knew of her past; servants lowered their eyes not because they were sorry for her but because they were in awe, and she no longer cared to befriend them, for their opinions no longer mattered. They knew naught of her except that she was a grand lady, and losing her shackles of shame left her feeling exhilarated. Now she was free to move, and to enjoy her wealth, status and beauty.

She heard a familiar voice and her reverie exploded, leaving only shards of bitter memories. Brandon's unmistakeable whiny voice carried on the breeze, and Alfreda sat up to listen.

"Lord Bishop, I came all this way straight from burying

my father to speak to the king, and now I am told he has gone back to the hall. Must I chase him all day?"

Alfreda, squinting against the sun, studied Bishop Oswald, and thought that he looked even more sour than usual.

He said, "Never mind that. We have work to do. You are bereaved; your father was a great man, but it is time to make you a greater one. With my help, you will outshine your father. With your help, I can…"

A gust of wind fluttered Alfreda's veil, and the rustling, so close to her ears, prevented her from hearing the rest of Oswald's speech. They began to walk towards her and she stood up, heart hammering somewhere near her throat. There was one aspect of her previous life which pained her still, and she must grasp this opportunity. As they approached, she took a step forward and touched Brandon's arm. "My lord, I was sorry to hear of the death of the Half-king. You are newly returned from East Anglia. Have you any news of my children?"

Brandon looked at first startled, and then, disgusted. He kept his chin up, but looked down at her hand until she took it away. Brushing his sleeve as if she had smeared it with mud from the river bed, he said, "Lady, when I was there I saw only my kin, those who share my blood, those who mourn. I do not recall that you ever mourned my brother. If you do not think of yourself as his widow, then how can his children be yours?"

He walked on and Oswald followed, pausing briefly to bring his face uncomfortably close to hers. His lips drew back as he inhaled and she shrank back, convinced that he was about to hiss at her. But he passed by without speaking, and she turned to look at the pair of them as they walked away. Once the momentary fear subsided it left only a burning hatred. She had only two desires; somehow to see her children again, and to exact revenge. Alvar might well turn out to be the man that she would always love, but it was only the king who could help her now. And she knew what she had to do.

She followed the courtiers as they wandered from the water's edge and back to Edgar's house. The men had not gone inside and it was evident that they were making plans to leave. The king's thegns had been mustered in the yard, and Lord Alvar and his friend were inspecting their war gear, running their thumbs across spear points and taking hold of shields, banging on them with the flat of their hands. Satisfied, they ordered the men into an extempore shield wall, lining up a few of the men who had travelled with them from the north into an opposing wall. Lord Alvar brought his arm up, held it aloft, and then brought it down as a cue for the two lines to advance. They met in the middle of the yard with a clash as the metal shield bosses collided. There was a plethora of loud grunts and plenty of shoving, but both walls held, with neither giving ground. Alvar gave the signal for them to ease off.

Edgar wandered over to Lord Alvar and whispered in his ear. Edgar stepped back, and draped his arm casually over Brandon's shoulder. Alvar spoke to the king's thegns and glanced around the yard. He spied his target and beckoned to a small boy, who came forward shyly and stood in front of the great lord, hands clasped behind his back, and his shoe tracing lines in the dirt. Alvar lifted his own shield from his shoulder, bent down, and handed it to the youngster. He showed him how to hold it by grasping the leather strap and keeping the shield across the body. He unsheathed the hand-saex from his knife belt and placed the blade into the boy's other hand, and then he gestured towards the shield wall where the king's thegns were standing in tight formation. The little boy nodded, perhaps with a little trepidation, for his teeth were clamped on his bottom lip. He stood for a moment, as if assessing the enormity of his task. He tucked his head down and set off at a run, hurtling across the yard and aiming for the central section of the wall. At the moment of impact, to a man, the king's thegns fell backwards, the wall collapsed, and the little boy emerged triumphant. The crowd whooped and cheered and laughed, and the boy beamed with pride. Alfreda tried to swallow away the lump in her throat. The boy was about the same age as her eldest son. She turned away but her path was blocked by Bishop Oswald.

Pointing to Edgar, he said, "It will do you no good to speak to the king about your children. See how Edgar loves our Lord Brandon."

Alfreda made as if to shoulder him aside, and he stepped back. She made her way over to where the king was standing, still with his arm around his foster-brother.

Edgar was addressing his men. "We need to ride north with the lords Alvar and Beorn. Right now, they think that you can be bested by a child. Let us show these northern lords how you really fight. We leave at dawn."

His words were met with cheers, and the sound of spears thumping against shields.

Edgar turned, saw Alfreda approaching, and smiled. "Now, I think, they are ready for a fight."

Alfreda knew that Oswald had followed her; she could hear the swish of his robes as he walked. Did he think she was so stupid as to petition the king immediately? She would get her children back, yes, but she would find another way.

"My lord," she said, "I saw the ships that you are building. Already they look as if they would scare away the mightiest Viking. Will you have them painted the same way as the dragon boats?"

Over her shoulder, Oswald hissed his irritation, muttering about ignorant women who did not know that the blue paint on the Viking ships was derived from a colour that came from Arabia and was very costly. To the king he said, "Lord, women know little about such things, which is how it should be."

Edgar slipped his arm from Brandon's shoulders, and turned towards Alfreda. He said, "Not at all. I had been wondering how we might paint our ships so that they are as fearsome as the Viking long ships. The lady has reminded me that I must now give it some thought."

He smiled, and even though his answer had been directed more at Oswald, she was gratified to note that his gaze had never wandered from her face.

Edgar continued to stare into her eyes as he said, "My lords, let us go within and take our fill of food and drink, for tomorrow we ride hard."

He swept his arm forward, said, "Shall we?" and directed her to the hall.

Alvar ruffled the lad's hair, and took him over to one of the king's thegns. "Get him something to eat. He has done us proud." Still chuckling, he walked with Beorn to the hall.

Beorn continued turning his head with the newcomer's instinct for observation. He pointed to Alfreda, gliding gracefully alongside Edgar and said, "The king knows how to stir the fire in the bellies of his men. And she knows how to stir his fire. If she was your mark, you had better think again."

Alvar deflected the comment. "She only did it to irk the bishop. Look." He nodded in the direction of Oswald, who was chewing his lip as if a wasp had just landed in his mouth.

Beorn said, "I do not like that man."

Alvar laughed and thumped him on the back. "I knew I was right to befriend you."

In the hall, he and Beorn settled their men on the mead-benches before taking their seats on the head table. Dunstan was not there and neither was the archbishop of York. Despite the presence of two other bishops, Oswald sat nearest to the king as if he were the senior cleric in the room. Apart from Alvar and Beorn, most of the other secular lords present were local men who held land in the south and southeast, and Lord Brandon took his place on Edgar's other side, as if he were the highest ranking earl.

When they were all sitting down, Edgar produced one of his rare smiles and publicly welcomed Beorn. "Now that we have a steadfast Northumbrian to share the drinking horn, every man is in his place, and my kingdom is truly whole." In a tone which was almost playful, he said, "Lord Alvar has not only kept the Welsh border safe, but has been riding round the north for a twelve-month, gathering men to my banner. Now he has come south, bringing me a pair of Northumbrian eyes, and on the way he found time to put down a band of wolf's heads who were bent on killing him and mocking my laws. To put it simply, to ask Alvar that a thing be done is to know that it will be done. Straight away."

Alvar sat back in his chair, Edgar's endorsement of his skills warming his ears and the back of his neck, and the ever-present sense of unworthiness gnawing at his belly. Edgar was lauding him, and yet his career had begun with the breaking of an oath. Was this why he tried so hard?

He had hardly had time to reflect since the wheels began spinning. He was hurtling along in a cart full of guilt, attempting to prove himself worthy and, as a soldier in peacetime looking for a purpose, he had tried his hand at politics. He had been so busy trying to justify the decision to abandon the Fairchild that he had barely stopped to assess how Edgar had acquitted himself as king. So far, the youngster had not had to defend his kingdom, but he had not sat idle and the burhs were fully manned, the ships nearly built, and the loyalty of the provinces assured.

Loyalty. It was the backbone of their society, his reason for swearing initially to the Fairchild. It was such an integral component of life that it heightened his determination to stand by Edgar, or forever be a man who broke an oath for nothing. So whilst Edgar's achievements were measurable, it made little difference; Alvar was tied to his king, come what may, even when the churchmen tried to pull Edgar away from martial concerns to those which better served their own interests.

And, as if reading his thoughts, Oswald spoke now, to downplay the attack on Alvar and Beorn, and to deflect Edgar's exaltation of their prowess. "Wolf's heads or not, it is godlessness which drives such men. These were not trained weapon-men, surely, but men who should spend more time in prayer. Church rules are not being followed and…"

Edgar nodded as if in agreement, but his eyes were shining as he interrupted the bishop. "We still need to ride there, to show them what we think of their craven attack. I have been blessed; the Vikings have stayed away from my shore. But even though there is no Viking threat, we should not sit easy. So I build up my fleet, I feed my weapon-men and, when we are threatened, we fight." When Oswald opened his mouth to protest, Edgar touched his arm. "Thus, men will know not to break my peace, and we gain time to spend on other things, as my forebear Alfred did. Learning and faith; these things matter. So we must spread out, to the borders and beyond, building monasteries as we go. Church and sword must weigh one as heavy as the other. I will lean as much on my churchmen as I do on my lords, and in this way not only do we strengthen the kingdom, but we draw them all together."

Alvar thought that, paradoxically, the methods of which Edgar spoke also kept the various factions apart, vying for power and his attention.

Edgar had spoken at length and with passion about building his kingdom into something more akin to an empire, strengthened by military might and an influential Church. Alvar was not naïve; he knew that Edgar would always play the lords against the bishops, striking a balance between those who must remain celibate and those who could found strong dynasties. The only question was whether Edgar realised the depth of division between the two sides. And, however convivial the evening, there was an absence of warmth. Edgar continued to praise, compliment and mock in equal measure. He spoke his mind and was never less than forthright, but he did not always disclose all his thoughts and rarely his feelings. Alvar thought again about another hearth, far away from the court, where there had always been a spare seat by the fire, where there was never any dissembling.

A servant knelt before him and offered a plate of summer pudding, egg custard, and shortbread, and Alvar realised that he must have chewed his way through the meat on his plate without noticing. The evening had turned into night. Jugs of ale and flagons of wine lined the tables, and the servants replaced them as soon as they were emptied. The jokes became obscene, the flirting more outrageous. Alfreda, forced by the East Anglians to sit further along the head table, had attracted a gaggle of admirers who kept her supplied with a steady stream of drinks and compliments. She repaid every gesture with the press of her hand upon the donor's arm, hand or shoulder, depending on their proximity. When Brandon stood up and went to speak to one of his thegns, she made her apologies to her new devotees and wriggled into the seat beside Edgar, where she applied the same gratifying technique every time the king spoke to her. She drank thirstily and frequently, staring at Alvar during every lull in the conversation.

Beorn, still keenly assessing all that could be gleaned from these new acquaintances, was quick to spot the incongruity. "Her arrow is aimed at the king and yet her sight is set on you. I have never seen a hunter so doleful about their kill. How do you feel about that, my friend?"

Alvar opened his mouth in quick response, but then closed it to consider his answer. Beorn was not overly perceptive; Alfreda's opinion of Alvar had never been in doubt. He had often wondered what odious act he would have to commit before she changed her mind about him, for she seemed to have decided long before she met him that she would like him. Alvar smiled bitterly at that. He could name straight away a woman who had been immune to his charms and he, never able graciously to accept a compliment, was inclined to assume that hers had been the correct assessment. With that, his thoughts took a morose turn, and the humourless smile dropped altogether. In answer to his friend's query he said, "No matter how loudly love might call, the path that must be followed often goes another way. The bed might even be softer there."

Beorn nudged him. "Well, bedtime is a long way off for us. Have a drink, friend, I am getting ahead of you." He whistled softly and waved his cup in the direction of the dais, slopping his drink. "See that?"

Edgar was on his feet and was holding his arm out, gesturing towards the door. "Lady Alfreda, walk with me."

Her features fixed in neutral expression, she nodded and stood up. She dipped at the knee to offer the tiniest curtsey, and followed him.

Bishop Oswald clutched the edge of the table and half stood up. He called out, "Lord King, you ride to a fight in the morning. Would your time this evening not be better spent in prayer?"

Edgar turned round and stared at the bishop. "No, my lord. That is what I keep you for."

Alvar laughed. Whatever sharp-pointed thoughts had pricked his brain this evening, the pain was fleetingly nullified by Oswald's mortification, as the bishop sank red-faced back into his chair.

Chapter Eight AD964

Winchester

Swytha shook her head and tutted. "She will not smile even a little."

Alvar grinned. "She is cross because she knows that she looked better this morning." It amused him, though, to see that even though Alfreda was dressed now in a drab, shapeless, homespun robe, she had managed to find a braided cord to draw it in around her slender waist. But it was still a dreary comedown for her, compared with the stunning attire of the earlier ceremony. That morning-gown, made from the delicate Godweb silk, had been the same red hue as her mouth, and the whisper of under-sleeve had glowed white like her lily cheeks. Alvar licked his lips.

Swytha frowned.

"What? I said naught…"

"You did not have to," she said. "Put your tongue away, brother, and remember that this morning the lady was wearing her wedding clothes." She looked forward again but whispered from the side of her mouth. "And that we are in a church."

The king was still dressed in his wedding costume; a floor length, shot-silk tunic, finished round the neckline and front opening with embroidery of gold thread, and the softest leather boots, so supple and comfortable that they would not withstand even a day's normal wear outside. Beside him, in her simple garb, Alfreda could now rely only on her looks and she gazed down at her plain dun robes and wrinkled her straight little nose. She put her head up and looked out into the crowd, her features fixed and giving no further insight to her thoughts.

Swytha wrinkled her own nose as yet more incense wafted over the congregation. "With first the wedding and now this, I feel as if I have been in this minster all day. My feet ache."

Alvar murmured in agreement and rocked on the balls of his feet. He looked across at Athelwold and marvelled how the abbot had changed since acquiring the bishopric of Winchester. He stood to their left, swathed in a blue chasuble bordered with the elaborate golden embroidery known as orphrey. Alvar felt again the dull ache in his belly. Athelwold's investiture as bishop of Winchester the previous year had been grand, opulent and every bit as boring as today's event. Alvar had looked at every face in the crowd as he shuffled and squirmed in the new minster, but none of the lords of Cheshire had made the journey south. How many times since then had he snapped at his thegns and officials, who kept him so busy at home, and cursed the Welsh who remained in their own lands and gave him no excuse to ride to Cheshire?

Bishop Athelwold lifted an elegant sleeve and put a finger discreetly under his nose to catch a drop of moisture. The woven silk shimmered exquisitely. He nearly outshone the archbishop, and, amongst these elegantly clad churchmen, Alfreda must feel dull indeed.

Except that today it would not have been difficult to outshine the archbishop; Alvar had seen thunderclouds less black than Dunstan's expression. During the preparation for the ceremonies, Athelwold, the champion of vulnerable women, had impressed Alvar and annoyed Dunstan all at once, arguing eloquently and vehemently in favour of Alfreda's consecration as queen. Alvar, no less concerned for Alfreda's wellbeing, and, truth be told, eager to exploit the opportunity to triumph over Dunstan, had pointed out the political advantages to be made. In Wessex, the wife of a king was seldom named queen; in Mercia, she always was. Edgar could bring his peoples together with such a gesture. Dunstan, comfortable for so long being the custodian of Edgar's sin, saw his leverage slipping away as Edgar repudiated the saintly Wulfreda. The king was smitten with the widow from East Anglia and he would have no other. The meeting had taken less than an hour. Alvar mused that wars had lasted years with less decisive upsets in the balance of power. And it was no longer a private matter; anyone looking at the archbishop and his sour expression would be left in no doubt as to how he felt about his task this day.

What was not so easy for Alvar to understand, though, was why Alfreda had agreed to marry Edgar. He had assumed… Well, no matter, he had been wrong before. But he was convinced that this was no love match, and he wondered why she would suffer another loveless marriage. It had been clear for some time that she saw some advantage in being Edgar's woman, but to be his wife? Once again, Alvar was surprised by what folk, even a beautiful woman like her, were prepared to do. Was it, in fact, he who was the fool, for all that he was prepared to do without?

Whatever her reasons, at least Alfreda would be able to use the title of queen for her whole life, and any future children would be named as high athelings, born of a king and a queen. He muttered under his breath. "But see how it sticks in Dunstan's throat."

Archbishop Dunstan's lips were drawn into a thin line, almost disappearing into the folds of his fleshy face. As he anointed Alfreda with holy oil, his arm moved in stiff jerks, as if tense muscles were fighting against the lightness of touch that was required to consecrate the woman as queen.

Alvar, too, winced, as the plain-chant began again. "Here is that din once more. I do not mind the scops when they sing, but these monks with their psalm-singing…"

Swytha rested her hand on his arm. "It will soon be over."

Alvar glanced again at Alfreda. She was well known for her love of the finer things in life, but this grim set of her mouth surely could not be merely the result of being forced to dress in a lowly fashion? As soon as Alvar and Athelwold were convinced that she was willing to agree to the marriage, they had both done what they could to strengthen her position. Pray God that they did not all find themselves wishing that they had listened to Dunstan after all.

Alvar, standing by the hearth in the crowded dining hall of the king's palace, turned as Alfreda walked through the doorway. She mouthed a few words as if in prayer as she searched the throng with her gaze, and he made his way to her side.

She rested her fingers on his arm. "Thank you. I felt as if I were drowning amongst so many folk whom I do not know." She gave him a regal nod and a practised smile.

"Why did you wed him?"

Alfreda put her arm down and blinked twice. "You have a blunt way of speaking, my lord."

He smiled. "Forgive me, my lady. I am becoming well known for it."

She put her head to one side and stared at him, as if in appraisal. She straightened up and gave him another smile, this time of friendship. "There is naught to forgive. I will tell you why I said yes to the match. The king wooed me and pledged riches to me and my kin."

"I do not believe you."

Alfreda lowered her voice. "You are right. The truth is that when the king asked me, I had many thoughts. I thought, who will say no to the queen? Who would dare to beat the queen?" Her head came up and she thrust her chin forward, but there were tears in her eyes when she said, "And who will take the queen's children from her?"

He swallowed hard. He knew that when she arrived at court her sons by Elwood of Ramsey had remained in East Anglia, but he had assumed that she had wished it so. Now he could see that Elwood's kin had a hand in the deed. "You have had many burdens to bear. I am sorry for you."

Alfreda breathed in, and her shoulders shook. "I asked the lord Brandon for news of my children, which he would not give me. Bishop Oswald warned me not to ask the king for help, and then the archbishop said of the wedding that if the king took the widow, he should leave the sons."

Alvar swore. It was no surprise that Dunstan would want Alfreda's sons out of the way, for he would not wish to see any full-grown athelings come forward to challenge the claim of Edward, the king's son by Wulfreda. But it was more an act of spite than an effective strategy; Dunstan's hopes for Edward were dependant on Alfreda's producing no more children. Whilst they would be younger than Edward, any future issue would rank more highly, being born to a king and his consecrated queen. Dunstan was forced to play a waiting game before he could see his hopes for Edward realised. Alvar said, "Sometimes I think that Dunstan might have fathered that child himself. It is no wonder that he would rather have eaten fire than see you named queen."

"Oh, you see it too. We think alike, so you will understand when I swear that no-one will gain from this match more than I shall, and that I will have many more children." She raised her voice. "I will need friends in the king's house, Lord Alvar. Can I know that you are one of them?"

He flashed a grin. "Lady, I was yours the first day I laid eyes on you."

She returned his smile, and for the first time that day the smile lifted high enough to return the sparkle to her eyes.

He gave a deep bow, backed away, and turned to greet his brother.

Brock had pushed his way through the crowd, his elbows out to the sides to protect the drinks in his hands. He handed a cup to Alvar. The noise in the hall rose and fell as shouts of laughter broke out periodically above the general hum of conversation. Brock nodded and reached up to speak nearer Alvar's ear. He said, "They are badly matched for height; I would say that she is taller by more than a hair."

Edgar had come to stand by his new wife. His blond curls licked round his gold coronet and caught at the soft bristles on his jaw. He stood a hip's width behind her so that his leg pressed against hers.

Alfreda turned her head and looked at Alvar. Her smile had gone.

Edgar's head was positioned such that he appeared to be whispering into his wife's ear. She gazed straight ahead and continued to stare at Alvar. Edgar's hand slid round her waist and stroked upwards almost to her breast and down almost to her thigh. He stepped away from her side, reaching for her hand. He led her through the crowded hall and most of the witnesses smiled their indulgence, for no man needed to have heard Edgar's words to know what was on his mind. Only Archbishop Dunstan glowered as they walked past him.

Alvar said, "I wonder if he is thinking right now of the day of the Fairchild's king-making?"

Brock rubbed his chin. "You could be right. This will be the second time he has lost out to a king's woman. Edgar the love-sick husband will not yield to Dunstan's bidding the way Edgar the youth has done."

Alvar looked again at the archbishop. Alfreda had thought to protect herself with this wedding, but ironically ran the risk of becoming the target of more hatred. If she was aware that Dunstan rarely gave up without a fight, then she was playing a dangerous game.

Dunstan stood up from his seat on the dais, and began to make his way across the room.

Brock gave his empty cup to a serving-boy and took two more drinks from him, this time choosing the specially prepared ceremonial mead drink known as bride-ale. He held the cups aloft, sloshing the contents, and offered one to Alvar.

Alvar clasped his brother's shoulder and said, "I find the mead too heavy in my belly this day. Find me some ale, I will be back soon."

Alvar elbowed his way through the crowd, impeded by the squash of bodies. He felt a foot under his shoe, but in the crowd could not direct an accurate apology. He followed Dunstan to the back of the hall. Away from the fire at the far end of the room, though the air was less smoke-filled, it was darker here and there were only a few couples, who, like Alvar, wished to stay in the shadows and not be seen. When he arrived, he wiped spilt ale from his sleeve and kept close to the wall, while the archbishop walked up to the door of the king's private chamber and waved away the door-thegn. The man hesitated, but was not brave enough to speak out against the wishes of the archbishop of Canterbury. All had seen the king leave the hall with his bride and knew his intent, and so it occurred to Alvar that they might not have barred the chamber door. Dunstan obviously thought so too, and reached out to push it open.

The royal couple had moved beyond the doorway only as far as it had taken to kick the door shut. Alfreda was standing, with her skirts gathered in her hands. The king was kneeling in front of her, his face between her thighs.

Alvar leaped forward to stand behind Dunstan and block the view from the rest of the hall. Dunstan's head turned as he looked from the motionless couple to the empty bed, still made and strewn with flowers. He must have envisaged that his admonishment would interrupt a coupling under the covers of the royal bed. Alvar leaned forward and looked past Dunstan's reddening neck. Alfreda remained as she had been when the door crashed open, her head turned towards the archbishop, whose ear-tips were now purple.

"F-f-fornicators!" he spat the Latin in his pulpit voice. When the echo died away he swept round and tried to quit the chamber. He pushed at Alvar, barely giving him a glance, but the earl was slow to move out of the way.

Alvar whispered into Dunstan's ear. "It looks as if the king no longer wishes to wear his hair shirt," he said, before he bowed low and stood aside to let him pass.

Alfreda did not move, but stared at Edgar. He was still on his knees; he looked up at her and said, "No man owns me. I *will* have you."

Edgar lowered his head once more, hands reaching to grab her buttocks, pulling her nearer his face, and Alvar stepped forward to close the door for them. As the door swung, the queen shuddered and bit her lip. Alvar secured the latch and walked back to the feasting tables, unable to shake the notion that Alfreda, at the moment of exquisite pleasure, had been smiling out into the hall; not at Edgar's head, but at Dunstan's back.

Alvar took his seat at the witan meeting and looked across at the queen. Her face was flushed but it was not from any warm afterglow. He had seen the look before, on the faces of men who had fought and survived their first battle.

She gave a tiny nod and he twitched the flicker of a smile. He turned at the touch of a hand on his shoulder.

"Here I am, come to take my seat amongst all the doughty lords of the kingdom. I hope they will be gentle with me." Beorn of Northumbria sat down beside him.

Alvar grinned. "They can see how tall you are, and I have told them how skilfully you wield a sword. I think you will have no trouble from them, *Earl* Beorn."

Beorn gave a shy smile in response to the use of his new title. "It still sounds odd to my ears." He reached up to move his hand over his shiny baldness. "It sounds odd to some others, too, given that I was not born in Northumbria."

Alvar chuckled. "Welcome to the mind of our king. He flatters the Northumbrians by giving them a lord who has lived amongst them, but he made you earl of York *because* you were not born there. He means to show your folk that his word is law in the north, and that they would do well to remember it."

"If he truly wants to keep his name in the minds of the north folk, do you think he might like to go there once in a while? I have a sore arse from riding all this way."

"Edgar knows how far away it is, my friend, which is why he sends me so often in his stead. Even I cannot say for sure where Northumbria ends."

Beorn folded his arms across his bulky chest. "I wish the Scots could say the same, but they seem sure that the border is much further south. Let us hope that Edgar's fleet and my weapon-men are enough to keep them away. The Greybeard of Chester shares my concerns, and I wanted to speak to him further, but I see that he is not here today."

Alvar looked around the hall. "No, neither is his thegn, Helmstan," he said. He scanned the room again, once more along every bench, and into every corner, and cursed his brain for not believing what his eyes had told him five times that day already.

Beorn continued. "The Greybeard has been unwell. He says that either the Scots or another winter will be the end of him; in the cold, his feet and legs redden and swell so that he cannot walk. Ah, here comes the king." He sought confirmation of Alvar's earlier instruction. "Wide awake?"

"Oh yes," Alvar said. Many a time he had watched as various members of the witan had fallen asleep and he would willingly have followed them into unconscious oblivion, but dared not, in case anyone wished to hear the opinion of the leading earl. The trick was to find something to engage the attention and focus intently upon it.

The archbishop was sitting next to Edgar, making a supreme effort not to look directly at his king, and Alvar would have granted away all of Shropshire to hear Dunstan's shrift that day. The older man flicked glances around the room, but he also avoided looking at the queen. Alvar had no such compunction and was rewarded by a flirtatious smile whenever he made eye contact with Alfreda. This, he decided, would be his distraction today.

Brandon, too, had difficulty keeping his eyes still. He sat up in his seat and stared at the doorway, only to slump down whenever anyone walked through it. Only when Bishop Oswald stalked into the meeting hall did the East Anglian allow his shoulders to settle and he sat back, relaxed, into his seat.

With Oswald's arrival the witan was complete. Edgar kissed his wife on the lips before he turned to address his audience in formal tones. "My kingdom is like a ploughed field." He nodded and his blond hair, curling wildly underneath his coronet, swished to and fro as he moved his head. "The oxen keep it furrowed, but the oxen need to be fed if they are to work strongly."

Alvar was tempted to make a joke about feeling the weight of the yoke, but he thought better of it.

Brandon cleared his throat and said, "Do you mean that we are not all pulling as we should, my lord?"

The others examined their nails, stared out of the window, or gazed at their knees, and Alvar chuckled.

Edgar smiled and adopted the tone which Alvar had heard him use in the nursery when talking to his son. "Far from it, far from it. I am blessed to have the wisest and most hard-working witan. Indeed I often hear of your tireless work in East Anglia, Foster-brother."

Brandon's shoulders came down and he looked across at Oswald, who nodded and smiled.

"No, my lords, it is time to feed you all once more and I think there is none so hungry as my lord of middle Mercia."

Alvar, distracted by the silent exchange between Oswald and his pet, now sat upright and looked at Edgar.

The king said, "The Scots are snarling, and the lord of Chester is old and ill. I need strong leadership on the northern edges of our lands and so I gift northern Mercia to Lord Alvar. And henceforth, he and Earl Beorn answer to no man other than me."

Alvar sat still and breathed hard as he tried to suppress a grin. He looked across at Beorn, and gave him a nod so tiny that it was little more than a downward movement of his eyes before he looked back up again.

Brandon's mouth gaped like that of a landed fish.

Edgar waved his arm and mouthed the word "Wine", and one of his thegns moved from the doorway. The thegn dispatched a slave-boy to the kitchen, then moved to the scribes' table.

Edgar said, "I have the new law code to show you all." He waited while the thegn collected a pile of documents from the scribe and handed one copy each to Alvar, Beorn, Brandon, Dunstan and Oswald.

Alvar scanned the charter. The prologue mentioned Edgar's desire to remedy the effects of the recent pestilence and famine. After laying out several measures to that effect, and making nationwide provision for the protection of property and the prosecution of thieves, the new law code stated clearly, as Alvar had promised Beorn, that the Danes would retain their own laws because of 'your loyalty, which you have always shown me.' Alvar would look more fully at the content when he had more time to study the document, but it seemed to be a measured and considered response to the problems which beset the folk of England, and it acknowledged fully the debt owed to the northerners. In the last clause, Edgar even managed to smooth Brandon's feathers, for, immediately after the command for Beorn to enforce this new law in the north, the final instruction was for copies to be given to Alvar and Brandon for distribution throughout England. They were the only three noblemen mentioned by name.

Edgar paused long enough for his ministers to read the salient points, then he cleared his throat. "Now, my lord Archbishop, how goes the work at Muchelney Abbey?"

The sudden change of subject caused everyone to look at Dunstan, just as the slave-boy came back with the wine. The door banged open and the archbishop flinched.

With a flicker of a smile, Edgar said, "My lord, be still; it is but a door opening loudly. What is there to fear from that?"

Alvar knew that this time, there was no need for the punishment of exile. This teasing remark was an assertion of Edgar's confidence to run his own affairs, and that he would not be cowed by the archbishop. This was all that would be said on the matter, ever. Alvar looked at the queen, who smiled and raised a perfectly arched eyebrow.

Dunstan gave his shoulders a slight shake and took a deep breath. "The work at M-Muchelney shows the piety of the m-m-monks of Glastonbury, my lord, and the fastness with which they cleave to God's word. They have wrought true wonders, with the abbot's house an outstanding sight. The rooms are flooded with light; the d-drawings on the walls are dyed with…"

"You are glad then. Good." Edgar held up a hand to silence Dunstan and directed his next question to Athelwold. "And at Winchester, my lord Bishop?"

Athelwold lifted his head, his features illuminated by a childlike smile. He had lost none of his enthusiasm for his reforms. "Well, although it has been less than a year since I became bishop at Winchester, we have sent away all the secular clergy and put in their stead monks from my beloved Abingdon…"

Alvar's attention had begun to wander as soon as Dunstan had started to expound on the delights of the decoration at Muchelney. He looked across at the queen, watching as she took a sip from her gold cup and made a show of licking her lips slowly before setting the cup down, and letting her hand slide down the stem before she let go.

"Winchester is now run wholly by monks, my lords."

Athelwold's voice penetrated his thoughts and at the mention of a monastic cathedral Alvar sat forward. "What about the clerks who were there before?"

Edgar allowed no time for an answer but turned to speak to Oswald. "What of the work at Westbury-on-Trim?"

Oswald licked his lips. "The building of the new church goes well and the abbot teaches the monks thoroughly. We work more slowly than Bishop Athelwold but I tell God what we need and…"

Alvar drummed his fingers on the table.

Oswald stared at him as though he were an irksome insect. "Is there something wrong, my lord of Mercia?"

Alvar said, "A new monastery at Westbury is no worry to me, my lord Bishop. But if any more of the clerks at Worcester were to go the same way as those here at Winchester…"

Edgar raised his hands for silence and stood up. "My good bishops, my heart sings to hear of your good work. A strong Church is a sign of a kingdom at one with itself. Who amongst us would not welcome that?" He looked round the room and made eye contact with each of them, but he allowed his gaze to linger a little longer on Alvar. "And so we are all glad." He held out his hand to Alfreda. "My lady, I think we are done here."

The scrape of chairs on the wooden floor drowned out lone voices. Brandon gyrated on his feet like a child fighting a full bladder. He spoke out loudly against the background noise. "My lord? My lord King? If I might speak?"

Edgar turned to listen. He lifted his fingers to cover the hand that Alfreda had slipped through the crook of his arm.

"The lord of Chester is not the only one who is ailing. The lord known as the Red Lord is not a young man, and his lands once belonged to my father." He looked down at the floor.

Alvar clenched and unclenched his fists. "The lands of which you speak are in Oxfordshire and Buckinghamshire, and they belong to Mercia. Your kin never held them by right."

Alfreda looked up at Alvar, raised her free hand and put her finger to her lips. She tugged the king's arm. "My lord, if you are all done here?"

Brandon shot a look at his elder brother, Thetford, who was lurking by the door, and then he tried once more. "But my lord, I was the only one who was not given any more lands."

Edgar opened his mouth but Alfreda said, "Dear husband, I should be tired after such a day as this, but I find I am not sleepy. Yet, I feel I should lie down for a while. Shall we, my lord?"

Alvar suppressed the urge to laugh. Edgar might feel the pull of loyalty to his foster-family, but if his cock led him in one direction, not even familial duty would turn him and make him go in another.

Alfreda led the king away, and Brandon left the room and went straight to his brother. They conferred, heads low.

Alvar rubbed his hands together and walked out of the room. As he passed the East Anglians he said, "What is wrong, my lord Brandon? I cannot believe that this is the first time you have been bested by a lady."

Thetford straightened up. "Have a care my lord, for we East Anglians do not forgive our foes."

"No? Neither, it seems, does the queen."

Alvar left the hall still smiling, but it was a brief and hollow respite. He had not yet overcome his aversion to the scheming and politicking of the court, and although Alfreda had persuaded Edgar to overlook Brandon's request, the victory was not complete as long as Edgar continued to allow the eviction of clerics. But another facet had been added to the long list of Alvar's duties, and for once it would not be the least bit odious; his new responsibilities would send him to Cheshire and he had no desire to linger at court any longer.

The light in the scriptorium was better than in some of the other outbuildings, but Brandon's mood would have darkened the brightest space. Dunstan allowed him to pace the floor a number of times and hoped that, by watching him, he could relieve some of his own frustration. The day's events had left him feeling as if he had been asked to swallow a drink made from hemlock. He waited while Brandon completed a few more circuits of the small building, and then swept his arm out to indicate the chair in front of him. Brandon sat down untidily, slumping forward and scattering the equipment from the writing desk onto the floor. Dunstan, torn between indulgence for his friend's mood and his abhorrence of any defacement of tomes of learning, stepped forward and knelt down to rescue the wax tablets and writing styli. A pestle and mortar, used for grinding the mineral pigments, had disgorged its fine powdery contents which could not be scooped up for reuse without contamination from bits of grit and dust. The ink pots had, fortunately, been empty, and Dunstan picked them up and laid them carefully back on the table.

"My lord," he said as he placed each one precisely, "We are all affronted by the heights which Alvar has now reached, but we must bide our time and wait until a way shows itself by which we can bring him and the king's wife back down." He stepped away from the table and paused to allow Brandon to respond. The earl looked at him as if he were having difficulty focusing and Dunstan had a brief, silent conversation with God, during which he assured his maker of his understanding that this was a trial; why else would one of his allies be as stupid as a mule while his enemy was sharp as a sword point?

He turned to Oswald, who, praise be to God, was possessed of a brain which worked swiftly and deviously. He said, "The law says that the hundred-moot must be held every four weeks, the borough court thrice a year and the shire court twice. Well then, let us look at this law and see how we can make it work for us. Your diocese is in the heart of Mercia. I think that there are many ways in which you can keep Lord Alvar busy within his own lands, and thus well away from the king?"

Oswald smiled. "As you say it, so it is done. Not only will I keep him busy, I will see to it that the wheels on our carts turn so slowly that he might never leave Mercia."

Dunstan nodded. "Good. And while you are away, I will take every chance that I can to whisper in the king's ear, to make him think about how often his wife's smile alights upon the lord Alvar. Let me plant the seed and I will water it well."

Brandon sat up as if waking. "What? Alvar and my brother's whore? Is this true?"

Dunstan tried to keep his tone light and to resist the temptation to address the man as if he were a particularly unresponsive pupil. "I do not know."

"Then why…"

Oswald said, "It does not matter if it is true. What matters is only that the king believes it."

Dunstan offered up thanks that if Brandon was his trial, then at least Oswald was his assistance, and that the bishop understood his intent. But it was a plan with scant chance of success. Without proof, it would be difficult to convince one as supremely confident as Edgar that he was a cuckold. Dunstan needed more. He said to Oswald, "While you are busy in Worcester, my lord Bishop, keep a wary eye and an open ear for anything that could be fashioned into a shovel to dig the upstart's grave." He kept the rest of the thought to himself, remembering his status as archbishop. *And bury the whore-queen with him.*

Cheshire

The chickens settled down to resume their pecking and the little boy ran at them again. He clapped his hands and they squawked and garbled and attempted to fly away, and he ran back to the fence to wait for them to quieten down again.

Out over the fields, the swallows twittered and chattered as they shot like arrows back and forth. Gytha came from behind the bake-house with a wooden bowl filled with wood-ash. "Siferth, it will be your bedtime soon," she said, but the toddler took no notice as he launched the chickens for a third time.

"Be good and I will show you where the new hazelnuts are growing. Next month we will pick them and we can eat them dried at Yuletide." She raised her voice. "Have a care; there is an ant bed over there and you are barefoot, little Helmstan-son."

He ran to show her his find. "Feather."

She sat down where the last of the evening sunshine was casting a warm spot on the ground, and picked up a saucepan. "Why did Leofsige bring out the trivet when he cooked outside?" She clicked her tongue, tucked a cloth into her belt and scrubbed the pan with handfuls of ash. "There was no need."

Siferth said, "Bad Leofy," and ran away again.

Gytha grunted. "He is a strong little man."

Káta reached out to catch two dandelion seed fluff-balls, stuck together and floating on the breeze. "Yes, I do thank

God for it. When I think what it took to bear him…" She gathered her cloak from the ground and draped it over her shoulders.

Gytha said, "We thought you both would die. All that blood lost, and you were so white. He would not feed and went yellow. Ha! Look at him now."

Káta smiled as Siferth once more sent the chickens pelting around the yard in confusion. "Yes, I think that both God and my mother's gods were watching over us that night." She opened her mouth to call again to Siferth and as she did so she glanced at the path to the stables. "See, Siferth; here is your father, come to tell you a tale, so you must go to bed if you wish to hear it." She stood up and watched as her husband walked wearily towards the house, each step slow and heavy, as if he were walking through wet sand.

The little boy ran to his father. "Offa, Offa!"

Helmstan brushed his hair out of his eyes with a muddy hand and scooped his son up from the ground. "Look at that, youngling; my fingers no longer reach all the way round you."

The little boy repeated his demand. "Offa!"

Helmstan looked over Siferth's shoulder, lowered his head to kiss his wife and raised his eyebrows in query.

"He wants to hear the story of King Offa; how he kept the Welsh out of our kingdom."

Helmstan said, "Ah, I understand."

"Siferth said, "Tell me, tell me."

Helmstan sighed. "Not tonight, my son." He adjusted his grip and said, "Come, put your feet through my belt and cling on. I'll take you to the hearth and tell you of another great man of Mercia, who was known as the Greybeard."

Káta touched Helmstan's arm. "Was?"

He said, "My lord died this morning."

"Oh, my love, I am so sorry to hear it. I know you loved your lord dearly." She stood aside and he carried the boy through the doorway.

As he walked past her he said, "Lord Alvar rode with me from Chester. He is with the horses, for he is worried that his steed is lame."

He went inside, but she stood by the door, shifting her weight from one foot to the other. She looked into the hall, then down the path towards the stables. The information had been delivered as if in afterthought, but she could not so easily dismiss it. "Gytha, what must I do?"

It was a name from another time, a time before she became a mother and her life was made complete. She had not seen him for three years and at that meeting, she recalled, she had been inexplicably angry that he seemed not to care that she was pregnant with a longed-for child. It should not have mattered to her whether he held any opinion, because the happy tidings had made her life with Helmstan all the more rewarding. Yet it had seemed to her that by telling him, she had shut a door without ever knowing if he even wished to step through it. But why should she wish to leave that door ajar? And why was her stomach now turning circles much as it did when the early flutters of pregnancy had first stirred in there? She repeated her plea. "What must I do?"

Gytha stood up and wiped her hands on her cloth. "What do you mean, Lady?"

After all this time there should be no reaction at all, and yet she was in disarray. She tried to attribute her state of agitation to the social requirements. "I should be with my husband; we are saddened by the Greybeard's death. And yet a great earl has come to be at our hearth and I would be no lady if I did not see to his needs."

Gytha looked through the doorway. "Lord Helmstan is playing with the child. You can leave him for a while. Let us go to Leofsige."

The cook said, "Lady, it is late in the day. It might not be the fare that the lord is used to, but I will do what I can."

"It is not a rare thing that our household grows to twice as many." Káta pointed to the beef he had set aside, marinating in vinegar and herbs. "We are rich enough to have that in our kitchen. You are the cook; do what you must."

Leofsige puffed his cheeks out and muttered. "I have already said that I will."

Gytha laid a hand on his arm. "My lady does not mean to speak so harshly."

Káta left them and walked down the lane, punching her hips as she went. "No, it will not do, to speak that way; it will not do." She stopped on the path and took deep breaths.

Dear God, what was it about this man that prickled her skin like a nettle rash? He had ridden away all those years ago leaving her to think that he was uninterested in her news, which was as it should be. She was the wife of his friend, nothing more. She sighed and slapped her forehead. Of course; that was it. She was angry on Helmstan's behalf, that Alvar had not visited the friend who missed his company.

She stepped into the stables and he stood up but made no greeting. "I do not think it is broken," he said to the stable-boy. "I will look at it again in the morning light."

Káta held out a hand that would not keep steady. "Lord Alvar, you are welcome, though it is a sad time for us all."

He stumbled forward, steadied himself, and took a step back. "My lady, forgive me, I could not see who it was in the doorway. Yes, it is a sad time."

He wiped his hands on his breeches and took her hand, held it for a moment, and then let his arm hang by his side.

He picked at a fingernail and she looked at the horses.

She patted the black stallion in the nearest stall and he stared at the floor.

He opened his mouth and she leaned forward and turned her head to listen, but he said nothing. The warm smell of sweat and leather was the same on every man who rode hard. She breathed it in as if for the first time. "Shall we walk to the hall, my lord?"

He nodded and followed her out into the dusk. Above the stable doorway, a red and white cloth flapped in the breeze, hung there to ward off hag-riding. "I do not like the thought of evil witches taking the horses at night and working them to death," she said, though he had not asked. The silence continued, magnifying the silliness of her remark.

The sun was gone and the sky grew dark and cold as quickly as a fire quenched with cold water. She shivered and pulled the light woollen cloak tighter about her body. From the corner of her eye she saw him begin to remove his own cloak and her stomach lurched as she waited for him to drop it around her shoulders. But he changed his mind, refastened his brooch, and his arms hung once again by his side.

"So you have a son?"

"Yes, we named him Siferth, after my father. He will not yet be abed, so you can meet him."

"I heard that you were unwell afterwards."

She laughed. It was too loud, and she took a deep breath. "That is one way to say it. It made a sword wound seem like a mere bee sting. Not that I know much of sword wounds…" She put her hands to her mouth. She was happy to talk of childbirth, but men were not so keen. He would think her such a silly woman, to clatter on.

"But you are well now?"

"Thank you, yes, but I do not think that there will be any more bairns." She chanced a look up at his face and saw nothing in the half light to give her any insight into his thoughts. Besides, how ridiculous to think that he would care one way or the other whether she were able to have more children. She kept her chin in the air, imagined that her mother was listening and said, "I must be thankful for what I have."

He glanced at her, and looked ahead again. He stopped on the path in front of her and she had nowhere to turn as he stared at her.

"My lord, is there something wrong?"

He shook his head. "No. I was led to believe that you had died whilst giving birth. I am glad to see that I was told wrongly."

They walked the rest of the way in silence, for she was too in awe of the earl even now to berate him. If he had, as he said, believed her to be dead, then he had all the more reason to visit his friend Helmstan. Why would he stay away? Unless…

She shook her head to free her mind of the madness that seemed to have landed therein. When she opened the door of the hall, Helmstan looked up from his chair. He kissed the top of his son's head and mouthed, "My love."

She smiled and sniffed, and turned to look once more at the man who was standing beside her, who came less than every other summertime and yet, when he did, disturbed her like one of Siferth's chickens. But somehow his presence always warmed and excited her, and even in the dusk and covered with grime, his face was so pleasing to her that if the price to pay for being able to gaze upon it was a little heartache when he left again, then so be it.

She said, "It will do my husband's heart good to see you, my lord. Do not leave it so long next time." She smiled at him, and knew that for the first time she was conveying genuine warmth.

"What? Well, let us hope that happier tidings bring me north in future. God, but I am weary to my bones from the sadness this day. Let us go to your husband and son then, and drink to the poor old Greybeard. Then I will get drunk and tell you all the latest tales from the king's house."

"Much of what goes on is, no doubt, not fit for my ears, my lord." She tried to keep a straight face, but failed.

He grinned back. "You are right. But I shall tell you anyway."

Chapter Nine AD965

Cheshire

Káta partially closed her eyes against the sun, and looked through rainbow-lashes at the brightness. Away near the woods, the incessant triple hoot of the wood pigeon announced that full summer had arrived, while beyond the mill the rising laugh of the curlew marked the way to the estuary, but, beside them, the downward slope of the riverbank offered shelter from the breeze, and the loudest noise here was the gentle chatter of the water. She turned to check once more that Siferth was safe above her in the field, and dangled her feet in the water.

"So must I wear my best kirtle?"

"No-one will be looking upon you, my lady. All eyes will be on the rich, good-looking earl and his new thegn."

"Do you think so?"

Alvar was lying on the grass beside her, with his hands behind his head. His legs were crossed at the ankles and he was chewing on a blade of grass. He turned his head, opened one eye, and grinned.

"Oh, I see now..." Her cheeks warmed; she felt a little foolish as she realised that he was teasing.

He chuckled and said, "Lady, when your husband kneels and swears the hold-oath to me as his lord, he could cluck like a chicken and no-one would hear, for they will all be looking at his lovely fair wife. You have no need for bright clothes."

"I will put some on, even so." Káta swished her feet one

more time and drew them up out of the water to dry on the grass. She lay back and smoothed her veil under her head. Arms outstretched, she pushed her fingers through the long grass, curling the blades round her knuckles. She pulled against their strength and allowed them to spring back up again. She was relaxed enough in his company to have begun to see why Helmstan valued his friendship so much. Alvar had an easy way of making her laugh and, where once she thought him arrogant, now all she heard were self-deprecating jokes about his exalted position at court. She had to acknowledge that he was, in fact, both amiable and affable. The doorway of possibility which had slammed shut when she bore a son left nowhere for wondering regrets to shelter, and had placed a barrier between her and any emotional danger. And, in an odd way, it had allowed her to begin to like this man. "And you; will you be the best clad lord in all Mercia?"

"I *am* the lord of all Mercia," he said.

She laughed. "As if you would let us forget it."

"No, you will never forget it, because I will be here more often, coming to the moots and overseeing the land. Before, I came only when time allowed, now I will come because I must."

She wagged a finger in the air, but with her eyes shut she could only guess that it was pointing in the right direction. "There you go again, always telling me how great a lord you are."

She sat up in a scrabble. In relaxing, she had forgotten how loose her tongue could also get. "I am sorry, my lord, that was not well said." Urged on by an honest desire to make amends, she held his gaze. "I was harsh to you when we first met. I thought that you were haughty, that you looked down upon us from a great height. Now that I know the happiness of motherhood, I would not envy the heavy burdens of a life like yours."

He smiled, but not enough to crease the skin around his eyes. "You have naught to say sorry for. If I seemed lofty, I think it was only because my tongue would not untie itself long enough for me to speak the right words. It is I who envies you and Helmstan, but you know this."

Káta wriggled her shoulders and lay with her eyes fully shut, feeling the warmth of the sun on her face. "I could bide here all day," she said.

"And I."

All she heard then was the chuckle of the river, and somewhere on the grass on the bank above her, a busybody bee investigated the clover. She wrinkled her nose at a tickle and raised her hand to swat away the fly. It tickled again, and once more she batted it away with her hand. When she felt the soft touch a third time, she opened her eyes. He had stopped chewing the blade of grass and had been brushing it against her face. Propped up on one elbow, his head above her face, he looked into her eyes. His hair fell forward and almost touched her cheek. With shallow half-breaths she tried to remain still, but her stomach turned a somersault and her chest rose and fell, so she held her breath.

"Mother? Mother?" Siferth tottered down the bank.

Alvar rolled away from her and sat up. She had the space then to do the same, and the boy toddled to her and fell into her lap.

Alvar reached out and patted the boy's head. "He looks like you; his hair is so fair."

"Do you think so? I see only his father's brown eyes. And he is like Helmstan, for once he knows what he craves he will have it then and there, or fight until he gets it."

"Much like all men, then, would you say?"

She smoothed Siferth's hair away from his eyes with the back of her hand, and stroked his face with her little finger. "No, it is more than that. I can see it in his eyes; he will forever be losing his heart to someone or something, because once he looks with longing he can see naught else."

"Uncle Var-Var, swim?"

Alvar ruffled the boy's hair. "Not today. I have something I must do with your father; I took but a heartbeat to speak with your mother first. Besides, she likes it not when I take off my clothes to swim."

"Oh, that was such a long time ago."

He stood up and crossed his arms, grabbing the hem of his tunic as if he were about to pull it off over his head.

She laughed and wagged a finger again. "Do not dare."

Siferth pushed his lip forward to form a baby-frown. He said, "Get Gytha swim," and scrambled back up into the field.

Káta stood up and watched him go. "You see, he will not sit while you make up your mind, and he will not rest until someone swims with him." She sat back down and gave Alvar another gently delivered admonishment, pointing at his dishevelled clothing. "You are wayward."

Alvar fastened his belt over his repositioned tunic. He grinned. "I am sorry, my lady. You said it was long ago, and so I took you to mean that you no longer minded my nakedness."

She bit her lip. If he did but know how beautiful she had thought his body when first she had laid eyes on him. "You should be ashamed. You are a bad teacher for my son."

He nodded, but grinned, making him seem less ashamed than a drunk staggering from one whorehouse to another. "My sister Swytha tells me so, too. As does the queen, and her bairn is still in his cradle."

She sat back. It was a relief to be able to change the topic of conversation, even if there was a nagging discomfort attached to the subject. "Tell me about Lady Alfreda. Is she truly lovely?"

He laughed.

"Tell me, is she comely?"

He folded his arms.

Káta said, "Is she fair as the lily? Slight like the Welsh poppy?" She got up, and gathered flowers from the grassy slope and the hedgerow beyond. She sat back down and dropped them into his lap. "Is she tall as the cowslip? Small like the clover? Prickly as the thistle? Tell me. Or have we found, at last, someone who is too grand even for a great lord like you?"

He held his hands up. "No more. I will tell you. She is…" He looked up. "Her hair is dark and she is tall, taller than the king, anyway."

"Taller than Gytha?"

"Yes, but not so…" He put his arms out to the sides, to indicate the Norsewoman's rounded figure.

"Oh, that is not kind."

"Well do not laugh, then."

"Tell me more about the queen."

He stared out across the river. "It is hard to find the words. Men speak to each other in ways that are not seemly."

"Simply tell me what you see, then."

He started again. "Her hair is dark; I know this because she always leaves a twist of it free from her head-cloth, as if she has put her clothes on swiftly, having come late from her bed. She is sloe-eyed, and those eyes are so big that she has the look of a helpless child. She gives freely of her smile and yet, when she bestows that smile, it feels as if no other man has ever seen it. And when she walks before you on those long legs, her arse swings like…"

"Enough." Káta laughed and covered her ears. "I have heard enough."

"I am sorry. I warned you I would be uncouth…"

"No, it was not that. I meant that I have heard enough to know." She hesitated, unsure whether it was her place to speak of such things. But he was waiting for her explanation. She sighed. "It must be hard to love a woman who is wed to another. Harder still, when she is not from the same rank."

She folded her hands in her lap and tried to calm her breathing. When she dared to look up he was staring at her, a bemused expression on his face, as if she had told him something of which he was not aware.

However many times she had been in this situation, she

never seemed to learn, and instead of keeping silent to limit the damage already done, as usual she felt her mouth opening to let more stupid words come tumbling out. "All I meant was, my lord, that I think I understand a little of what you feel." Too late, the words were there, hanging in the air, waiting to be interpreted. Or misinterpreted. Dear God, what had she said? Her cheeks grew warm and she looked away.

He sat up and took her hand in his. Her only live sense then was that of touch; the warmth of his hand and the rough patches on his palm, the strength in his fingers.

"Lady, I would never..."

He said something and she did not hear properly, for her own thoughts were too loud. But she was certain that he spoke of loyalty, of wanting what cannot be had, of accepting what was not to be.

She could not lift her head, but stared at his hand, for if she looked at it, he could not move it away.

Then he spoke of what it was to be married, and she knew his hurt, for Alfreda was now the king's wife and forever lost to him. Wasn't that what he meant? She looked up. "I am sorry, my lord. I had no right..." Káta blinked back tears and said, "I am blessed. My husband is a good man." She pulled a little with her arm and waited for him to stand.

He did not release her hand. "Yes, he is a good man."

At last, he let go, and still she could feel where his fingers had pressed against hers.

He stood up. "And now I know why you look away from me, and you will understand why I ride away from you."

Helmstan knelt before Alvar, clutching a gold cross between his joined hands, which he presented for his lord to hold while the oath was sworn. "By the Lord, before whom this hallowed thing is holy, I will be steadfast and true to Alvar and love all that he loves and shun all that he shuns, after God's law and the world's law and never, by will or by thought, by word or by deed, do aught of what is loathsome to him, as long as he upholds me as I am willing to earn and fulfil all that our understanding was, when I bowed to him and took his will."

Alvar accepted the oath, raised his thegn up to kiss him, and reflected that the duty to keep his man as he deserved probably did not include harbouring the occasional daydream in which he swapped his life for his. He waited for Helmstan to get properly to his feet again and he looked around the hall, used until now by the Greybeard of Chester, held in the name of kings who never came. There was a large gold cross on the wall; he looked up to the ceiling, projected his thoughts beyond it and silently apologised for his lust and envy. And, while he was about it, for most of the other five deadly sins as well.

Alvar handed Helmstan the items of heriot, glad that they had chosen the war gear together. He stroked the new, dent-free helmet and he tested the hinge on the cheek-plate. He leaned forward to pick up the shield. It was the usual round, with an iron boss and leather strap, but the lime-wood was covered with leather, painted to Helmstan's own design, with curling motifs and dragon heads. Alvar gave Helmstan the sword, pattern-welded from twisted iron rods, which would mark him out as a rich and powerful thegn.

Many men had come this day; men who, like Helmstan, had sworn oaths to the late Greybeard and needed a new lord. He scanned the benches to see if any man remained who had not yet come forward to be placed under his protection. Káta sat among them, with Siferth on her lap. Her gaze flicked from her husband to his new lord. She looked down at the boy and adjusted her veil, but the action was idle habit, not nervous fiddling. Siferth wriggled off her knee and as she ran across the room after him, she looked over at the dais once more, her face bright and her cheeks uncoloured. These days she walked tall and let her sleeves fall back; she was like her flowers near the river, showing their petals to the sun.

He, too, felt as if he had been standing taller, divested of a dull ache, which had eased the moment he was able legitimately to return to Cheshire, and then been completely dissolved by his overwhelming relief to find that she was alive.

He found her changed, more confident because she had a child, and markedly different from the woman whom he had so recently left in Winchester, a woman whose confidence grew the more men lusted after her. Alfreda had realised her ambition, but Alvar sensed that an ache lay gnawing at her heart, even now. Káta, however, had fulfilled her role and felt worthy. If marriage put a woman beyond the reach of other men, then childbirth moved her still further. Káta was a contented mother, and he was no longer a tongue-tripped fool in her presence. He dared the occasional joke about his status and, whereas once she would have reacted with distaste, now she seemed to understand that he was poking fun at himself. Gone was the shy mouse, and she was bold enough to tease him as if she were no longer cowed by his status. Yes, motherhood had completed her, and there would be no more misunderstandings.

When he reviewed their conversation that morning, it was a condensed version. Two comments, which he knew had originally been separated by time and context, now sat together in his memory and would not shift.

'It must be hard to love a woman who is wed to another. Harder still, when they are not from the same rank.'

'It is I who envies you and Helmstan, but you know this.'

Káta walked back to her seat, the recalcitrant Siferth waving his arms and legs about, deploying the only defence available to a small child being lifted from the ground. She looked at the group on the dais once more and when she smiled, her blue eyes flashed like a glint of sunlight upon the water. When her smile was directed at him, Alvar felt the hot light as if a candle shone upon his face, but found that when she turned away, she took the flame with her and he was thrust back into the cool of the shadow. Down by the river, though, her smiles had been for him…

"My lord?"

"Hmm?"

Helmstan grinned. "I must thank you again for this heriot. I am proud to hold this smooth new helm, and this linden shield with not a dimple on it." He paused. "My lord, nay, friend, is something worrying you? Your thoughts seem to be in a place far from this hall."

Helmstan was wrong. Alvar's thoughts were very much in the hall, although they might as well be flying around outside, for they were un-catchable, nonsensical. But, whatever rope of sense these twisted threads of ideas eventually made, one thing was certain; there was naught to be done. Whatever his destination, all paths were blocked with tree-falls. "Naught is wrong, my friend. All is as it should be."

Helmstan waved at Káta as they moved across the crowded hall. He said, "My lord, after all these years of friendship, it means a great deal to me to swear as your thegn. I loved the Greybeard well, but you know, I hope, that you will always find me at your side, ready to do your bidding. Ask me aught or ask me naught, I will…"

Alvar fiddled with his arm ring. "I thank you for your words, but there is no need."

"But I want to have it said. I know that you will look after these folk well, and that you and I will stand by each other through thick and through thin…"

"Enough, man." Alvar ran a finger around his neckline to loosen his tunic. Either he was getting fat like his brother, or the room was too airless. He stared around the room and his gaze alighted on a small figure, hunched in a chair near the door. "Ah, there is the Greybeard's widow; I should speak with her on this day."

He walked away with only as much haste as was seemly, pausing on the way to receive words of congratulations from thegns already bound to him, and those who had knelt before him that day.

Brihtmær, a thegn of Chester, slapped him on the back and said, "Well, my lord, Mercia is yours. What else can you yet wish for?"

Alvar managed a grin. "I crave only to walk through this green field of life without stepping in any cow shit, though I fear it is not a wish that God will grant me. Come, let us find a drink."

Chapter Ten AD966

Cheshire

In the brew-house, Káta was checking the progress of the latest batch of ale. "With Helmstan away, we will need no wine from Chester and can make do with our own ale for a few weeks," she said.

Young Haward ran in, flushed and panting. "Lady, my mother sent me to ask for some newly churned butter. My sister's fever has cooled and she would like a little to eat."

"Run and find Siflæd in the churning room. Take what you need of the newest butter, and tell your mother to give your sister some barley bread, too. It will help to rebuild her strength."

From the brew-house Káta made her way down to the river and called on Wyne the miller to enquire about grain stores.

"Some of the older bags were worm-riddled, my lady, but we have enough to see us to next harvest. I must warn you though that it might not grind too well."

"Lord Helmstan is away so we do not need it ground so finely. Sift and sieve, and we will make the best of what we have. But tell me if you find any more weevils. Once the crop barns are empty we must see to it that they are clean for when the sheaves come in."

Beyond the mill, Burgred the herdsman's youngest daughters were standing in the river while they washed their clothes, and Káta dropped down beside them on the bank to help.

The elder of the two, Wulfflæd, said, "We have been laughing about old mother Leofwaru. She has lost her wits altogether now, my lady."

Edith, the youngest, said, "She upped and kissed the priest, full on the mouth; said he was her long-dead husband." She giggled again as she splashed the kirtle back into the water.

Káta wrung out an undershirt and left it on the stones by the water's edge. "I wish I could stay longer, for it is good to be outside with friends, but…" She hauled herself up the bank and walked with heavy feet through the fields to the hall.

"Gytha? Gytha? Where is she… Oh there you are. We will go to Oakhurst tomorrow. Hild's bairn is due soon and it is a while since I have called on old Goda."

"He cannot see you; why worry?"

"That is not kind," Káta said. "When I have spoken to Leofsige about our food, I will do my sewing, and then we must set to on that loom." As she walked out of the room she said without turning, "And do not wrinkle your brow; you know it has to be done."

In the morning, they took the path through the woods to Oakhurst. At the edge of the village they stood aside for the slaughter-man, who was moving on from the hillside settlement, having butchered their animals for them and been paid with a few cuts of meat which he could then sell on. They held their noses and made faces until his wagon of carcasses was out of smelling range.

In Oakhurst the villagers waved and shouted their greetings. Among the cluster of small dwelling houses, women were grinding corn in the sunshine that penetrated the clearing while their children played beside them, skilled in the art of avoiding the quern stones. Old blind Goda, propped up against a wooden sheep pen, was talking to the youngsters and directing them in their game as if he could see what they were doing. An older woman, her sleeves pushed up, prodded a tub full of woollen cloth with a wooden pole and stirred to ensure that the red dye from the madder root took hold. "It is hard going this time, my lady."

Gytha stepped forward and peered at the mixture. "When I lived in Northampton, we used stems of ladies' bed-straw to turn the cloth red. It takes well, and if you use it there is no need for the first salt-boil."

Káta said, "Or we can buy some more madder root from Chester. The best comes from over the sea and seems to work better. Let me know if you want me to get you some."

Hild came from behind one of the buildings. She walked with the side-to-side gait that came with the last stage of pregnancy and leaned heavily on the ever-present blackthorn stick. "As you can see my lady, this bairn is in no mood to be born yet awhile," she said.

Káta said, "You must be weary. I know you were hoping to have it weaned before harvest."

Hild shrugged. "It would not be the first time that I have brought a bairn to the fields with me." She lowered her voice. "It should be here by week's end, and yet it does not kick as much of late."

Káta exchanged glances with Gytha. "What you need is red-berry leaves, boiled up in water," she said. "I have some dried among my healing leaves; I will bring them next time and help you make the drink, then I will stay with you all day to help you."

"All day?"

One of the other women looked up and sat back from the quern stone. "I think our lady is like us, and needs to keep busier than ever when her man is away."

The midwives and the other women stared at Káta, dread blanching their faces. "My lady, what have you done?"

Káta looked at each of them in turn. "We have all prayed to Christ, and left gifts for the goddess Freyja too. It is nearly three weeks over the time and the bairn is not moving as it should. We all know this is not good. This was all I could think of to do."

She had not told them where she was going, but when she came back from the heart of the forest with the hagtesse they had hissed at her and crossed themselves.

"I know that she stinks. I know that she looks like she lives in a hedge. I know, too, that every one of you thinks that she is a witch. But how can any of us know what it means to live on your own, with no kin or neighbours nearby? Who among us would wish to live beyond the warmth of the hall-hearth? We need someone who is skilled at helping with childbearing and..." She looked at their anxious faces. Adherence in the villages to the folk-ways was not as fixed as the fear of pure evil. They had every right to defy her; they could report her to the priest, or to the reeve.

The women looked at each other, and when a low moan inside the house rose to a wrenching scream, they looked back to Káta. Mawa, the eldest, stepped forward and took Káta's hand. "You speak the truth, Lady. The folk-ways are older than any of us here standing and we need this woman's help. We only wish that we were as fearless as you are. We cannot know what the priest will do..."

"I will go to mass with no guilt in my heart. I brought this woman here for the sake of Hild. I do what I need to do for my folk; all the gods that ever were should know this." Káta took a deep breath. "On my soul be it, then." She stepped back into Hild's house.

The old woman was standing with her arms folded and her chin up, but with her gaze turned towards the sick woman, who no longer squirmed, but lay still, moaning weakly.

Káta said, "Do what you must."

Káta waited for the priest outside his church. She stood under the ancient yew that must have been a sapling before the Christians ever built their church on the holy land, and she thought wearily about the day's events. After all her travails, Hild had been delivered of a dead baby, and soon there would be a fresh mound of earth in the churchyard close by the walls of the church. The old woman had said her spells, and worked to stave off the infection which threatened to send the mother the same way as the child. The hagtesse had told the women that she could do no more; that the Wyrd sisters, or the Norns as Káta's mother would have known them, would weave the fate as they willed.

The sinking sun cast long shadows across the churchyard. One of them moved; the priest was behind her. Unable to meet his gaze, she said, "Hild has borne a dead bairn." She sighed, but it became a shudder as she struggled to keep the sob from her throat. "She might soon follow the child into the next world. Please do what you can for her and her child." She looked up at him, waiting for his response.

The priest expressed no surprise. Death, particularly that of a newborn or its mother, was no rarity, but nevertheless he frowned. She had expected him to. The babe had not drawn a single breath, and thus had died without being baptised. Priest Wulfsige was a good man, always driven by vocation to provide succour to his parishioners. But he was not a brave man. She was confident that he would agree to bury the infant in the small reserved area under the eaves of the church, but with every such request Wulfsige grew more reluctant, aware that he was breaking the law. She reached out and pressed her hand on his arm. She could feel him shaking. "Hild might not live. It would comfort her greatly if she could go to God with the knowledge that her bairn lies in the eaves-drip."

Priest Wulfsige chewed his lip, plainly struggling to reconcile his duty with his conscience. "Do you really believe it?"

It did not matter what she believed. It was the way things had always been done. In the end, despite their prayers and best efforts, God had chosen to take the babe. None of them wanted to think of that small soul in purgatory, so why not give it the chance to be washed with drops of water from the church roof? It might just serve as enough of a baptism to send the child to God. She said, "What harm can it do?"

Wulfsige gave a little whimper of a laugh. "You have not met the bishop of Lichfield, my lady. The laws are clear…"

She released his arm. "Please," she said, "Hild needs you." She left him to gather what he needed, confident that he would find the courage to minister where it was most needed. She stepped from the churchyard out onto the lane that would take her back to Ashleigh. Any hand-wringing over the day's events would have to wait; the hagtesse would be safer if she had an escort back to her home in the forest, Hild's children would need food, and it was Káta's duty to oversee the arrangements.

Gloucestershire

"I never thought so see you attending so many hundred-moots, my lord. Not when you have the right to send others in your stead."

Alvar glanced at Thegn Wulfgar's twisted profile, and stared out ahead. "I must watch the bishop, or let him be a wolf in the fold. The man sticks to me closer than my own shadow." Not for the first time, he recalled Edgar's words. *'Dunstan is my confessor… I cannot call off his hound.'*

"It must be goading to you, my lord."

Alvar grunted. "And you, too, I should have thought." Wulfgar's cheerfulness was so ingrained that he seemed able to forget that Oswald was a thorn in his own side, too. Wulfgar's folk were descended from an ancient tribe, older than the Mercians, and possessed of the independent sense of identity so hated by the bishop.

The road to the folk-moot gathering at Bledisloe Tump crossed a high ridge, and cut between forest on one side, and open land which sloped to the river below. Wulfgar looked down the hill. "Ah, well, we Hwicce from the dale look to our great lord to keep our foes off our backs. And we will love you even more if you give us good food and too much ale, much as your father did…"

Alvar laughed. "Love me more, eh? Is that a kindness or a threat? Never fear; I shall see to it that my hall-boards always groan with food. You will never be short of fodder."

He looked over his shoulder. "The only men at your back today are your fellow thegns and my stewards." He pointed to the scribe. "And one holy man will not harm you. As for keeping the bishop away, he should not gift any land without my leave, but…" The truth was that in his new ship-soke of three hundred hides of land, Oswald enjoyed private and total jurisdiction in an enclave of authority within the very heart of the earl's lands. Alvar's fingers tightened around the slack of the reins and he squeezed the leather.

Wulfgar said, "I hear that he is still busily giving land to his kith and kin. The wonder is, that being such an ill-mannered man, he has so many friends. I, for one, have not forgotten that he once called me a *'twisel-tooth'*." He turned and grinned at Alvar, showing his uneven teeth. "Although my wife is more upset about my broken nose."

Alvar smiled. "Hmm. That might be because you broke it falling drunk from the mead-bench." He lifted his leg away from the saddle to scratch his inner thigh. "And there will be none of that whilst we are with Oswald. Settle yourself for a boring few days."

"You admit that it will be dull, so I ask again; why do you come? Why not do as the other great lords do?"

"I am happy to let my thegns speak on my behalf in other hundreds, but I would have Oswald go no further than my eyes can see." Last time he had turned his back, Oswald had decided to take every third penny paid in tax, which traditionally had gone to the lord of the area and was known as the earl's penny. "I will not let him have any more from me." He waved away an irritating fly. "I cannot be everywhere," he grinned at Wulfgar, "Because my lands are so vast. Yes, you do right to bow to me," he said in response to Wulfgar's mock gesture of respect, "But whenever the hundred-moots are in the bishopric of Worcester I will be there, watching him." He clenched his jaw. The meetings were held every four weeks, and it left him little time to do anything else. He cursed the bishop under his breath.

His profanity amused Wulfgar, who broke into his notorious laugh. It began as a gurgle that caught in his throat and sounded like accelerated hiccups.

Alvar grinned and glanced skyward. "The weather looks threatening. We should get off this ridge, for I could do without a wetting. Let us see if we can outride the rain as well as the bishop."

But at the Tump, Oswald and his group of scribes were already sitting on the wooden platform at the top of the mound, with every piece of their luggage unpacked around them. They made a play of shuffling along the bench to make space for the new arrivals. Alvar decided not to snap at the bait but waited while they fidgeted and sorted the documents spread over the table top.

There was no room left for the king's reeve when he arrived, and the delegation from the cathedral stared ahead as if to defy an order to move again. They sat in a line, hands clasped over the paunches that padded out their habits.

Alvar laughed. "Lord Bishop, do the brothers forgo as much as they should? It strikes me that if they went a little hungrier we would have room for Reeve Sihtric to sit alongside us."

Oswald looked down at his own slender frame, then stared at Alvar. He flicked his hand and the brothers all shuffled along again.

The king's reeve sat down and said, "Shall we get to business?"

Quills in one hand, pen knives in the other, the scribes were equipped to commence, but seemed in no hurry. Alvar sat forward, head in hands, and tapped his fingers against his cheeks. Why did they not have their wax tablets and styli, with which they could write quickly, to copy out at a later time? To keep him waiting, and make him fidget, whilst they wasted expensive vellum and precious time. Well, he could play that game too. He grinned and stretched out his legs, picked at a snagging fingernail, and whistled. The monks conferred, shrugged, and looked at Oswald. The bishop's pale eyes narrowed before he gave a small nod.

Alvar nudged Wulfgar. "At last we begin."

First to be called was a plaintiff called Thurferth, who accused his neighbour, Leofstan, of stealing two sheep from his flock.

Alvar addressed the local official, the hundred-man. "Is Leofstan here to answer?"

"He is, my lord," the hundred-man said.

Thurferth swore his oath that he made the accusation with honesty and in good faith, and Leofstan was called forward to answer the charge against him.

He stood in front of the platform, his back to the gathering, and spoke the traditional oath with a raised voice so that those behind him, as well as above, could hear. "By the Lord, I am guiltless both in deed and thought of the wrongdoing which Thurferth says I have done."

Alvar said, "Who will speak for this man?" The light dimmed and he glanced up at the sky, where dirty clouds were rushing to the muster.

The hundred-man stepped forward and gave the names of those who would bear witness for the defendant, and one by one they were called upon to give their oath.

"By the Lord, the oath is true which Leofstan swore."

The case was dismissed. The hundred-man gave the name of another defendant, one Wynsige, who had failed to appear to answer a charge of theft. "This is not the first time that he has been called to answer."

Alvar decreed that compensation should be paid to the plaintiff and ordered the payment of a fine, half of which would go to the hundred and half to the king. "Is he a thegn, this Wynsige? Yes? Then sixty shillings will go the king and sixty shillings will go the hundred, and if after thirty days the shillings have not been paid, then Wynsige will become outlaw and be named wolf's head."

The next case involved a man who had been caught

stealing from his neighbour's house. Wulfnoth accused Ealdstan, and brought forward witnesses who swore their oaths.

"In the name of almighty God, so I stand here by Wulfnoth in true witness, unbidden and unbought, as I saw with my eyes and heard with my ears that which I say now with him."

Alvar spoke to the bishop, but projected his voice so that all might hear his judgement. "Lord Bishop, house-breaking is a wrong which cannot be redressed by payment of silver. I therefore give him over to you, that he may go to ordeal."

Oswald echoed the theatrical tones. "The man Ealdstan will go to the church of St Mary's, where he will fast for three days, after which he will yield to ordeal by hot water." To Alvar he said, "And there is no doubt in my mind that his hand will blister and not heal."

There remained the collection of various rents, fines, and taxes, and the hundred-man again came forward to make payments to the lord, the bishop, and the king's reeve. The money was counted and recorded by the scribes, who made piles of the pennies and scratched the numbers onto their documents. A fat blob of rain landed on the platform table. The scribes held their pens in mid-mark and looked up. Two more drops smudged onto the vellum, diluting the charcoal ink, and the late afternoon gave way to an early evening as the sky darkened and the summer rain fired down on the gathering. Villagers, petitioners and witnesses, scattered in moments, and left the dignitaries to protect their paraphernalia from the rain as best they could.

Wulfgar, already mounted, wheeled his horse around and shouted, "My lord, come and keep dry at my house."

Alvar waved a hand in gratitude and said to Oswald, "We go to Munford; you know it?"

Thunder rumbled like a slow bellyache and Alvar leaped onto his own horse, and raced the others down the hillside to Wulfgar's manor in the valley.

The men ran through the hall door, stopped, looked at each other, and laughed. The need to rush was over and they flicked their sleeves and shook their feet. Wulfgar's young wife, Mildrith, waved from the far end of the hall and continued with her directions to the servants to pull the trestle tables into the centre of the room. Alvar raised his hand to wave back and wiped water drips from his nose. The fire cast a welcoming glow, and he unpinned his cloak, rubbed his hair with it, threw it on a nearby bench, and made his way to the hearth. He tried to sit beside the fire but his breeches were stuck to his thighs. He was still peeling them from his skin when the bishop and his entourage arrived, in a scuttle that was neither a run nor a dignified walk.

Oswald joined Alvar by the hearth and they both sat down. Alvar shuffled his chair sideways and stuck his legs out at an angle to ensure that the bishop had plenty of room. "I am not like a monk. I do not mind who sits beside me."

Oswald shook water from his hand. "Believe me, I have never thought of you as being like a monk. No, I think of you more as a silly youth who likes to play children's games."

"Really? Is that not like the fox calling the wolf cunning?"

A serving-boy approached. "My lords, my lady Mildrith begs forgiveness that there is little more than broth, bread, and cheese this evening. There is wine, though, if the lord and bishop would like it."

Oswald scowled and opened his mouth, but Alvar laid a hand on the boy's arm. "Tell Lady Mildrith that I will eat heartily this night, and that I will gladly slake my thirst with her ale, for though she has been lady here for only a three-month, I know it to be well brewed here."

Oswald sniffed and moved closer to the fire. "I will have wine," he said to the boy. He rubbed his hands together and held his palms to the heat. "We will go to the Tibblestone in the morning, to be there before the lark rises. I hope that the men of that hundred are not so lawless as those we dealt with today."

Alvar's men were still throwing off their belts to loosen their wet tunics. They shouted to each other as they dried off. Servants were hurrying round the hall and conferring with their superiors who, in turn, took instruction from Mildrith and Wulfgar.

Alvar shook his head. "Forgive me, Bishop, but in this din I think I misheard you."

Oswald said, "No, you did not. I said lawless."

Alvar raised an eyebrow. "This hundred is mostly a law-abiding one. Yes, there was theft and house-breaking, but no house-burning or murder, and never once have tolls or tithes not been paid."

"That may be so, but they live unchristian lives. I will have words with the priests, for they should speak more of Christianity and do more to quell heathenism."

"They do what they can and they look to their flock. What more would you ask of them?"

Oswald suppressed a sneeze. "They must be harsh, brook no wrongdoing. I heard of a Cheshire thegn's wife who has the mark of the Devil on her hand. It is said that she gave shelter to a pagan witch, who cursed and killed a newborn. And yet the priest did naught. At Lichfield they are working for me, to find the proof and give me the names. In London this year a witch was thrown from the bridge. This is the way to put a stop to these things."

The thundering hooves from moments before now echoed in Alvar's chest. He put his hand over his heart. His sister-in-law did that when she watched her little ones climbing trees that were too high, or riding horses that were too big for them. He was used to seeing to the needs of those who depended on his protection, but this was a new sensation; he could only guess that it was fear.

He stared at the bishop through narrowed eyes, took a deep breath, and lifted one foot to rest on the other knee.

"I, too, have heard of this woman. It is my understanding that the mark on her hand came about during a mishap with a saw. A dear friend once told me of the Bridestones on Cloud Hill in Cheshire, where folk say a Viking and his Saxon bride were hounded and killed. Have we not gone beyond such deeds, where folk are damned ere we hear the truth?" Alvar paused to scratch his nose, as casual an act as he could think of. The strength of his reaction had surprised him. Unfortunately, the slight lift of Oswald's mouth into what passed for a smile indicated that it had provided some useful intelligence to the Dane, too. And only when Alvar saw the bishop smile had he understood, finally, exactly what it was that he had revealed.

He tried to steer the conversation not to a new path, but further down the road a little. "At least the folk here will follow the law of the moots. Be thankful for that, for most of the men who live here do not even deem it to be a real shire."

Oswald raised his eyebrows. "What are you saying to me? How can they not, when all England is shired and always has been?"

"Not in Mercia. The shires here were new even in my father's day. The folk here long for the old days and yearn for their old-rights."

The bishop sniffed again. "I am bound to be sick with cold." He kicked the hearth-slave. "Stir yourself, thrall, and get this fire burning hotter." He turned back to Alvar. "You speak of old heathen ways, I think. The king will not like this, you know. He wishes to have one strong kingdom. There are no worries like this in East Anglia. There, the folk are lawful and Christian."

"Pig shit. Brandon shows you his white teeth so much that you are now blinded by him."

"My lord Alvar, you must not speak to me in this way. I am a man of the Church."

"I will keep it in mind, if you do." He looked Oswald in the eye and held his gaze until the bishop turned away to stare at the flames. "East Anglia was always more tightly bound to Wessex; Edgar knows this, and he also knew that he had to let the Danes in the east keep their own laws. Edgar knows a little, too, about Mercian law."

Oswald sneezed. "Mercian law, West Saxon law, they are but one thing."

"No, they are not. The folk here feel that most keenly, and it must not be forgotten."

"But this is tiresome. Must I call all these folk Mercian, then? Are we not all English?"

Alvar grinned at the unintentional irony. "Some of us are. I think you will find, lord Bishop, that in this dale, and all along the Severn, they call themselves not Mercian, but Hwicce."

The bishop rolled his eyes, and went to his seat at table.

Mildrith adjusted her veil, and smoothed her skirts. She served the head table and did not sit down, but whispered to the servants who kept up a relay to and from the kitchen. Alvar kept his hand-saex away from the table and used Mildrith's cutlery instead, wiped his mouth on the napkin provided, and refrained from retrieving any dropped food. He smiled and gave Mildrith an encouraging wink.

Wulfgar turned his lopsided face and scowled. He pointed at Alvar, mouthed, "You," drew his finger across his throat, and barked out his yuk-yuk laugh.

Alvar smiled back, but he was troubled by his earlier conversation and could not resist glancing at Oswald, even though the bishop's face was a mask. Had he got away with it? Perhaps he had let nothing slip, after all. It was a strong reaction, but only because he had not, until now, been aware of the strength of his feelings. For that reason, it was possible that he was magnifying something which was, after all, of little consequence to Oswald, who continued to eat in silence, staring straight ahead.

The Tibblestone marked the crossing of the roads which passed through the hundred and was an ancient and sacred meeting place. Alvar leaned against the stone and curled his toes against the wet that seeped through his boots from the previous day's rain. He should have waited for Oswald and his clerks to rouse themselves, for few people had gathered yet for the court meeting, but had he watched them any longer he would have loaded the monks' carts for them. A few stall-holders had arrived, eager to take advantage of the day's gathering, and he watched as a cloth merchant draped his samples over willow hurdles spiked into the ground. Further down the road, a metal-worker displayed his pewter brooches and trinkets, no doubt hopeful of selling his inferior but affordable jewellery and accessories to the poorer folk of the neighbourhood. Soon the air would be filled with the smell of bread and hot broth when the food sellers arrived, but for now, Alvar widened his nostrils to breathe in the scent of the damp ground, turned his face to the sun as it started its climb into position, and guessed at the hour.

"My lord, may I speak?"

Alvar looked down and nodded at the thegn, Goscelin of Worcester.

"It is about my brother, Leofwine, and his kin. You might know him? No? Well, he was one of the clerks at Worcester before he was put out to make way for the monks. I did what I could to help, but I have only a few hides of land myself so I could not do much in their time of need. They are finding it hard, my lord. Many had their own lands elsewhere, but my brother is not a rich man and…"

Every muscle in Alvar's back knotted into a ball, each one knocking against the next and sending a pull of tension down his arms and into his fists. "Tell him to go to my house at Upper Slaughter," Alvar said. "Have him make himself known to my steward there and he will be given work and somewhere to sleep. When I am back there, I will make a gift of land, enough for his needs and for the needs of his wife and children."

Goscelin sagged onto his knees in the wet grass. "My

lord, I thank you. My brother will weep with gladness at these wondrous tidings. You are a great and kind…"

The bishop's train arrived. Alvar silenced Goscelin with a wave of his hand and beckoned him to his feet. He pushed himself upright away from the stone and stood up straight. Striding up to the bishop he said, "Come, my lord, we have many tales of lawlessness to hear this day."

Oswald continued to oversee the unloading of the chests and furniture from the carts.

"Hmm, I thought so. What form does the wrongdoing take?"

"Theft. Of land and belongings, with no payment."

"Well that will never do." Oswald put a hand out as if to steady one of the boxes. "Take care with that, Brother Oswi." He turned to look at Alvar. "So, this is another lawless hundred after all."

"No, lord Bishop, the lawlessness of which I speak is not in this hundred. The wrong has been done by the bishop of Worcester, and the men whom you have wronged are the clerks of the minster who have been put out of their homes and thrown off their land. I warned you that this would not do."

Oswald turned round. His mouth twitched, his cheeks grew red, and a vertical line dug a channel into his forehead. He stared at the younger man and smiled, though his thin lips lifted only from a downward arc into a straight line and the furrow on his brow remained. "You are a hindrance, but you are right, Lord Alvar, when you say that there is much work to be done. For when I have done with these hundred-moots I must go to see the lord Brandon. There are many fens in his earldom where we need to build in the name of the wondrous St Benedict." He tilted his chin so that his mouth came closer. His eyes gleamed like a hearth-fire given life by a taper. "We will build and we will strengthen the Church and we will strengthen Wessex. We will build and drive the heathen folk from the fenland. We will not stop, nor bow before our foes. We shall…"

"Those lands do not belong to you, you mad old goat."

"Not belong? It might be that those fenlands were once in Mercia, but they are not now, nor will they ever be again. God has a greater need for them." Oswald's breath came in rapid bursts and his nostrils whistled as he expelled the air. He swallowed, and when his breathing slowed he said, "And so do I."

"To stop me having them?"

Oswald sucked another breath into his wraith-like body. "You can believe what you wish, my lord. There is naught that you can do."

Alvar clenched his hand around his sword hilt and took a step forward.

Oswald marched to the standing stone and called for a scribe to produce a document, from which he proceeded to read. "And we bid that every priest keenly upholds Christianity and wholly quells every heathenism; and forbids well-worshipping and witchcraft and spells and all that is done at or near trees…"

Wulfgar came to stand by his lord. "The old weasel is bent on killing our ways and taking all our land. What is to be done?"

Alvar, angry and fearful, could only thank God for the sliver of composure that kept him rooted to the spot rather than indulging his sudden lust for butchery. He shook his head, and spoke through a jaw that would not fully open. "I have been wrestling with the thought that forever in hell would be no time at all, if it meant that I could slit Oswald's throat." He took a calming breath. "Whilst I might have the king's love, I do not think Edgar would forgive me for slaying his bishop. He wants the Church rebuilt and strengthened, so he needs Oswald; that is the burden we must bear. The Church will grow strong, and England with it, and the old ways such as yours will soon be no more."

Wulfgar grunted. "The giving of a name will not make folk like mine feel English."

"You know this, as do I. And so does Edgar, but Oswald

does not care."

"So we are toothless as bairns?"

Alvar slapped his hand on Wulfgar's shoulder. "Oh, my teeth are sharp enough. We must bide our time, but all will be well."

He glared across the grassy sward at Oswald, who turned and met his gaze with a stare from eyes that flashed cold enough to burn.

Chapter Eleven AD967

Cheshire

"You are early; here we are with the haw blossom barely out. We do not usually see you before full summer." Káta put down her wool-combs and patted the stool next to her. "Here, sit, and leave your men in the hall. They are making a mickle din in there and I would not be able to hear you." She picked up her spinning. Each time the spindle dropped to the floor, she gathered it up, wound the thread round it and dropped it to spin once more. "Not only have you come early, but Helmstan says he has had many letters from you over the last few months, each one asking after me." She looked up and smiled.

Alvar, his face to the sun, squinted as he said, "Lady, I would be here more often, but I need to watch that snake Oswald like a hawk watches a hare." And he could not have come earlier, for fear of leading Oswald straight after him, so he had stayed at home and watched the watcher, plaguing Oswald by following him everywhere, much as the bishop had been doing to him this past year or more.

"So which is he then, your bishop, a snake or a hare?"

She kept her head tilted over her spinning, but looked up and smiled. A strand of hair broke loose from her veil and fell across her forehead. He wanted to reach forward and brush it to one side for her. He filled his nostrils with the waft of lavender before he sat back and said, "It is not kind to tease." But being teased was a small price to pay for seeing her well, and free from harm. Helmstan's letters had been full of assurances, but visual proof was better, being irrefutable and not subject to being outdated.

"I have a hare," said Siferth. He did not turn his head, but picked another piece from the log pile given to him by the woodsman. He added it to the top of his tower. "He lives in the field."

Káta leaned forward and spoke in a conspiratorial whisper. "I think it might not be the same one that he sees each time. But I will not shatter his notion."

She gathered up her spindle and repeated the spinning process. Her hands did not shake, even though she must know that he was staring. She had fetched the extra stool from the hall herself and weathered the looks of his men with a gracious smile. She still often looked down at the floor when she spoke, but sometimes she met his gaze now when they talked, and he was able to see her eyes as well as the downward sweep of her pale lashes.

He spoke quietly. "You seem to be burdened with few worries these days."

She said, "When you have a child, your own life becomes meaningless. I go to mass every day, for his sake; I would not want any of my wrongdoing to come back on him. No-one ever speaks of what I once did."

"Oh my lady, thank God. That is… I meant to say…" He clamped his mouth shut. She was referring only to the well-worshipping. She did not know that he was aware of the hagtesse, and he had no wish to alarm her. "You have had no trouble with your priest?"

She shook her head. "I barely stepped outside the law, and I do not think God minds. How can he, when he gave me the child?"

He agreed. "I know many men who think naught of stretching their own beliefs into a new shape if they need to." Certainly, Dunstan and Oswald were not above rewriting canon law when it suited them. "Maybe I should follow that lead sometimes. If I were not so unbending, I might find it less hard to get what I crave."

She laughed and brushed the loose tress away from her face. He wanted to take off her veil and place the hair back behind her ear.

She said, "You forget that all sins will be answered for in the afterlife. If you wander too far from the path of righteousness there might be a reckoning."

"Lady, sometimes I think it would be worth it."

He stared at her until she blushed, shook her head and looked away.

Her words came at a new speed. "Well, you speak of stretching, which is what I will need to do to my hall if we are to fit all these men in for the night. The new bower is not finished, as you can see." She waved a hand towards the new guest-house, where two men were planing and filing the upright green-oak timbers of the new building. Inside the hall, the noise increased and as it fell away, Wulfgar barked out his laugh. She winced and said, "You have brought nearly a whole fyrd and one of them makes a din like a kicked mule. So, now that I have fed and watered them, will you tell me why you are here?"

"When will Helmstan be back from his hunt?"

"As I told you when you came, he will be back any day now. Do not play with me any more, my lord." She leaned over, placed her spindle by her feet, and rested her hand on his. "Why are you here? It was not merely to ask after my welfare."

He cleared his throat, pretended an itch on his ear, and brought his hand up from under hers. "I need men to fight with me in Wales, while Earl Beorn is dealing with the Scots. Edgar wants the northern and western marches secure. There has been unrest there."

"And you would have my husband's life laid down."

"Lady, you know that I would not ask if there were any other way. But the king looks to me as earl of Mercia to keep the borderlands free from..."

She slapped her hands down on her knees. "Oh, stop there. If there were any other way? You love naught better than a fight, and you know that Helmstan will be the first to offer you his sword. You will even hope that the fighting lasts, so that you can get the full sixty days owed from the weapon-men. You are like an eager child."

He could only take the rebuke with good grace. He would not insult her by pretending that wars in Wales did not offer opportunities for fame, and for booty to be distributed to allies and kinsmen. It was an enjoyable and profitable pastime and he was, as she said, as excited as a small boy.

On cue, Siferth walked over to Alvar. "Lift me up and spin me," he said.

"I thought you would have forgotten that," Alvar said, but he scooped the boy up by his legs and whirled round, while Siferth flung his arms out and shrieked and whooped.

Káta spoke through her own laughter. "Put him down before he is sick."

After a few more turns, Alvar set the boy down and Siferth giggled and tottered like a drunk towards the builders, who laughed, turned him round and pushed him back towards his mother.

Alvar sat back down. "You do not mind? I thought you might be over-chary with him."

"Even if I were, it looks as though you have done it before, while I was not looking." She put her hands up, palms towards him. "No, keep your 'sorry' for another day." Leaning over, she picked up a bowl from under the stool. "I do not know if he will want to eat this now though."

She stirred the mush of boiled rosehip with her finger. "Siferth, will you eat this before the wasps settle in it?"

She licked the puree off her finger, and Alvar ran his finger round the neck of his tunic. He coughed. "You do not fret over him much, then?"

She rested her hands in her lap. "I nearly died bearing him. God willed that we would both live; He is not going to take him away from me in the middle of a silly game."

Alvar nodded. He said, "I understand. Only when you

have fought hard for something do you earn the right to hold it dear. That is why I..." That was why he could only sit and talk with her instead of lying in her bed. He shook his head.

"What is it?"

He coughed out a laugh. "I only meant that I should not be thinking of soft pillows on the eve of a fight. I must earn my rest first."

She nodded her understanding, but her quizzical frown betrayed that nod as a polite pretence.

He shuffled his stool back so that he could lean against the cook-house wall, stretched his legs out, and disturbed a foraging chicken. "And what about me, my lady; will I be taken from my child's game, as you call it?"

She gave him a long, slow smile and he shuffled in his seat, at once warmed and yet too hot.

"You think to tease me. Will you die in the fight, you ask? Well, who would take you; I think that both the Devil and Christ would claim you as one of their own."

"Then truly I cannot be harmed by any Welshman's spear."

"Oh, you may laugh now, and you may laugh loudly, but you will not laugh again if you bring Helmstan or yourself home wounded."

"Lady, it was only a meal, not a big gathering. The woad-dyed one was pretty enough; you could have worn it."

Káta, wearing only her linen shift, danced with the red and yellow shot-silk gown and ignored Gytha's attempts to catch her and brush her hair. "But this one was brighter, do you not think? The Godweb cloth was not cheap, and the workings on it are pretty."

Gytha sniffed. "I think you would have looked good in either. Now, are you going to let me comb your hair?"

Yes, I will sit. Aah! No need to wrench my head from my shoulders."

"Sorry. But if you had not worn the head-cloth I would

not have needed to use so many hair-needles. I do not know why you worried so much about tonight. Leofsige told me that you were clucking in the kitchen while he was cooking. You do not usually do that."

Káta sat up straight as Gytha worked the carved-antler comb through to the ends of her hair. "Lord Alvar is a great and wealthy lord and should have the best food. To have an earl eating in our hall brings my husband a higher standing, and I was acting in his stead. I did not wish to shame him."

Gytha puffed out a snort of air.

"I gave out the drinks myself and did not spill a drop, like thus." Káta picked up the water jug, lifted it high and splashed the liquid into the cup. "Not one drop."

"And you are proud of yourself? I do that every day. Now sit still."

Káta sat back and hugged herself. "I do not feel so worthless now that I know I can do the right things in front of such a lord," she said.

Gytha tugged on a tangle. "Maybe you will go to the king's house now, sometimes?"

Káta sat up straight. "There is no need. Besides, there are too many other high-born ladies there."

"So? You have shown what you can do. You have the best clothes…"

"No, I like it better here; when it is only… I mean that it is not so hard. I can make believe that everything belongs to me when I am here."

Gytha sniffed, pulled the comb through the separated hair and said, "That will do." She placed the comb on the table and held a taper to the fire. When it caught the flame, she held it up to light the wicks in the wall cressets and said, "I do not know what you mean, Lady. All this does belong to you." She threw the taper into the fire.

"Naught; forget what I said." Káta climbed into her bed. She brought her knees up to her chest and wrapped her arms around them. "When I was little I would let my mother think I was sleeping. When she had left the room, I would open the hangings, and think of a comely king, or fair-looking lord, who would come in and sweep me away. It was but a game, but it was such a lovely way to go to sleep. Did you ever…"

"Me? I keep too busy to find time for love." Gytha reached up to draw the bed-curtains.

"No, leave them…"

She woke, but did not open her eyes. She could not tell if she had dreamed; there was no distinct vision to recall, only a lingering contentment that she was in no hurry to chase away. She lay under the blankets and stretched out her arms.

"Be still, you dim-witted hound. Burgred, fetch him back; he is on the net."

Káta heaved herself from the bed, opened the shutter, and peered out into the sunshine. The dogs were padding over the hunting-nets as the men tried to fold them away.

"Kat! Dearling!" Helmstan waved. "We have boar for the spit tonight and none of us wounded in the hunting of it." He stepped over the dogs who meandered round his feet while their tails thrummed. "Here comes the man who saw a hart and let it get away. You should get yourself a bow made of yew, my friend." Helmstan's laugh boomed out across the yard.

The young thegn, Lyfing, said, "My lord, my bow is as long as a man, and is harder than most. Yet the ash yields in my hands like a soft woman."

Helmstan looked up at his wife and smiled. "He speaks as if he knows what a woman feels like. With tales like that, we should have him as our scop. I will be with you shortly, my love, but we have a wounded hound and a lame horse to see to."

Káta laughed. His face was flushed and grubby and he was in need of a shave, but he did not look ready to sit down, like the boys who raced in the fields every summer and needed a few moments to slow to a stop. "I will not call you from your games yet awhile," she said.

She grabbed her clothes and threw them on over her shift. Gathering her hair forward over her shoulder, she braided it on her way outside as she rushed to try to make up lost time with her chores.

Alvar was outside the bake-house, supervising the loading of provisions onto the pack horses. She opened her mouth to speak, but left the words unsaid as Helmstan hurried back up the path from the stables and caught her up in an embrace that lifted her off the ground.

He bent his head and whispered in her ear. "This is not much of a homecoming my love, I know. But keep our bed warm for me when I come back again."

He set her back down, and her cheeks throbbed at the thought of Alvar as witness. But his back was turned as he took more dried meat from Leofsige and he had not noticed.

"I must say, Helmstan, that if the thegns of Chester give as many men and as much food, we will soon be strong enough to meet aught that we might find in Wales." He bestowed a charming smile on Káta but the skin around his eyes did not crinkle. "I thank you for your warm welcome, Lady."

"What? Oh, it was naught, my lord. We are always glad to see you here."

His smile remained in place, but he looked past her.

The men mounted their horses and Káta begged one indulgence, turning to gather what she needed from the pile by the door. "It will stop the evil one pulling at the bridle and will stop your horses falling," she said. She presented each of the riders at the front of the column with a switch made from ash. She reached up to give Alvar his stick, but though he took it, he did not meet her gaze. The sun hurt her eyes. She took a step back to allow them to depart, and blinked to lose the black circle that blurred in front of her eyelids.

Gytha appeared at her side. "What is wrong, Lady?"

"Naught is wrong. Here you see a lady waving off her

man and his lord, and hoping that her man gets time to rest at Chester before he moves on. All is as it should be. Anyone who thinks otherwise is a dull-wit." She brought her sleeve up to her eye, wiped it, and went to attend to her duties.

After seeing to the upturned bucket in the milking shed, and helping Gytha on the loom, she spent the day checking the stores and provisions, making sure that they had enough for their needs while the men were away. After that, with fewer folk around, there was nothing to prevent her catching up with her mending tasks, and the need for neat stitches kept her thoughts busy as well as her hands. But as night fell she put down her sewing, unable to do more without the light, and let her gaze wander to the window. Had the sun also shone all day over Wales?

When Siferth asked that night to share her bed instead of Gytha's, she agreed; he cuddling up for warmth, she for comfort.

North Wales

Helmstan put his hands to his ears. "Stop! Enough names! I brought you one weapon-man from every five hides of my land, I am here in this rainy spot, and that should be enough for you. I do not care why I fight; I only wonder when I can go home and get dry."

Alvar halted his list of the warring Welsh princes. He nodded at Helmstan's man, Lyfing, as he made his way towards the latrine ditch. When Lyfing had walked past, he answered Helmstan. "You are right. All you need to know is that there are many sons of the Welsh leader, Idwal, who are now set against one another, and Edgar has sent us here to be the fox in the hen-house." He had taken the commission without question or hesitation, but it was not the way he preferred to fight. To him it seemed a misuse of men and resources, as well as being morally questionable, to lay waste to the land whilst the inhabitants were engaged elsewhere. But he had his orders. "Think of us as Edgar's big foot, stamping down heavily on small ants who might think to bite us."

"Have we not stamped enough? It has been weeks." Helmstan stretched out his big hands and warmed them, holding his palms towards the flames, and rubbing them together from time to time. "I understand that we are here to make mischief, but where can it end? We are fighting neither for one side nor the other. Must we keep on until one lot of Welsh wins out over another; what if that takes more than the sixty days?"

It was a reasonable question. Alvar only wished he had the answer. His instructions were to show the sons of Idwal that whenever they rose up to take arms, the English would be there, breathing threateningly down their necks. But how to end it? They had wreaked destruction up and down the peninsular called the Lleyn, and wherever they had met any Welshmen with a mind to fight, they had persuaded them otherwise. Perhaps Helmstan was right and it was time to go home. The men would, by law, only serve sixty days and if nothing was resolved by then they would have to leave anyway. He looked around him. Knowing the Welsh liking for an ambush, they had set up camp at a site which left them less vulnerable to attack, but more open to the weather. The day's rain had subsided enough for them to light the fires, but the ground beneath them was soggy, a sodden mix of slippery leaves, sopping grass and twigs that would never snap, only bend. If the weather was as bad on the other side of the march, then the harvest might be under threat. With that thought, Alvar leaned forward and slapped his hand down on Helmstan's thigh. "You are right. It is time to go home."

Helmstan looked up. "The clouds are gathering. How far will we get before nightfall?"

Alvar stood up, trying to remember how far they were from the settlement of Nefyn, and how long it would take them to get back over the border. They'd not ridden a direct route from Nefyn, but had taken a detour to rout a band of Welshmen who had challenged them on the road. "How many miles was it to the..." He turned at the sound of shouting.

Lyfing was running back from the latrine ditch, pursued by half a dozen Welshmen. Alvar, Helmstan and the rest of the men leaped to gather their weapons, and Helmstan scooped up a spear. He ran to give the spear to Lyfing who, as soon as he had a weapon in his hand, turned and faced the enemy. With a spear but no shield, he stood his ground, jabbing at the intruders, keeping them at bay until Helmstan found his footing and began slashing with his sword, and did his best to protect them both with his shield. It was only a matter of moments then until Alvar and the others were able to join them, and a hastily established shield wall gave strength and protection. To Alvar and, no doubt, all of the men there, the clattering of the shields coming together was the most comforting sound they could hear on the battlefield. They fought as one, until they gained ground and the wall altered to form smaller, tighter formations. Lyfing was engaged in a scuffle with a Welshman; he was forced to keep back, poking with his spear but unable to come forward because he had no shield. Helmstan rushed round Lyfing, reaching with his sword, and stabbed the adversary in the shoulder. The Welshman went down, but even whilst on his knees, he thrust forward with his spear. Lyfing jumped out of the way and the man's swing brought his body round. For a moment he was facing the other way. Helmstan stepped forward, went down on one knee, and brought his sword across the man's throat, standing up and booting the body forward away from him. Immediately he stepped back, retreating behind the wall, dragging the brave but increasingly vulnerable Lyfing with him. As the wall closed around them, the man next to Alvar slipped on the rain-soaked grass. He fell, and a tall Welshman came forward through the gap. Helmstan slashed at him with his sword until Alvar could adjust his footing. Helmstan's sword thrust had severed the man's arm muscle and his arm hung useless. Alvar finished him off with a blow to the skull, and the Welshman fell back. Alvar and Helmstan continued to hack and push, standing close and working in unison.

A cry went up from somewhere behind them. "My lords, the bowmen; look out!"

Cheshire

Káta stepped out of the widower Brunstan's dwelling. She sniffed, and smelled the subtle change in the air that signalled the beginning of the end of the summer. The harvest was due in, and there was enough of a cool breeze in the evenings to warrant the wearing of a light cloak. She turned at the sound of footsteps as young Haward clattered over the footbridge.

"My lady, thank God I have found you," he said. He leaned over and looked down at the ground while he caught his breath.

"What is it? Is your sister unwell again?"

"No, beyond the ridge… The men are coming home"

Káta felt her shoulders lift. "Oh thank God. I will run back and tell Leofsige."

He touched her arm. "No, my lady. There are wounded among the men; it is not food they need, but your leech-worts."

"My leaves and herbs are at Hild's house."

"Yes, my lady."

She put her fingers to her temple. "Are her sons among the wounded?"

"No, my lady, I saw them walking with the others. Shall I fetch your things and bring them to you?"

"Yes. Yes, thank you."

Káta lifted her skirts, urgency compelling her to run out

of the little valley, but fear slowing her steps back to her own manor. The resulting hurried walk pounded her shins. The path-side brambles scratched at her ankles, but she put the pain away, to suffer later. At Ashleigh, she shouted to those in and around the hall. "Look lively, stir yourselves. The men are coming home."

Gytha put down her besom and walked towards the doorway. "When?"

Káta glanced over her shoulder at the gate. "Now."

They came in at the speed of the slowest man's walk; even those who were unscathed and on horseback moved at a weary pace. Káta and Gytha scanned them all and went to those who at first glance seemed most in need of help. One of the horses had been pulling a litter, and Káta went to tend the man who was lying on it. She dropped to her knees, lifted back the blankets of fur, and saw the closed-eyed face of her husband.

Helmstan, roused by her gasp, spoke in a drowsy whisper. "Do not be worrying about me, Wife. It is but a wounded foot, swollen too sore to let me ride." The corners of his mouth lifted a little. "My lord Alvar is glad to tell all who ask, that a Welsh arrow struck me whilst I was fleeing."

Her shoulders relaxed and she smiled. Then she pursed her lips, stood up, and folded her arms. "And where is the man who led you into this?"

"Thank you for worrying, but I merely have a slight sword wound to the shoulder. It only broke the flesh and is not deep."

She looked up at Alvar. He smiled, but blinked with slow-moving lids. He had one hand on the reins and the other arm in a makeshift sling fashioned from a linen undershirt. It was darkly stained with blood.

Káta's mouth was dry. Her head thumped from the ache of anxiety, and her stomach, tied in knots of fear since she first heard that there were wounded amongst the men, now gurgled to remind her that she had not eaten all day.

"Gytha, which of these halfwits should I see to first? The

earl is hurt the worst, but during a game of his own making. My lord husband is not so badly wounded, but did not bring it upon himself; he merely followed his lord."

A few of the men sniggered.

Gytha said, "Your lord needs to be taken to his bed and a bolster put under his foot. *His* lord needs a new binding for his wound, and some chicken broth with marrow and melted butter."

Káta turned round to the men and smiled. "Yes, laugh, for you are home, and you are alive. You are blessed, be glad. Leave your swords and spears." Young Haward had arrived with her medicine stores and she set him to work collecting all the weapons. "Send the swords to the smith for sharpening and ask him to put new hafts on the spears. Then find what you can in the bake-house to fill your belly." She smiled. "By way of thanks for your help."

The sun had almost set and they shepherded the men into the hall to warm by the fire. Two thegns helped Káta settle Helmstan into his bed and she inspected his wound.

He sat up on his elbows. "I must go to the hall. There are deeds that I must speak of and there must be a gift-giving. These men fought well…"

Káta pushed him down flat again. "You will bide in your bed for a week, otherwise sitting on a gift-stool is all you will be strong enough to do for the next year." She put aside all notions of restful sleep. "I am the one who must be in the hall." She planted a hurried kiss upon his brow and went back to the hall.

Someone must have helped Alvar from his horse, for she found him already seated on one of the cushioned benches.

"Gytha, can you bring me a candle-staff?" She picked up a chair and sat down in front of him. "I made light of your wound. Is it sore?"

"It smarts, but only like a bee sting. It will be but another scar soon enough, to go with all my others."

She cast her gaze downward, reminded of her comment years before, when she had compared childbirth to sword wounds, and hoping that he would not offer to show her any of these other scars, but he seemed bent on behaving himself and no lewd comment came forth. Small wonder, for by the time Gytha placed the candlestick on the table, Alvar's head had slumped forward and he was fast asleep.

"When I sat up all night and watched you sleeping, it was so that I could see to your needs after you were wounded. I did not think to have my kindness repaid in this way. For days now you have... Will you hand me the shears?" She cut the thread and put the scissors on the ground. "My lord, you sat while Gytha and I swept the floor and put down new straw, then you followed me when I went to fetch the loaves and even tried to help me with your one good arm. Have you never seen a woman sewing before? Even now I feel you staring at me as I stitch."

"Like a cat looks upon a mouse?"

She rested her mending on her lap and looked up. "No, it puts me more in mind of... I had a gosling once, which hatched out and took me for its mother. It, too, followed me all about."

He sat still on his stool, his good arm raised to shield his eyes from the sunshine, but despite his efforts, the grey eyes squinted as he looked at her. He said nothing, but a smile twitched his lips.

She made a few more stitches and said, "You were never so keen to keep near to me before."

"I was never so near to death before."

"Forgive me for laughing, but did you not say it was but a bee sting?" She stabbed at the cloth with her needle. "Well then, I will speak while you listen. I have no tales, but I believe that the scop has been sent for to proclaim the boldness of young Lyfing. My lord will call him first up to the gift-stool to reward him for his fearlessness. Is it true, then, that he stood in death's way that my husband might live?" She pulled another stitch through the cloth. "This linen is unsmooth. My husband needs new... My lord, is it true, that Lyfing…" She looked up, but he had gone.

Káta tutted, made a few more stitches and sighed.

Gytha walked by with her arms wrapped around a cluster of logs. She slowed, but did not stop. "What is wrong, Lady?"

As Gytha walked on, Káta said, "I spoke as if I thought him a blain, always with me. But now he has wandered away and it feels more like a butterfly has flown off."

She left her mending on the stool and looked about outside, but concluded that he was busy elsewhere and would find her if he chose to. With the household still swollen with the men not fit yet to go home, she needed to be in consultation with Leofsige more frequently, and went to the kitchen to discuss the day's meals with him. The cook-house was always warm and Káta was glad not to have bothered with a veil that morning. A tall figure stood by the table and she called out as she stepped inside the dark building.

"Leofsige? Did you hear me?" It took a few seconds to see after the brightness of the outdoors. It was Alvar, not Leofsige, who was standing beside the table, gnawing on a lump of bread. She paused with one foot forward, her upper body turned ready for retreat. "You do not have to fetch your own food, my lord. Speak out at any time, and my folk will bring whatever you crave."

"I thought that eating would take my mind off this." He pointed to his wound. "It itches." He stuffed the last of the bread into his mouth.

"You must keep using the cleansing salve that I gave you, at least until the whole wound has scabbed. It is a shame that we have no shellfish in the summer, for that would make your blood good again. Leofsige will bring you pease, honeyed and peppered. You must eat it all." Made braver by this demonstration of expertise, she took a deep breath and moved into the room. "I need to look over my healing things." She opened the communal herb box and pretended to count, before taking a key from her belt to open the lock on her spice store.

She checked the contents of the box and he chewed the last of the food. He took a sip of ale, but still looked at her even as he raised the cup to his lips.

"You have been staring at me for days now, my lord. If there is something you would do or say you are nearly too late, for my bed-ridden husband will soon be on his feet again."

"Nearly?"

She dropped the saffron onto the table and tried to scoop up the expensive strands. "I... I only meant that you have had the three days welcome that is owed to you in law. Not that we would not be glad to offer you a longer welcome; and the wounded, and our hall is yours for as long as…"

He took a step towards her and though her fingers shook, she managed to lock the spice box and return it to the side table. From there, she hoped to make her escape. She turned round. He was standing before her, his expression the same as on the day he had ridden out of the manor to Wales. He looked into her eyes and she could not turn her head.

She looked down. "My lord, I…"

He put his good arm on her shoulder, placed the wounded one on her waist, and bent to kiss her on her open mouth. He caught her bottom lip between his own lips and held it there for just one heartbeat.

He turned on his heel and walked outside.

She ran her finger along her lip and cursed her inability to tell indifference from passion. She had been taking only half-breaths, and now she snatched air into her lungs and held onto the table to steady herself. Her cheeks were hot so they must be red, and the shake in her hands would mark her out to anyone as an adulteress, so she stayed a while in the cook-house. She checked the stocks, looked to see which of the dried meats Leofsige had soaked ready to be cooked, and measured portions of dried beans and peas to be added to the pot. When at last she felt able to step outside, she took a few deep breaths, put a hand up to check that her hair was in place, and made her way back up to the hall.

Once, she had hinted that her feelings for him were more than they ought to be. But, rightly, he had not responded, and she thought that they had both forgotten about it. Yet now he had kissed her. Why? Wasn't it the queen whom he loved? Hadn't he said as much, down by the river that day? She touched her fingertips to her lips. She might at one time have thought of that kiss as a gift. What on earth was she supposed to do with such a gift now?

Her mending was still on the stool. The yard was empty save for a solitary chicken, until Leofsige came out of the hall frowning and carrying a large purse of coin.

Káta said, "Have you seen Lord Alvar?"

"Gone, my lady. He gave me this for the feeding of the wounded men, then he upped and left."

Chapter Twelve AD969

Winchester

The baby's squalls broke the silence once more and Alvar looked round the hall. Brock smiled, but others looked peeved. Alvar leaned forward to whisper to his brother. "If any man thinks ill of her bringing the bairns with her, he should look at the king and think again." He nodded towards Edgar, who smiled at Alfreda and received a half smile, half lip-licking invitation. "It is not hard to see why Edgar will give her aught she asks for."

Brock chuckled. "Nor is it hard to see why you keep staring over there."

"Where else is there to look? I am bored. Beorn is not here. I do not blame him though; Northumbria is a long way off and he is busy fighting the Scots. Apart from you, who is there to amuse me? Brandon is a dull fart and the Red Lord of Oxford is not red any more, but old and grey and speaks only of his aches and twinges. Bishop Athelwold is asleep," he looked behind him, "And I find I cannot look at Guthrum without staring, for I have seen thinner necks on a bull."

The Viking sailor, mercenary and proud of it, was standing against the wall, arms folded. Many were wary of the man who furnished Edgar with a fleet and yet who was tied to the king only by the money paid to him as a hireling.

Brock began a laugh that ended as a cough. "Yes, it is a little like having a bear to keep watch over your house; those within are almost as frightened as those without. I must say though, that like so many others, I should also give up the witan and sit at home by my hearth in my old age. I swear I have aches and twinges to match those of the Red Lord."

Alvar signalled for drinks. "That is not so, brother. You are young yet and…"

Oswald and Brandon were seated nearest the window, heads bent together. In the sunlight, Brandon's hair gleamed gold. He looked young next to Oswald, but he must be… Alvar counted the years. If Brandon was twenty-six, the same age as Edgar, then Alvar was… "Thirty-three. Can it be? And that makes you almost fifty."

"What?"

"Never mind, I was but reckoning out loud. Now, what do you think those two are speaking about?"

Brock shrugged. "From the way they keep sending black looks over here, I would say you have done something that they do not like."

Alvar waited for his brother's coughing fit to subside and said, "Naught new there, then. It seems I upset the East Anglians even whilst I sleep." He sat back. "Dear God in heaven, will this witenagemot ever be over and done with? Four days of laws and land-gifts and my legs are set fast, bent forever."

Brock's shoulders shook, but he kept his laugh in. "Go and wander, then, for they will be some time yet, I fear."

Up on the dais, the scribes were still bent into a huddle with Edgar and Dunstan. Alvar stared beyond them to the view through the window. The royal palace nestled between the old and new minsters, close to the ancient Roman town wall. He sniffed and wrinkled his nose, never at ease penned in behind the old fortifications of the empire. Monks swarmed like black ants on the busy route between the great hall and the bishop's palace, but aside from them and the occasional view of a guard out on the wall, there was nothing of interest to look at, the market stalls being all pitched to the northeast of the town. Alvar sighed and stood up. He eased his legs, rubbed his backside, and moved behind the fan of chairs spread in front of the dais. He walked over to the corner of the hall and bowed before the queen. He tickled the baby lying in her lap, and sat down. The child by her feet looked up at Alvar and smiled, and the earl scooped him onto his knee.

Alvar ruffled the boy's hair. The youngling was named after his grandfather, Edmund, but Alvar addressed him by his nickname. "Leof, I swear you grow heavier by the day." He turned his head to look at the queen. "You are well, lady?"

"Well enough, though I do not like this hall, with only one room off it. I have grown used to larger buildings, like the houses in London. However, the king keeps me rich in sundry tokens of his love, for here you see I have given him not one, but two athelings." She smiled proudly at her newborn son, before reaching across to the boy on Alvar's lap. "And this one so like his father."

Alvar bounced the four-year-old up and down on his lap and the golden curls bobbed as the child moved. "Sometimes they can be fair like the mother, not the father. Soon he will be asking to swim and be swung in the air." He swallowed hard. "God grant that…" He coughed. "God gift it that little Leof will be as strong a king as Lord Edgar has been," he said.

In the opposite corner, also behind the semi-circle of chairs, Prince Edward was sitting with Abbot Sideman, his tutor. While the abbot's head was bent low over a book, Edward began to tease a spider that was quivering in its web on the wall. Blowing gently on the silky fibres, he tempted the spider to shoot towards the vibrations, and pulled on its legs before letting it retreat so that he could torment it all over again.

"His very being is what stops me from letting these children far from my sight," Alfreda said.

"Edward is the king's eldest child, but there is no man here who would harbour thoughts of wrongdoing in his name. Your sons are the athelings, not him."

"No, you do not understand, my lord. I spoke of Edward himself. Only last week I found him gripping so tightly onto Leof's arm that he brought tears to my little son's eyes. But I think I know why he behaves so badly; it must have been hard for him, wrenched away from his mother." She stared off into the middle distance.

"Lady, I think your thoughts fly to your own sons, growing up so far away in East Anglia." Alvar knew that Alfreda had worked hard to get her older sons returned to her, but whilst she might have given up hope, she was probably ignorant of the reason for the continued separation. No doubt Edgar would have been charming in response to her requests but he was no fool; he would not welcome to his court the fully grown sons of his queen. Adults who could claim atheling status would be a threat to his kingship and certainly to that of Leof. He said, "You might be right. Edward might feel the loss of his mother as keenly as your own sons do, but a child can be sad without feeling the need to make others weep. From what I know of Edward, he is a bad-tempered youth who makes it hard for men to love him."

Alfreda said, "I think he craves what my new sons have. I think he would have the warmth of his mother."

"I think he is a little shit," Alvar said.

As if to prove the point for him, Edward chose that moment to complain to his tutor of boredom. The gentle Sideman explained that the benefits of watching the rudiments of statecraft would be visited upon him, "One hundred-fold when you become king."

"No. Will not listen." In a movement quick enough to confuse the eyes of witnesses, Edward brought his hand up and slapped the abbot across the face.

The king, in the centre of the semi-circle and with his back to that corner of the room, was still speaking to Dunstan and had not seen, but, looking over Edgar's shoulder,

Dunstan saw how many among the lords and officials stared, and then squirmed in their seats as Abbot Sideman now attempted to ease the boy from his sulk and persuade him to leave the room. The servants cowered against the walls, and Sideman had to hiss his whispers against the silence.

Dunstan watched as Lord Alvar handed the atheling Leof back to his mother, and made his way over to Edward. He placed a hand on Sideman's shoulder and then spoke to the boy in such low tones that it was impossible for him to be overheard, but when he had finished Edward stood up and left the room without saying another word.

Alvar sat back down next to his brother, Lord Brock. Dunstan, released from the king's attention, took a moment to study the lord of Mercia, and wondered whether he should adjust his opinion of the man he had long since condemned as self-serving and amoral. The quiet efficiency with which he had quelled the disturbance was admirable in itself, but Alvar had eschewed to inform the king, thus denying himself both the opportunity to earn any plaudits for calming the disturbance and to point out the obnoxious behaviour of a child of whose very existence, by his own admission, he thoroughly disapproved.

The scribe nearest to Edgar cleared his throat and prepared to read out the details of the next document, and Dunstan noted the boredom displayed by the warrior earl now that he was forced to sit still and listen once more. Lord Alvar flicked his middle finger against his arm ring, creating a clinking sound, which alerted the good bishop of Worcester.

Bishop Oswald leaned forward and said, "Does it all take too long, my lord of Mercia? Such a shame, that we must wait while it is written. This is bad enough, but then it must be read aloud two times, for those who do not understand the Latin."

Lord Alvar looked at Oswald from under raised eyebrows. "What need have we for the Latin? The true gift is when the turf is cut and handed over to the man by his lord. How many Romans do you see at this witenagemot, lord Bishop? I see Saxons, Angles, Mercian Danes, I see Norsemen. I can speak to them all and they understand me."

Dunstan sniffed. A few more learned Europeans and a few less uncultured northerners would be more to his liking. At least the barbarian Northumbrians had had the good grace to stay away from this moot.

Brandon, seated to Oswald's right, smoothed his hair and said, "My lord Bishop has lent me one or two books. I read them in the Latin, for I do have the book-craft."

They all looked at Alvar, who appeared unimpressed. "My lords, had I the time to spare to read books, I would not waste it by reading books."

They nodded and smiled, and Oswald turned to Dunstan and mouthed the word, "Oaf."

Dunstan, aware above all of the dignity of his position, only felt able to acknowledge the comment with a slight nod.

The scribe read the details of the land grant. "Given this day to Ælfwold, ten hides at Kineton, Warwickshire…"

Lord Alvar sat back and folded his arms.

The scribe continued. "Sit autem praedictum rus omni terrenae servitutis jugo liberum tribus exceptis rata videlicet expeditione pontis…"

Oswald opened his mouth.

Alvar said, "Yes, thank you, but if I did not know that such land comes free for a lifetime with naught owed but the upkeep of bridges and the rebuilding of walls and earthworks, I would be a sorry sight for an earl, would I not?"

Oswald shut his mouth.

Dunstan found himself wondering for the second time whether it wasn't time to revise his assessment of this bone-headed soldier.

The scribe finished in English. "These are the edges of

the land: from Wellesbourne to the furrow, from the furrow to the ditch, from the ditch on the edge to the made road, from the made road to the foul pit, from the foul pit to the springs, from the springs to the edge of Mercia, from the edge of Mercia to Grundlinga-brook, along the stream, from that stream to Fidestan…"

Now Lord Alvar looked like the fox that got the chicken. No wonder; Dunstan knew from his days as bishop of Worcester that the edge of Mercia to which the charter referred was that of the boundary between old Mercia and the land of the Hwicce. He had always counselled Edgar to express his gratitude of the peoples who helped him to gain his throne, but, in acknowledging their ancient borderlines, did the king need continuously to feed the Mercians' self-importance?

In only a few more seconds, the witan resumed its business. Dunstan felt the tension leaving his hunched shoulders. This was church business, and, as such, far less vexatious.

A scribe nudged the sleeping Bishop Athelwold, who snorted, pressed the knuckle of his forefinger into his eyelid and rubbed hard. He stood up and introduced his new treatise. Dunstan smiled. The bishop had been working on his *Regularis Concordia* for some time, worried, as all the reformers were, that some monasteries were embracing the rule of St Benedict less quickly than others. Athelwold eloquently outlined the need for uniformity, and announced the new rules, which decreed that all bishops would live with the monks, that all churchmen would forgo the right to write a will, and Dunstan nodded as each point was declared. But he sat forward as swiftly as if he had been thrown out of his chair when Athelwold presented a bound volume of his new monastic laws to the king's wife, and informed her that the complete work was dedicated to her. Dunstan concentrated on the emerald on his ring, polishing it vigorously with his thumb. His sanguine mood was fading away, to be replaced by the familiar irritation that the wrong people, secular people, immoral people, were benefiting from Edgar's reign.

He turned his head at the sound from beyond the door.

A man was shouting and there was a scuffle outside in the antechamber. More shouting followed and the door banged open. A king's thegn rushed in, but kept his hand on the open door, jerking to a standstill when his arm extended back fully. "Lord King, Sigehelm of York is here and says he must speak to you forthwith. I told him that he should not..."

The king said, "Bid him come to me. I will hear him."

The thegn stepped back into the corridor and pulled the door half shut. After a few muttered words Sigehelm of York hurried into the chamber and bowed low before Edgar.

"Lord King, I bring grim tidings. Some men from York rode many miles to the town of Thanet, with naught on their minds but to sell their wares and make a fair penny. Little did they know what would betide them there." Sigehelm stared around the room through rapid blinks as if realising for the first time that the hall was full of nobles.

Dunstan said, "Get on then, man, and tell us. W-what did betide them there at Thanet?"

"The men were set upon my lord, badly beaten, their goods stolen and their gold, too. I have seen their wounds with my own eyes, and have brought with me twelve men who will swear an oath that I speak the truth."

Edgar's nostrils twitched. He put a hand on Dunstan's and beckoned Lord Alvar to join them in a huddle by the dais. He did not frown, and his voice stayed at its normal pitch, but his speech came sibilant through a jaw held tighter than usual. "We cannot let this lawlessness stand. Townsfolk and craftsmen do not have hearth-fellows or thegns. I am their lord, for they have no other. I will deal with this wickedness in such a way that no man will ever think to do another such foul deed. I will have it known that all men are free to ride in my land without fear, be they Englishmen or

Danes. What say you, my lords?"

Dunstan looked across at his friend Oswald. It was never good news when Englishmen displayed their dislike of any men they deemed foreigners. He nodded and said, "I will go to the bishop's house and hear the sworn oaths of the twelve witnesses, my lord, although I know in my heart that this man Sigehelm speaks the truth. It must be d-dealt with, as you say."

Edgar nodded. Without turning his head he said, "Lord Alvar, I would hear your thoughts."

"These men of York were about lawful business and their robbers laugh at you, my lord. No man must ever think that he can do such evil and not be brought to answer for it. This law-breaking must be dealt with swiftly."

Edgar nodded. His brow remained un-furrowed but a bead of sweat hovered there. "I knew that we would all be as one on this."

Dunstan felt his mouth wrinkling as his teeth clenched. God forgive him but his pride bristled when Edgar spoke as if he and the earl were apples from the same tree.

Edgar put his hand on Dunstan's arm. "Dear friend, I know that I can leave the kingdom in your hands while I ride to deal with this."

The compliment pushed Dunstan's shoulders back and brought him up to stand tall. But he slumped almost as quickly when Edgar's words echoed in his head and this time, he listened to them properly. An archbishop ruling in the king's stead might wield power for a short while, but the glory would fall on those who showed impressive martial strength. The upstart must not ride with Edgar. "Lord King, Guthrum the seaman takes plenty of your gold. Is it not time that he earned it? If you go to the aid of Norsemen with a Norse fleet, you will prove how mindful you are of your debt to the northerners."

Edgar nodded and strode off towards Guthrum. The leader of the mercenary fleet nodded while Edgar spoke, but one foot began inching forward immediately and he was ready to stride away as soon as the king had finished talking.

Bishop Oswald leaned nearer. He smiled at the archbishop and said, "So Edgar is sending Guthrum to Thanet. Not the lords of Wessex, or Mercia, but the Norseman. He sends ships, not the fyrd. Did the lord Alvar hurt himself when he tripped over his pride?"

Lord Alvar revealed his coarse nature with his answer. Grinding his fist into the palm of his other hand he said, "Bishop, I will not speak my thoughts; it would only show me to be the swearer of foul oaths that you already think I am."

The bishop laughed and smiled at Dunstan once more.

Lord Alvar breathed in through his nose so hard that his nostrils flared. "But do not worry, Bishop Oswald, for one day I will twist your smirk like a rock bends a ploughshare." He sat back and worried away at a loose piece of skin by his fingernail.

Dunstan laid a calming hand on Oswald's arm. It was clear that Alvar was agitated by Edgar's decision to leave him behind. With Edgar away and Dunstan left in charge, Alvar would be isolated. And so would the king's wife.

There was a loud snorting noise and the Red Lord's head, grey and bent and fragile, rolled forward and jerked up again.

Edgar strode back to the dais, rubbing his hands. "Guthrum has gone to make ready, so we must not be far behind. Alvar, get your men from all over Mercia; we will go in with so many weapon-men that they will rue the day. Oh yes, and when we get back, I will gift the Red Lord's lands to you. He grows old and tired. He has told me himself that he has the bladder weakness that always leads to sickness in an older man."

Dunstan heard a strange, high-pitched squeak and knew that it had emanated from Lord Brandon. He noticed that Lord Alvar wasted no time, even forgetting to bow to his king before he ran out of the hall.

Men began to stand, scraping their chairs back while

discussing the day's events as they filed out of the hall to relieve themselves before the feast. Servants came into the hall to drag trestle tables from the walls and set them up, and kitchen-hands walked through with plates of bread and jugs of ale and wine.

Brandon came to stand next to Dunstan and the older man sensed that he was shaking. Brandon addressed Edgar. "Lord King, if you have a moment before you leave?"

Edgar looked at his wife and then at the door to his private chamber. "I was thinking that I might…"

Brandon spoke at the same time. "It will not take long." He, too, glanced at the queen and was rewarded with an icy glare. He swallowed and his Adam's apple bobbed. "Lord King, Foster-brother, it was always my hope that the Red Lord's lands would come back to my…"

Alfreda placed a hand on her husband's shoulder and moved her thumb in a circle of massage. She whispered close to his ear and then smiled and looked down at the floor, where she moved her foot from side to side and let it brush Edgar's shoe. Her actions were so redolent of another king's wife, an evil influence, that Dunstan found the name Jezebel whirling round his brain like a taunting sing-song.

"Yes, my love, you are right." Edgar lifted her hand and kissed it. "I will speak to the bishop about Peterborough." He said to Brandon, "My lord…"

Dunstan noted that he did not reciprocate and call him his brother.

"My wife spoke earlier to our friend Bishop Athelwold, who wishes to rebuild the abbey at Peterborough. She has reminded me that you would be thankful indeed at the thought of another great abbey growing strong in East Anglia." He stared at Brandon for a moment. "It is a great gift, is it not?"

Brandon made another peculiar noise.

Edgar said to Alfreda, "Shall we go now my love? Can a woman be brought for the children for a time? I will need to leave soon."

In the opulence of Bishop Athelwold's palace Dunstan felt comfortable. If ever he could not be at Canterbury, then Winchester was an acceptable substitute. Fine wine in ornate gold flagons had been left for them on tables covered with decorated linen cloths. The chair cushions were soft, with smooth coverings that were a salve to his aching legs. But no amount of luxury or bodily comfort could soothe their fractious spirits this day. He and Oswald silently sipped their wine and Dunstan knew that Oswald was seething just as much as he. Alvar had the Devil's own luck and Dunstan needed to pray strongly if he were going to find a way to bring him down and remove this block to the Lord's work.

Oswald put his cup down on the table, where its base sat precisely over one of the flowers on the patterned cloth. He dabbed at his lips with a napkin and placed it, neatly folded, back on the table. "If one wishes to hurt a man, then one must find what it is that he truly cherishes. Only two things matter to Alvar: his land, and his lineage."

"Go on."

"There is an abbey in my diocese. Evesham is in need of reform. It sits on land held by Lord Alvar that was once held by his great and hallowed father. It would not be much trouble for me to find a way to argue that the land was stolen by his father and that it should come back to the Church."

Dunstan took another sip of wine and swirled it round his mouth before swallowing. It warmed his throat briefly before slipping down his gullet. He remembered Alvar's father. The family power base was southwest Mercia, the former kingdom of the Hwicce in the diocese of Worcester. In one deft manoeuvre, Oswald could weaken Alvar's power base, deprive the earl of prized revenue, and tarnish the name of his esteemed father by branding him a thief. Oh yes, that should hit the over-mighty lord where it hurt most.

Dunstan broke a long-standing habit and reached to pour his own wine. "Another drink, Bishop?"

Chapter Thirteen AD972

Shrewsbury

He glanced at Brock's chair. He looked at the new steward. He gazed at the table where Brock and he had sat with Beorn of Northumbria last month, the day before Beorn travelled northward to resume his tussle with the Scots. Again, he looked at Brock's seat. If he were a man who ever thought he could be wrong, he would have listened to his brother's complaints of aches and pains. Now the empty chair no longer groaned under Brock's barrel-weight, the man was in his grave, and all joy had gone from Alvar's life.

Helmstan leaned in towards his lord and said, "I see where your eyes wander. It is hard for you to be in this meeting room without him, I know."

Alvar stared out across the meeting chamber, nodded once, but could not speak.

Helmstan said, "How is Lady Alswytha?"

Alvar swallowed hard and tested his voice with a forced cough. "Swytha is a rich widow, for she held land in her own right, too. But she was wed to the man for thirty years and they loved each other well." He cleared his throat again. "I held her while her tears fell, and I held her as she told me that she could not weep hard enough to get out the sorrow from inside. I thought that she would break from the sadness, and I did not know if I had the strength left in my arms to hold her if she did." His voice cracked on the last word and he coughed and repeated it. "Did."

Wulfgar, seated to Alvar's left, said, "And barely was the burial over than the monk from Evesham came."

Helmstan leaned forward to see past Alvar. "Evesham? Why?"

"The monk came to tell our lord that the abbey was to be rebuilt; that they were taking back the lands which his father stole and that our lord was now keeping unlawfully."

Helmstan exhaled with a whistle. "Truly, my lord, they did this?"

Alvar looked straight ahead. "I read their page of dross and threw it into the fire. I was in no mood to… And yet…" Only afterwards had the thought come; so many loose threads that, of a sudden, could be caught in his mind and made into a rope: no sooner had he knelt to receive the Red Lord's lands in Oxfordshire and Buckinghamshire than word came from Evesham. All of the secular monks put out, and Alvar's father declared a petty thief on the very day Brock was laid in the ground.

"And yet, my lord?"

"I think that there are those who sought to kick me at a time when most it would wound."

On the other side of the room, Oswald and Brandon leaned in with symmetry and spoke in low whispers. Oswald's parchment face barely moved, but Brandon nodded at the older man's every word.

Wulfgar said, "And you must have been hoping to see the back of Oswald, now that he has become archbishop of York."

Who could forget the tales which had filtered back from the continent, of Oswald's majestic progress to Rome? One of Brock's last worries as steward was establishing who was responsible for his lavish spending on his slow journey to the pope.

Alvar snorted a laugh. "Yes. I thought I was rid of him. I even teased Beorn about it, telling him that from now on he would be the one to feel Oswald's breath on his neck, while the old crow filled York minster with his kin. Little did I know."

Helmstan said, "I did think it was not lawful, to be both a bishop and an archbishop at once?"

"Maybe he could not bear to leave me?" Alvar smiled and shook his head. "No, it is not lawful. All of us believed, rightly, that in order to go to York he would have to leave Worcester behind. This is church law. And I found myself once again thinking how some men can bend the shape of their beliefs to fit their wishes. But at least I know why Edgar let Oswald become archbishop at York."

Wulfgar leaned across the table, picked up the jug and splashed ale into their three cups. "Go on, my lord."

"Firstly, he had given more land to me and did not want to tip the scales too far on one side. Secondly, the archbishops of York have long been a law unto themselves. This way, Edgar can bind York to the south whilst keeping an eye on Northumbria. It is but another show of his strength within his kingdom."

Wulfgar drained his cup. "Earl Beorn will not like it."

Alvar gripped his ale cup, but he had yet to lift it to his lips. "Our lord King always gives with one hand as he takes with the other. Beorn's bitter brew will be sweetened by the new law. As one of three leading earls in the land, his standing in the north is at least the same as Oswald's."

Helmstan said, "I nod to Edgar's wisdom. He now has two men in the north who have ties to him and to the south. They will watch the northerners and each other. Beorn's heightened standing will mean that he is mightier than ever and it should, as you say, sweeten the stink a little as the bishop breathes his stench all over York."

Alvar's cheek twitched. "That might be so, but Oswald still tramples all over Worcester. I am not rid of him either."

"You can come to Cheshire any time you like, my lord, where we will not speak his name."

"Does Wulfgar not work hard when I send him?" Alvar raised his cup, but it slid through his hand. He put it down and wiped his palm on his breeches.

"Yes, my lord. We work well together." Helmstan exchanged a glance with Wulfgar. "It is only that you seldom come yourself now."

"I am needed near Worcester. Riding to Cheshire takes time that I can no longer spare. I am not a man now who has time to play." Alvar stared ahead, but on either side of him he was aware of the shrugs and raised eyebrows.

The general hum of lowered voices faded away, as awareness grew that the king was ready to reconvene the meeting.

Edgar looked round the room and smiled at each of his councillors, before his gaze settled on Bishop Athelwold. "Now we will have written down the gift to our beloved Bishop Athelwold of the aforesaid land at Barrow-on-Humber, this to be given to help to build up the abbey at Peterborough."

Brandon squirmed in his seat and bobbed up and down.

"My lord of East Anglia, you would speak?"

Brandon ran a hand through his hair and smiled at the gathering. "I would let it be known that I am following your lead, lord King. As you have given land to Bishop Athelwold to help Peterborough, so I will give land. My house is at Upwood, so I have no need of my father's lands at Ramsey. The house, the land, all of it, is henceforth gifted to the archbishop of York, where he can begin to build an abbey."

Wulfgar hissed. "Oswald in the fenland? My lord, they cannot."

Helmstan said, "It might be only sodden marshland, but it was always Mercian, and many folk who live there still think of themselves of Mercian. And besides, Oswald's reach is spreading far too far."

Alvar said, "I know." He put his hands on the table with a thump. "My lord King, after Peterborough, this is one step too many."

Edgar sat motionless in his chair. With pointed reference to Alvar's new title, he said, "Is it, my lord of middle

Wessex?"

Our lord King always gives with one hand as he takes with the other. Alvar could only smile wryly as he recalled the conversation that morning, when Edgar told him that he had shown '*Kindness beyond reckoning in looking after the widow we know as Swytha. You have overseen Brock's lands since his death, and now I gift those lands to you.*'

Alvar filled his lungs and held his breath. He exhaled in a slow, controlled, silent whistle. He had let himself believe that Mid-Wessex was the sweetener against Oswald's continued presence at Worcester, perhaps even Edgar's acknowledgement that Evesham was a crime scene. But Ramsey? This was moving the fight to a new field.

Oswald stood up and went to speak to the scribes. They waved their arms in a flurry of black sleeves and pen feathers.

Helmstan spoke out of the side of his mouth. "They do not understand. Ramsey is in the fenland that once belonged to Danish Mercia. It should come to you, my lord."

If it was even within Brandon's gift, being in disputed territory. Alvar said, "Oh, they understand. Believe that, if you believe naught else in your time on earth."

Edgar leaned forward while Dunstan spoke. He nodded, and sat back.

Dunstan stood up to address the council. Sixty-two now, he stood less steadily and kept one hand always on the table, but his back remained straight and he held his head erect. "My lords, we of the Church can only give thanks that our most righteous and God-fearing king and his wom..." He coughed and his jowls wobbled. "And his queen, help us to grow strong. Who among us d-does not also long for a mark of a strong England? Truly, I say to you all..."

Wulfgar said, "Look over there; I would dearly like to take Oswald's smirk and shove it up his arse."

Alvar said, "You will have to get behind me and wait your turn. God forgive me but I see this not as their gift to God but their threat to me. Bishop Athelwold barely misses stepping on my toes on his way to Peterborough, but Oswald takes a knife and sticks it deep into my gut while he cuts the grass at Ramsey."

He stood up to push his chair back. He looked around the room, sighed and sat back down. "Stamp my feet and tell my woes. But to whom?"

Wulfgar touched his arm. "My lord?"

"Brock is dead and Swytha has taken herself off to a nunnery. Even if Beorn were here he would goad me into a fight before he would lead me out of one." He looked at Helmstan. "And the only other…"

Helmstan raised his head. "Yes my lord?"

And the only other one who would soothe him was forbidden to him, for he had crossed a line that would see him in hell. "Naught." He clicked his fingers at a serving-boy. "We will have drinks here. Wulfgar, you must remember that as one of my leading thegns you do not have to fetch your own ale now." He rested his legs on the empty seat opposite. Edgar was right; this morning he took his seat as lord of all Mercia, from Cheshire to Worcestershire, and as lord of Oxfordshire, Buckinghamshire and Mid-Wessex. He should rest at that and be glad. He raised his cup and drank a silent toast to all those who had once gathered there. He caught the queen's gaze. "There sits another who has little bliss in her heart."

Helmstan said, "It was hard for her to lose her beloved Leof, and I would wish that fever on no-one, never mind a little child, but do you see how she now behaves with the other atheling?"

The queen was sitting with her ladies and had her youngest son, Æthelred, on her lap. He wailed and squirmed, but Alfreda held him clamped.

"When my Siferth was barely more than a cradle-child he would find many things to do that need little thought but a lot of daring. Æthelred is nearly three; he should be off his mother's knee."

Alvar slapped Helmstan on the back, harder than he

meant to. "Forgive me my friend, but you must know how dull it can be for childless men to listen to such tales."

He stood up and did not answer when Helmstan said, "Then why do you go to the queen…"

As he approached, Alfreda gave Alvar an empty smile and moved along the bench to make room for him. He sat down and fiddled with his garnet ring. He was tempted to pick the child up, but he knew that where once he could have scooped Leof onto his lap, he must leave Æthelred with his mother, for the boy would tolerate no other.

"He misses his godfather Brock," she said.

"You are kind to speak of my loss before your own. We all miss my brother," he said, "As you and yours grieve for Leof." He touched her cheek. "So soon after your father's death, it was an unkind blow."

Alfreda allowed her tears to fall. She fingered her necklace. "I am now to be known as the lady of all nuns and worship must be said in my name, yet death stalks us all, and prayer is no shield against loss."

Alvar stared at the necklace, a circle of coloured glass beads in groups of three, separated by gold triangles, set with garnets. At the centre of the circlet hung a gold round, engraved with animal symbols and set with blue glass. There was nothing wrong with displaying the trappings of wealth, certainly no bishop he knew ever dressed shabbily, but there was something about the look of the queen that sat incongruously with her new title as defender of nuns, and at odds with her mourning. It was as if she had become so used to the potency of her feminine allure that she no longer knew when best to display it and when to minimise it.

"I had heard that Athelwold's book named you thus. But I will not lie and say that I will ever find time to read his work."

"It seems there is never enough time…" She controlled a sob, but could not continue.

He reached forward and placed his hand on her knee. "My lady, I cannot give the answers you seek, for only God can do that. But as winter comes near, summer will always follow and you must look to the living; your son needs his mother, and your king needs his queen. And you are not friendless."

She squeezed his hand and the boy on her lap said, "No. *My* muv-muv."

She said, "You are a true and kind man, my lord."

He sat back and smiled. "Do not tell my foes, for were we all to become friends, what a salt-less meal life would become."

"Your foes are my foes," she said. "Do not forget that Brandon stood by and did nothing while I was broken by his brother's hands. Oswald and Dunstan have no love for women, for are we not but weak sinners? Of the churchmen, only Athelwold has been kind to me. And yet Edgar loves us all, whichever side we stand. I am closer to him than any and even I do not understand how he does it."

Alvar lifted one side of his mouth into half a smile and puffed air through his nostrils. "I could tell you, but there is a bitter feel in my mouth this day, and my words might be soured from it. Let me say this; that he gives us all a reason to love him and he deals, mostly, with even hands. Yet not all are in thrall to him. Our neighbours to the west and north…"

The queen touched his arm with her free hand. "Oh yes, this is something of which I had half heard. My lord, will you tell me? My husband came to our bed last night in a sore temper and I could not lift his mood."

He said, "I do not know if anyone can. In Wales, the sons of Idwal are still fighting each other. One of them is now king of Gwynedd and is a mean, dark little man with many foes. He holds one of his brothers in a cell, which I hear has not pleased his nephew. And last year, the king of the Isles, whose name is Maccus, harried Gwynedd and now his brother, Gothfrith, has done the same."

"But why would the Welsh with all their fighting make Edgar so wroth?"

Alvar shook his head. Edgar was indignant that any man would dare fight so close to English lands, and had spoken to Alvar of his desire to broker peace in return for gratitude, or even servitude, from these neighbouring lands. But it was the effrontery of the Scots which had turned the king's mood sour. "It is not only the Welsh that vex him, though they do not help. In Scotland, the son of the king of Strathclyde has killed the king of Alba, which is nobody's business but their own, but…"

"Yes?" She shifted the wriggling Æthelred from one knee to the other, but the child would not be appeased, and whined until she lifted him up so that he could stand on her knees. He bent his legs and bounced up and down until she winced.

"But there is a man, Kenneth, who is kin to the slain king of Alba. He moved in when both kingdoms were weakened by the fighting and now claims to be king of both Alba and Strathclyde. He thinks this makes him mighty enough to have some of Northumbria to boot." He forbore to mention that Kenneth had also taken the son of Beorn's deputy as a hostage. The queen had burdens enough, without learning of yet another displaced son.

"And Northumbria belongs to Edgar. Little wonder, then, that my husband would not be soothed last night. I began to think that he no longer finds me fair."

"Lady, only madness or a sickness of the soul would keep a man from craving you."

Her hand went to her veil. She forced the child to sit back down on her lap, and sat upright. She smoothed her dress over the curve of her bosom. "I thank you for your kind words, my lord."

"I speak the truth; that is all." He looked over his shoulder. "I must go back. Edgar will not let these things rest and we have much to speak about."

"Ah, has this something to do with Dunstan's great show; a second king-making? Can such a thing be done, do you think?"

He grinned and said, "Edgar wills it, Dunstan craves it, and I say let it be done. Therefore, it will, indeed, be done."

He slapped his hand down on her knee and the child Æthelred's lips quivered.

"Lady, let me not be guilty of the sin of pride, but Dunstan's show will be merely the gilding of the hilt. It is I who will put the edge on the blade." He glanced back at Oswald's carrion flock. "And it will be keen enough to shear any black feathers and stop their flight."

She tilted her head to one side. "Oh, yes? I feel there is more to this tale than you are willing to give me."

Dunstan's sermon was over, and several lords stood up to stretch their legs. Husbands came to talk to their wives, and Alvar winked at Alfreda.

He stood up and shoved his thumbs under his belt. He raised his voice and said, "If you want to see real strength, lady, look not to the west with Dunstan next Pentecost, but let your eyes follow me to the north."

Chapter Fourteen AD973

Bath

The sun shone in a cloudless sky and cast beams of radiance through the window lights. Dunstan smiled with satisfaction; God had blessed the day. The archbishop breathed in deeply, joyful to be in this place. The abbey, rebuilt by King Offa, had been the only thing about which he and the debauched late king had agreed; the Fairchild had told Dunstan that the abbey church was marvellously built. Now, the community was being reorganised by a devout anchorite who had been busy transforming it into a strict Benedictine chapter, and Dunstan was elated. On his way to the abbey, the archbishop had stopped briefly to marvel at the ruins of the Roman baths. The magnificent upright columns were all that was left of the building though the springs remained. He knew that many of his countrymen still shied away from the place. He was scornful of such superstition, passed on through the generations from ignorant pagan Saxon invaders who had come from the old country and been frightened beyond rational explanation by the towering walls and stone buildings, so alien to their culture but so representative of the aspirations of the Roman Empire. Empire. He liked the concept. Edgar had been negotiating and threatening in order to coerce all the kings of neighbouring lands to stop fighting each other and bow to his higher authority, and what better way to symbolise that than to stage this coronation? Edgar's first had been a rushed affair, not nearly public enough, and Dunstan was determined that this time the folk would witness a spectacle. He would give the scribes something to fill the pages of their chronicle, the history of their people which had been begun on the orders of that other great king, Alfred.

Edgar looked at once magnificent and humble dressed in his alb, a simple white gown. Dunstan nodded approvingly, glad that he had persuaded the youngster to adopt the clothing of the newly baptised at Whitsun, for was this not a form of initiation, or rebirth? Edgar's blond curls, lively as ever, softened his face, which was not so boyish now, lined as it was from his habit of bringing his eyebrows closer together whenever he was concentrating. And he was indeed no longer a boy but a man, thirty years old. This fact also pleased Dunstan, who delighted in the coincidence that he was placing the crown of the empire on the head of a king who was the same age as a clergyman must be ere he acceded to a bishopric. From either side came the sweet sound of the boys singing the psalms, and every now and again, a fresh waft of fragrance would billow across from where the archdeacon stood, swinging the incense holder. The crowd stood in ecstatic silence, smiling blissfully. Dunstan's spirit was almost replete.

The only irritation, like a bur caught in his sandal, was the sight of the king's wife and her bastard child. The woman had dressed herself in homespun, but Dunstan was sure, even with his limited knowledge of women, that her cheeks were unnaturally pink, and he was certain it was no accident that there was just enough hair on show beneath her veil that no man could be in any doubt as to her dark-haired beauty.

He breathed in deeply, listened for a moment to the mellifluous voices, and offered up one more silent prayer of thanks. The presence of that woman would not distract him from his task. Edgar might have dubious taste in women, but his devotion to the Church and the cause was unquestionable. This ceremony would mean as much to him as it did to Dunstan.

Now it was time for the oath. Dunstan had searched the scriptures and drawn inspiration from the anointing of Saul and David by Samuel. He had written the oath for Edgar and, although the king would swear it in Latin, Dunstan would ensure that all men who mattered would know the nature of Edgar's promise: first, that the Church of God and the whole Christian people should have true peace at all time by Edgar's judgement; second, that he would forbid extortion of all kind and wrongdoing to all orders of men; third, that he would enjoin equity and mercy in all judgements.

He anointed the beloved head with the holy oil, chanted the Latin as he put the crown firmly in place, and led Edgar to his throne. He turned, ready to deliver his sermon. The crowd cheered. The good folk of the English shouted and danced, the boys sang louder and Dunstan stood serene, happy to wait for them to quieten down. While he waited, with his fixed smile, he allowed himself a moment of personal triumph. He had given them a magnificent ceremony; an oath, the anointing, the investiture, and the enthronement. All that remained due was the homage. *Well then, Lord Alvar. Better that, if you can.*

Chester

Alvar kept his gaze fixed upon the small boat and said, "If either one of you breathes a word of this, I will feed my hounds with your freshly roasted ballocks."

Wulfgar, speaking with an audible tightness of tone, said, "Forgive me, my lord, but I do not understand. You have ridden at the head of all the weapon-men of England, leading them the whole way from Bath. They would forgive you for being frightened, would they not?"

Helmstan emitted a strange sound, like a chicken being throttled. In a quavering voice he said, "No, Wulfgar, you have it wrong. Our lord is not frightened, but worried; worried that when he spews he will ruin his fine clothes." He barely got the final word out before his laughter got the better of him.

Alvar turned and glared at them.

Helmstan wiped his eyes and sniffed. "I am sorry, my lord. I merely wonder what the king will say if his leading earl will not…"

"I did not say I would not get in the boat. I only said that I do not trust it to hold us out of the water."

Wulfgar cleared his throat. "My lord, all these folk…"

"Yes, yes, I know they have all come here to see. It is easy for you; all you have to do is stand here on the wharf and watch as I sink."

Wulfgar looked back at the crowd. Despite the long wait, their enthusiasm had not yet waned. He shook his head.

"They are still throwing blossom into the road. They have waited all this time to hail the king. Why then is this meeting being held on board ship, where they will not be able to see?"

Alvar muttered to himself. "I have begun to ask myself the same question." He wrinkled his nose, already feeling nauseous. The idea had made sense at the time when it was first mooted. First, the ceremony at Bath would hark back to the days of the Roman Empire, while the subsequent muster of all Edgar's weapon-men and their procession north would demonstrate his military strength. Edgar was laying claim to a larger realm, and Bath was the perfect setting. The Roman ruins would stir up memories of the Roman notion of Britannia, but, more pertinently, Bath was one of the burhs built by Alfred and it lay on the border between Wessex and Mercia. The ceremony would provide yet more proof of Edgar's desire to favour neither one former kingdom nor the other, and ensure that the streets from Bath all the way to Chester were lined with folk who had every reason to support a king who had demonstrated his love for all his peoples. Now the paying of homage on board a ship of Edgar's fleet would be a potent reminder that he also ruled the sea around his kingdom. Alvar took a deep breath and a last look at his companions. He handed Helmstan his sword. "Speak to God for me." He leapt into the tiny boat. Wishing that his sins took less time to repent, he spent the short voyage from the estuary to the open sea engaged in negotiation with the Almighty.

The little landing craft glided alongside Guthrum's clinker-built ship, where the Viking captain waited to welcome Alvar aboard. Alvar ducked his head to avoid a low-swooping gull and tried to steady himself. The smell of salt and ropes and tar was an unfamiliar mixture and he swallowed hard. "How do seafarers ever learn to stride about on these things?"

Guthrum grunted a laugh. "For me, it is dry land that does not move enough. Look merry, for you will be the only one. See, over there on the steerboard side."

Alvar glanced at the assembled dignitaries, most of them pallid and frowning. "I see what you mean."

Guthrum bowed before backing away and Alvar stepped forward for the formal greetings. The boat rolled and he lost his footing. He righted himself and looked up. The gulls gleamed silver where the sunshine brushed their wings. As they rose and dived, they called out; he heard their cries as laughter, directed at him.

The king and his councillors were seated behind a raised platform. The small table in front of them was covered with a red cloth worked through with gold thread. The edges of the material flapped in the breeze and only the heavy gold plate and lumps of lead used as paperweights for the charter books stopped it from taking off. Edgar's expression was unreadable, but next to him Oswald, Brandon, and Dunstan had all fixed their mouths into humourless smiles. Each man puffed his cheeks now and again and with each push of air, patted his stomach.

Alvar was amused. If merely stepping aboard had churned his guts, what had they all suffered, sailing round the coast from the earlier ceremony? "It looks as though the waters from Bristol were somewhat less than smooth?"

They did not reply.

He chuckled, taking a natural pleasure in knowing that however sick he felt, they undoubtedly felt worse. In life, such knowledge was usually as good as a cure.

Months of planning and preparation had led up to this moment. Surely the religious ceremony had been a triumph and doubtless Dunstan would lose little time in telling him all about it, but for now the archbishop would have to sit and suffer the display of martial and diplomatic power. Whilst Dunstan had been writing sermons, choosing his finest vestments and deciding which psalms were to be sung, Alvar had been deep in negotiation with Edgar and the various kings and princes who ruled the surrounding kingdoms and islands. By means of persuasion and not a few open threats, a peace had been brokered and an agreement reached that saw them all gathered this day, ready to do homage to a king whose fleet blocked the estuary and whose fyrd had recently marched the length of the country, showing its might to all who lived in its path. Dunstan might yet feel worse before his nausea subsided.

Alerted by the cries of the young prince Æthelred, Alvar turned to look at the queen, who was sitting next to Bishop Athelwold. The boy squirmed on his mother's knee, but she kept a tight grip and delivered an alluring smile. God, but the woman was beautiful, even after giving birth to four children, losing two and burying one. Her smile had altered slightly since the early days, showing her pretty teeth, but not reaching to her eyes, so that they remained wide, unaffected by ageing creases.

Alvar smiled back, but sobered in a heartbeat as he nodded his greeting to the Northumbrians, Earl Beorn, and Earl Wulf of Bamburgh, both grim-faced. It seemed to Alvar that Wulf had the harder task, keeping Beorn from killing the man who was standing between them, restrained on either side by their white-knuckled grip. Kenneth of Scotland, captor of Wulf's son, stared ahead, not in defiance but with the certainty of a gambler who knew the pattern of luck at the gaming boards.

Of the other men waiting to do homage, there was no mistaking the identity of Maccus, Norse king of the Isles, and his brother, Gothfrith, the men who had been attacking the Welsh of Gwynedd. They were both wearing rows of gold arm bands, and round their necks their amulets glinted through their braided hair and beards. The brothers were standing like sailors, their legs apart, planted on the deck.

To their left, but not close enough to exchange snarled insults, stood the Welsh. Alvar greeted Iago of Gwynedd and his nephew Hywel ab Ieuaf, and spoke to them in Welsh, expressing the wish that they might spend enough time in England to allow them to dry out after all the Welsh rain.

Hywel stared at Alvar with black-brown eyes. He said, "I can tell you that this morning the sun was shining, west of Hawarden. I can also tell you that your Welsh is truly bad," he said in perfect English. He took a step forward. "I would speak with you alone, after."

Alvar nodded. He bowed to the last of the kings.

This was Domnall of Strathclyde, who looked up, gave a brief nod, and hung his head again. After the blood-feud between the two Scottish kingdoms, Strathclyde was his no more and nominally in the hands of his son. Alvar glanced at Beorn's Scottish prisoner. Kenneth of Alba, who had taken such advantage of the quarrel, was appraising Domnall as if he were a wolf eyeing up its prey, and Domnall was standing, stooped, with the air of a man already defeated.

Edgar beckoned Alvar and spoke with the language of ceremony. "My lord of Mercia, manifold are the things for which we owe you our heartfelt thanks. You lead all our weapon-men and you even speak Welsh. Now that you are here, it is to Wales that we look first." He smiled at the Norse brothers. "King Maccus of the Isles; I already knew that you and your brother Gothfrith are skilful seamen, but I can see from your clothes that you are also both rich men."

Maccus smoothed his moustache and Gothfrith flexed his biceps.

Edgar's smile vanished and left no trace that it had ever been there. "However, I speak to you as seamen. Look at all the ships in my fleet. I think you are shrewd enough to understand that it would be a shame if you and I had to fight." He raised his hand. "No, do not answer me yet. King Iago, my Welsh neighbour and friend, I am glad to see you here. Today you have come to swear hold-oath to me, and that means that whenever Gwynedd is in need, you will be able to call upon my help."

Iago paused only to shoot a look of hatred at his nephew, an action which pricked Alvar's interest, before he acknowledged Edgar and mumbled a few short sentences in Welsh.

Two gulls craw-crawed overhead; they circled the boat, caught the wind and rose higher into the sky. Edgar shook his head. "I heard only the word *Saesneg*."

Alvar translated. "King Iago said simply that he understands what you say, my lord, but his English is not good enough for him to answer you other than in Welsh."

"I thank you once more, Lord Alvar." Edgar turned back to Maccus and Gothfrith. His voice remained quiet but there was menace in his tone, a sharp blade cutting the air. "So, let us put it all together. You have seen my fleet, and you have heard me say that Iago is a friend who can beckon English help whenever it is needed. Therefore, it would be madness, would it not, for any more of your ships to sail to the shores of Wales, bent on harrying and burning?"

Alvar looked at the brothers and his hand twitched on his empty scabbard, but their arms were no longer folded, hanging now by their sides as they shrugged their recognition of their impotence.

Taking advantage of the momentary silence, King Domnall of Strathclyde stepped forward so quickly that he almost stumbled.

"You are keen, my lord," Edgar said.

In a low voice, Alvar said to Guthrum, "Keen, yes, but not as a man to a mead-bench."

"No, indeed," the Viking said, "More like a thief wishing to have his neck stretched and let the lingering be over."

Domnall wanted only to submit to Edgar before he turned his back on his life. "I go to Rome," was all he told them. He bowed and stepped back to the very edge of the ship.

Edgar turned and fixed his gaze on the last of those who had come to swear an oath of loyalty to him. Edgar said, "So now we must address you as King Kenneth, for Domnall has stepped away and bequeathed you his kingdom."

One corner of Kenneth's mouth twitched.

"And yet," Edgar said, "There are things that kings must do, and there are things that kings must not do. You have Earl Wulf's son, I am told. You must give him back."

Kenneth shook free from the Northumbrians' grip and raised his chin. "I have Lothian, too, which also does not belong to me. Will you make me give that back?"

"No."

His brinkmanship having backfired, the smirk melted from Kenneth's face.

"My lord, you must." Beorn pushed forward but Wulf held his arm.

Guthrum leaned in close to Alvar. "Lothian is not within Edgar's gift, is it?"

Alvar sniffed and concentrated on his breathing, still unaccustomed to the strange smell and gentle motion aboard ship. "Maybe not, but hark at his words now." Edgar would find a way to twist the situation to his advantage and demonstrate how far his reach extended.

Edgar smiled at Kenneth, but it was merely the baring of teeth, devoid of all warmth. "Before all these witnesses this day, I give you Lothian, for which I know you will give thanks. I know, too, that you will acknowledge that the land south of the Tweed belongs to the ancient kingdom of Bamburgh and, therefore, to England. Thus, you will swear to harry it no more."

Kenneth looked to his left and right, and breathed in until his chest rose up. He caught Edgar's gaze and stepped forward and, even as he knelt, he kept eye contact with the king of the English.

Guthrum stared ahead but leaned his head to whisper. "Did I hear that right? Has Edgar given something that was not even his to give?"

Alvar coughed and slid his thumb and index finger down the sides of his mouth to suppress his smile. "Edgar knew he could not get Lothian back, but he made it look as if he has gifted it to Kenneth. And all these kings must bear witness that Kenneth bowed down to Edgar for it and swore to stop attacking Bamburgh."

Kenneth stood up and turned to face the assembled nobles. Alvar thought of a wounded stag he once shot, who turned into the forest and lived to fight another day.

Edgar stared across at Alvar, who nodded his satisfaction. The Welsh had conceded that they were subordinate, admitting that they would need to call for English help if attacked. The Norse brothers had agreed to stop their harassment, and Kenneth had been forced to acknowledge where the border between England and Scotland lay. This was a good day's work.

With the formalities done, the hardier amongst the gathering began to shuffle around the deck. Bishop Athelwold stumbled over to Alvar. "Hold on to me, Bishop, if you will, for I think I have the way of it now, and can stand on this thing without falling. We might yet get back to the staithe without a soaking. Did all go well in Bath? Dunstan looks pleased with himself, so I guess that it did."

Athelwold clung to the earl's sleeve. "The archbishop rises above such thoughts. This was done for God and king and not for his own ends. You should not speak so…" He arrested his gentle rebuke and clasped his hands together. "It was a sight to behold, indeed. Gold everywhere, singing such as you never heard…" He twinkled a smile. "I am boring you. Let me say then only that it was all that we had hoped for."

"So, must we call him Edgar Caesar, now?" Perhaps he was being unnecessarily harsh. Dunstan's second king-making, all done with much ceremony and his beloved psalm-singing, had, apparently, been a triumph of spectacle. But this thing done here today, where so many kings bowed to Edgar, this surely would be the stuff of hearth-tales, the sealing of Edgar's power and strength.

Athelwold patted his arm. "Do not let pride put clouds in your eyes, my lord. Could it be that one ceremony gave strength to the other? If Edgar did, indeed, come here as

Caesar, does it matter who gave him that name?"

Alvar nodded his head to concede the point. But it was not easy to acknowledge that his lifelong foe might have been a help and not a hindrance in this instance. It seemed that his hatred had grown over the years and now matched Dunstan's in intensity.

The bishop continued. "Besides, I hear you have greater work yet to do?"

Alvar offered his arm again as the boat lurched. "You mean the mints?" He resisted the urge to joke that the new uniform coinage should carry the head of Caesar upon it. "Edgar wants every penny in the land to be the same. It will take some doing, but now that this day is over, I can begin to think on the best way to…"

Athelwold convulsed.

"Lord Bishop?"

"Will be glad… Get back… To shore…" The bishop tightened his grip on Alvar's arm and turned to vomit over the side of the ship.

The borough walls guarded an empty space; all the townsfolk were down by the quay. The town reeve was standing nearest the water, waiting for the royal party to disembark. Behind him, every baker, potter, and tanner cheered and jostled. A big man who smelled like a tree-wright stepped backwards and trod on Káta's toes. Across the road, the goldsmith was standing alongside the minter; even rich men had turned silly in the sunshine. The horse-thegns stepped forward with the steeds and the dignitaries mounted. They took their weapons from their deputies and sheathed them for the short journey. The crowd roared and cheered. Káta jabbed her elbow back after yet another push from behind.

Siferth stood on tiptoe and said, "Which one is my uncle Alvar?"

"Oh, can you not wait until they ride by us? You will see well enough then."

Siferth kept his gaze on the procession. "I do not know why you are cross. I am the one who should be irked after being deemed too young to ride alongside my father. Here they come. I can see the white nose on father's horse. Will the lord Alvar hail us with a wave, do you think?"

The cheering around them grew louder as the riders neared, and Siferth rocked on the balls of his feet. Káta tutted and tapped his arm.

The crowd resumed the flower throwing and raised their voices in light-hearted jeers as the Welsh princes rode by. "Go home to your wife and sister. They are the same woman!"

The younger one took it in good part and leaned forward from his horse to bow to the crowd; the older one, whom some said was his uncle, glowered at the throng and spat curses at them in his native tongue. "Ciwed! Tyrfa ddireol! Dafad!"

Helmstan sat tall on his new bay stallion, the white blaze flashing bright in the sunshine. He turned to his left in time to nod to his wife and son, and Káta raised her arm to wave, but the richly dressed man who rode next to him kept his eyes on the road and did not once turn his head.

Alfreda held her son in front of her on the white mare and smiled at the crowds. As she passed by, Siferth drew in his breath and said, "Mother, the queen is so fair and lovely."

Káta brought her arm down and covered her hand with her sleeve. "Oh, these folk all look pretty, but pretty does not get the stew cooked."

"They are stopping now. Will they go on foot through the town do you think? The man who is helping the queen from her horse, is that Uncle Alvar? She looks lovely when she laughs, does she not, Mother?"

Káta sniffed. "All women look more comely when they laugh, it is well known. I can see why they say she is tall, but other than that…"

The elegant earl of Mercia had aged little, although

perhaps if she were closer, she might see whether his hair had begun to grey. Again, from a nearer vantage point she might have seen if there were any embossed decoration on his expensive boots, but there was no escaping the piercing glare of the sun's rays, caught by the jewels on his sword hilt and bouncing off in a blink-inducing beam, nor could she ignore the shining silk of his tunic, shot through with threads of gold that glinted and winked with his every movement. Although he must be nearer forty than thirty, he stood with a straight back and square shoulders. He took the queen's proffered hand, and bowed low.

Siferth turned to Káta. "Are they not both fair-looking… Mother, what is wrong?"

"Naught. I am hot and tired, that is all. Come, let us go and find your father; soon it will be time to eat."

Alvar walked into what he still thought of as the Greybeard's hall, hung up his sword, and a young man immediately stepped away from the wall, touching his arm to gain his attention.

Hywel ab Ieuaf of Gwynedd had a face which presented a paradox. He had no lines or wrinkles yet this, perversely, gave him an appearance of perpetual sadness. He said, "A word, Lord Alvar?"

"As long as it is in English, this time."

"I would rather have it that way, yes. As you know, my uncle's English is not good, and what I have to say to you is not for his ears." Hywel stared at him with dark brown eyes, barely blinking.

The familiar tug of excitement grabbed at Alvar's stomach, but he did not move so much as an eyebrow. "Go on."

Hywel said, "Our laws tend to set brother against brother. When men die, they do not leave land to the firstborn, but to all their sons. So when a king dies, this means that brothers fight to the death." Three Yorkshire thegns walked by and he raised his voice against the strengthening background noise. "Five years ago…" He shook his head and grabbed Alvar's arm, pulling him nearer to talk without shouting. "Five years ago, my uncle Iago locked my father away, and now dares to call himself lord of all Gwynedd."

"So Iago and the other sons of Idwal are still at one another's throats; naught new there. It must make your life in the rain-soaked hills a little less dull, but what has all this to do with me?"

Hywel waited as two king's thegns walked past on their way to find their seats. He leaned in closer, brushing Alvar's cheek with his hair as he spoke into his ear. "I mean to overthrow my uncle and free my father, and to do that I have need of English fyrdsmen. You fought my uncles six years ago. I wonder if you would fight again, now, with me."

Alvar put his tongue to his lip and stared beyond Hywel. He said, "When I fought your uncles I was stirring up trouble for both sides. In truth, I care little for the Welsh." Hywel's eyebrows shot up in mock surprise and Alvar chuckled. "But I am drawn to a man who dares to talk of wrecking a cave when the bear is standing so nearby." He nodded towards Hywel's uncle. "You and I will speak some more, away from other ears, before you go back to your homeland."

He turned away, and Beorn pushed an ale cup into his hands. "For a man, who like me, has left it too late to find a good seat, you are nevertheless looking cheerful."

Alvar drained the cup and wiped his mouth with the back of his hand. "Old friend, lately I have been feeling every one of my thirty-seven years. I have buried too many kin, lost too much land, and had to sit too near to Oswald at too many moots. But today I have watched a great man settle his kingship for once and for all. Edgar is living his forebear's dream. Alfred would be proud to see how Edgar's fleet sails round the shores every year, and to see the new silver pennies which are to be struck with Edgar's head on them…"

Beorn feigned a yawn.

"And today I have been offered a fight." He noted with satisfaction that Beorn closed his mouth and looked attentive once more.

"Oh yes? Need any help?"

But Alvar saw something else which did not please him and he put up his hand to silence his friend. "What is that mirk-mouth doing now?"

Archbishop Oswald had stopped on his way to the dais and was standing by the back wall of the hall. He was deep in conversation with Kenneth of Scotland, and by the manner in which he was holding his hand up to his mouth and whispering into the Scot's ear, it was clear that this was not innocuous gossip. It would not be beyond Oswald to stir up a wasps' nest if he thought that Alvar's political tableau had triumphed over Dunstan's coronation.

Alvar said, "He is too cunning to let us overhear, but let us get nearer; we might hear some of it."

"Mother, you could have spoken then."

"The lord Alvar is not to be yelled at as he goes by. Besides, he would not have heard me above this din. I will speak to him, but if you keep beleaguering me, it will be you that I bellow at, not him."

Helmstan said, "What is this?"

Siferth opened his mouth, but Káta said, "Your son is yet another who has been smitten by our queen's twinkling eyes. He wishes to go to the king's household as his thegn, but I told him that he would need to speak to the earl about such things." She looked to her left and glared at yet another couple who tried to squeeze onto the bench.

Helmstan said, "Really? I must say that I had always thought you would swear hold-oath to the lord Alvar when the time came. Still, to be a king's thegn is to be worthy. I will speak to my lord."

Siferth smiled. "I thank you, father, for it will mean that I can…"

Káta put her hand up. "I have said that I will do it. You are three years off being a man. Why must we have such a to-do about this?"

Helmstan lifted his arms, palms up in query, and Siferth said, "She has been in an ill-mood all day. It is the heat."

On the other side of the hall, slouched in his chair, Beorn grunted. "So, all our borders are safe. But while the fleet is watching the shores, who will watch the archbishop's stronghold?"

Alvar helped himself to another drink. "Ah, so you have not delighted in working alongside Archbishop Oswald at York? Have you not found him to be a good and God-fearing man?"

"He is a thief."

Alvar held the cup at his lips but did not drink; he set the ale down and laid a hand on Beorn's arm. "Speak softly, my friend. There are too many eyes and ears in this hall."

"It is too loud in here for any man to hear if we do not want him to." Beorn tore a chunk of bread and chewed it as he spoke, spitting crumbs across the table. "I was made an earl so that I could be a sixth finger on the long-reaching hand of Wessex. But, whilst I am the king's man, I have at least lived there all my life and know their ways." He took a mouthful of ale. "Since his arrival in York, Oswald has shown only his greed for land and a yearning to make his kin rich."

"So, he is doing the same things in Danish York that he has done in Mercian Worcester. Throws out the clerks, gives land to his kin?"

Beorn nodded. "He has built no new abbeys, but his kith and kin swarm the land like a horde of wasps." He shrugged.

Alvar leaned forward to refill his cup. "I share your loathing. But for now, let us drown our woes in drink until we care only to go a-whoring but are too numb to do it."

They drank cup after cup of strong, locally brewed ale

until Alvar's legs lost the ability to carry him outside in a straight line. He staggered into the night air, his only purpose to find the latrine or another suitable spot where he could empty his bladder and resume his drinking session with Earl Beorn. A woman came towards him, her head down and her arms folded. It took too long for his brain to tell his legs to move, but before the collision she looked up and took a side-step.

Cross-eyed with the effort as he tried to focus, he said, "Lady Káta?"

She paused in the doorway, but kept her back to him. She had not heard, and he stepped away. But then she spoke.

"Yes?"

He turned. She was standing with her arms wrapped across her chest, her hands hugging her upper arms.

He stood, swaying, and smiled at her. "How are you?"

She waved her hand as if it were not important. She spoke quickly. "I am glad that I have seen you. My son, Siferth…"

"I know his name."

"Wishes to be a king's thegn when he becomes fourteen. It seems that the queen has won his heart."

"Tell him to come to me." He suppressed a belch.

"That is the thing, though, my lord. He does not know you well enough to ask such a thing."

He scratched his head. "Not know me? He knows me right well…"

"Would you know him? Could you pick him out from among the many men in that hall?"

"I could never forget those looks." The boy looked too much like his mother.

She said, "You have not been these five summers gone."

He winced. "No, you reckon wrongly. It was only… Yes, it has been. It was… The right thing to do. I took something which was not mine."

She slapped her hands down by her sides and moved

forward, and he took an involuntary step back.

She raised her face to his. "Is that it? You dull-witted man! All this time you have kept away because of that? And I thought that you were playing with me, that it meant naught to you. Now you tell me that you felt guilty?

He shook his head. "I am sorry, lady, I am in my cups. If you could speak a little more slowly?"

She took another step towards him and jabbed his chest with her finger as she spoke. "You took naught. A gift is not theft." She walked off and left him gaping like a landed fish.

She blended into the world of other people, while he stayed behind in the silence that she had left. As he stood there, still swaying, someone knocked into him on their way past, but he did not look round, and dismissed the apology with a wave of his hand.

Siferth glanced up when his mother hurried back to her seat. "Mother, you look red. I thought you went outside to cool down?"

Káta arranged her skirts beneath her. "I spoke to the lord Alvar."

Siferth wriggled on his seat. "What did he say?"

"He said that you should speak with him but it would be better, I think, to leave it until a time when all are not drunk."

Helmstan laughed and said, "It might take some time before the men in this room are sober once more. I … What is Kenneth doing?"

Siferth craned his neck and sat up in his seat. He pointed at the dais. "Father, is that the Scottish…?"

"Ssh." Helmstan cupped his ear.

Káta looked around. Others, further along the bench, who had also seen the movement, had stopped talking, but as Kenneth swaggered to the edge of the dais he had to shout for quiet. The noise of the chatter swelled like a wave and receded.

"I was wondering," said Kenneth, in dramatic tones

worthy of a scop, "Whether you good folk of England like it, or like it not, that your king is such a short-arse?"

The quiet became absolute. Helmstan's hand was on his scabbard, moved there by instinct even though his, like every other sword in the room, had been hung up. Around the hall, thegns and earls leaned forward, one hand on the table, ready to leap up. The women looked on open-mouthed and the guards at either side of the doors moved closer together. The group of dancers, halfway through their tumbling routine, came to a standstill in front of the dais. They looked to their left and right and sat down on the floor, hugging their knees to their chests. Káta was afraid to breathe, lest she be the only one. She brought her hand up to her mouth, but withdrew it when she saw one of the churchmen staring at her. In the scandal of the moment, she had forgotten how distasteful some folk found her scar. She let her hand fall slowly, lest it make a sound in the middle of the awful silence.

King Edgar rose cat-like from his chair and moved to stand next to Kenneth. He turned to face him only after he had looked out at the crowd. He held out his hand and gestured towards the door. "I see that you are indeed fearless, King Kenneth. But though I know that every man believes it, I would have my folk see it too. Would you like to fight me outside, or shall I ask these folk to stand aside and we can fight here, before them all, in this hall?"

The Scotsman was the first to break eye contact. Káta dared to breathe again. Kenneth looked around once more and nodded to the men whom she had seen flanking him earlier in the day. "My lords Beorn and Wulf, it was kind of you to bring me here, but I think that I will make my own way back, and I think that I will leave now." With a perfunctory bow to Edgar, Kenneth left the hall. In the quiet he left behind, the echo of his footsteps rang round the high space of the roof timbers.

Then the din erupted like dogs after sniffing the scent, and Siferth had to raise his voice. "Father, Edgar is so strong and fearless. But what of the queen, is she in need?"

Helmstan shook his head and Káta said, "I tell you for the last time, the lady has enough men slavering around her; you do not need to worry."

Alvar approached the doorway to find his way barred. At sight of him, the guard lowered his sword and they both had to stand aside for Kenneth who hurtled through the door as if he had left all his courage behind him in the room. Alvar stared as the Scotsman retreated. He said, "Was our malted ale not to his liking?"

The door-thegn tested a grin and rolled his eyes.

Alvar chuckled and made his way back into the hall. At first sight, all was as he had left it. But if Kenneth had gone, then there must have been a scuffle at least. All his men had resumed their drinking but he knew that, to a man, the Mercians would have put their hands to their empty scabbards, ready instinctively to fight. He was about to go and congratulate them whilst squeezing them for information, but Dunstan came and stood in front of him.

"You are to blame for this. You are t-too proud, my lord. What were you thinking, to talk the king into taking such risks? The ceremony at Bath was enough. This was your doing and you left our dear king open to threat."

Scratching his head, Alvar said, "He looks all right to me." He weaved his way through the press of people, who were still on their feet and boastful of all the things they would have done had they been required to fight. Beorn told him what he had missed.

Alvar let out a low whistle. "Now we know what Oswald was up to. He poked Kenneth until he barked, and it was done to make me look bad. Dear God, how much they must truly hate me, if they were willing to let Kenneth fight Edgar, whom they claim to love." And now they would hate him all the more, because Edgar had emerged looking invincible, having appeared to find the incident amusing.

But Oswald was not, for once, shooting looks of hatred

at him. No, indeed, he was smiling. That in itself was enough to send a chilling shiver down Alvar's back, but when Oswald looked away he followed his gaze to find the old crow staring at Káta. With deliberate exaggeration, Oswald continued to stare at her whilst making a show of pulling his sleeve down to cover his hand in an elaborate mime, a parody of her self-effacing habit. Alvar felt the sweat cooling on his spine. Oswald knew; knew who she was, and how valuable she was. To both of them.

Beorn had been speaking. "At least we have moved on from the days when the kingship was being fought over by spitting youths. Edgar's kingdom is so strong that there will be no need to split it upon his death, which is a good thing. Not like when he and his brother were young. And when you have done scratching your arse, you will see what I mean."

Alvar ripped his gaze away from Oswald. "What?"

"I say thank God that Edgar is strong. His sons, unlike him and the Fairchild, are only half-brothers and even less likely to love one another. And look at them; young Edward is grimmer than a whipped thrall, while Æthelred looks as if he has yet to stop sucking the queen's tits."

Chapter Fifteen AD974

Near Rhuddlan, North Wales

He felt no pain at the time of impact, just a forceful blow such as a man might inflict with a powerful punch. The hurt was only to his dignity, to be on his arse in the Welsh mud, and he twisted round, aware that his mount might not have been so lucky. His thwarted attempt to stand upright forced him to look down; his thigh was skewered on the same fallen tree branch which had sent his horse sprawling.

Wulfgar knelt at his side. He nodded at the nearest man, drew his finger across his own neck and pointed to the horse. He turned back to Alvar and said, "My lord, this must be pulled out."

Now the pain arrived, late but potent. It came in throbbing waves and drove deep into his thigh muscle. It clutched at his breath. "Would you… Have me… Bleed to death?"

"My lord, we cannot leave you stuck to this tree."

Alvar closed his eyes and jammed his teeth together as the pain stirred a fire at the site of the wound. He said, "I will not die here. Pull it out then, but get me back to Mercia before I breathe my last."

His fate lay in the hands of others and he surrendered. He knew that his leg must at least be free of the branch, for he was now lying on a litter. Dragged, pummelled, across country, he gave thanks that they had been out of the mountains and on their way home when the accident happened. He could not tell daylight from dark, for his vision was cloudy even when he strayed over the border between sleep and wakefulness. He thought he heard Wulfgar joke that, "You can die now if you wish, my lord," and reasoned that if he heard true then they must be back in England.

He smelled wood smoke, from a makeshift camp or a settlement. He listened, waiting for the sounds which would tell him which it was.

Wulfgar said, "Your father told us to come; he says that your mother has some skill at healing."

A youth, whose voice Alvar did not recognise, said, "Where is my father now?" His tone wobbled with the erratic squeaks and falls that marked him as no longer a child and not yet a man.

"He is still at Rhuddlan and will ride on after he has met Prince Hywel there."

"We have had no word all summer; my mother would be grateful for news."

"It has been hard, but Hywel has fought off his uncle. Although we sometimes went into the hills they call Eryri, we left it mostly to the Welsh, for we found the land hard, wet and unforgiving. We helped Hywel by keeping Iago running hither and thither, so that he always had two foes to fight. But the Welsh have a liking for playing smite, run, hide, and they played that game on us a little to the west of Rhuddlan. We had to ride at speed through thickly wooded land, and that can harbour its own threats, as my lord found out."

"My mother will be glad to know that my father is unharmed."

Unseen hands lifted Alvar from the litter and laid him on a more comfortable surface. He closed his eyes and heard nothing more.

A woman was weeping quietly. In a tone suggesting desperate prayer, she said, "I could not bear it if he were dead."

"Where am I?" He could not move, nor see her.

"You are in my bed."

"Then I must truly be in heaven, for there is nowhere sweeter."

He opened his eyes. He was, indeed, in a bedchamber. The room had bare walls, but the scent of dried herbs floated up from the floor. On a bedside table, a plate was piled high with chunks of barley bread and new butter. He smelled it without interest. Furs lay piled on the bed despite the season and Káta, seated beside the bed, fussed with the covers to straighten them. She leaned across him to prop his pillows and he caught a waft of lavender. As she sat back, a tress of soft blonde hair brushed his cheek.

His mouth was dry. He swallowed several times and attempted speech. "My hand is stinging."

"That will be where I smote you," she told him. She sniffed, and moisture glistened on her cheeks.

"Was I…Was I speaking aloud?"

"You were."

He stared at the ceiling and tried to recall. "I am sorry; I thought it was the speech one hears only in sleep. You were right not to stand for it."

She sniffed again and stood up to fetch a cup of water from the table. With her back to him she said, "This is the second time you have come to me thinking that I will put you back together. Do not think to keep doing it."

He said, "But I saw how skilled you were all those years ago, when that herdsman hurt his leg in a similar way. Where else would I go to have my wounds tended?"

She came back to the bed, lifted his head with her hand, and held the cup to his lips. "That was such a long time ago. You are older and I am wiser."

His head flopped back against the pillow. The liquid soothed his parched throat and sent a cooling sensation travelling down the inside of his chest. "Lady, your words wound me more than any Welsh tree. But tell me; this pillow is soft and it feels like I am lying on laths made from silk, not ash. Am I truly in your bed?"

"You are. We never put the roof on the new bower-house after you stopped coming to see us, so there was nowhere else to put you. And that youngling, Wulfric, who fetched us that day to Brunstan when his leg was bad, is the full-grown man who heaved you into it." She lifted the covers to look at his bandage. "When they brought you, it seemed that you would not live out the night. We made you as restful as we could. I even ground up dried horse dung and put it on a linen cloth over the wound to bind it. At last we stopped the bleeding, but not before you had soaked all of my bed sheets."

"I can only thank you for letting the horse-shit dry; many would have thrown a steaming turd on me and left me to rot. You, at least, have a good heart."

"Yes. And as I hear from those words that you are truly yourself again, we need no longer speak of things…" She stood up.

He reached for her hand but missed. "No, Lady, let us speak of them, for once and for all time."

She went to the table at the side of the room.

He slid his hands under the blankets. "We cannot keep running from this."

Káta picked up a wash cloth and dipped it into a water bowl. She wrung it out and said, "Well, you cannot run, and that is the truth."

He moved his head from side to side and beat his hands on the bed under the covers. "Oh, if I could only…" His voice was low; his words little more than a mumble. "I love you."

She stopped wringing the cloth, but stood with her back to him, so still that he could not be sure she was breathing. It was the moment when, if she had not heard, he could pretend it was never said.

With the slowest of hand movements, she placed the cloth back in the bowl, wiped her hands on her skirt, and turned around to face him. "What did you say?"

The moment of safety gone, he blundered on. "You are the woman I crave. It is a good thing I never took a wife, for she would have suffered. I love you; I think I have loved you from the day I first saw you. But you are Helmstan's woman and I will never do aught to mar that."

Her tears fell again. She did not smile, but there were no lines on her brow, and she tilted her head as if to welcome the wash of tears on her cheeks. "I am Helmstan's wife, and I will love him and ever be true to him."

What a fool. "Oh God, forgive me, I should not have said…" He held out his arms, but punched the bed again.

She took a step forward, but kept one hand on the table behind her. "No, my lord, hear me out. If it could be any other way I would hold you now and keep you from ever leaving me again. If I could be yours, I would."

He raised one arm and she came to him, holding her right hand out until her fingertips brushed his, but she came no nearer.

"Then it is said, and it is known." Exhausted, he closed his eyes and slept.

"Come at me again, and go at my left leg, to get under my shield if you can. Then we will learn some more downward blows to the head and shoulders."

"And then can I do it with an iron sword?"

Propped against the wooden fencing of the paddock, Alvar shifted his weight until his leg was comfortable again. He nodded at Siferth. "You might as well learn how to wield a man's blade, although not one that has been near a whetstone. But for now, this will keep your mother from becoming wroth with us."

"Is that what you think?"

Alvar, caught out in clear breach of the rules of his rehabilitation, put on what he thought was his most endearing smile, with little hope of success.

Siferth stopped his run up and scraped to a halt in the frozen mud. "Mother, it is only made of wood."

Káta put her hands on her hips. "It could be woven cloth for all I care. Your uncle Alvar is a sick man and you should not be asking him to come out in this weather to play fighting games with you." She exhaled through her mouth and pointed at the breath-cloud. "It is too cold today."

Siferth lifted his chin, an act of defiance less meaningful now that he stood a head higher than his mother. He had his father's build and his mother's looks and Alvar waited to see who would win the battle of wills.

"Uncle Alvar tells me he is well enough, and I believe him."

"Oh yes? Did he tell you how he needs to get his strength back after losing so much blood? Did he tell you how long it would take for the wound to heal? And then does he know how long it will be before his leg is as strong as it was?" She turned to Alvar. "When I stopped you leaving before the first snow, it was not so that you could do this instead."

He pushed his hair out of his eyes. "I am barely putting any weight on it, I swear to you. And the youngling wishes to learn these new skills. He will need them."

"You see, Mother, Uncle Alvar is right. I must learn how to do these things, and I must learn it from the best."

She turned round again. "Oh, you have him eating out of your hand." To her son she said, "When are you thinking you will need these skills? And why?"

"So that I can keep the queen from harm."

"Oh; her."

Siferth made a few thrusts through the air with his wooden sword. "I know that you like her not, Mother."

Káta leaned back against the fencing and looked at Alvar. "No, my son, you are wrong."

Alvar raised an eyebrow. "Is that so?"

She did not drop her gaze. "Sometimes, one small drop of knowledge is enough to calm a stormy sea of envy. I am wise enough to let you go to the queen, for I understand that while you might love her, it does not mean that you no longer love me, any more than my staying here means that I do not love you. Go, with my blessing."

Siferth said, "Thank you, Mother."

A warmth from his belly spread through Alvar's body until it burst out as a grin that threatened to split his face. He said, "Yes, thank you."

She lowered her voice to a whisper. "I was not speaking to him."

Alvar made a grab for her tiny hand and squeezed it. "I know."

"Mother. Mother! Look at what I can do."

She turned her head to look at her son, but kept eye contact with Alvar until the last possible moment. She said, "Well, if you must learn, then as you say, you should learn from the best. But if my lord gets broken again…"

Káta walked back to the enclosure gate.

Siferth said, "Mother spoke as if she were teasing, but she must think that you are a great man, for she is keen not to have you sick again."

Alvar grinned. "Your mother is a wonderful woman."

Káta pressed each item into his hand. "You must put this salve on, for there will yet be swelling, more so after a hard day's ride. And I showed you how this must be boiled up to a brew. I know that they have Leeches in the south, but it is hard to step in and take over where another has begun the healing. It will be sore for many weeks yet and even after that you might still have twinges." She looked up. "I am speaking too swiftly."

He stepped outside, put the things into his pack, and beckoned her from the hall doorway. She stepped towards him but her legs felt unsteady. A gust of wind slapped her dress against her legs and she pulled her cloak tight round her body.

He reached out and lifted her chin. "I will see that no harm comes to him. He is the son of my best-loved thegn, and his mother is most dear to me. You must not worry."

He dropped his hand and she kept her face tilted towards him. She tried to meet his eyes, but had to look away, for the tears were hot and ready to boil over. "I know you will look after him. But I…"

Helmstan came striding out from the hall and Siferth followed him, a smile pinned to his face, and his eyes wide like a child's on its birthday.

Helmstan rubbed his arms in an effort to keep warm against the wind. "The snow has melted but you should find the roads hard enough to ride before it all turns to mud."

Káta held her arms out to Siferth but he glanced up at Alvar and wriggled from her grasp. "Mother…"

His father laughed. "Now we know that he is full-grown, if he will not wear his mother's arms."

Káta clamped her hands to her sides until Alvar and Siferth had mounted their horses. Alvar nodded to her and Helmstan, and before the horses clattered out of the gateway, Káta released the tears. She and Helmstan waved long after the riders had stopped casting backward glances.

Helmstan said, "I know it is hard for you my love, but he is old enough to be with a foster-father and I know of no other man whom I would entrust with my son's life."

A sob broke from her and she flung her arms round his neck. "Oh, you are a good man. There is none better."

Chapter Sixteen AD 975

Deira (Yorkshire)

Alvar prayed that Earl Beorn had not retreated to Earl Wulf's territory in the ancient kingdom of Bamburgh. A ride of any great distance these days aggravated his damaged thigh; he did not want to arrive at Beorn's residence only to ride yet further north. From Leicester they took the old Roman road from Doncaster, through Castleford and on to Tadcaster. The terrain was the usual shrouded, water-logged hell pit that he found so hard to navigate and he did not trust the warty, withered old man who guided them. But he had chosen this route to avoid the ferry crossing at Barton-on-Humber and now had to rely on this little warlock to steer a course through the sodden misty marshland. Brandon, who was so keen to please and so familiar with murky fenlands, would have felt more at home here. But the task had been asked of the lord of Mercia and duty had saddled his horse.

Wulfgar was riding beside him, with Helmstan close behind, leading a party of twenty Mercian thegns. Too many, Alvar thought, but it was *'Better to have them and not need them than rue the day they were left behind.'* It made sense; more so than the finger of doubt that tickled his spine and would not be stilled. The July sky darkened. The rain, which all day had threatened to fall from the solid grey cloud, broke free in a vertical assault that attacked the backs of their necks before they had a chance to pull on their hooded cloaks. In the humid afternoon, many had been riding in only their breeches and undershirts, but they were no cooler when the rain came, and as the thunder growled and lightning rent the blackened sky, they quickened their pace when told that a short gallop would see them to their journey's end at Wighill.

Alvar had not sent an advance rider, but he was sure that Beorn knew he was coming. Would he wait for him?

They slithered to a halt outside Beorn's hall and dismounted. Alvar wiped at the smell of wet mud in his nostrils. He detailed a party to stay with the horses and took only Helmstan, Wulfgar, Brihtmær of Chester, Aswy of Shropshire, and Ingulf of Worcester into the earl's hall with him.

The premature evening rendered the inside of the building gloomy. The fire in the hearth burned low, and in the corner of the room a whistler was playing a mournful tune on an apple-wood flute. It was a popular instrument in York, but Alvar found the tone too morose and he hoped that he would not have to talk over the noise. He and his men took off their sodden cloaks and shook them before handing them to a servant who set the garments by the fire to dry.

Earl Beorn was seated upon the dais. A gold arm ring was hanging loose around his wrist. He was touching the fingertips of both hands together and allowing the ring to slide from one wrist to the other and back again. As Alvar approached, he let the ring fall to the table where it whirled, clattered, and lay flat. Only when the noise died away did he speak. "My lord Alvar, how do you like our northern weather?"

"It is a little wet for my liking." Alvar's words came out as if his voice belonged to someone else. He coughed.

"Be thankful, then, that you did not have to fetch me from my house in York; the dale will most likely be flooded by morning."

It was a poor effort at humour and with the mention of York, Alvar had no need to make the pretence of a smile.

"You know then, why I am here?"

"I do." Beorn signalled the piper to stop. "What I do not know is what you are going to do."

The silence was an oppressive successor to the awful music. Helmstan and Wulfgar kept rigid guard either side of the doorway, and the other thegns stared at the food and drink on the table, though none reached forward to take it. Beorn remained motionless and looked at the lifeless arm ring on the table. Away from the warmth of the fire, Alvar smelled for the first time the musty dampness which must have pervaded the hall at his every visit. A lump in his throat, his companion since he left Wessex, quivered in his windpipe. His head throbbed from the strain of keeping his eyes dry. The musician sat with the pipe now harmless in his lap and Alvar felt the stilled air begin to thicken until it pressed his bones. "God's ballocks, man, what were you thinking? The king is dead; you should be with me and the rest of the witan while we choose an atheling as the new king. Instead, we hear that you made straight for the archbishop's house and tried to kill him."

Beorn tried a grim joke. "At least with me at York, you cannot blame for the king's death."

"I wish I could. It would tell me how a man of three and thirty, strong and healthy, dropped down dead after no sickness." Alvar jumped onto the dais and threw himself into a chair alongside Beorn. They stared out into the hall. Alvar waved at the other men who were waiting by the hearth. "Eat," he said.

Brihtmær and Aswy helped themselves, while Ingulf took some bread and cheese over to the men standing guard by the door.

Beorn looked round. "What news from Wessex?"

Alvar shook his head. "The queen is at her wits' end, in deep mourning. As are we all, but that does not stop the fighting over which of the athelings will become king."

"Æthelred must be the one. It was written in law. His mother is a queen."

"She is a queen, you are right. But she is a queen who is hated by Dunstan. We have much to argue about before it is settled. And before we speak about it, I have to deal with you. Why did you do it?"

Beorn waved a hand and a servant appeared from the shadows, darted over to the thegns' table, and came back to the dais with some ale and two cups. Beorn waited until the drinks had been poured. "I can only say that a black madness came over me. When I heard that Edgar was dead I thought only of his beloved Oswald, who was an arrow in my side. I thought of how he sat in York, taking land from men who held it freely from me, forbidding the clerks from getting wed or even to make wills, so that their land would go back to the Church upon their death." He drew a deep breath, sighed and lowered his head. "I had too much to drink and I rode to York not knowing what I meant to do when I got there. Thank God that I was too drunk to wield my knife with any skill. Either that, or the ale that stirred my wrath also washed it away."

"You are truthful at least. And it is to your credit that in the end, you stayed your hand. After years of all his doings and having to watch him build all those monasteries, I do not know if I would have had the strength to withhold."

Beorn laughed, but it rang hollow, like one sharp beat on a drum. "Then it would have been my task to ride to fetch you. Either way, we stand together. Even so, you are far too steadfast in your friendships, and that might not be wise for you any more."

"Do not worry, my friend. Your Northumbrian shit will not stick to me." Alvar laughed too, but there was no force behind it and the sound melted away. He said, "Standing true to those I love has not come cheaply. I do not think I have any more to lose." In the silence that followed he stared at Beorn's fire. Like every other man and woman in England, Alvar valued the hearth as a source of heat, giving not only warmth to the body, but drawing to it the company of others that helped to sustain the soul. But sometimes, a hearth alone could not make a home.

Beorn spoke again. "I would not have sat here waiting for any other man to come and tell me my fate. But I willingly waited for you, my friend. So tell me, what must I do? Am I to swing from a rope?"

"Not while I draw breath. You are sent from these shores, forever to be thought of as Nothing. It has fallen to me to witness your leaving, never to come back."

"I wish to God that I had thought it all through before I brought this shame on my kin." Beorn sighed. "But I knew it would come to this, even if I hoped otherwise." A shutter blew back from the window and hammered back and forth as the wind swept round the hall. Beorn sat forward and placed his arms flat on the table. He gave a formal speech. "My hall is dim; God has sent the darkness and the rain, and now I must go to the faraway, where there will be no hearth-fellows. We must all float with the ebb and flow of life, but I wish I could bide here to tell the tale's end. Have I time to share a drinking horn with you one more time, my beloved friend?"

"A ship lies in the Humber and will make sail upon my word. I will stay here until you leave."

Beorn drained his cup and the servant leaped forward to refill it. "Leave it man, I will do it. And fetch my horn." He spoke to Alvar once more. "You do not believe I would leave?"

"I believe that you would go. Your word is always good enough for me. You know why I am here. I am here to make sure that word does not spread too far. Canterbury does not want it known that there has been a threat made upon York."

Kingston, on the Thames

"I will do to him what Beorn threatened to do to Oswald. I will wring his neck until his eyes burst out… Strip off his wretched skin with my hand-saex and spill hot wax on his heart… Pull out his stammering tongue and nail it to the hearth and grind his bones into tinder…" Never, even on the battlefield, had he been so enraged. It was as if his anger had been simmering in a cauldron for all these years and now the fire had been stoked enough for the whole pot to boil over.

They were in the queen's bower, well away from the meeting hall, but still Alfreda looked anxiously over her shoulder. When she spoke it was with a voice unknown to him, cracked and hoarse from crying. "My lord, I beg you to still your wrath."

"What?" Alvar stopped and looked at her. Her eyes were lost in dark circles, painted by the sleepless nights following the death of her husband and protector. Æthelred was pale and frightened and a poor substitute for his father, but no-one in the witan had ever pretended that either of the two princes was ready to be a king. No-one had expected Edgar to die.

Alfreda looked at the floor. "Dunstan said that there must not be another wrangle over the kingship. He said that the land must not be weakened by Edgar's death, and must not lose that which the king and the Church had made strong." She lifted her head. "My lord, will you sit down before you wear a hole in the floor? Your limp is worsening, and I need you strong and whole."

Alvar panted as his journey from shock to anger ended in stunned curiosity. "How was this thing done? Why did no man put a stop to it?"

"Being an anointed queen did me little good, for Dunstan would have no son of mine on the throne. Edgar wore his hair shirt for the sin of Wulfreda, so in Dunstan's eyes, a son born of that match is worthy to be atheling. Wulfreda was of royal kin so her child is throne-worthy; therefore my son is not. There were not enough who would speak for my son, and too many who would name Edward as their king." Alfreda tapped her fingertips. "I will reckon them up for you. Oswald stood with Dunstan, and wherever the Dane stands you can be sure that the lord Brandon will be stuck to his side, and he brought the lords of Essex with him."

Alvar counted too. "But my thegns in the south, Wulf in Bamburgh, all of Mercia, would have stood by Æthelred," he said. "We all would have followed Edgar's wishes."

The queen dropped her gaze again. "Bishop Athelwold stood by us, as did my late father's Devonshire kin, but…"

"Mercia was not here." He slammed his fist into his other palm. "No, they saw to it that I was not here. What a witless empty-head I have been. Beorn, of course, could do naught, but Wulf could have ridden south given time." He looked up as the door opened and he nodded when Siferth came in. "But Wulf was never sent for, was he? And I… I, daft turd that I am, dragged my sorry arse and all my men to Northumbria, stayed there long enough to see Beorn gone from our shores, and for Dunstan to put the king-helm on Edward's head. God curse him for a word-breaking heap of shit."

"Uncle Alvar, my lady…"

"Has often had her ears warmed by your uncle's curses, Siferth; do not worry," Alfreda said. She put a hand up to push her hair from her face. "Lord Alvar and I have always had an easy way with each other and this will carry on, I am sure, now that we…"

Alvar sat down. "And you, youngling; what will you do now?"

Siferth came to stand behind the queen. "I have sworn to Lord Æthelred, Uncle, as have many here who once were thegns to Edgar. You can sleep restfully to know that my queen and my lord Æthelred are well looked after. We would lay down our lives."

Lives? He was still some months shy of his fourteenth birthday. "I am glad to hear you swear it, although if I think about it there is not one among you who is old enough to shave. Do not be stirred, I am teasing you. I know you are steadfast. As to your sword skills, well, you were taught by the best." He grinned at Siferth, noting how the boy had broadened across the shoulders.

Alfreda gave a high-pitched laugh. "Come now, Lord Alvar, this is too much like fatherly pride; it is almost as if Siferth were your own son. And there is no need for such silly talk, for I will be safe enough with y…"

Her mood lurched again and the haunting shadows washed across her face. He wondered if her lighter tone reflected nothing other than a monumental effort to turn his attention back to her and away from Siferth.

She said, "My lord of Mercia, my dearest friend, will you bide here in Wessex with us for a while?"

He looked across at her. Her breathing was easier now, as was his. He shook his head. "My lady, whatever Siferth says, I cannot sleep restfully, and I am not a hound that lies down to have its belly scratched after a kicking." Alvar bowed low and stalked off.

Dunstan was in the writing-house with Oswald and several scribes, whose hands were stained with vermilion ink. As Lord Alvar crashed into the room the scribes attempted to collect their parchment and leave. Oswald backed two steps nearer to the far wall, his gaze fixed upon Alvar's sword arm.

Dunstan, though, looked at the intruder and smiled. He opened his mouth and heard his voice ringing out sweetly, lubricated by the hour he had spent this morning singing in the chapel, giving thanks that although his beloved Edgar had gone, at least Alvar's power had been buried alongside him. "My lord, I know that you have some words for me, but I will speak first, as I fear that there might have been a small misunderstanding."

"For which you have earned my undying hatred." Alvar stepped so close to him that Dunstan had to shuffle backwards. "But by my leave, speak on."

Dunstan swallowed. He bolstered his resolve with the memory that he'd initially crowned Edgar in similarly hurried circumstances, years before, and thus the precedent had been set. "I may be g-guilty of the sin of pride, but I have shown that you, as one man, are not England, nor do you speak for the whole land. There has been no brawling over the kingship, and we of the Church are free to go on with our work as before." He held out a hand. "I know that Edward is not yet the king that he could be, but I can lead him, as can Bishop Sideman, who has been a good teacher to him all these years. No, my lord, I am glad of how things are, and if I must stand and take a tongue-lashing from you, I say it will have been worth my while." He shut his mouth and kept his head erect, waiting for the verbal onslaught.

But Alvar stood back, folded his arms, and stared at him, saying nothing. In the silence that followed, Dunstan withdrew his proffered hand and looked across at Oswald, who shook his head and shrugged.

Still Alvar remained silent and they began to fidget; Dunstan fiddling with his sleeve-ends and Oswald with his fingernails.

Alvar spoke at last. "Now what?"

Dunstan struggled to keep his smile from wavering. "M-my lord?"

"Now what will be done?"

The archbishop folded his hands in front of his gown. He had seen a challenge where there was none. Alvar's question was surprising in its simplicity, but he was happy to explain. "N-now you will swear hold-oath to King Edward, and our lives will g-go on much as before." *And then it does not matter if you wed Edgar's widow. For, having sworn to Edward, you cannot then fight on her son's behalf. I have won, Earl.*

"No."

This time the smile slid away and Dunstan felt his heart hammering. "My lord?"

Alvar stepped closer, looked him in the eye, and spoke in tones barely above a whisper. "That youth is not born of both a king and a queen, and he is a snivelling shit to boot. I will not swear to him. So I shall tell you what is to be done now. Now you will feel the might of Mercia, and you will learn what a strong and worthy king could stop, that a child-king cannot."

He turned round and pulled the door shut behind him, and the only sound was the echo of the door-slam.

Dunstan stared at the space that Alvar had occupied but a moment before. He said, "Archbishop Oswald, I am left with the feeling that we might have overreached ourselves."

"Edward is king. There is naught that Alvar can do about that now."

Dunstan wished he shared his friend's conviction. "If, or should I say when, he weds the widow Alfreda, he will fight hard in the name of her whelp and if he wins, he will become king himself, in all but name."

Oswald laid a hand on Dunstan's arm and the archbishop was surprised by the strength of the grip.

Oswald said, "You and I have never played together at the gaming board. I fear I would beat you, for I know when to hold back and play my last piece."

Dunstan was tired. "I am sorry, Archbishop, you have lost me…"

"Alvar will not wed the king's widow. I know that his

heart lies elsewhere, and I am going to show him what happens to ungodly women."

Dunstan shrank back. "Dear God, what has been unleashed this day?"

Oswald said, "Do not worry. He is a beast with sharp teeth, yes, but not cunning. He will be easily snared, and I know how to lure him. And by the time I have dealt with this other woman, Alvar will not dare to wed the queen." He bowed and quietly left the room.

Dunstan sighed and looked around the room. An empty scriptorium was a rare sight, and the silence was unsettling. The gentle grinding of powder, the schwoop-click of the pen knife against the feather, the tapping of the ink pot, and the scratching of the nib on the vellum, all these were comforting sounds of continuous devotional industry. In one menacing flash, the heart had been ripped from this central core of religious activity, leaving naught but a shattered shell. Dunstan stepped forward to right an upset ink pot and crossed himself.

Part III – Gerīpenung (The Reaping)

Chapter Seventeen AD976

Evesham

The smooth-skinned novice stumbled through the doorway, and the book slipped from his hands. Illuminated pages fluttered to the ground, and the gold lettering glinted in the sunshine. He stared up at the earl, but made no attempt to stand up or to retrieve the book from the mud.

Alvar leaned forward in the saddle and patted his horse's neck. He looked down at the monk and said, "I can wait while you gather up each leaf, Brother." More than likely, it was the money from his patronage which had paid for it, but the young man would have no recollection of this earl and would see him as wrecker, not benefactor.

A volley of loud bangs echoed round the courtyard and the young monk scrabbled backwards on his knees.

Alvar said, "It is only the crack of stools and benches being thrown on the fire. Your brothers would rather see the wood burned than someone else have it. You think that I mean you some harm, but I am only here to see to it that you leave."

The novice remained on his knees, but he began to scrape up the pages. Alvar saw now that the gold leaf illuminated the pages of the bible. "I mean no harm to that, either, or to the walls of this abbey. I would put back what belongs here, that is all."

More monks came through the doorway, chivvied from

the other side by Helmstan. They bunched together in the courtyard and shuffled their feet as if unsure which direction to take, but there was no fear in the older men's eyes. Like rats running out of a wet ditch. They would find another warm nest soon enough.

Helmstan said, "Wulfgar has gathered the last of them from the church, my lord. Shall I ride a way down the road with them in case they try to come back?"

Wulfgar walked up behind him. "They would not get far." He stood in front of the group of monks. "Tell your abbot that all the Worcester and Gloucester thegns are on the roads, helping our lord put this land back how it was."

Alvar turned his head and looked out beyond the gate. Further down the road nearer the river, shouts and screams rose up, the words lost in the air, but the meaning clear. He wrinkled his nose as the thick smoke billowed not just from the bonfire, but from fires which had been set in the village. The wind brought the black clouds; they wafted round the abbey and turned day into night as they passed. He closed his mouth against the taste.

Helmstan said, "The folk here blamed the bad harvest on last year's fiery-tailed star. They are hungry and have no love for the abbey, where the monks have grown fat on food rents while others starved. Our men, as well as chasing the monks, might be called upon to safeguard them. It might help that they are abroad on the lanes."

Alvar stared at the road. "Or it might help to blacken our names."

Wulfgar said, "My lord, I found someone in the church who wishes to speak with you. Shall I bring him hither?"

"No need." The group of monks parted, and Oswald stepped between them to stand in front of Alvar. "I will not be brought before this man as if I am the law-breaker. I am here. And I would have some answers."

Wulfgar brandished his sword and waved it close to Oswald's chin. "Shall I end it here and now, my lord?"

Alvar said, "No. I am not a murderer. All that is done

here this day will be lawful."

Oswald made a snorting sound and gestured with his arm. "You call this lawful? Turning holy men out onto the road?"

"I am giving this land back to those to whom it belonged. I am merely righting a wrong."

Alvar pulled his horse round and looked down without lowering his head. Oswald was shaking, but whether through anger or cold, Alvar did not care. Another chair went on the fire, and newly fuelled, smoke-disturbed embers floated over them. Each of them squinted, but neither wiped their eyes. Alvar's cloak hung open.

Oswald pulled his cloak tighter against the wind. "You speak of the law, but you have sent weapon-men out onto the lanes without the king's leave. And if he knew what you are doing to these holy brothers…"

"Enough." Alvar sniffed. "For too many years I have heard you say one thing, watched while your hands do another. Edward has no love for, or belief in, the ways of the folk in the old kingdoms. This was something that his father, a great man, understood. As to whether your Edward loves the abbeys, I know not nor care. He is not his father, and his father is not here. What will, or can, Edward do to stop me?"

The tips of Oswald's ears glowed red. "He is your king."

Alvar leaned over in the saddle and brought his face nearer to the archbishop's. "No, he is not my king. He is the thing that you and Dunstan made. And when you stepped forward to put the king-helm on his head, against the wishes of Edgar, you shoved me too far." He sat up straight.

"Lord Alvar, your elbow…" Oswald knelt down to pick up his mitre from the mud.

Alvar stared at the older man. "You see, Archbishop? It is not hard to put something on a man's head. It is even less hard to knock it off again."

Oswald wiped at the headdress. "You have made it unclean." He lifted his head to glare at the earl. "I hope you are proud now."

Alvar had to turn away, for his eyes stung from the smoke and were watering. He swallowed; all he could taste was the bitter smoke of the fire. The wind that whipped it up was sharp as it blew round him, and yet he was not cold.

Oswald walked round to stand in front of Alvar's horse. "You cannot burst into the grounds of an abbey like a wild hound."

Alvar looked the older man up and down. He flared his nostrils. "But I am a wild hound." He sniffed again. "And you are no more than a chewed cloth that I have spat out. It is ended." He said to Wulfgar, "Take him to Worcester and lock him in there."

"You will burn in hell for the deeds done here this day."

"Then I will see you by the Devil's hearth, my lord Archbishop." Oswald had transformed a cathedral chapter into a monastic priory. Now it would become his prison.

Cheshire

"Mother, Evesham was only the beginning. He gave the land to his brother's eldest son, and all the old clergy have been brought back. From there he went to Winchcombe, where he threw out the abbot and all the monks. Then he went on to Deerhurst and Pershore."

"Has he gone mad?" Káta wrapped her cloak around her body.

"Are you cold? We should go inside."

She shook her head. "No, I am not cold. It is only that I... And does your father stand with him on this?"

"He does. But Alvar is not mad. He has seethed for years about losing his lands and his rights to them. He worries, too, about the folk who live upon them."

Káta gripped the edges of her cloak. "There will be an ache in his heart. His loathing for Oswald and Dunstan was well known, but he will be wroth with Edgar, too."

Siferth stepped nearer. "What do you mean; why would he be wroth with Edgar?"

"For dying." She looked up, hoping to see a glimpse of sun, but the winter sky was a solid grey. Ice lay like broken glass around the edges of the puddles. She sighed and walked back along the path towards the enclosure gate. Siferth skipped along beside her.

She wanted to ask him about the rumours; that when the abbey at Evesham was attacked, the stones fell and the whole building collapsed. Underneath the stones, the grave of Saint Egwyn had been exposed, and it was said that his skin was as fresh and pink as if he had never died. Stories like these, true or not, served the monks' cause, not Alvar's. At such hard times as these, it would not do to have the folk turn against the lords. She stopped and put a hand on Siferth's arm. "I do not know how it is elsewhere, but here we have had to bulk our dough with pease and beans, or go without bread. I have found folk eating riddled meat and unripe foods. The children have sore skin and eyes, and their gums bleed. If others, like us, have the loosening bowel sickness and they are as weak and hungry... Will they stand by Alvar or will they turn back to the Church?"

He held her hand and they walked on. "They will not turn back to the Church. Yes, many are unwell. Many are starving. But many were also forced to sell their land to the Church for less than it is worth."

He told her then of the folk-moots, packed full of those men who were now landless. Alvar had heard the pleas of many men whose kin had been coerced into bequeathing their land to the Church, so that any surviving kin would be left with no means of a living when their relatives died.

Siferth stopped on the path in front of her. "You are right, Mother; lots of folk think that the world is ending, and maybe they think it is God's doing, but the food rents owed to the Church make their hardships worse." He laid his hands on her shoulders. "These folk look to Alvar to give them back their lands and rights. And who will stop him now? The monks mourn Edgar, but they must have thought that Alvar's power would also die with him. Yet Alvar has the weapon-men behind him, and he is the only one with the skill to lead them. Oswald is locked up in Worcester, and no man can say how Edward will blow."

Oswald locked up in Worcester. Thank God. Hunger was not the only demon stirring the folk. Comets and the death of kings terrified everyone; none more so than dear Wulfsige the priest, who, after all these years, had lost courage and gone running to the bishop of Lichfield with his tales. His departure was soon followed by the arrival of a deputation from the bishop of Worcester, demanding to know the provenance of her scar, and making clear their knowledge of her association with the earl, with whom she was overheard conversing at Chester, in what they called an over-familiar manner. She could not recall, but they said there was a monk who knocked into Alvar, who had heard their every word. The things of which they spoke had happened so long ago, but Edgar's death was like slackened reins, and all horses were free now to run after years at the tether. News of the attacks on Evesham and elsewhere sent her inquisitors scuttling back, with naught from her lips to damn her, the folk who lived under her protection, or her loved ones. And now that Oswald had been incarcerated, she could breathe a little more freely.

Her son was smiling, and his flushed cheeks were not due to the cold weather alone. She said, "You speak as if it is a game. You are barely fifteen and you have your whole life still to live. But the earl will be known forever as a man who harries monasteries. When men have food once more in their bellies, will they still follow him then?"

A gust of wind blew across the enclosure and the paddock gate banged against its post. Káta stepped from his grasp to shut it. "This needs to be tied with twine. I will tell Burgred to fettle it." The wood banged against her fingers. "Aah!" Why did knocks always smart more when the hand was cold to begin with? She wrestled with the gate and in a low voice she said, "String will not do. Too many things have come loose that cannot be tied together."

A drop of moisture bubbled at the end of Siferth's nose. He sniffed it away. "You worry too much about Uncle's good name. I was there, Mother, at Ely, with the queen. I heard Bishop Athelwold speak of him as a great patron of Abingdon and Glastonbury. Think on this: the abbeys that he has laid to waste all belong to Oswald."

Káta dredged her knowledge of the southern part of Mercia and brushed imaginary dirt from her hands. "Well then, this madness will soon blow itself out, for there are not many more of Oswald's houses left for him to go at with his cudgel." She looked at him, noting the sheepish expression. "What?"

"It has gone a bit further. After Deerhurst, things got stirred up."

She caught her breath and stood still on the path. "What has Deerhurst to do with it?" All she knew of Deerhurst was that it was the ancient spiritual home of the Hwicce. Thegn Wulfgar often spoke to Helmstan of his proud heritage.

"Alvar got it back for them."

She shook her head. "But I do not see…"

"The Hwicce land is the heart of old Mercia. Whenever two athelings have fought for the kingship, Mercia has always supported one atheling and Wessex the other. The Mercians are now rising up, as they did when they put Edgar on the throne."

Her mouth was dry and she coughed. She needed no lessons in Mercian history. Helmstan refused even to acknowledge the new geographical shires, designed to transform Mercia from an independent kingdom into just another administrative area of Wessex. "So this is not simply a matter of restoring the monasteries?"

"Maybe it was for Alvar, in the beginning. Let me say it this way: he and the Mercians may not wish for the same things, but they are going forward as one. A fight cannot be far away. Now that Edgar has gone… I heard Bishop Athelwold say that the hound is without the huntsman and runs unfettered."

Káta put a hand up to cover the lump stuck somewhere between her throat and her chest. Swallowing brought no relief. "What say the East Anglians? You were there, at Ely."

Siferth laughed. "Brandon said that he and his brother Thetford were as one. My lady the queen said that they needed to be, for each of them was less than half the worth of Alvar." He slapped his thigh. "She is most witty, is she not?"

Káta sniffed. "Her word-craft is good, but I wonder that she has need of it when men fawn over her like lovesick…" She looked up. "Never mind. I only wish to know when there will be an end to this silliness, so that my husband will come home. And who is there to see to the lord Alvar, for he needs someone with him who will…"

Siferth pulled his spine up straight, and took a deep breath to inflate his chest. "I am there when Lady Alfreda has no need of me. And Father is always by his side. I do not know what makes you say such things, Mother, for…"

"Do you know, I think I will go within, after all. This wind gets a hold of my bones like a bramble-thorn to the ankle." She looked down at her hand, where her nails had dug four red crescents in her palm. "Let us go and speak of things more blithe, for I would make the most of you while I have you here. Did I tell you that Eadyth comes oft-times to beg tidings of you? Some weeks she is here on a Thursday, only to come again on the Friday. She is a pretty little thing."

"Mother, you do not need to shout; I am only standing by your side."

Káta smiled in apology. "Sometimes though, my son, you need loud words so that you cannot hear the din of the stillness."

Shropshire

Dust flew up around their faces. Ground which was once fertile moist mud had been turned to barren powder by the continued lack of rain. The thatch on the roofs was as dry as tinder and the air was depressingly devoid of the stench of animal dung. Alvar and Helmstan exchanged glances and Wulfgar spoke for them all.

"There will be no food to be had here. Much longer, and we will be eating our own horses."

Alvar could only nod. Soon, they would no longer have the strength or resources to continue patrolling the land. It was unreasonable to expect even his own estates to continue to provide food and supplies for his entourage. The folk of this settlement had packed what little they had left and moved away. The door of the tiny wooden chapel hung open, occasionally clattering against the wall. There was naught but cold ash in the smith's furnace, and baskets which should have been in the storage lofts lay empty, some upturned, on the ground. In the burial ground next to the chapel, numerous mounds of freshly dug and repacked earth spoke of the recent deaths. Alvar said, "Come. There is naught for us here. We'll go on to…" Before apprising them of their destination, he stopped to listen. "Down by the river; shouting."

They kicked their mounts into a gallop and hastened to the riverside. Once there, Alvar needed no time to assess the situation. A young monk, black habit enveloping his wasted frame, lay slumped against a tree trunk. The blood from the head wound that had killed him had stopped flowing, and a red trail stretched from his temple to his chin. The prize for which he had been slaughtered, a cow with bony haunches, stood nearby, pathetically scratching for grass on the parched earth. The source of the shouting was the two men, perhaps friends, perhaps not, who had seemingly set about the monk and were now fighting over the booty. Wulfgar leaped from his horse and grabbed one of the men, pulling him away from the other, and dragging him roughly to his feet.

The man turned to face Alvar, staring up from eyes sunken into his head. His cheekbones were sharp, foreshowing the skeleton he would eventually become. He retained an air of defiance. "He wants to kill it for its meat."

The other combatant stood up, hand-saex still poised. "He wants it for milk. Hah! As if a starving beast can be milked. We will die of thirst ere he gets his way."

Alvar could only concur. "Slaughter it and share the meat. When your bellies are full, make your way to Shrewsbury. Tell the reeve there that Lord Alvar sent you. Nowhere is thriving, but the towns are not as badly off. Maybe you will fare a little better there for a while."

They did not look impressed with his advice, but he could do no more. Yet if he could not put this right, then who could? This was not what he'd been about when he embarked on his mission, nor was this situation good for England. He knew he was watching Edgar's legacy slipping away. The laws and structures that Edgar put in place must be adhered to, otherwise it would all have been for nothing, and they would all have to admit that the success of the kingdom had rested on the one man. As soon as he could, Alvar would need to get back to the seat of Government and swallow his pride.

Cheshire

Káta stood by the table in the kitchen and stared at the bare rafters. Just twelve months before, she had met Hild in the lane. Káta had been to take some of the surplus cheeses to the folk who lived beyond the mill, and had also left them two flasks of milk. She smiled to recall Hild's incredulity that the flasks had contained whole milk, rather than the leavings from the cheese-making. Káta had laughed then, assuring the other woman that the yield was abundant. Leofsige had feared for his head, with so many cheeses smoking above him in the kitchen, although it was true that his head was nearer to the roof than most.

Now even the tallest man in the land could walk round her kitchen without fear. This year, there was no spare cheese, and there would be precious little to put into the stores for the winter. They had turned the hunting dogs loose to fend for themselves, but one had returned last night, starving and diseased, and had not survived the night. It needed to be buried or burned, but Leofsige, one of the few men left on the estate, had gone out foraging in the woods for her, steadfast in his loyalty, and desirous to see her well fed. She had teased him before he left, telling him it felt odd to send a bear to catch a hare, but he had been determined, as cook, to find something for them to eat. And while he was gone, he said, she could watch the cauldron and add water as necessary to keep the stew bubbling nicely, and he would bring a bit of meat to add to it.

Trying to ignore the fact that the stew consisted, essentially, of the water, she ladled more in, and gave the huge pot a good stir. Despondent, she unlocked her spice box, thinking how nice it would be to add flavour to the meagre meal, but she knew even before she lifted the lid that she would find little inside which would enhance the taste. Shaking her head, she closed the box, wondering why hope had ever triumphed over knowledge. She reached out for her leech-worts, briefly entertaining the notion that some of her healing herbs also tasted pleasant. But the thought was banished as quickly as it arrived, for she would never forgive herself if she ate anything that might help an ailing villager. She was not that hungry, yet.

Since the herbs and potions were on the table in front of her, she reasoned that she might as well check them for freshness and potency. Spreading them out in front of her, she began her inventory. She had plenty of dried elderflowers, and there might still be some berries worth picking. The garlic bulbs were ready to be pulled; garlic was always a good standby for headaches and sore throats. There should still be some heartsease to harvest, and she could dry the whole plants to keep in her store. It was too late in the year to collect any more nettle because it needed to be picked before flowering, but the meadowsweet would still be in flower and the blossom was useful not just for flavouring ale, but for easing pains in the joints of the elderly. When the kitchen door opened, she called out to Leofsige that she might need to send him back out again. "I will need some more elderberries, some feverfew, comfrey, oh and marigold."

"Would that be so that you can cast a spell with it?

Káta felt instantly cold, as if all the blood had drained from her body and out through her feet into the earth. Her heart began to knock loudly as if it, too, wanted to leave her body. She turned slowly, swallowing in an attempt to reintroduce saliva to her mouth. Standing in the doorway, the monk from Worcester was staring at her, his hands tucked into his sleeves. He exuded a sense of confident calmness which she was desperate to emulate. Lowering her chin slightly, she inhaled deeply and said, "You are always welcome at my house, Brother, although I must say I had not thought to see you again so soon."

The monk stepped into the room and she saw that he had not travelled alone. Two henchmen were visible just beyond the doorway and the noise of horse tack rattling and the scuffing of hooves suggested that there were more men waiting in the yard.

The monk, whose name she did not know, moved nearer. "We were not able to finish our business last time. Our beloved Bishop Oswald is locked up and cannot leave the minster, but we can still do his work for him." He raised his hand, preventing her speech. "And, before you ask, the lords Helmstan and Alvar are, as far as I can gather, busy over in the east, more days' ride away than it will take us to get to London."

Flexing her legs and trying to stop her knees from buckling, she said, "London?"

Panic created a loud noise in her head, making it difficult to hear his words. He explained something about taking her to trial, gave some reason for the location having to be London and she nodded but knew, even as she did so, that she had not listened properly. He repeated the charges against her. The crimes of brewing herbs and reciting curses to ward off nuisances such as wens were risible, given that every woman in every parish used such things in the absence of a Leech. They were no more than spoken orders that the wen would 'Shrivel as coal on the fire, shrink as muck in the wall, and waste away like water in a pail and become smaller than a worm's hipbone'. When he came to his last, though, she grew indignant.

"Well-worshipping? No, never. A simple rite carried out by the well; that was all. And it was so many years ago."

He smiled. Had she not known the reason for his

presence, she might have thought his expression benign. "You do not deny it?"

"Would it do me any good?"

"And what have you to say of the foul-smelling woman whom you brought to the house of another during childbirth, ensuring that the child was stillborn and could not be baptised?"

Outrage fuelled a burgeoning defiance. Káta lifted her head and said, "I say that without her, Hild would have died along with her child. The bairn was laid to rest in the eavesdrip, thus receiving water from the church roof and God's blessing. I am a Christian woman, Brother. Folklore and heathenism are not the same thing. If you came out into the world from behind your prayer books more often, you would know this."

The smile froze. "If, as you say, you are a Christian woman, then you will have naught to fear from ordeal." He turned and took a step to one side, allowing the men to come into the room.

Her bravery evaporated. "You mean to shackle me?"

"No, lady. Not unless we need to."

They would not let her ride, but made her walk between the horses. Not only did this make for a hot, uncomfortable and smelly journey, with dust and flies swirling around at her head height, but it also consigned any plans for escape to the realm of fantasy. Helmstan's rank spoke for naught now, and she was being treated like a lowly churl. She took no exception to her loss of status, but it reinforced the awareness that there was no-one to swear an oath for her, no-one to speak on her behalf, no-one to come to her rescue. The path led them further and further from Ashleigh, from the place which had given her welcome and shelter for all these years. Every impulse urged her to struggle, resist, run back to the haven of her home. With every step forward, the ball of fear in her belly expanded so that waves of dread rose up into her chest and set her heart hammering.

They came to the Chester road, but they would not turn north. From this point, there would be naught that was familiar to her; the terrain of fields, forests, and hedges would be similar, but not known. Would she ever be allowed to come home?

The horses came to a halt and, above her, the men began to mutter. Peering from her restricted vantage point, she strained to see around the beasts and ascertain why they had stopped. Ahead, the path had been blocked at the entrance to the woods. Parched trees had been felled, no doubt with ease, and laid across the track. The barrier had been supplemented with twigs, lumps of earth, stones and a brown lump that looked as if it might be a dead dog. Káta put her hand up to her mouth. With the path blocked, they would have to find another way round, either through the woods, or back to Ashleigh to take the road south of Oakhurst. Had Leofsige organised this; was he lying in wait to effect an ambush? Hope flew back from its banishment and lodged with a tentative grip in her mind, lifting her spirits and calming her heartbeat.

Flanked by the two lead horses, she had no choice but to turn when they did. The rider of the black stallion to her left leaned over and said, "I do not know why you are smiling. If we cannot get you to London, then we will do it here."

Káta could not look at him but stared at the ground, at a tiny patch of earth where four browned blades of grass stood proud of the dry, sand-like mud. The space between each blade was too vast, as if the earth were gradually balding. Káta continued to focus on the tiny area, while the icy shard of terror worked its chill all the way down her spine.

The rider of the black stallion called out to the monk. "We will have to find another way round. If not…"

If not, then what? Had he made a gesture, bringing his finger across his throat? Káta tried to swallow, but her mouth felt as if she had used her tongue to sweep the hall floor.

The monk urged his horse forward; she heard the hooves moving and his voice became louder, nearer. "My lord is the archbishop of York and the bishop of Worcester. He bade me bring this woman to trial, no more or less than that. Let us see what lies beyond that grove."

Káta kept her head bowed, but glanced up. To the west of the blocked pathway through the woods was a small cluster of trees that stood slightly apart from the rest. Beyond them lay the road to Oakhurst. Inhaling deeply in a bid to still the noise from her pounding heart, she wondered if, that way, also lay her rescue. Shuffling slowly between the two great beasts she found that her fear was punctuated by the most prosaic thoughts, beginning with the awareness that, up close, horses stank. Then she wondered idly who would watch the stew pot, and how long it would take before the untended cooking fire caught hold and sent the kitchen up in flames. When Gytha returned from visiting family in Northampton, would she find Ashleigh razed to the ground? Lost thus in a diversionary reverie, she was slow to the realisation that the henchman on the stallion had stopped to dismount. He came round between the horses and grabbed her forearm, pulling her out into the relatively fresh air. She breathed deeply, ridiculously pleased to be away from the smelly flanks. But the man's face told her all she needed to know about his plan. The monk might be intent on sticking fast to the exact specification of Oswald's orders, but this man was clearly a little more enthusiastic about the remit. Bored by the delay, he no doubt sought to salvage some fun from the day. He stretched his mouth into a horrible line, part smile, part grimace, and marched over to the nearest tree, striding so forcefully that she had to scrabble into a run to keep from stumbling.

The monk began to shout. "I will not be part of this. Further, I will not answer for it. This is not what was asked of us."

But though the monk would not be part of it, it was clear that he would expend no effort to help her either. Horribly fixed in the present, with no thoughts of domestic detail to distract her, Káta was despondently aware of the sound of the rest of the escort galloping away, and she knew that this was the point at which her life would end, here against this oak tree, and that this man's contorted face, etched with pleasure and hatred, would be the last she would see.

He reached the tree, turned on his heel and threw her round, so that her back smashed against the trunk. He held one hand across her throat whilst he fumbled at his belt for something. Káta closed her eyes. Either he was intent on raping her first, or he was reaching for his hand-saex. Whichever it was, she had no wish to see.

She heard something odd, thundering, but not hooves. Her assailant uttered an odd grunt of a sound and jerked forward, pressing his weight against her. She opened her eyes and was aware of a flash of something black and long. Widening her eyes, she saw the light brown bumps along its shaft, where the spikes of Hild's blackthorn stick had long ago been cut off and smoothed. Hild raised the knobbly stick high, brought it down in a wide arc and struck again, this time with so much force that the man slipped away sideways and fell to the ground. Before Káta could think about wriggling free, she heard a high-pitched song and saw a glint of something shiny, and then she looked down to see Leofsige's cleaver embedded in her attacker's back. Now her mind began to dwell again on stupid details that came flooding back into her thoughts, and she stared, wondering why there was no blood oozing from the sides of the blade.

Hild stepped forward and gathered Káta into her arms. Sobbing, she repeated, "My lady, oh my lady, my lady," and Káta, still focusing on the mundane, thought it peculiar that her own eyes remained dry.

Leofsige put his huge foot on the corpse and tugged the meat cleaver free.

The blood began to ooze. It did not pump, as it would from a living body, but spilled its all in a steady flow, much as an upturned jug would empty its contents and then stop.

Káta watched it for a while and then shook her head. "What must you think of me, that I did not thank you straight away for my life. Dear friends, how can I ever repay you?"

Leofsige continued to wipe the blood-sticky blade with the edge of his tunic. Without looking up, he said, "We love you, Lady, and would die for you. Now, word must be sent to Lord Helmstan."

It was as if she suddenly thawed. The freezing fear had been banished and now came the fire of anger. "No! He must never be told. If he knows, he will come home and the lord Alvar will come too. I will not be used as bait to turn them from their course." She could not even begin to contemplate which of them would be the most angry. She must endure in silence, because she knew how much Alvar had already given up and she would not suffer to see him lose any more, not on her account. Furthermore, he would feel guilty if he knew that his duty had taken Helmstan away from her at such a time; the man seemed to take responsibility for the wellbeing of the whole world. She did not want that on her conscience, she who was not his wife and all the more dangerous to him because of it. And how would it all be explained to Helmstan? She would die before she caused him any pain, or one second of doubting her love. "Never tell them, never. Do you understand me?"

Hild's arms were upon hers and the woman was making shushing noises as if soothing a teething child. Káta paused for breath and only then did she feel the tears running down her cheeks, the snot in her nose, and the scratchy feeling at the back of her throat that indicated how loudly she had been shouting. She sank to her knees, still supported by Hild who knelt with her, and she rocked back and forth, permitting the tears to flow. "They must not know, they must not know."

East Anglia

The wind was incessant and Alvar was growing tired of the endless need to flick his hair away from his eyes and mouth. Crouched beneath his blanket, he looked out across the boggy, featureless landscape and grunted. "I wish I could stop the wind with my shield and push it back whence it came."

"The folk here call it an idle wind, that does not bend but goes right through." Wulfgar smiled his crooked smile and hitched his blanket up tighter round his shoulders. Nodding at the sodden coverlet he said, "This wool has been my wind-shield since we got here and it is soaked through. Are you sure you want this land back? You have only to say the word and I will turn this whole fyrd about, and we can be back in my dale by nightfall." He rubbed his back.

"Too many years have passed for you to tell me now that you have no belly for a fight." It was a teasing comment, of the type used by them all to keep spirits up, yet Alvar could not look his friend in the eye; he was not ready to admit that the fire in his own belly had not long since been extinguished.

Helmstan stepped from his tent. "I would like to get on with it. It may be a godforsaken marsh, but by rights it is Mercian land and it is time we took it back."

"The lingering might soon be at an end. Look to the

south."

Wulfgar and Alvar stood up and discarded the woollen blankets. Awareness grew among the other men and they gathered round their leaders. The East Anglian fyrd was approaching from the direction of Ramsey. The richly clothed, well-equipped noblemen were easy to pick out but Alvar, his eyesight not as sharp as in his youth, squinted to make out the identity of the bishop who was riding with them. "It is Athelwold; he must have been at Ely when we sent that monk there to find Brandon." He kicked dirt over the fire. "I give them this; they have brighter wits than I thought." If the East Anglians were determined to avoid a battle, they could have done worse than bring with them the one holy man for whom Alvar might have lowered his weapons. However, it was unnecessary, for he had no intention of wielding his sword or his spear. He had already decided to bring things to a conclusion; this was merely a show of strength to complete the restoration of lands to the secular lords, which he considered to be the first and best step to helping the hungry, by giving them back the means to scratch a living from the land. The army at his back had gathered from a different source than his own anger and attached itself to him like a nest of wasps growing larger and larger. He would use the strength of numbers to wrest back the land, but from here it was his plan to seek out Edward's council and begin to extract order from chaos. Meanwhile, like two cock birds, he and the opposing forces must display their feathers and crow their challenges.

The East Anglian fyrdsmen came to a halt and their leaders moved their mounts ten paces forward. Alvar grabbed his helm.

"My lord, your byrnie?" Wulfgar held out Alvar's mail coat.

Alvar took the heavy body armour from him and put it on, giving Wulfgar his helm to hold while he slid the mail on over his head. The other thegns followed suit, whilst the wealthier freemen fastened up their padded jackets and picked up their spears. A horse-thegn brought Alvar's stallion. He mounted up and urged the animal forward. Behind him, his army clanked and rattled as it followed him.

He led his men across the marshy ground, until the two delegations were close enough to exchange words. Here, he called his men to a halt and copied the East Anglians, as he and his leading thegns also moved forward by ten paces. Behind him, his soldiers formed a colourful shield wall that painted the bare landscape, while the banners snapped back and forth in the wind.

The lord of Thetford, Brandon's elder brother, was the first to speak. "You must put an end to this madness. Stop threatening God's churches, and leave these lands at once. If you do not go, we will drive you from here."

Alvar looked at him for a moment, but spoke only to his friend. "Lord Bishop, I am sorry that you have been brought here to witness my deeds. I would have you know that I do not bring this fight to God, or those who serve Him, only to those who would hide behind His name."

Athelwold opened his mouth but his words flew away with the buffeting wind. He brought his horse forward until he was level with Alvar. "I had thought to find you fully wroth, swinging your weapons and bent on doing harm. But I can see in your eyes, my lord, that your temper has blown itself out." He lifted his arm. "You must go now to the queen, for the lady Alfreda has need of a friend. And our young king is in need of wise words from a man who can teach him." He leaned in closer. "You know as well as I do that the folk thrown off church lands are not the only ones who are starving. We should do naught to make any man's burden heavier." He paused, as if considering whether he had said enough to press his point. "You hold sway over this land. All are watching you, waiting to see what you will do next." He gave a sad smile.

Behind them, Brandon leaned forward to catch the bishop's words. He nodded, his head bobbing like a delicate flower-head in the wind. "Yes, yes, you must go back. Do not bring shame to your rank of earl."

Alvar smiled at Athelwold, marvelling that one so aged could still sit so firmly astride a horse. In tones just loud enough for the bishop to hear, he said, "Your words are well meant, but not needed. You speak my thoughts. But allow me one last boast?"

He lifted his head and shouted across to Brandon. "The lord of East Anglia is so keen to see my back. I can only guess that he is frightened to fight me."

He sniffed and looked around him. Wulfgar was right when he said that with a hard ride they could all be sleeping in Mercian beds come nightfall. He said, "Peterborough can wait. My men will leave and you may tell the brothers within that they are free to go about their day's work with no fear." He moved his horse forward and spoke so that only Athelwold could hear. "I have been riding long and hard, only to come to this wilderness. It is as if the glee-man teases me with his hiding games; I feel that he has opened his hands and they are empty."

Athelwold reached out and patted Alvar's hand. "You have not found what you sought, my son. Nevertheless, your wrath is quenched, and God will lead you to the right path now."

Alvar put a hand to his stomach. "Odd, but I feel hunger. I have not craved food nor slaked my thirst for so long. But now…"

"You were numbed by a death, and now your body is reminding you that the death was not your own. Go home. Live. Put this kingdom back together."

Athelwold turned his horse and as he drew level, Brandon and Thetford pulled on their reins and moved back towards their men. Alvar, Wulfgar and Helmstan turned their horses back towards their camp.

They drew level with the ranks and Wulfgar leaned over to set the news murmuring along the line. Cupped hands sent the whisper through the throng, but behind the shield wall, Godere, a thegn of Chester, shouted out.

"No! This land is Mercian and we will have it." He leaped onto his horse and rushed to meet them, his sword unsheathed.

Wulfgar said, "What is he thinking?

Helmstan shook his head. "What does he mean to do?

As Godere moved towards him, Alvar lunged forward from his saddle to stop him, but missed by a hand's breadth.

Helmstan stood up in his stirrups and reached out with both arms. "I have him." He caught the edge of the saddle cloth and twisted round with it as Godere rode by. The thegn had gained speed; the cloth ripped through Helmstan's hands and he fell from his horse.

As Godere thundered closer to the turned backs of the East Anglians, divots of soft fenland soil flew up. Thetford turned round and manoeuvred his horse so that he could face Godere head on. He, too, raised his sword, but as Godere crashed at him, sword arm up and ready to strike, Thetford threw down his sword and snatched a spear from his guard. He held his shield ready to deflect Godere's blow, but when Godere was near enough and raised his arm to strike, Thetford held the spear up and thrust it into Godere's unprotected side. The spearhead pierced Godere's byrnie as quick and clean as a kingfisher dive, breaking the surface as if it were water. Momentum carried Godere's torso halfway down the shaft. Thetford let go and Godere thumped to the ground.

The soldiers stared. Only the banners broke the stillness as they slip-slapped in the east wind. Athelwold made the sign of the cross, Brandon bowed his head. Thetford dismounted but stayed by his men.

Someone in the Mercian fyrd struck his spear shaft against his shield. Others joined in and the rhythmic thumping stirred Alvar from his daze. He ran, and skidded onto his knees by the fallen thegn. He leaned over Godere's face, but felt no breath. Brandon and Athelwold came to stand by the body.

Alvar said, "He is dead." He stood up. "My lord

Brandon, you and I will speak with your brother about this man's wergild."

Brandon flushed. "My brother will know what he has to do. He is a great… "

Alvar put up his hand and Brandon flinched. "You…" Alvar uncurled his fist and put his arm back down by his side. "You must tell him, my lord Earl." He turned to the bishop. "Before you offer up this man's soul, I will hold to my oath and take my men from this field. But listen; do you hear how they shout? Their feelings are strong. This is not merely a fight between earls; this goes much deeper and will take a lot of healing." He began to walk away. "I will send men to take this poor man's body, but now I have a wounded thegn who needs my help."

He ran back to Helmstan, who was lying where he had fallen. Wulfgar was on his knees beside him.

Alvar said, "Any broken bones, friend? Your wrinkled brow tells me that there are." He knelt down and felt along Helmstan's legs.

Helmstan said, "No. I had the wind knocked out of me and I will have a sore arse tomorrow, but otherwise I am whole." He twisted his head and looked towards the cluster of people gathered round Godere's corpse. "I wish, though, that I could have stopped him. He was a good thegn, but his tongue always took him further than his thoughts might have led him. Now all I can do is to get his wergild for his widow."

"I have already said that I will speak to Thetford about it. He may be brother to the earl of these lands, but he need not think he can kill a thegn without amends. Here, give me your hand and let us get you back on your saddle. Can you ride?"

Helmstan's chin jutted forward as if his teeth were clenched, but he nodded.

Alvar clicked his fingers for a runner to fetch Helmstan's men, and he and Wulfgar helped him to his feet. Helmstan leaned on them as they looked once more at the bloodstain on the fenland soil. Helmstan allowed Wulfgar to lift him back into his saddle.

Alvar said, "Ride home, friend. Have that sweet wife of yours look at those wounds that you are hiding from me, and come back to us when you can."

Flanked by his men, Helmstan left the field. He sat bent over the saddle, one shoulder higher than the other. He disappeared beyond the line of tents and Alvar shook his head.

Wulfgar said, "When he first fell, he was holding his side. I could see that it was hard for him to breathe."

"I know. I saw it too."

Chapter Eighteen AD977

Gloucestershire

In his great hall at Upper Slaughter, Alvar was sitting at a table on the dais with Wulfgar on one side and his steward on the other. He glanced down and re-read the document in his hands. Set on richly embroidered cloths, the finest candlesticks cluttered the table in front of him, and his two favourite hounds were lying sprawled behind him on the floor, their tails occasionally thrumming against the bottom hem of an enormous wall-hanging and causing a cold draught. Brandon of East Anglia and his brother were sitting side by side, facing him. Next to them were representatives for Ely Abbey, three monks whose apparel was the only drab cloth in the room. Brandon was looking past Alvar to the wall behind him and his cheek twitched when Alvar said, "You did not think to find such rich gold wall-hangings in my house. Did you think that with no woman of my own, my house would be bare?"

Brandon put his hand to his face as the colour bled into his cheeks.

"You do not answer. That tells me that I am right, then." Alvar sat forward and stared at Brandon, but the younger man looked down.

Lord Thetford leaned forward and opened his mouth, but Alvar gave him no chance to speak.

"So, to business." He slapped the document with the back of his hand. "It says here that King Edgar gifted forty hides of land at Hatfield to the abbey of Ely." Alvar looked up.

The monks answered with enthusiastic nods.

"It says further that the land was rich in wood, and would therefore give the good brothers endless timber and firewood."

Again there was vigorous nodding.

"Then Brandon of East Anglia and his brother took the land, saying that it had been stolen from their father."

The monks shook their heads whilst Thetford gave one, emphatic nod.

"Now the good monks wish to buy back the land which was their only woodland. Have I understood this right?"

One of the monks cleared his throat. "My lord, we offer in its stead, thirty hides at Hemingford which were willed to the abbey by Wulfstan of Dalham."

Alvar wondered who this Wulfstan was, and whether he had bequeathed the land willingly.

But Thetford said, "We could have settled this matter ourselves."

Alvar said, "Really? If, as you say, that land was stolen from you, then you are also saying that King Edgar was a thief."

Thetford glared at him dismissively. "King Edgar did not know at the time that it was stolen, but that is not the point. As to the monks' offer, I know that the land at Hemingford was not the only land bequeathed by Wulfstan. He also left the abbey six hides at Wennington."

Alvar said, "Holy hell. You crave that, too?"

Thetford said, "And more besides, because those two together would still not be worth the land at Hatfield."

Alvar was determined to settle all these disputes lawfully. "If I were you, my lord Thetford, I would stop my bleating. I have been told that Godere's widow has not yet been paid her man's wergild. I give you thirty days. If you foul my hall with falsehoods today, I will shorten it to fourteen." He glared at Thetford until the other man accepted the threat and sat back.

Alvar turned once more to the monks. "What else have you got?"

They bent their heads and conferred. They looked up at Brandon, glanced at Alvar, and huddled together once more.

Alvar slipped off his garnet ring and twirled it over his thumb and back to his fingertip. "Brothers, if we could have an answer before dusk… These good lords must make their way home to East Anglia." He grinned at the accused.

Brandon said, "It is kind of you to think of our plight."

Alvar continued to smile at him.

Brandon's jaw dropped slack. "Oh, you meant that we must begin our ride home, for there is no welcome at your hearth this night."

Wulfgar let out a snort. Alvar clicked his fingers, and servants came forward to pour drinks into gold cups.

One of the monks raised a hand. "My lord, if we must… There are five hides at Welling which we could offer."

"How came the abbey by these?"

"They came to the abbey through the wrongdoing of Wulfwine the cook and his wife, Alswytha. It was lawfully written and witnessed."

Alvar sighed. "I knew a woman, once, of that name. How filthy this world would look to our Swytha now. My lord of East Anglia, we have heard little from you. What do you have to say?"

Brandon sat up and smoothed his tunic, and Alvar glanced behind him to where the smaller of the two hounds thumped his tail, waiting in the same way to be noticed.

Brandon patted a pouch full of documents. "Should you care to read these, you will see how many acres of land the abbey now holds which were taken unlawfully, or else not bought for their full worth. It is not hard to believe that the land at Hatfield came to the abbey in a likewise way."

Alvar grunted. He agreed. They had suffered at the hands of Ely almost as much as Worcester's land thefts had plagued him. Could they see it, though? "How does it feel, now that you tread in my shoes?"

Brandon shook his head and looked at his brother.

Alvar said, "I can see that you do not understand. As at Worcester, so at Ely? No? Well, so be it." He stood up, pushed his chair back, and delivered his judgement. "Hatfield will be given back, in return for Hemingford, Wennington and Yelling." As Thetford tutted and blew, he said, "Let it be written. And do not be sent like children to me again."

Outside Alvar's hall, the overhang of billowing willow trees shaded a cool green sward. A light breeze carried the song of a thrush from the orchard. Alvar stood on the soft grass, closed his eyes, and breathed in the cleansing air, deep and full.

Wulfgar joined him. They stared at each other and gave in to their laughter.

"God, if I died today, the first thing I would do at heavenly gate would be to thank the Lord for giving me this morning." When Alvar had vowed to restore order through the strict application of the law, he had not expected to derive amusement from it.

Wulfgar wiped at his eyes with his tunic sleeve. "Truly they looked as if they had come before the hangman, did they not?"

"I think that they would rather see the hangman than have to sit before me. Ely has become like Worcester; they could not see what I meant by that, but now they know how it feels to have their land taken from them by the Church. What a sweet taste. East Anglia bows to me, and Oswald is penned in Worcester. Oh, life is good."

He had not seen the visitor when he first came outside, but now the young rider dismounted and approached them, hanging back while they laughed again and thumped each other on the back.

"Lord... Alvar?"

"Yes, I am he. You find us in a merry mood, so I am bound to say yes to whatever you ask."

"No, my lord, I have not come to ask anything of you."

The youth's arm seemed too heavy to lift as he pointed without precision to the tether-post. Next to his mount, head down, a pack horse was grazing on the sweet grass.

Alvar looked where the boy pointed. The sight stole his laughter; a pail of water over a drunk's head. "You bring me heriot?"

The boy nodded and looked at the ground.

"Whose is it?"

The pack horse raised its head to reveal a white flash on its nose. Alvar exchanged glances with Wulfgar, and Wulfgar ran over to the beast. He looked at the painted shield and then at the finely engraved sword. He picked up the helm and turned it over in his hands, fingering the dents. Alvar let out his held breath, but only snatched at another one.

The boy handed him a written message, but it lay unopened, unnecessary, in Alvar's hands, as Wulfgar stumbled the few steps back to them.

"It is Helmstan's. It is Helmstan who is dead."

Cheshire

"He all but fell from his horse after riding from Peterborough that night. It was hard for him to breathe and when we got him to his bed, we found that two of his ribs were broken. We bound him tight, and he lay abed all through winter, and we thought that he would heal come springtime. It was a hard winter, as you know. Many folk starved." Káta looked up. "We lost Burgred. And Brunstan."

She lowered her head again and stared at her hands. "We took care that our lord did not go hungry. But he never regained his strength. His breathing grew hoarse, even though we gave him cheese with dry bread to help his weak chest. Then the fever came to Ashleigh." She fidgeted in her chair. "So many were sick with it, and we did not let them near our lord but he had no strength. A cough came that would not be soothed, not even with honey and dill seed, and it worsened, and brought with it so much blood…"

Siferth reached forward and took her hand. "There is no more to tell, Uncle."

Alvar swallowed to shift whatever was stuck in his throat. He blinked and turned away. The hall was full of more bundles and belongings than there were people, and it seemed that as well as the house staff, many villagers had been finding comfort from sleeping in the hall since the death of their lord.

He took a steadying breath and turned back to Káta. "My lady, what can I say to ease your hurt?" Helmstan had bequeathed most of his lands to her, knowing that Siferth would be gifted his own by the queen, and there might be some comfort in the realisation that she was wealthy enough to take care of all their dependants. But when would she surrender to personal grief?

"I did worry, because I should have burned the crop when he died; folklore says that in this way the house and those who still dwell within will be safeguarded." She looked up at him. "But my folk were hungry."

"Lady, you fed your folk. You are wise enough to know when folklore is wrong and when it is right. Look to yourself now. Your folk will not mind."

She gave the smallest of smiles. "I know that. I thank you for your kind words. I did not know what to do. You have ever been so… And Helmstan was always… It is harder than I thought to be on my own after so many years."

He counted on his fingers but she stopped him.

"Twenty, my lord. We were wed the year after you were gifted your earldom."

"For almost all those years he was my steadfast thegn. And he was a friend for even longer. You are right, Lady, it is hard to be without him."

They sat together by the fire. The light from the windows sank away and the hearth-fire lit the evening.

Siferth was the first to break the silence. "I think I liked best the tales of Offa and how he fought off the Welsh. You would have liked those too, Uncle. Then there was Penda, who fought the Northumbrians and all Christians. And I liked the tales of the lady of the Mercians and her husband, the lord Ethelred. Father said to me many times that he hoped that Lord Æthelred would become as strong a leader as his namesake. And there was the Greybeard, my father's lord. How saddened Father was to lose his lord…"

Káta offered no memories to share. Instead, she stared into the fire and smiled. "Yes, he liked that."

Alvar sat forward. "My lady?"

She shook her head and settled her hands in her lap. Her head moved first one way and then the other. She gave a small laugh and said, "That was ever his way."

Alvar pushed his chair back. Though the hall was full, Káta was somewhere on her own and he felt he should not be watching. He did not wish to add to her misery and he searched his memory for a harmless anecdote, one which would not initiate fresh pain. He slapped his hands on his thighs. "Wales. Did I ever tell you? One time by the fire, he told me that I must have a soft arse if I had a need to sit so near the heat and leave him to freeze behind me. That was after he had stepped in the path of a wounded boar and put his sword through it before it could kill me. Once he found a finch, dropped from a nest, and he kept it warm in his great hands all night. And he was the only one who did not whinge about the cold wind at Peterborough…" The next word felt solid and would not pass his throat. Alvar, like Siferth before him, fell silent.

"I find myself thinking," Káta said, "How I never minded when he was so often away from home. So to stop the weeping, I play a game, that he is away again now and that any time I will hear him riding in, but it does not work, for I know in my heart that he is gone."

"Mother, can you not try to get some rest?"

Alvar said, "You look as if you have had many sleepless nights. You do not look well. Will you have a nap?"

She nodded and stood up. "If I can. You will bide here a while?"

Alvar looked at Siferth.

"Uncle and I have to ride to a witenagemot, Mother. We must leave at morning light and even then we will be late getting there."

"The queen will be waiting for you."

"Yes."

"Then I must thank you all the more for making time to come when you have so little of it, my lord."

He reached for her hand. She tightened her fingers around his and he covered them with his other hand. "How could I not?"

Kirtlington, Oxfordshire

It was dusk when they arrived, but all around were the signs of a settlement swollen to twice its size. Tents were flapping in the breeze, pitched next to new buildings with unfinished roofs. Horses had been tethered too close together outside the stables. Alvar said, "I will warn you now that all the men of the witan will ask you about your father but do not worry, for I have not forgotten what it was like to lose my mother when I was fifteen. I will not leave your side."

They rode through the gateway and Alvar put his head to one side. "That is not the din of a merry gathering. He looked about him and said, "It looks as though you will be spared the ordeal of speaking about your father. Something is not right here."

They handed their horses to a groom, and Alvar waylaid a monk scurrying across from the church to the hall. "What is going on, Brother?"

The monk stopped, looked at Alvar's fine clothes, and gave a deep bow. "My lord, at midday the bishop of Crediton fell down dead."

"Sideman? Good God, that was unforeseen. Edward will be heartbroken to have lost his teacher."

"The king is more, how shall I say, wroth, than upset, my lord. Forgive me." The monk hurried inside.

Alvar and Siferth followed him. Inside the cramped hall, the air was warm. Most of the onlookers were pressed against the walls, seeking to distance themselves from the argument. King Edward was standing on the dais, red in the face as he shouted at Dunstan, who was standing with his head bowed.

"I am the king, do you not understand that? I say it will be Abingdon."

"I hear you, my lord, but the g-good man's bishopric was, after all, Crediton."

Alvar spotted Wulfgar amongst the reluctant witnesses and went to stand next to him. "What was the taper that sparked this fire?"

"It is barely believable," Wulfgar said, turning his head as if looking for a means of escape. "They are fighting like hounds over the bishop's bones."

"What is there to fight about?"

"From what I can gather, Sideman wished to be buried at Crediton, but, and here we can only wonder why, Edward has said that his body should be taken to Abingdon. Dunstan seeks to make him think otherwise."

Alvar shook his head. "This is not a worthy…" He was distracted by the frantic look of despair on the archbishop's face. Dunstan stared at him as if in silent appeal, and Alvar knew that they were both recalling the incident so many years ago, when the then bishop had fought with the Fairchild over the bones of the late king, the Fairchild's uncle. Nothing that had happened in the intervening years had loosened Alvar's notion of right and wrong, and if Dunstan needed his help to ensure that the bishop was buried in the spot he had requested, then so be it. If Dunstan was finally realising that he could not manipulate every king, Alvar was not in the business of gloating.

Siferth said, "His folk are hungry, fighting for their old-rights. Many things lie rotting for need of settlement by law, and look how the lord Edward whiles away his time."

Alvar grunted his agreement and stepped forward, intending to make his way to the dais.

But Queen Alfreda came to stand beside them. "My stepson was in a sore temper anyway; this afternoon he shouted at me so loudly I thought my ears would burst."

Little Æthelred clutched her hand and said, "It frightened me."

Alvar looked once more at the dais and he laid a hand on Alfreda's arm. "What did Edward say to you?"

She shuddered. "He sought me out when the bishop died and told me about the night two years ago, when they came to tell him that his father was dead, and how once he heard that he was to be king, he knew that he had no more to fear from me or mine. But then he put his mouth right near to mine and cursed me, saying that I oft-times came into his sleep, even now." She shook her head. "My son is no longer a threat to him and he knows this, so I do not understand what he meant about his dreams."

It was not hard to explain. Alvar said, "You took his mother's place and he knew that he should loathe you, but you are lovely to look upon. You are all that is needed to fill a man's sleep with yearning. He will not have known which was strongest; his hatred of you or his longing for you."

"No, that cannot be. Truly, do you think that he felt…?"

"I do not know why you wonder at it. He is not the only man in the witan to think of you in that way."

Alfreda tilted her head and patted Alvar's arm. "I have always known that some…" She looked up and her smile faded. She released her hold on him. "My lord, you are not yourself this night."

Siferth was leaning against Alvar as if he would fall if he stood alone. Alvar reached round and dropped his arm over the boy's shoulder. "My lady, forgive me. We have come here at the saddest of times."

Alfreda looked from one to the other. "Indeed you look like you share a sadness that is deep and dear to you both." Her gaze flicked over both of their faces once more. "No, it cannot be. Siferth is not… Is not your son… Do you have a wife elsewhere?" Her mouth creased as her face shrank into a frown. "I wonder that you have the time, Lord Alvar." In even terser tones she said, "Although I understand now why you have been so long away from court these past two years, when we have needed you here."

Wulfgar turned his head, wrenching his gaze from the spectacle on the dais to look at Alvar. Siferth broke free from Alvar's grip and stood with his chin raised in front of the man he called 'Uncle.' Alfreda squinted as if in expectation of a powerful blow.

Alvar looked at them all in turn and said, "No, my lady. For the last two years I have been in the saddle. But I only wish that I could say yes, for the truth is that this youth's father was the most steadfast, stalwart, and hard-working man that ever lived and he rightly loved his son, for he knew the man that he would become. I would be proud to call Siferth my son."

Wulfgar lowered his shoulders and exhaled. Alfreda inclined her head and left them to their grief.

Siferth smiled and said, "Those were kind words, Uncle."

"It was but the truth, youngling. You know me, I always speak the…"

Edward's shout was now a screech. "I am your lord King and I will speak the king's words. For once in my life I will not be told what to do by a churchman, living or dead!"

Alvar glanced around the hall at the other men of the witan. They were either looking at their shoes or had developed a sudden interest in their ale cups. He was sure he spoke the thoughts of many of them when he said, "Holy Jesus, he is not yet sixteen. Can we only hope that he goes the way of his forebears and decides against living to an old age?"

Chapter Nineteen AD978

Calne, Wiltshire

Bishop Athelwold looked up, his eyes swimming milky with age. "You swore to me in the winter of last year that there would be no more of this. Now here we are with only two weeks until Easter-month and all is far from well." His old friend met his gaze with a small smile that wrenched Alvar's guts more than any knife blade. "Edgar's was a peaceable reign but, free from Viking raids, you all turned in on yourselves. Now, without Edgar, it falls to you to put a stop to all the wrangling."

Alvar looked around the dingy hall at the assembled witan members. Many thegns had come, not just from the local area, as was usual, but from all over the country. It was a visible demonstration of the strength of feeling throughout the land, but it made for a crowded meeting hall. Some grimaced as they sat down on wobbly chairs, while others ran their hands across badly planed table-boards. Some late arrivals came to the top of the stairs and squinted in the poor light of the upstairs chamber. Few of them spoke.

Alvar turned back to the bishop and said, "I gave you my oath that there would be no more fighting, but there is still much unrest. I seek only to calm it." He waved his arm in a wide sweep and said, "Look at them; they are in a grim mood indeed. Here are men who have watched starvation kill their kin, their friends, and their thralls, while all the time food-tolls must be paid to the monasteries, and they have come to ask Edward to put it right."

"You have stirred them up."

"No. They came to me." Alvar shook his head. "This was not of my doing, I swear to you. In Edgar's day, men sought me out, knowing that I had the king's ear. Edward will listen to no man but Dunstan, but men with grievances still come to me because they know that I will not sit idly by. I have served kings all my life. I wish to do so again but…" He held his hands up and let them fall to his sides.

His old friend nodded. "I understand. Some say that Dunstan might be rueing the day that he set the king-helm on Edward's head."

"Will he heed us now, do you think?"

Athelwold sighed and put his arms out, palms up, lifting one then the other like weighing pans. "He feels he must stand true to the man he made a king, but he also knows that Edward would leave him like a lamb before the wolves."

"That is all I can ask for; that he might listen to what we have to say."

Athelwold shook his head. He stood up and leaned on his wooden staff. "I have given you more hope than I meant to. The archbishop would rather hold hot coals than stand before you all and tell you that he was wrong."

"I thought last year that I had felt the frost begin to thaw."

"Then you were mistaken. And whilst you might have blunted Oswald's teeth, you have not stilled his tongue. He sends many letters from Worcester outlining his wishes, and Dunstan reads them all."

Alvar said, "Then I must keep on listening to what my heart tells me."

Dunstan and the other bishops entered the chamber and Athelwold went to join them.

The other witan members made their way to their places. One said, "I should not be climbing stairs with my old weary legs. Why has Edward brought us here? Can anyone remember the last time a moot was held here?"

His companion said, "It is so dim in here that I can barely see my way to my seat. And it stinks."

Alvar looked around him. The straw on the floor was clean but not evenly spread. "I do not think the household knew we were coming until yesterday."

Edwin, the new young earl of Kent, tugged at a warped shutter but it stuck fast. He banged it with his flat palm and swore. "By the holy bloody rood..."

Alvar said, "It is a shame it is so stiff; you look as if you would like to shut someone's head in it. Tell me; are the Rochester monks still cursing you to hell?"

Edwin walked over to him, bending low to avoid a beam.

Alvar looked at the younger man's spotty chin, and circled his aching shoulders; the shutter was not the only thing grown stiff with age.

Edwin said, "I was as even-handed as I could be at that hundred-moot last year, but the monks were so sure of my finding in their favour that they were cross when I did not. All of a sudden, I was accused of stealing their land. It was a little unforeseen, to tell you the truth."

Alvar smiled at the understatement. "You are not the first to come to me with such a tale. I only wish I could say that you will be the last, but that rests with the archbishop and whether he will heed us."

Edwin grinned. "You have a way of getting men to see things your way..." He closed his mouth and bowed low.

Alvar turned round. Edward shuffled past them, his newly acquired broadness of shoulder dragging his body into a hunch; a puppy trying to control its adult body. In the small room, chairs collided as men scraped them back. When Edwin of Kent sat down, he put his elbows on the table and it rocked on uneven legs. Wulfgar tried to stretch his legs out and only succeeded in kicking Alvar. Alvar said, "Get a window open before we all choke for want of clean air."

Wulfgar waved to a serving-boy. The lad could not get through the jumbled mass of tables, so Wulfgar pointed to the window and mimed the action.

Dunstan remained on his feet and as the coughs and murmurs subsided, he looked round the room and focused on Alvar. "My lords, I would have all words spoken out loudly this day, not whispered in dark corners."

Alvar nodded and stood up. "As you ask, so shall it be. Every man here knows my thoughts on the theft of Mercian land and my rights therein, so there is naught new to tell about that. But other men, from beyond Mercia, have come to me seeking redress. Leofric of Ramsey reports how Archbishop Oswald ate and drank like a king there, while outside the abbey, the folk starved. My own thegn, Wulfgar of Munford, has kin from Worcester who were made homeless by the archbishop's own kin from the east. Thegn Ethelnoth's lands were taken from him and given to the abbot of Malmesbury these three years gone." He took a deep breath and swallowed, but the musty air stuck in his throat. He coughed. "I also hear of folk whose land at Taunton was taken from them and given to the bishop of Winchester, and that even though our good queen, the lady Alfreda, spoke on their behalf, they are still homeless and hungry."

Many shouted their agreement and pointed fingers at Bishop Athelwold but Alvar, always less comfortable attacking the queen's champion, looked down at a dirty stain on the floorboards and poked it with his foot. He looked up when the clamour subsided and he put out his arms. "These men would have their land back, my lord Archbishop, and they are but a few of those who have been wronged in this way."

Dunstan cast another glance around the room, as if to assess the mood of the men gathered there, and shot a look of appeal to the silent Edward, who remained seated on the king-stool and picked at his nails.

"My lord Alvar, these are b-but one or two tales. Tales,"

he emphasised the word, "Which have not been heard in law. They do not speak for the whole of my lord King's lands."

"Oh, I can give you more. A thegn in East Anglia, one Alfric, unable to settle a debt, had his land given to the abbey at Ely."

Dunstan shook his head. "If I find it hard t-to accept your words as the truth, it is b-because the lord Brandon, who is lord in the lands of which you speak, does not come to me bearing the same tales."

A shout came up from the back of the hall. "He is too busy taking land for himself."

Alvar turned, but the heckler remained faceless in the crowd of men who nudged each other.

Dunstan waited for quiet. "All I am saying is that not all the carls are with you in this. We hear nothing from East Anglia, or Essex, or from Northumbria."

A Northumbrian voice called out. "You saw to it that Earl Beorn is too far away to be heard!" He was applauded with whoops and jeers directed at the figures on the dais.

Again, Dunstan waited for calm.

Edwin of Kent left his seat and went to stand next to Alvar. "You will hear from me, my lord. And I stand with Mercia on this."

Wulfgar got to his feet. "I, too."

One by one, thegns from all areas stood up, declared their agreement and went to stand near Alvar. Brihtmær of Chester and Aswy of Shropshire moved to their lord's side as expected, but Osmund of Suffolk came too. Wedwine of Ramsey left Brandon's side, and brought his own men with him. Soon, only a handful of men remained in their seats as the witan members stood to join the Mercians in the centre of the room. The malcontents stood in defiant silence and Alvar waited for Dunstan to admit defeat. He looked at the king, who was sitting slumped, with his head forward.

Alvar nudged Wulfgar and pointed. "See how idle Edward is, to sleep while…"

Wulfgar opened his mouth to reply, but then he touched Alvar's arm. "My lord? Do you hear it?"

Alvar tilted his head to one side and listened to the slow rumble as it grew louder. He looked down at his feet. The rumble gave way to loud creaking, the floor moved, and he put a hand on the table to steady himself. Around him, men turned to each other, shook their heads and frowned. A splintering crack followed the creaking as the middle section of the floor gave way. Alvar saw the realisation on Wulfgar's face a second before they, and all those who had been standing with them, were hurled with the falling timbers to the floor below. Lengths of oak tables fell through after the hurtling beams and rotten floorboards; chair legs speared men who lay helpless, injured or worse by the fall. They lay, innocent killers of those under them, those who had dropped first and were buried before they died.

The sound of crashing timber subsided and a cloud of plaster-dust rose and fell. In the silence, another sound, an unearthly groan, grew louder, until one final beam broke off and landed on the top of the heap. It came to rest, tottered, and the higher end wavered before, with one last creak, it settled.

Alvar lay still while he waited for the tell-tale pain to manifest itself. When none came, he felt along his arms and as far down his legs as he could reach without sitting up.

"Wulfgar?"

A muffled voice came from below him. "If my lord would shift his arse from my head, I would find answering him less of a hardship."

The long silence broken, men began trying to move, calling out to friends or crying out in pain. No longer able to hear his friend, Alvar shuffled around and found Wulfgar pinned down under a floorboard. He shoved the wood away from Wulfgar's chest, sat him up, and held his arm around him until he was happy with his breathing. He helped him up and they scrabbled at the fallen timbers so that they could free others who were still trapped. Rescuers began working from the other end of the lower room and, as he and Wulfgar dug with their hands, Alvar shouted out. "Thegn Wulfgar and I are here; keep coming this way as you can. Delve deep, for many are hidden."

Above them, Dunstan was the first to stir, and scrambled out onto the only beam which remained intact throughout the length of the broken section of the floor. He peered down at the pile of bodies and splintered wood, and turned his back on the scene.

Wulfgar said, "How swiftly these churchmen run."

But Dunstan's voice rang out. "My lord King, Bishops, follow me down the stairs. You, king's reeve; gather your men and go in to help those who have fallen. You, there; send riders to the abbeys at Bath and Malmesbury. Bring back monks who have knowledge of healing. My lords, I will see you safe down the steps, and then I must go and help in any way that I can."

Alvar raised an eyebrow. "Who would have thought it?" He spat dust and wiped his mouth with his sleeve, and looked around him to see what needed to be done next. The fallen men attempted to get up, and those who were unscathed or only wounded moved away to reveal those who had not been so fortunate, crushed under the weight of timbers and bodies. Alvar and Wulfgar lifted each dead man as soon as the body was freed.

On the other side of the lower chamber, King Edward could be heard berating his clergy. "I look to you to shield me from harm, but I could have been killed here today."

Dunstan said, "My lord King, you were not killed, but many have been. We must look to those who need our help, and offer up prayers for those who are beyond such earthly cares."

"No." It could have been another piece of falling timber, but the subsequent crack sounded more like a hand on a face. "All of my life I have had a man of God telling me what to do. Even when I became king you all told me that you knew best, even after I was a man grown. And now my lords fight as they would never have done in my father's time. They make it known that they would have that gristbiter Æthelred as their king. All I have so far to show for my kingship is starvation and fighting and roofs falling in."

Edward's voice rose higher and the unwilling eavesdroppers lowered their gaze and returned to their search, grabbing at the debris in silence. Alvar kept his head low, listening for moans under the noise of Edward's screeching.

"This is God's doom on my witan. They are gutless men who would not know the hue of a dog turd. And speaking of little shits, where is that weak brat and his whore of a mother? Why were they not here to feel God's wrath... Was this her doing? Did my stepmother mean for me to die here this day?"

Bishop Athelwold spoke now, his elderly voice cracking. "Lord King, the lady Alfreda is at her house at Corfe. She will be greatly saddened by this sorrowful news. She is a good Christian woman and will spend many hours kneeling before the altar, praying for these lost souls."

"Liar. All through my kingship that bitch has sat and smirked, biding her time until the day her whelp can take my king-seat. Well they will not have it!"

Wulfgar let out a slow whistle. "Surely he will not strike the bishop now?"

But there were no more raised voices. They redoubled their efforts to free those still trapped and to remove the bodies of those who were beyond help.

Alvar took up one end of a beam, Wulfgar the other. "One, two, three, heave." They hurled the wood to the side of the room and knelt down to pull out Osmund of Suffolk, bloodied, but alive.

Alvar said, "I wondered where you had gone. First you were standing beside me, but then you went away."

Osmund grinned. "I thought I would go downstairs for a while, my lord, but I was too idle to walk the long way."

"While you were gone, we let some more light in."

Wulfgar pointed to the hole above them and laughed, but it was a trickle, not the torrent that usually chuckled forth.

Alvar turned to tackle another pile of rubble. "I do not think that there are any bodies underneath, but we should look anyway."

They clawed at the mass of ruptured timbers and clumps of plaster, until the floor was visible beneath it. Alvar wiped dust, sweat and blood from his face, and stood up to ease the ache in his back. He turned and met Dunstan. He swallowed to find some moisture for his burning throat.

"Lord Archbishop, it looks as if we have met in the middle."

Dunstan inclined his head. "Sometimes it is the only way."

Alvar returned his gaze and they both nodded.

"Lord Alvar, do you think you can ride? Our lord King has taken off in a temper and without his thegns. We will d-do what needs to be done here; I need you and your men to fetch Edward back, for he needs to be seen with his folk at such a heart-rending time."

"Do you know where he was going?"

"He said that he needed to kick out, that his lords were all lying in a heap, and his bishops would all only offer him the other cheek. I think he has gone to Corfe."

Corfe, Dorset

Alfreda sat back in her chair, put the cup to her lips and sipped the mead, enjoying the sweet warmth as it slid down her throat and heated her belly. In the three years since she had been widowed she had learned to take the time to savour even the tiniest pleasures, otherwise the nights stretched out, and offered only boredom followed by an empty bed. In the days of her marriage to Elwood, she would have welcomed the chance to sleep alone. But she had learned from Edgar first to believe in, and then to use, her allure. With that lesson came the realisation that Alvar appreciated her beauty every bit as much as her husband did. She delighted in the knowledge that both men were keen to have her. Thus she would spend the evening in their company and come bedtime she would be so aroused that it never really mattered that Edgar was not the man of her dreams. It had sweetened the bitterness of the drink she had brewed for herself.

A cry went up from the other side of the hearth, where Siferth and some other thegns were volubly engaged in a table-game. A cleverly strategic move had been greeted with grudging respect, heads in arm-locks, and drink spilt. Siferth called for more drinks, but none was forthcoming. A small slave-boy lay asleep by the fire and Alfreda leaned forward to kick him awake. "See to the drinks. Now."

The boy scuttled off to fetch new jugs of ale, and Alfreda smiled at Siferth, who raised his cup to her in acknowledgement. When the boy came back, his legs wobbling under the weight, Siferth drained the refill in one long swig, wiped his hand across his mouth, and held his cup up for replenishment.

Alfreda sat back in her chair. She would have a word with her steward about the lack of care paid to her thegns' needs. Siferth had served her well, and she would not have her hospitality found wanting. The young man had been her one source of solid comfort through her dark hours.

In the depths of mourning she had clung to the hope that with Edgar dead, Alvar would at last declare his feelings. But whenever she revisited in her mind the fraught meeting after he came back from overseeing Beorn's banishment, she saw the indifference on his face to all but her sadness. Her hands made fists on the side of her chair as she recalled how he'd ignored her overtures, and the thought had passed through her mind that he was, in fact, every bit as uncouth as his enemies had declared. He had fussed around Siferth so much that anyone would have thought that it was the boy, and not her, who had been bereaved. This had led her to accuse Alvar of fathering Siferth, but she knew she was wrong. Alvar had always been too devoted to her and to Edgar to have any life beyond court. And she could not be envious of Siferth, for he had more than made up for the slight by showing such loyalty to her.

She had spent enough moments alone to realise that her status was a weapon with two edges. Her power as queen was dependent first on Edgar and now on being the mother of the atheling. Her elevated position as royal mother would only last until such time that Edward had a child. Then who would defend her? Once upon a time she had assumed that person would be Alvar, but there lay yet another puzzle: whilst she was beginning to accept that Alvar might not, after all, want her, she was at a loss to understand why. Her title had kept her protected in a physical sense but it had not saved her emotionally. It had been so obvious that Alvar was attracted by her beauty so she had no idea what had gone wrong, and she had no other weapon in her arsenal. She had learned to use her looks, and it was the men in her life who had made it perfectly clear that this was the only way a woman like her could survive, so Alvar's rejection was a mystery to her.

Another shout went up from the gaming table and Siferth stood up, punching the air with his free hand. His other fist was still curled tightly around his ale cup and he made his way over to Alfreda, taking a few more sips as he walked. He indicated the chair next to her with a nod and a raised eyebrow.

She leaned across and patted the seat, smiling. "You do not need to ask before you take a seat beside me." As he sank onto the cushioned seat, she wriggled on her own chair, adjusting her kirtle so that it lay flat across her belly, and tugging it down slightly by her bosom.

"A drink, my lady?"

She turned her head so that she could look into his eyes. "Why not?" She patted his hand. "You are always so thoughtful, seeing to my needs." She sat back and gave what she hoped was a convincing laugh as she looked out across her hall. "Are we not truly blessed, with games and laughter, and all these beloved thegns?"

A man would not starve or even complain if he ate fish every day of his life. But give him the taste of deer meat, washed down with the exotic wines from over the sea, and the fish would begin to lose its flavour. And Alfreda, who knew what it was to have an attentive man in her bed every night and to wield power over the lives of those who had crossed her, felt the noise of her happy hall ringing hollow in her ears. Yes, why not get drunk?

She looked at Siferth. "Why do you not bring your friends here, too?"

Godric, vanquished at the gaming table, came at Siferth's signal and sat on the floor, his legs folded up under him. Alfreda looked down at him. He was not yet twenty, but his deportment gave him the slow confidence of one much older. His soft brown hair was shorn close to his head and shone like smooth mole-fur. He seemed to be staring at the mead-bench and she thought she could detect the object of his attention. One of her wards, Edith, sat nibbling daintily on a small piece of bread, her round cheek-apples bobbing up and down as she chewed. Ulf, another of Siferth's companions, wandered over to join the group and playfully cuffed Godric round the ear before he sat down next to Siferth.

"Your aim forgets the reach of your lowly arrow, Godric."

Godric laughed. "There is no law that forbids me to look. I know she is too high-born for me, but she can be mine whenever I sleep."

Alfreda touched the top of his velvety head. "It is within my gift, you know. She is my ward, after all."

Godric wriggled round and rested his forearms on her chair. "Truly? Can you do this, my lady?"

Siferth said, "My lady can do aught. For is she not the true king's mother?"

Alfreda looked down at her lap. "Then pray to God that my little Æthelred stays strong and healthy. For without a husband of my own, what would I do if aught befell my boy or worse, if Edward were to beget sons?"

Ulf stood up and bowed low, wobbling more than a little as he straightened up again. "I will wed you, my lady."

She laughed, as he had intended that she would. "You? You are a mere sapling."

Godric slid forward and hooked his leg round Ulf's, causing him to sink to his knees. Godric said, "He is not man enough to take care of you. No, Lady, I will wed you."

She gave a gasp of mock outrage. "But what about my poor ward?"

But Godric and Ulf were now engaged in a play fight, rolling over by the hearth like two overgrown pups. Siferth chuckled into his ale cup.

She kicked him playfully. "What of you? Are you taking no part in this?"

He grinned. "Let them fight; when they are both spent, there will be no man but me to take your hand, fair lady." He clapped his hands. "Piper! Play for us."

With the dusk had come a low mist that hovered above the ground in the gap between the hills and chilled him with its clammy white tendrils. Alvar stopped to blow on his hands. They were raw and still bleeding, peppered with splinters. Only a fool would tell Dunstan that he was fit to ride with such injuries; only an old fool would take off with so few men.

Brihtmær of Chester said, "You are deep in thought, my lord?"

"I think my brain must have been shaken by the fall. It will take more than three men to herd one sore-tempered king. Wulfgar's backside was hurt more than his pride, stopping him from leaping into the saddle, and he sits now by the hearth at Calne. Was I a madman not to do the same?"

Brihtmær said, "The night is too early for us to know the answer. But you were called upon to ride here and so you came. You would not have done otherwise."

"But with so few men?"

"We brought all we could, my lord. It might be that we need no more."

"I pray that you are right." The daylight was all but gone, and Alvar led the way towards the shadowy outline of the queen's house on the hillside.

The guard at the gate nodded and bowed, and Alvar, Brihtmær, and Ingulf of Worcester entered the enclosure. The hall door opened, showing a glimpse of the warm welcome that might have been theirs on any other night, beckoning fatigued visitors to the bright and cheerful hearth. A figure staggered out, ale cup in hand, and greeted a companion by the stable block. The door slammed shut.

Brihtmær handed his reins to a stable-hand and said, "Is that not your foster-son, Siferth of Ashleigh?"

Alvar nodded, but put a finger to his lips.

Siferth called out to a friend. "Godric, what kept you? I thought you only went to piss out all that ale."

The other man said, "I did, but one of the horse-thegns told me that the silver mare was about to birth her foal, so I went to see."

"Well come back in, the glee-men have begun telling their riddles. The queen keeps guessing most of them and beating me, so I need help if I am to win. And she told me not to be away for too long, so we must hurry back. See, here is Ulf come to find you too." Siferth threw an arm round each of the other men's shoulders as they made their way back to the hall. He tried to reach round to his ale cup over Godric's shoulder and the three of them zig-zagged across the courtyard until Siferth pulled them to a halt. "Uncle, is that you?"

Alvar slid from the saddle. "It is, youngling. I am weary, but it does me good to see you again, even if…"

Siferth seemed to be vaguely aware that certain niceties were required and he waved his arms about. "Godric, fetch a horse-thegn for the lord Alvar's steed." He stilled his flailing arms. "Uncle, what are you doing here? I thought you were with the witan at Calne."

Alvar held his hands out to touch Siferth's shoulders, but the rough wool of the cloak snatched at his cuts, and he let them hang back by his sides. "I seek the lord Edward. Has he been here?"

Siferth looked into his ale cup. He tipped it up, frowning at its emptiness. "Odd. I did not think I had drunk so much." He hiccupped. "How have you lost the king? Have you missed him in the mist?" His drunkenness exaggerated the quality of his joke and he folded over, hands on his thighs, laughing in a way that was less a sound, more an undulation rippling up and down his body.

Alvar took a step forward. "Siferth, is Edward here?"

Siferth shook his head as if to swill away the ale. "Why would you think that the king is here? He would no more come to the queen's house than…"

A mounted figure moved away from the enclosure fence, out of the shadows and into the light of the brazier. "I would come if I thought my king-helm was loose on my head."

Siferth bowed low and his cup clattered onto the ground. "My lord King, I… That is to say, the queen…"

Edward leaned from the saddle. "Stop gabbling. I will see her now. Bring her to me."

"My lord… I do not think that you should…"

Alvar reached up to put a hand on Edward's arm, and kept his eyes wide against the pain. He said, "My lord, I am glad to see that you are calmer than when you left Calne." He lowered his arm and nursed his hand behind his back. "We know how upset you were to lose so many good men."

"Not you, though. Shame." Edward spat on the ground by Alvar's feet. "No, my lord, I am not calm. Here you see a man who has gone far beyond wrath and can look coldly through the red mist clouding the eye."

Alvar glanced at the hall, where the door was shut but unguarded. He scanned the yard. Godric, whom Siferth had dispatched to fetch a horse-thegn, was now on his way back from the stables with a groom. The guard at the gate looked on; he was leaning against the gatehouse wall, relaxed with one foot over the other, but his spear was in reach and his thumbs were tucked into his knife-belt, close enough to reach the handle in a hurry. Soft giggles betrayed a couple enjoying the privacy of the darkness, and the fire still glowed in the smithy. It was not a fyrd, but there were enough witnesses to make Edward think twice before he acted rashly. Alvar clicked his fingers and his own thegns, Brihtmær and Ingulf, walked over to stand beside the king's stallion. Alvar turned to the groom. "Here, take my horse. You, Godric, is it? Come and help Siferth and the others to see to Lord Edward's steed."

As Alvar walked away, Edward called out. "Lord Alvar, I do not need all these men around me. Why have you put them in a ring here?" His voice became a bark. "And whither do you go that makes you show your back to your king? Do not think to hinder me."

Alvar stepped back to them. He nodded at his own men, and to Ulf and Godric he said quietly, "Hold him." He raised his voice. "My lord Edward, I am merely on my way to make sure that the welcome in the hall befits you, and to tell the queen that she must come to greet you."

Alvar smiled, bowed low, and walked to the hall door. He was breathing in shallow gasps. He must not run; the hounds only gave chase when the prey bolted and he must keep space between Edward and the queen. He groaned and held his breath when Edward shouted out anew.

"You shits! I know what you are trying to do. Let me through or I will ride over you. I will see the queen, so move your arses or be knocked to the ground."

Godric said, "Is the Devil within him?"

The horse whinnied and Ulf stumbled as they all tried to hold and soothe the nervous beast.

"No," said Siferth, "But he uses his fists when he is wroth."

"I will see the bitch. Now."

Alvar backed towards the hall and reached behind him to bang on the door.

Siferth said, "My lord King, I know that it is the drink speaking through you. The queen is not a…"

Edward lowered his face to Siferth's and said, "I am not drunk and she is a whore. She stole my mother's foot-hold in my father's house and she wants my kingdom for her by-blow son."

Siferth said, "No, I will not let you speak so. She is a true and good woman and I would lay down my life for her."

"You might have to."

Alvar rolled his eyes and turned round as the hall door swung open. He said to the door-thegn, "Get your lady.

And be swift."

Alfreda came to the doorway and smiled. She put a hand to her head and patted her headdress. Even in his urgency, he found time to notice how absurdly pleased she seemed to be to see him.

"Lord Alvar, you are most welcome; we have pipers, harpers, riddlers and glee-men here, and more than enough ale. Your foster-son sees to it that my hall is always lively. He looks to my needs well." She continued to smile at him, but drew the tip of her tongue across her lips while she waited for him to speak.

Alvar stepped forward. The warmth of the hearth beyond was a few impossible steps away. But behind him, the shouting continued. He said, "My lady, the lord Edward…"

"The king, my lord? I have not seen him since Yule. What makes you think…?" She looked past his shoulder. "Oh sweet holy Jesus."

Alvar turned again to look back at the yard. Edward's sword arm, raised above his head, was a blur against the darkened sky. He leaned forward out of his saddle and brought his arm down. Behind him, the glow from the brazier lit his empty hand, but too late to show the lack of weapon and stay Siferth's dagger. The blade slammed into Edward's back.

"Siferth. No!" Alvar ran.

Edward sat back and reached round to feel under his shoulder-blade. He rubbed his fingertips together and looked at them. "Christ, you have killed me."

His horse reared and broke free from Godric's grasp. Ulf jumped aside as the front hooves came down, and leaped up to try to reach the reins. Ingulf dived for the tail but missed and landed on the ground, and the stallion ran. The guard at the gate stepped forward, only to spread flat against the gateway as the beast gathered speed. Edward, with only one hand on the reins, struggled to keep his seat and was still within view when he slipped from the saddle. His right foot

369

caught in the stirrup, he was unable to push himself clear, and as the panicked beast continued to run, it dragged Edward along behind.

Godric and Ulf stood and gasped for breath, then ran off in pursuit of the horse and its injured rider. Ingulf and Brihtmær ran to attend to the queen, who stood in the doorway with little Æthelred by her side. Siferth did not move, but stood with the bloodied knife in his hand. He continued to stare at it even as Alvar uncurled his fingers and took it from him.

"Uncle, I..." Siferth surrendered; he stumbled forward into Alvar's arms and sobbed.

Alvar let the knife drop to the ground and held the boy. Once, years ago, Brock's eldest son had broken a cart wheel. His world was over and yet he had clung to his uncle, unshakable in his belief that grown men can mend all. Alvar struggled to keep his thoughts in the present, so alike were the cries in this dark night.

Ulf and Godric returned, their faces white in the moonlight. Godric opened his mouth, and the queen's scream began before he had finished his words.

"The king is dead."

The queen screamed again, little Æthelred wailed as he clutched her skirts, and Siferth slumped to the ground with his head in his hands.

Ulf said, "We followed him over the bridge and up the hill and the horse would not stop but kept going and we did not think we could catch up to him and it was not until we reached the settlement on the other..."

Alvar held his hand up to silence him. This was not a time for explanations, or even protracted thought. He must act. "Siferth, come here and kneel before me. You will swear hold-oath to me as your lord." He reached behind him and clicked his fingers. Brihtmær pushed a gold cruciform brooch into his hand. "Swear," Alvar said again, "On this holy thing..."

Siferth stuttered the words of the hold-oath.

Alvar lifted him, gave him the kiss and said, "Now you are my man. Do you hear me? *My* man." To Godric and Ulf he said, "Show me."

He followed them as they led him away from the royal settlement, round the west hill, past a line of trees, black now against the purple sky, and through a cluster of small dwellings. Beyond the one-roomed houses they showed him a well. The king's horse was standing nearby.

Alvar peered into the well. "Oh, tell me you did not."

They looked down at the ground. Ulf said, "My lord, we were frightened. We did not know what to do. We thought it best if folk could not see the bod… The king's…"

Alvar shifted his weight from one foot to the other; the grass was springy beneath him and he longed only to lie down on it. "Wareham is near here, I think. Fetch a monk from there. Have him bury the body."

"Uncle?"

He looked up. Siferth had followed them, like the runt seeking the warmth of the rest of the litter.

"I could not go into the hall, for I have lost the right to sit by the hearth. I will have to go far away. If I am even allowed to live…"

Alvar walked up to him and placed a hand on his shoulder, forbearing to wince. "You know that I will do what I can. But to take the life of a king…"

"He would have done harm to the queen. I could not let him. I had to stop him."

"The queen." Alvar ran back to Alfreda's manor. "Brihtmær, find my horse and one for Siferth, too. We must get away; the queen must not be washed with Edward's blood."

Alfreda watched them ride out. Why would he leave her? Was he not her protector? She'd been a widow for three years, flirting with silly boys just to keep her skills honed, and tonight he had knocked on her door. He had come for her; for one joyous moment she had thought her wait was over. But now the king was dead, killed in her yard, and Alvar was gone. There would be no salvation. She stared out at the brazier. The flames licked and crackled, agitated by an evening breeze blowing across the courtyard, and illuminated the bloodstain on the ground. Edward's blood. The fire stirred memories of a burning building, and a chance of a new beginning. So many years had passed since then, most of them good ones. But it had all come at a heavy cost, for she had lost three of her four children. Two cruelly kept from her, one taken by God, his little body burning with fever one moment, cold and dead the next. Her son was still convulsing with sobs beside her, and his shuddering body radiated warmth. She clutched him tightly. "Ssh, there, there, it will be all right." The king was dead, and there would be salvation. Alfreda put her free hand up to tidy her veil, looked down at her last remaining son, the atheling Æthelred, and repeated her words. "It will be all right."

Calne

In the pallid morning light, tree-wrights were chopping fallen beams and boards, and dragging the smaller pieces to bonfires. Wounded men hobbled around outside the king's hall and helped where they could. Many more, still torpid with disbelief, remained seated on rescued stools and chairs, and gazed at the wreckage.

Alvar wrinkled his nose at the smoke and put a hand up to bat away the flying embers. He left a listless Siferth in the makeshift infirmary. Outside the lodge for the clergy, he waylaid a monk. "Tell the archbishop that I would speak with him."

The monk went inside and Dunstan appeared, dabbing at his mouth with a napkin. The smile of greeting fell from his face. "The king is not with you?"

Alvar spoke in a voice made gruff by smoke and fatigue. "Lord Archbishop, I would speak with you right away. One to one."

Dunstan indicated the way with a sweep of his arm. They went inside and past the clergy who were sitting at their breakfast tables. Some ate with enthusiasm; others, faces dirty, looked too shocked to eat well. Dunstan knew he must speak to them soon; one, in particular, had remained mute and hungry since the collapse, and he was no use to God or the injured in that weakened state.

In a private chamber at the rear of the building, Dunstan

offered Alvar a cushioned chair and the earl fell into it. He mentioned how warm the room was, commented on the smell of incense and he blinked slowly, as if the pungent air were pushing heavily on his eyelids. Dunstan's bed was piled with soft furs and gold embroidered covers, pillows and cushions, and Lord Alvar looked, covetously, it seemed to Dunstan, at the feather-soft haven. As always when he travelled, Dunstan had brought with him many wooden caskets decorated with gold. On the table next to Alvar lay a particularly beautiful reliquary and the earl leaned his head on it.

Dunstan tutted, but he shrugged and said, "It will not be the most ungodly thing you have ever done." He cleared his throat. "Well? Why have you not brought the king back with you?"

Alvar sat forward. "My lord Archbishop, I have ridden hard miles from Corfe, and in all that time have not found the words to tell you in a kinder way than this: your king is dead."

Dunstan lost all control of his head. He stopped blinking and his mouth gaped open. His head was shaking; his ears were not working properly.

"No, my lord, it is not a lie. I only wish it were."

Dunstan regained control of his faculties. He sat down and said, "I will call for food and drink and then you must tell me all."

He listened, even now not really able to believe, as Alvar told him a tale that was as tragic as it was shocking. When he had dispatched Alvar and his men to bring Edward back, his only concern was that Edward might dirty his own name by frightening or, and it was only a possibility, assaulting the king's widow. How had it come to pass that Edward was dead, killed at the hand of thegns who loved the queen so much that they would kill and die for her? Was his assessment of Alfreda proved wrong, or right, by this turn of events? He must conclude this meeting rapidly, for he had much to say to God in the privacy of the chapel. He crossed himself, murmured a prayer and said, "What must be done?"

Alvar moved his head from side to side and raised his shoulders as if to ease the ache there and in his neck. "A king has been murdered, and the killing calls for the payment of wergild and a hanging. The king's kin should hunt down the killers."

"But if he has no full-grown kin…" If he had no adult kin then the responsibility would fall to someone who acted for the royal family. But the royal family was divided. Who would act for Edward's side? Brandon? There was no-one, in truth, who could stand against Alvar.

Alvar held up a hand. "The thegn, Siferth, who wielded the blade, is dear to me."

Dunstan slumped in his chair, accepting the inevitable. Alvar would fight on behalf of Alfreda and her thegn, and none could stop him.

"You should know that I am his lord."

Dunstan demurred. "I was given to understand that he is Alfreda's thegn."

"I made him swear to me. He is my thegn now, and I am bound to protect him."

Dunstan opened his mouth and shut it again. It was one thing to fight on Siferth's behalf, but with the ties of lordship came shared responsibility. Alvar had made himself vulnerable, and laid himself open to accusations of collusion in a murder. Why would he make such a sacrifice? He must truly love this thegn, to act so selflessly. Reluctantly, Dunstan acknowledged that the action went deeper than mere love. By moving to make Siferth his thegn, he had negated the need to arrest him. With a legitimate reason not to draw his sword, he was guaranteeing a peace which would only be broken should someone choose to accuse Alvar directly of murder. His reputation might suffer, but the kingdom would be mended. Alvar was putting duty before all personal considerations and, belatedly, it occurred to Dunstan that it was this tendency that had helped to make

Alvar so indispensable to Edgar.

He sat back and, though his overriding emotion was sadness, he gave in to the urge for a small chuckle. "Once, I thought you to be no more than a brute with a sword. But now…" He shook his head with only a tiny range of motion as he finished the thought. Edgar had brought Alvar to court because he wished to use his loyalty and his military skills and yet now, the soldier Dunstan had dismissed as unimaginative had found a way to solve this monumental crisis by deliberately, and publicly, sheathing his sword. Loyal yes, but clever too, and Dunstan, his lifelong enemy, found that he welcomed the opportunity to speak to the man as one statesman to another, a part which Dunstan had hitherto been so fond to play as a solo role.

A serving-boy brought a flask of wine. Dunstan offered some to Alvar, who shook his head. "You will not have a drink?" Dunstan took a sip from a gold cup. "What of the athelings?"

"There is none as throne-worthy as Æthelred. The witan would not bind themselves to any other."

"Then he must be brought to Kingston this day, named king by the witan, and given the king-helm."

"No."

The archbishop frowned. "But we cannot linger. This land was being rent asunder even before Edward's death; we must have a king."

"We must not be too swift. Otherwise, men will think that this killing was done for Æthelred and in his name. And…"

Dunstan leaned forward. "Yes?"

"It will hurt you to hear this, but there are few men in the witan who will shed any tears for Edward. His slaying might turn out to be the thing that brings us all back together." He sighed. "There should now be a time of stillness. Let us wait awhile, rebuild this place," he nodded towards the smouldering courtyard, "And then rebuild the kingdom."

Dunstan looked up at the ceiling and rubbed his chin. "Do you really think you can keep the blood from Æthelred's hands, make him king and bring all the lords together?"

"All are tired of the unrest. Too many died yesterday."

Dunstan crossed himself. "It was God's doom on a land grown lawless."

Alvar was quick to give assurances. "And we will answer to Him. Edgar strove always to be even-handed, but kept his lords and his churchmen ever on the wrong side of each other. With no strong king to bind us, look at what we have done." He looked up. "All of us."

Dunstan sighed and nodded. He took another sip of his drink. "And so?"

"And so… It is over. I will take Siferth to his mother and you will do naught while I am away. Can I have your word on that; that I will not come back to find I have missed yet another king-making?"

"I think that you and I have reached an understanding, Lord Alvar. I always wondered why Edgar leaned as much on you as he did on the holy mother Church. Your deeds this day have shown me your keen wits, and your wisdom."

Alvar raised an eyebrow. "Did I hear you right?"

Dunstan nodded. "Yes. I see now why Edgar kept you close for all those years."

Alvar gave a slow smile. "I will thank you, my lord, for I know that those words did not come easily." He coughed and fiddled with his garnet ring. "Oft-times I have cursed your earthly ways, thinking that you should have stayed in your minster, and busied yourself only with holy books, but now I find it a blessing to have some of the burden lifted." He sat back in his seat, pushed his legs out straight and crossed his ankles. "We must also speak of shifting the body so that there can be a fitting burial. I left word at Wareham for the monks to bury the body, and I left enough silver to see it done and to still their tongues."

"Still their tongues?" Dunstan knew that in the race to

find answers to problems, his mind was losing, his thoughts turning at a much slower pace than the earl's.

Alvar explained. "It is a busy port. The ships would be better to come and go without the seamen knowing who is buried nearby. Also while I think on it, the witan must be sent home. There were more than enough woes here even before I brought back these awful tidings. Men will not wish to remain at a gathering at such a time."

Dunstan said, "Again, you think of things that I would not. But will you speak with the witan before you leave, so that we can make sure that they are all willing to swear to Æthelred as their king?" He rose to his feet. "Meanwhile, I will have him and his mother brought here."

"Send my men. The lady will not come otherwise."

Dunstan opened his mouth to answer, but closed it again. Alvar's body was no longer supporting his head. Reclining in the chair since he first sat down, he had appeared to be tired beyond endurance and now his eyes had closed, taking him on the short journey to complete sleep. Dunstan stood up as silently as he could and made his way to the chapel. He had many things to ask God, a dead king's soul to pray for, and many sins, not the least of which was pride, to atone for.

Cheshire

They had set out from Chester in the first silver and grey light of the morning, before the sun had repainted the colours onto the earth.

"I do not understand why we could not come last night."

Alvar patted Siferth on the back. "It is good to hear you speaking once more. I feared you were struck dumb forever. I did not want to frighten your mother by coming at nightfall. It is bad enough that I come at winter-tide."

"Why?"

She always teased that I only ever come here in the summer…" Alvar scanned the path that ran to the woods. "No, she is not here."

"You never told me, before we left, what will become of me."

Alvar pulled his cloak tighter. Although the sun was rising in a clear sky, spring was in no hurry to arrive and they walked on a hard frost. "No, I am sorry, I did not." He had been too busy sending word about Edward's death and notifying the kin of all those who had died at Calne. But he should have found time to speak to the boy and he rested his hand on Siferth's shoulder. "You will keep all the lands you held from the queen, otherwise we might as well shout your guilt from the bell towers and the world would think that Alfreda and her son are guilty too. But you are best kept out of the way of wagging tongues so for now, you must hide out here; there is enough room for you on your mother's lands." He let go of Siferth and took a last look along the path. "Come, she is not at the church or the mill this morning. We must look for her nearer home."

Alvar turned to go across the fields to Ashleigh but Siferth touched his arm. "Uncle, will you go on ahead of me? I am not yet ready to see the look of shame in my mother's eyes."

Alvar smiled. He barely had to lower his head to look at Siferth, for the lad was as tall now as his father had been. His eyes were brown, but they were the same shape as his mother's, the lashes the same shade of light brown that framed Káta's eyes. "There will be naught in her eyes to match the fear that I see in yours now. You must believe me on this. But yes, I will go on without you."

He set off, with the rising sun at his back. The trees cast long shadows, with his amongst them, across the length of the field. He walked down the slope towards the little gate that would take him to Káta's hall and with every step, his shadow shortened so that it was small against that of the trees. He turned his head; Siferth was standing at the top of the hill, fiddling with his cloak pin. Alvar looked back towards the manor and saw her.

She looked up, gathered her cloak tighter around her body and continued to walk along the path at the same measured pace.

He stood, fidgeted, and strode out towards her. His steps carried him quicker than her pace though they were no greater in number. They met at the gate and he opened it for her.

"You have something bad to tell me," she said.

She would not thank him for prevaricating. "The lord Edward is dead. Siferth wielded the blade."

She said nothing, but stepped forward and put her head against his chest. He put his arms around her and held her. They stood together, while overhead the rooks screeched out their early morning cacophony. His thoughts turned from his task to the warmth of her body, and he breathed in to rob her of her scent before she moved away. She broke free, but kept hold of his hand. She took a few steps away from him before she released him and her fingertips brushed the very ends of his before she finally let go. She did not look back, but said, "Tell him to come to me. He looks cold, standing up there by himself."

Inside, she sat with her hands in her lap, while Siferth related all the details of the evening in Corfe. She stood up, walked to him and held his head against her belly.

She said, "You acted to spare the life of one who was dear to you. This was not murder. Make your settlement with God if you must, but I have no fears for your soul." She walked back to her seat.

Alvar caught her arm. "God is one thing, but I think it is your forgiveness which means more to him."

She smiled and sat back down. She beckoned Gytha, who walked forward and bent her head towards Káta's. Káta whispered a few words to her, and the Norsewoman nodded and left the hall.

"I told Gytha that she and the others will have to do without me today. I wish to spend the day with my son and with my…" She arranged her sleeves. "What tidings have you brought that are not so sad?"

She listened for hours as Siferth told her of his life at court, her lips drawn into a line that was a poor imitation of a smile and faltered with every mention of Alfreda.

Alvar patted her arm and whispered his assurance. "Her hair is greyer than yours."

He was rewarded with a full smile but it faded again when he told her about the disaster at Calne.

"Who was wounded? Wulfgar, Brihtmær, Aswy of Shropshire? I would know of all Mercian thegns and lords."

He repeated the list by rote; the names of the wounded and those who were unharmed. "And Aswy came away with a slit over his eye, Wulfgar with no more than a sore arse. I think that God may, after all, be a Mercian."

"Did you ever doubt it?" She smiled and beckoned to a

little slave-boy to clear the tables. When the lad had finished, she nodded her thanks.

Outside, the short March day was all but over, spilling low red light through only the west window. Alvar slid down in his seat, legs straight. Káta's fire was warm and lively. "Hearth and home, there is naught better," he said. He closed his eyes.

Káta nudged his foot and he opened one eye. She pointed to Siferth, who had lain down on the bench next to the wall. The boy was fast asleep, curled up like a child.

"I told him that he had naught to fear from telling you. You were always one to take whatever life throws your way. He will truly rest now." Alvar slouched down in his chair again and wiggled his toes in the warmth of the heat from the flames. Káta's folk had fed them well and now the hall was quiet. There was nothing left to tell or do and his eyelids dropped down again. He snapped them open, though he knew it was the beginning of a fight he would lose.

Káta smiled at him. Her words came like an echo caught in the air from so many years ago. "And will you be spending the night with us, my lord?"

He had no flippant answer for her this time. "I do not think I could shift from this seat if it set on fire, my lady."

"That is a shame. It seems you have forgotten how warm and soft you once found my bed."

He lifted his heavy lids to look at her, to read her face, and be sure that he had not misunderstood.

There was no mistake, for Káta was on her feet. She placed a cloak over her sleeping son by way of a blanket, held out her hand, and led Alvar to her bedchamber.

"Will you have a drink, my lord?" She stood at the table and clutched the jug with white-knuckled fingers.

"No, I think not. Is it too cold in here? Shall I fetch more furs?"

"You are cold? I will pull the shutters."

He moved to the door as she moved to the window, and the whole space of the room was between them. He smiled at her and she looked down at the floor.

"This will not do," he said.

"You are right. How can we do this?"

"You could begin by putting the ale down."

She stared at the jug as if she had forgotten it was there and she rushed to set it back down on the table. He stood behind her, took hold of her elbows, and turned her round to face him.

She laid her hand on his chest, flat against it with her fingers spread; he closed his fingers round hers and held them there. With her other hand, she stroked his face. "I know how you look. I have looked upon you for a lifetime, but…" Her fingertips moved along his chin, across his eyebrows, the curve of his smile, the outline of his ear.

He lifted a coil of her hair and felt its silkiness before he brought it to his nose to smell again the delicate fragrance of lavender. He reached out to explore her face, but she clasped his hand and turned it palm up. "These wounds have not healed well. Did you put on any salve or bindings?"

He looked up at the ceiling. "How black and white is a woman's world… I have been a little busy these last few days."

"Then it is as well that I am here to kiss them better."

She took up both his hands. She touched her soft lips against the palms and each of his fingers, one by one. He felt no pain, but a warmth that spread along his arms down his body to his belly and beyond.

He lowered his head and nuzzled her face until she lifted it to his. "Your mouth is sweet, lady, but it is not where it should be." He leaned his head to one side and dipped forward, but she moved her head the same way. He tried again and placed the lightest of kisses on her mouth.

He straightened up and laid his hands on her shoulders. He slid them down the length of her arms, caressed her fingertips and then let them go. She put her hands on his chest, palms flat, and swept them across his front and around his upper arms.

He nodded towards the bed.

"Is it time?"

"Oh, yes." It was a hoarse whisper. He cleared his throat.

She said, "I could stand here all night. To be able to feel, to…" She reached up on tiptoe, put her nose to the indent between his jaw and earlobe and breathed in deeply. "After all this time."

"Lady, I fear that if I do not lie down, I will fall down. But we do have all night and I am in no mood, nor young enough, to be too swift."

She took a step back and the smile faded. "I had not thought."

"What is it?"

"I, too, am not as young as once I was. I have borne a child." She lowered her head. "You might not like what you see."

"Lady, we have let enough time go by. I crave only to know you, now, before I sleep and wake to find it was not real after all." He laughed.

"My lord?"

"Forgive me. I am so tired it feels like I am in my cups. I have loved you half my life and you are standing before me, welcoming and willing. God must love me, after all."

She took another step back as he flung off his clothes and stood naked before her, his tunic, breeches, belt and leg-bindings scattered across her chamber. She looked down at the floor but he lifted her chin and said, "Lady, I saw you looking at what I have for you. I would have a kindness now from you."

She squealed and ran for the bed, but he caught her arm. She tugged at her robes and he said, "Let me help you."

She giggled as he tried to pull her kirtle and under-dress over her head at the same time. She stood naked before him and the laughter stopped.

Reaching up, she embraced him, her fingertip tickling his skin as she traced the lines and scars on his back. He smiled when the movement slowed down; she had found the most recent, the shoulder wound that she had healed.

"It will do," she said. She stepped closer. "I have craved this for so long. So many years, so many wishes."

He caught hold of the hand and drew it to his chest. "No more. This time is ours, and no-one can take it from us.

She began to speak, as if to express a doubt, but he put a finger to her lips. He said, "Lady, I am not going anywhere."

"I know. But only if I hold you can I believe that you are really here."

He said, "I am here. And I wish to know what it is to kiss you."

"You have kissed me two times, my lord. You must not be greedy."

"No, I will not steal any more kisses like a thief in the night." He moved his mouth nearer hers. "I would have my fill after a long fast." He put his arm round her waist and drew her to him. "I will have them to own, open-mouthed." He shut his eyes.

She put a hand up to his face. "Look at me," she said, her gaze fixed on his. "I will not turn away. I can look at you whenever I wish to, and I will not look away. Give me your eyes."

Shrewsbury

Alvar found Alfreda calmer but not relaxed. Her tone was at once resentful and belligerent.

"I never thought to say it," she said, "But I stand with Dunstan on this. A swift king-making was called for. It could have been done at Eastertide, and I would hear from your own mouth why you would not let it be done."

"My lady, I…" He held up his hands when he realised she had not finished.

"For I will not have my son done out of a kingship a second time, my lord."

She drew her lips into a pout, and feathery lines puckered her mouth. He could not recall a time when he had seen her so cross. She was still beautiful but there was no denying that she was getting older. He smiled; they were none of them young any more, for all he had spent the last few days behaving like a lustful youth. He stretched out, put his hands behind his head, and thought of the day before.

He had told Káta that he felt like one of her cats, stretching out in the sun, with no purpose than to rest. Two weeks of her company and of lying in her bed had brought him to a hitherto unknown state of tranquillity.

Alfreda leaned forward. "My lord, do you heed me?"

He smiled. He had ignored his yearning for Káta for so long that all he wanted to do, now that he had the taste, was to drink from the cup forever. But yesterday he had taken his leave of her. The witan was gathering and reluctantly he informed her that he must ride to meet them. Yet she had merely smiled, acknowledged the fact that he was needed, and told him that she would settle for what she now had, and would make the best of it. He was to go, with her blessing and love.

Alfreda tapped her foot. "My lord, why are you grinning like a simpleton?"

"Forgive me, my lady, I was thinking about better times." He shook his head and sat forward. "Lady, let me spare you all but the truth. If your son is made king now, everyone will say that murder was in our minds all along. Time is our friend, not our foe. There is no other atheling, and therefore no threat to Æthelred's claim."

"But a land without a king is weak," she said.

He took her hand. "Can you truly not see, Lady? Your son is but ten years old. He will need grown men to rule in his name, the same men who hold the kingdom for him now. Putting a king-helm on his head will not change that, but it will allow us to put everything to rights for him before he becomes an anointed king. Let the mistakes be ours, not his."

"You are all like wolves, bent on tearing one another's throats."

"No more."

"Truthfully?"

"Yes."

The other witan members filed into the chamber and he grinned and sat up straight. Two weeks in bed had also restored to him something that he thought had fallen away with the timbers at Calne. A familiar excitement jumped in his belly.

The queen said, "I would have a little more from you than that before I sleep unworried in my bed."

Alvar said, "All land disputes will be settled, but only for those who have already come forward. No new cases will be heard. I have agreed that I will put up with Oswald as long as he shows me all his gifts of land before he grants them."

The archbishop of York hobbled by and they exchanged a nod. "I have even said that I will do my best not to be unkind to Brandon, but it is not easy." Alvar grinned. "Sometimes I itch even now to set fire to his breeches to see if the man can leap without being told to."

Brandon sat down and looked at his lap. "My lord of Mercia wishes to play with fire, because he knows he is on his way to hell and needs to get used to the heat."

Alvar chuckled and Brandon raised his head, surprised at the reaction. He looked bemused, like a failed hunter who had finally and unexpectedly made a kill.

Dunstan settled himself into his chair. "I know that I speak for all here when I say that we are gladdened to see an end to the fighting. We c-can all look forward to the days of another strong kingship such as Edgar's, he who ruled over a peaceful land, and died in his bed and not with a sword in his hand."

Æthelred had perched himself on the king-stool, where his legs dangled, too short to reach the floor.

Alvar thought back to the days of the boy's father. At the age of ten, Edgar's character was already formed. Where he had been a well-risen loaf, Æthelred was but the lump of soft dough. God grant them the years needed to guide and shape him. The thought wearied him that his work was still not done, his duty to the royal house not yet fulfilled.

The archbishop of Canterbury twirled his cup round in his hands. "There is one thing I would say to you though, my lord Alvar. You have worked hard to keep the blood off the queen's hands and away from our young king. But what of the danger of your own name being besmeared? I know it was a risk that you were willing to take but…"

Bishop Athelwold sat forward. "My lord Archbishop, you do not believe that the lord of Mercia was, in any way, guilty of…"

Dunstan set down his cup. "No, I do not. As I told the earl, I have in these last weeks begun to see a little of what Edgar saw, that behind the foul words and the loud roar, there is a sharp-witted wisdom and a willing ability when things need to be done."

"My lord, you must stop. My cheeks are reddening."

The queen raised her eyebrows. The pursed lips had released into a smile. "They look as bold as ever to me, my lord."

Alvar grinned. "Well, my lady, if I must have only one sin, then let it be pride."

Dunstan coughed and said, "Be all that as it may, I ask again how the lord Alvar will banish any suspicions that he was behind the king's death all along. For if he were now to make an unwise match…"

The queen sat forward as if his answer was important to her. Did she think…?

Alvar sat forward too and rubbed his hands together. "My lord Archbishop, I am flattered beyond reckoning by your praise, but you need not worry about any fingers pointing at me. I will not be here. Iago of Gwynedd wishes to steal back the lands of Hywel ab Ieuaf, and Hywel has asked for my help once more." He grinned at the archbishop.

Dunstan rolled his eyes heavenward. "I was too swift with my kind words. You still like nothing more than to ride off with your sword in your hand."

A low chuckle echoed around the room. Only Alfreda sat like Lot's wife, her expression frozen into one that suggested the final thwarting of her plans.

Gwynedd, North Wales

The Mercian army came through the pass of Bwlch Mawr, and Alvar and Wulfgar dismounted. Alvar let his horse find what grazing it could and he scrambled down the hillside by the waterfall that tumbled down Gyrn Goch Mountain to the sea. He sat down with his legs stretched out in front of him and leaned back on his elbows. Below him, the monastery at Clynnog Fawr nestled on a small stretch of flat land between the hills and the sea. A pretty little pebble beach gave way to bright, blue water, and away to the northeast lay the island that the Welsh called Ynys Môn. He closed his eyes and let the sun warm his face.

Wulfgar scrambled down the slope to crouch beside his lord. "Hywel's men are on their way back from Aber, my lord. I saw them on the road."

"Good. We need do naught before he gets here. The hare we caught; is it on the fire yet?"

"I told them to fetch it to you when it is done. So, now, tell me why I am on my arse on a Welsh hillside, soon to be upsetting some old Welsh monks?"

Alvar brushed his hair from his eyes. He must ask Káta to cut it for him when he returned home. "You must ask Hywel about that one. I have no answer."

Wulfgar frowned. "What is wrong, my lord?"

Alvar sighed. "Iago has gathered men to him from Dublin, ready to sail to help him. That is why we made ourselves seen at Aberdaron, to frighten them off by waving at them from across the water and showing them that Hywel is not alone." He glanced at Wulfgar's knotted brow and smiled. "But I do not know whether I want to be a part of what happens next. The monastery down there has strong ties with the House of Gwynedd. To harry this place would be as big a blow to Iago as the harrying of York or Canterbury would have been to Edgar. And I am in danger of becoming the thing that men like Oswald hated me for." He laughed. "I can see you have no pity for the Welsh though."

"Not after they cursed me with ringworm, warts and wens." Wulfgar eased from his squat to sit down. He rubbed his knees. "Do you think we have grown too old for this?"

Alvar put all his weight on one elbow as he scratched his chin. "Truth be told, I knew I was, even before I came. But I am lord of Mercia, so it behoves me to oversee any fighting that goes on anywhere near the border. I thought I had enough fighting years left in me," he sat up and shook his arms, "But my bones have begun to tell me otherwise." Come, let us go and find Hywel and shake the ache from our arses."

"Mildrith told me that I would have more than a sore arse if I did not come home whole, and she did not understand why I laughed."

"I was told something like that." Alvar put his hand up to his hair again to push it out of his eyes. "I never gave it much thought before. For years, whenever you spoke of Mildrith, or any other man spoke of his wife, I had naught to say back. But now…"

"What do you mean?"

Alvar said, "It is a new feeling and it makes me smile. After all these years, I have someone to go home to."

He ran down the hill to greet Hywel. "It is a wondrous sight, this land of yours, Welshman."

Hywel nodded. "Why do you think we are always fighting over it?"

Alvar laughed. "All that bloodshed over a lovely view? I

think not. You Welsh make our English fights look like children's play. I am glad I am not wearing your uncle's shoes this day."

"My uncle Iago thought he was safe from me. He believed that when Edgar swore at Chester to be a friend to Gwynedd, it meant that every English king thereafter would uphold that oath. His unlawful hold on these lands died with Edgar."

"Many things died with Edgar."

"I do not think that the ships from Dublin will unload now that they know you are here. You and I have fought well together. I hope that I can ask for your help another time."

Alvar looked out through his long fringe, first to the sea in front of him, then to the mountains behind him and then to the ground, where the road ended underneath his feet. "Ha! Do you hear him, Wulfgar? Youngling, I am too old for this. And I am no murderer of monks. It is bad enough that many at home already think it of me. So I will stay while you see off the sailors from Dublin and then I will go home. Besides, you will not need my help again."

Cheshire

"I told him that if I sought to bind him to me with my bodily strength, then it was but a forlorn hope. This kingdom will always have a stronger grip on his heart. Even so, a fyrd should be home before the first winter shower falls."

From the top of Elfshill Káta looked at the Welsh hills in the distance, where the snow lay in the gullies and made the rocks beside them seem darker and sharper. The air was clear and there were no clouds in the sky. She put out a hand. "They look so near that I feel that I could reach them with my fingers."

Gytha shouted up from below. "Lady, does he come?"

Káta shook her head and made her way back down to the halfway point.

Gytha leaned against a tree and panted. "He might bide in Wales until the thaw. He might be with Thegn Aswy in Shrewsbury. You should not worry yet."

Káta blew on her fingers. "Come, we must see if the road to Chester is hard enough. I need to speak with the bone-carver before Siferth's wedding. I want him to make a bride-gift for Eadyth. Should we buy wine as well as mead for the wedding, or the Welsh-ale, do you think? Oh, do not let me forget that I said I would send Wulfric some garlic. And old Leofwaru needs some more hemlock, for she says she cannot sleep. Shellfish… Do you think shellfish would do to go with the bride-ale?"

Gytha laid a hand on her arm. "Lady, he will come. You must not worry."

Káta turned a full circle on the path and sighed. "I know that in life we must take all, the thread and the thrum, but sometimes I wonder if it was real. Now he is mine and I can be his, yet never has he felt so far away."

Chapter Twenty AD979

Kingston

The archbishop of Canterbury strolled past with a beatific expression on his face. He said, "Folk have spoken to me today of yet more wondrous things."

Alvar smiled at Dunstan's conspiratorial nod. He whispered to Káta, "Do you hear how he speaks to me as if we were childhood friends?" Dunstan, erstwhile enemy, now embraced Alvar as a member of a government which had been validated by miracles associated with Edward's shrine. He had been pleased with Alvar's idea to move Edward's remains a year after his death, reburying the murdered king with all due ceremony. Sightings of saintly apparitions and stories of miraculous healing suggested celestial approval for the new reign. Raising his voice to answer the archbishop, Alvar said, "I heard many such tales along the road to the reburial at Shaftesbury, my lord. The tales will only grow in the telling."

"It is the hand of God which drives the folk to this shrine, His wonders to witness." Dunstan smiled again and lifted his nose. "Ah, spitted hog. I find that it is hungry work, overseeing a king-making. I will t-take my leave, my lord." He glided off towards the dais, where a gold embroidered tablecloth was fluttering in the breeze.

"He stands upright for an old man," Káta said.

"He has lost none of his stern ways though, as those folk over there are about to find out." Alvar pointed at the estate workers whose tools and carts were littering the way and impeding progress.

Kingston was a royal manor expanded once more, as new buildings sprang up around the hall and next to the chapel of St Mary. Many remained unfinished, so that even after the new king's crowning that morning, builders were still labouring with their T-blade axes to dress the new timbers. Joiners were turning alder-wood bowls on their pole-lathes even as the hogs roasted on the spits. Servants rushed to lay the trestle tables and dragged yet more chairs from the hall, while the builders yelled at them.

"Watch out for that spade."

"Look out yourself; this food is for the king. And he will not want to eat it to the din of your hammering."

"A new king brings a new household, needs new bowers. Where would you be without us? Throw me a loaf, you lovely thing… Oh, beg forgiveness your Holiness."

They all fell to their knees as Dunstan walked by. He paused briefly to cast a withering gaze at the detritus.

Káta laughed and walked with Alvar towards the tables. "What are these wondrous things of which Dunstan spoke?"

"Oh, folk healed from sickness, walking again after years of being bed-bound…"

It was the usual list of miracles associated with hallowed burial places, and Alvar tested her to see if she was listening. "Leaving gifts for trees, bathing in a well…"

She tapped his arm. "Do not tease me. So the folk of Wessex are as silly as I once was. Now that Edward is reburied, the tales will find a home, as you say. I wish I had been there with you."

Alvar guided her to the shelter of an oak tree. He placed his hands on her elbows and said, "I could not have found time for you, my love. I rode at the head of the fyrd; I oversaw the burial and was busy all the day."

A Wiltshire thegn wandered by. "Good day to you, my lord Alvar. The sun shines for our new king."

"Yes, it does. Good day to you, Goding."

Káta wriggled from his grip. "You are mine, but I do not have you."

"What? I am sorry, I did not hear…"

She clamped her teeth onto the corner of her bottom lip and looked down at her feet.

He said, "You spoke in a whisper…" And it brought echoes from the past, of a young wife, newly wed and tongue-tied. But this was not that woman. She wore a gown of blue which matched the colour of her eyes. Her fur-trimmed sleeveless coat was fastened, against the mode, with the Celtic-copper brooch that he had given her. Not weak, recycled Roman metal mixture, but only the best for his woman. "How fair you look; a truly great lady." He held out his arms.

She walked into his embrace and he kissed the top of her head. He said, "My love, forgive me. You have me now. Edward is buried, this time with all care owed to him, Æthelred is made king this morning, and what a lovely morning it is."

The clear spring sunshine was warm but in the shade, a breeze blew reminders of the winter and Alvar was glad of his cloak. He looked down at Káta and dropped an arm around her shoulders. "You are shaking. Is it merely from the cold? You must know that you have naught to fear?"

She lifted her chin. "Do not worry about me. I will sit with Wulfgar's Mildrith while you are about your business." She squeezed his hand.

He gazed into her eyes. "Lady, I am ever filled with wonder, not only at your loveliness but at your strength." He lifted her fingers to his lips and held them there as she began to walk away, so that her arm was outstretched before he released her. He called after her.

"Have I not truly learned now how to woo a lady?"

She did not turn, but put out a hand behind her, waving it to and fro.

"Is that all? You think I have come so far and no more?"

This time she turned and smiled. She hailed Mildrith,

linked arms with her, and they walked away. He tucked his thumbs into his belt and whistled as he made his way to the row of seats nearest the dais.

The tables for the nobles were laid with linen tablecloths held down only by the weight of the gold plates and cups. The ground was strewn with fresh cut flowers, banners danced in the breeze, and under the shade of an ash tree the harper plucked his strings while the pipers blew and children ran about at their feet.

Alvar turned to greet Wulfgar as he fell into step beside him. "Is it not a great day?"

A giggling child ran from behind the tree and Wulfgar hop-skipped to avoid her. "It will be for you, my lord. Other men might not like it."

"What, do you think Lord Brandon will not wish me well?"

Wulfgar made a play of scratching his chin. "Hmm, let me think…"

Alvar knew the answer. He was about to be called forth, recognised as Æthelred's foremost advisor, and handed control of a long-disputed area in Buckinghamshire. If he were Brandon, he would be peeved, to say the least. He said, "I should not wallow in it, for pride is a sin. But to have a real, legal hold now over Buckinghamshire… Good God, man, you are louder than those beams they are hammering. What are you laughing at?"

"I cannot believe it; can you think of nothing else that makes this day so sweet? Is that not your lady, come to watch you being named most doughty earl of Æthelred's kingship? She must think a lot of you to ride all this way. I have never seen her in Wessex before."

"Christ. I had not thought." On the very day he had met her, so many years ago, he had been struck by her lack of affection, her reluctance to preen like the ladies of the court. Alvar stood still. Wasn't that why he had always loved her? She had stayed away and she had remained free of the taint of politics, she had never learned to hate, or to dissemble. She had changed, yes, but only to become a stronger version of herself, capable, stoic, compassionate, sensible. Selfless.

Wulfgar turned round and walked back three paces. "My lord, you are grinning as though your wits have flown away."

"She has come to be with me." And for no other reason.

Wulfgar laid a hand on his arm. "Yes, lord, she is your lady. Come now; stir yourself. Right now you look less like a leading earl than an addle-brained child."

They took their seats before the dais and Alvar said, "And the king looks as if the Devil himself is about to ride in."

The young king was seated on the king-stool. He was still dressed in his full-length coronation robe. His hand was at his temple, and he twisted a tiny piece of hair round and round his fingers. His mother the queen sat beside him, wearing a gown of deep red silk. Today her hair was contained within its headdress and her smile was serene. The royal couple was flanked by the two archbishops. One smiled, one did not.

A thegn stood behind King Æthelred and beckoned Alvar to come forward. Wulfgar touched him on the back and Alvar stood up, stepped nearer the dais and sank down on one knee, head bowed.

When the murmurs subsided, Æthelred cleared his throat. "Lord Alvar, you come…" He coughed. "My lord you come before… Before…" The boy looked across at his mother.

She rested a hand on her son's shoulder and said, "My lord, you come to stand before us that we might give to you a gift of land, the first of our kingship, for we would show you, and all who are here this day, that we owe you a great deal." Alfreda paused and looked at her son, but Æthelred stared straight ahead so she continued. "We know you to be a stalwart lord to your folk. We know you to be a true man to your king. We know you to be a wise teacher to the king.

We would have it that all men here this day know of these things, and know that they are the truth."

Alfreda nodded to the scribe, who read out the boundaries of the gift of land at Olney in Buckinghamshire. Alvar remained on one knee, but looked up and held out his hands.

The young king handed him a twig. "I give you this token from the aforesaid land, that all may see your ownership of it."

Alvar smiled, hoping to soothe the boy's nerves, but Æthelred clamped his mouth shut and his bottom lip trembled.

Alvar stood up and walked back to his seat. He looked at Brandon and opened his mouth to speak, but pushed out the air with a half-sigh, half-smile. He put his tongue to his lower lip and sat down. Brock would have been proud, not only that his little brother had been so honoured, but that he had let go of an opportunity to goad Brandon. He sat back to watch the rest of the gift-giving.

But Dunstan stood up and cleared his throat.

Alvar said, "I do not have the strength for one of his sermons. I will wander about before I fill my belly."

He stood up and walked over to the feasting tables. He hailed a tall man standing by the roasting-spits. "Thored, it is good to see you. I was sorry beyond belief to hear of your father's death. Earl Beorn was a good man and I loved him well."

"It was hard for him to bear being sent from these shores, to be away from all those whom he loved. I think he welcomed the illness when it came. He spoke highly of you, my lord, you above all others. He said it was you to whom he owed his life."

Alvar clapped the younger man on the back. "It is good to see you here, and all the sins of the fathers forgotten. Edward's men are here alongside Æthelred's, and old wounds are healed. It is a good beginning for a kingship."

Thored nodded and turned away to take his seat. Edwin

of Kent and a companion came from the seating area.

Alvar said, "I see you are still lame. The leg is not healing well?" Not all things were forgotten, for there were many reminders of the tragedy at Calne.

Edwin shook his head. "The stiffness will not go. But I can ride a horse, so there is hope yet. And I have learned to keep away from stairs." He nodded to the young man beside him and grabbed his elbow to bring him forward. "You know Ethelmær?"

Alvar squinted. "You look as if I know you…" He dredged his memory until the name made sense to him. This was the nephew of the Fairchild's young bride. God, how many years had it been since their annulment was engineered to allow Edgar to strengthen his claim to the throne? "God's bones; seeing you here as a man grown, it makes me think of all the years that have gone by since the Fairchild's time."

A gentle touch on his shoulder made him turn. Alfreda was standing behind him.

He took a step back, turned fully, and bowed low before her. "My lady. It is a great day for us all."

She inclined her head. "It is. Although I must say I do feel every one of my years when I think that I have been queen in the lifetime of three kings now."

"Lady, you are as young to me as on the day we first met."

"You are a liar, but I thank you for your kind words." Her smile faded. "In truth, I have to thank you for so many kindnesses. What I owe you goes beyond reckoning."

He held a finger to her lips. "Lady, whatever I have done for you, I did with gladness and always willingly."

She placed a hand on her mouth and traced the path his finger had taken. She smiled and laid her hand on his forearm. "We would have made a good match, you and I, do you not think?"

Everyone had expected that they would eventually wed. He wondered whether if, at times, he had assumed the same thing. He might even have believed that he was in love with her, except that he had never in fact stopped to ponder it. Yes, she was beautiful, but the more her beauty became her salvation, the more something withered within. Besides, his heart had always belonged to Káta, even before he was aware of it. He had always found it easy to flirt, but then it was easy enough to tell a beautiful woman the truth, to compliment her. It was with Káta that he was so tongue-tied, because it mattered.

Alfreda was waiting for an answer. He raised an eyebrow. "My lady, I could never have hoped to reach so high. And the witan would never have said yes to such a match."

It was a lie. He had held the country in his hands, there had been no-one left to stop him had he chosen to take the queen.

But this beautiful, damaged woman nodded, acknowledging defeat and retaining the one thing to which she had clung tenaciously; her dignity. "It is true," she said. "You might have become too strong as husband to the queen." She raised her chin, gave a little shake of her head and fixed her face in a smile. "Yet look at you now; lord of all Mercia and beyond, leading earl of the witan, nearest to the king's ear and, I believe, the richest among us. What is left for you now?"

Alvar looked over her shoulder. "The one thing that in all that time was forbidden to me," he said.

Káta was sitting at the table with Mildrith and Wulfgar, and had kept a space open for him to join them.

Alfreda followed his gaze. A fleeting expression threatened to betray her thoughts before she composed her features into an unfathomable mask. "Ah, I see."

He rushed to fill the silence for her. "And there is something you must do, too."

Once again, a king was dead before reaching the age of twenty, and now his brother was the new boy-king. When folk read the chronicles many years from now they would think the scribes had mistakenly written it twice. But this was not the same story. Edgar had leaned on him so heavily that Alvar had been caught off-balance when relieved of the pressure, but Æthelred would not call on him in the same way. Alvar looked around and saw many younger men, men who might one day do for the king what he had once done for Edgar. But in the meantime, if ever there was a role for Alfreda, it was to be the guiding hand behind the throne. Her most redeeming trait was that she had always been a fierce and loving mother. He took her hands and said, "Sons might be born, but you will always be the mother of the king. No-one can take that from you."

She raised her chin, took a deep breath and put the smile back on. "Indeed. And will you stay to help us?"

It had been his lifelong role to sweep up the mess which others had left behind, and he had sacrificed an important thing along the way. God grant him enough years to make up for all the time lost and wasted. Æthelred was crowned; Alvar had done his work.

"No, my lady. I am going home."

Chapter Twenty One AD983

Gloucestershire

With their backs to the little wooden church, they crossed the stream at the ford and made their way towards the house. Káta ran her hands through the rosebay willow herb at the edge of the path. "The fireweed has blossomed early this summer."

Gytha grunted and moved her basket to the other arm.

"Let us go home through the orchard."

"Why, Lady?"

"I like it there. It is pretty."

Gytha shook her head. "It is all as one to me. But if you wish to go, then we go."

Káta said, "We did not have groves like this at Ashleigh. Here I can sit and watch the wryneck and the owl looking out from the pear blossom."

Gytha pointed up at the trees, where the fruits hung, heavily plump. "The blossom has all gone, Lady, both from the pear and the apple. Next you are going to tell me that you like the apple-wine they make here, even though I know you find it bitter. Or instead of finding silly reasons not to go back to the house, you could simply go and ask him if it is true." She rested her basket on an upturned cart.

Káta's cheeks grew warm. "You know me so well, dear friend. Yes, I can put it off no longer but must go and ask him."

Gytha nodded towards the house. "No need. Here

comes the lord now. I will go and find work; I have seen that look in his eyes before." Gytha shuffled away.

Alvar strode into the orchard and put his arms round Káta's waist. He lifted her off her feet and held her just high enough to kiss her mouth, while her feet dangled above the ground.

When he put her down she said, "It is true, then?"

He had the grace to look shame-faced.

"But why must it be you?"

"Hywel has asked for my help. Not for the help of the English, but for me. We have fought together before, as you know."

"That was to get his uncle out of Gwynedd and you helped him to get back his kingdom. But this is elsewhere in Wales and it has naught to do with you. This Deh… Deheu…"

"Deheubarth. It is in the lands of Einion ab Owain."

"Whoever he might be. This is not about kingship, but yet another fight over land."

"Yes," he said with ingenuousness, "All fights are about land ownership. But we cannot afford to lose Hywel as a friend. Æthelred is growing, but is still tied to his mother's skirts. I must look to our borders, keep them strong, make sure that no man thinks our land weak, and tries to take it for himself."

She sat back on the edge of the cart and he knelt on the grass before her.

"Besides, you would not want me growing fat like Brock did."

She poked his hard stomach. "There is no danger of that. Why can you not go hunting, if you are restless? I would rather have you wrestling a boar than a horde of Welshmen."

"I have sent word that I will go. You would not want me to withdraw my promise and show my word to be worthless."

He was staring up at her with those light-grey eyes that

were so hard to resist. No wonder his mother had indulged him. At this moment he looked like a child pleading for a new wooden sword.

"What I want is to have you here, unharmed, alive." She looked up, but could not see or hear any of the birds that she normally found in the orchard.

"Hywel and I have a long-standing friendship. I owe it to him." He sat back and rested his hands on his thighs. "You have never worried so before."

"You have never been so old before."

He laughed. "I am not yet fifty."

"You are nearer to it than forty. As for me, I am a grandmother now and that makes me feel old even if you do not."

He jumped up and his knees cracked. "Ride with me, then."

"Are you mad?"

He picked her up again, twirled her round, and planted a kiss on her forehead. "Come to Ashleigh. You can see Siferth, Eadyth and the bairn, and bide there until I come back."

He set her down on the ground, but she clung to him and rested her head against his chest. "I would look a forsaken old woman indeed, would I not, standing each day atop Elfshill watching for you?" She locked her fingers behind his neck and tilted her head back to look up at him. "I am your woman now, and I will bide here until you come home. There would be little for me to do in another woman's house and I need to be busy whilst you are away. And mind you come back whole, for I have told you before that I am not going to keep sewing you back together like so many bits of ripped cloth."

He kissed her again, this time on the mouth. "I will come back, and you will not have to heal me. Upon my oath."

She rewarded him with a small laugh that was meant to sound jolly but came out shrill. "I was once so in awe of a great earl that he only had to tell me things for me to believe them to be true."

He smiled, his head to one side, so keen to go off that she could only think of a puppy going on its first hunt.

She stamped her foot and released him. "Oh, it is in your blood. Go and gird yourself if you must, even though your knees crack and I see you holding your stiff back."

He ran off towards the house and called for his man, Steapa, to make the carts ready.

She laughed and called after him. "Slow down, or you will wear yourself out ere you get anywhere near Wales."

He turned and ran backwards for a few paces. "I have strength and more to spare. I will show you tonight in bed; you have my word on that."

"May God make it so." She put her hand up, waved until he was out of sight, and brought it down to clasp the other hand as she prayed that her great earl still had the power to make all his other promises come true.

"Where in merry hell is it? I told Steapa to shine it for me; I might as well spit in the wind."

Káta passed Steward Heanric on the stairs and smiled. "Is he making your life harder? I will try to calm him."

"Bless you, my lady." Heanric paused. "I have grown used to his outbursts over the years. Besides, they have been few and far between, and went away the day you came to live here. Indeed, I have not seen him like this for many years. Not since King Edgar died."

She patted him on the arm. "When things rip, there is always a loud noise." Alvar was torn and it was making him testy, the pull of his friend's call vying with the desire to stay at home with her. And in response, she struggled with both elation at the strength of his love for her and the heartbreak caused by his leaving.

She tidied her emotions away into the very back of her mind and marched into the bedchamber. "My lord, what use will it be to shout so loudly that you can be heard in Rome? What is it that have you lost, you silly old man?"

Alvar continued to throw clothing out of a chest and did not look up. "My helm. The one the Fairchild gave me when he made me earl. Steapa has taken it and not put it back. I would get more work out of a gnat. He is such a slack…"

"Oh be still. Look what you have done."

Alvar stood up and looked around the room. "What?"

Jewelled plate and chalices were still rolling along the floor, upended from the long table at the end of the room. Tunics and breeches, tipped out of clothing chests, had formed into crumpled heaps and the furs and blankets from the bed lay in a pile on the floor.

Káta bent down to pick up the clothes. "The helm is still with the smith, having the knock beaten out. They should do that with your head."

She sat down on the edge of the bed and folded each tunic and shirt, smoothing out the creases with her palms with increasing force.

"What is it, my love? You are cross and I am sorry I made a mess, but that is not why you are upset." He sat down on the bed beside her and tilted her chin with his fingers. "What is it?"

She stood up and went to the table. Picking up a cup, she twirled it in her fingers. "It is naught. Such a little thing. I spoke of being your woman…"

He leaped up and came to stand beside her. "But not 'wife'. That is it, is it not?" He took her hand and pulled. "Come, sit. Come on."

She followed him back to the bed. "Really, it is naught."

He sat her down and put his arm around her shoulders. "No, forgive me, for I should have said all this a long time ago. And it is I who am in the wrong."

She opened her mouth but he put up his hand.

"No, hear me out. There is a ghost between us, my love. Not an unwelcome one, but he is here. Once, I thought myself not worthy of your love…"

She began to demur.

"No, I know now that it is untrue, for I think I earned the right to love you by giving half my lifetime for it. But you were once wed to a thegn of mine who was unwavering in his loyalty. If I were to wed his widow, would it not look as if I were glad of his death?"

She turned and laid her head against his chest. "Oh, my love, I will not tell you that I never loved the man, for I did, deeply. But I have loved you for so long and I will not throw away any more time. I am glad to have you near; I need no more."

"When you came to live here, in my house, I should have…"

She put her hand up to his lips. "When I came to live here I gave my life to you. I did not look back on my old house. How could I ever go forward if I looked back? Here, with you, I have all that I…"

He sat forward, clapped his hands and lifted her face to look at him. "We could become handfasted. As the Danes do."

"To wed, but not in a church? I like that thought."

She put a hand out to touch his greying hair, and ran her palm along his jaw line.

He turned his face and kissed her fingers. He looked behind him at the expanse of comfortable bed. "Are you busy this morning?"

She tapped his cheek. "Do you think of naught else?" She turned. The clouds had moved away from the sun and by the window a misshapen form was glinting on the floor. "Oh, the glass is broken." She prodded him and went to kneel down to pick up the broken pieces.

"I do not know why you are cross. I can get another one made."

She sat back on her heels. "This Gloucester glass is so pretty; I had never seen it before I came here." She reached out to the largest shard and her fingers shook. It was not a time for things to be broken. All was mended and should stay like that. She breathed in, stood up, and turned to wag a finger at him. "Swear to me. Swear that you will get me another." She pulled her face into a smile that her mother would have been proud of. "And then I will let you go off to your silly fight."

He grinned and looked again at the bed. "Is that all? Well, if you are selling things cheaply this day…"

Glastonbury

Wulfgar's laughter was subjugating his breathing and it was hard to catch every word he said. "One of them had been having a shit… Sorry my lady, but his arse was still hanging out. They all looked so startled, sweating on their lips and brows. They made it so easy for us that all we had to do was stroll in."

Káta moved to her left and he stopped to wipe his eyes.

"Have I told you that bit already? I will speak on, then. They were all standing there and could not get to their spears in time. We had come upon them so softly and silently that my lord said it was like taking bread from a bairn. Then their leader came forward and spoke in Welsh and my lord answered, first in Welsh, and then in English. He looked him right in the eye and said, 'I say again that you are a dull-wit, but I can forgive you for that. Where you have gone wrong is in being a Welsh dull-wit, for there is no cure for that.' We were meant to be taking their weapons from them, but all we could do was stand and laugh."

Káta laughed too. "What must they have thought? To be met by an Englishman wilder than they are, who can speak their tongue and curse them in their own words."

"He teased them then, telling them what he was going to do with them. And they believed him."

She thought of her lovely new glass palm-cup, brought by the foundry man from Gloucester only yesterday. "So they should, for every one of my lord's oaths has been fulfilled. They must have heard this and known it to be true."

"In truth, lady, I do not think they knew what to make of our lord. Is that right, never left an oath unfulfilled? I had not ever thought of it."

"Oh yes. Many foul curses, none of which, blessedly, have come true; but always kept his word. After that first time, when he left the Fairchild, he never broke another oath. Even before he left to fight this Welshman Einion, he swore to me that I would not have to sew him back together when he came home." The last word caught in her throat.

Wulfgar held out his arms.

She fell against him, her head on his chest.

"Lady, I know I have told you many times, but you must believe that he willed himself to keep alive; that he always hoped to get back."

She tried to speak, but the words would not come and she shook her head. His arms, wrapped around her, were strong and she drew comfort from his warmth. Yes, Alvar would have tried to get home. He had a mightier will than any man living and no matter how badly hurt, he would have forgotten that he was but a man and he would have tried to drag his tail back to England. She clenched her fists and beat them without power on Wulfgar's chest. This one time, may she not be wroth? No, not even now. Others would be more bereft than she, for she had learned long ago how to love him and yet be without him. She looked up as Wulfgar's tear dropped down and wet her cheek. She said, "Thank you for bringing him home to me."

The other mourners had moved away from the graveside to allow Alvar's widow to grieve alone for a while, but Wulfgar refused to leave her side for a moment. She leaned against him, unsure if her legs had the strength to take her away from her lord this one last time. She stared down at the mound of new earth, so close to the grave of his brother Brock, and his king, Edgar.

Brandon was the first to return to pay respects to her. He said, "I have been at my father's grave, for he too was laid to rest here."

"Then my lord lies among the great and the good." She looked back down.

"I could never hope to be as great an earl as he." Brandon said.

He moved off towards the abbey church and she smiled. Had he been speaking of his father, or Alvar? She looked down. "Did you hear his words my love? I wish you could tell me what you think of them. Oh love, I have so much to say, and no-one to tell."

Káta smelled the calming fragrance of lavender. She looked up, and Alfreda stepped forward to take her hand.

The queen said, "We have not met."

Káta bobbed her head in acknowledgement of the other woman's rank. She said, "No, but you know my son, Siferth."

Alfreda's eyes widened as if she had been startled, and then her brow creased into a frown. Finally she nodded, and in a small trembling voice she said, "I did not know you were his mother."

Tears spilled down the queen's cheeks but Káta heard self-pity more than sorrow in her words. Alfreda said, "If I had been more humble, if I had stayed more, well, more like you, perhaps I would not have lost him. Those of us who flew too near the king had all our feathers torn. But you stayed away; you were unscathed."

The dagger that had been twisting in Káta's heart since they brought Alvar's body home had made such a bloody mess she wondered how anyone could look at her and not see it. Was she still so good at making the best of things? There were so many truths she could tell the queen, but decided against all bar one. "We are not so different, you and I. We have buried two husbands each and have done little to earn our suffering."

Alfreda nodded. "We watch them fight and die and we are helpless. I tried to play the game and I lost. It was you who won. I could have learned much from you, if I had only known what he truly craved." She lifted her chin and turned to walk slowly away, sending another waft of lavender into the air behind her.

Káta stared after her. "She wears the same blossom-water as I do."

"Yes, my lady."

"He never said." She looked at Wulfgar. "Being with her made him think of me."

She started to count all the nights she had lain awake, kept from sleep by jealousy. She shook her head and said, "No, that way lies madness."

Wulfgar said, "From the way the queen fights hard to put one foot ahead of the other, I would say she mourns nearly as strongly as you do, my lady."

"I would say that we all feel the loss." Bishop Athelwold's voice was feeble with age. He said, "I never thought to outlive him." He laid a hand on Káta's shoulder and looked down. "We who lived through Edgar's kingship knew that he was guided by God. We thought those wondrous days would go on for ever. We were wrong."

Káta lifted a hand to comfort him, but closed her fingers in the air and put her hand back by her side.

Athelwold said, "Folk have asked me if the new king will ever be as mighty as his father. I think that kings are only as strong as the men who surround them." He sniffed. "Sometimes it is but one man who makes the difference." He looked down at the grave. "We are all the worse for his death."

Káta dared to touch his arm. "Will you bide here a while longer, my lord Bishop? I fear how it will be when folk stop speaking of him, for then truly it will be as if he is no longer here."

Athelwold wiped a tear from his eye. "Folk will not stop

speaking of him, for he was a great man who was true to all whom he loved."

She laughed and he flinched. "Forgive me, Bishop. They will stop, for is it not the Church who writes the histories? But you are right; he was steadfast like no other. His whole life was spent in duty to those whom he thought he owed it and in the end, he even gave his life in the same pursuit. How bittersweet that he died whilst helping a Welshman, of all folk. I am sorry that I startled you, but I know that Alvar would have laughed louder than I at that thought." Her laughter turned to sobs though the sound barely changed. Her legs felt as if the bones had melted and she leaned back against Wulfgar.

Bishop Athelwold said, "You must believe that he lives on in heaven, my child."

She wiped her tears with the back of her hand, the same action that Siferth used when he was little. "I only hope that in heaven he will find a warm hearth and hall, strong mead and stronger friendships."

The bishop lowered his voice. "You do not fear for his soul, child? That God would not… Is this why you now shiver and shake?"

She lifted her chin. "No, my lord. Winter was always hard without him, but now I do feel the cold all the more. He was always too busy to let the years get in his way and moved about as if he were still a young man. It is too calm now without him. I wish the wind would blow hard and bring with it snow and rain, for in this stillness I fear I will never be warm again."

"You had but a short time together."

"No, my lord. We loved for a lifetime, and we were together long enough to tell each other so. We shared many tiny moments which we strung together over the years to make a life that we could both remember." She clutched Wulfgar's arm. "I cannot step away. Only twice have I turned my back on him. Once when I blushed at his nakedness in the river and once when he thought he had done wrong by kissing me. How do I turn away now?"

She looked up at the trees. The smallest of breezes set the leaves trembling. She gathered her cloak about her and nodded. "It is time to go." The shiver whispered through the browning foliage and one leaf broke free. Spiralling as it fell, it landed feather-light on the ground, and all was still.

~ * ~

Afterword/Author's Notes

Alfreda remained the power behind the throne. Right up until her death, she continued to exert a strong influence on her son, and is cited as being the woman who brought up her grandson. She has often been portrayed as the wicked stepmother who arranged the murder of King Edward the Martyr. Many historians now believe that the deed was carried out by a group of Æthelred's young thegns. It seemed possible to me that one of those thegns was a young man like Siferth.

King Æthelred grew up to earn his epithet, "Unræd" (Unready). The bad counsel to which that title refers is a reflection of the quality of the earls who came after Alvar and his contemporaries, and Æthelred's reign proved the truth that kings are only as good as the men who surround them. Brandon had five adult sons, but none succeeded him in East Anglia. Younger men rose through the witan, gave a weak ruler bad advice, and within twenty years of Alvar's death, the king was in exile.

This story is based on historical fact. All of the main characters, apart from Helmstan and Siferth, Wulfgar, and the rest of Alvar's thegns, existed, although I have changed some of their names because many of the original Anglo-Saxon names are hard to read, and harder to pronounce. I've adapted them so that they don't make the gaze 'stick' on the page too much. But for those who know about this period and/or long for authenticity, here is a list of the characters with their original names in brackets:

Alvar (Ælfhere)
Káta (Eadflæd)
Brock (Ælfheah)

Alswytha/Swytha (Ælfswith)
Bridd – meaning 'fledgling' (Ælfweard)
Abbot Athelwold (Æthelwold)
Elwood of Ramsey (Æthelwold)
Brandon (Æthelwine)
Thetford (Ælfwold)
Alfreda (Ælfthryth)
Edelman 'Greybeard' (Æthelmund)

I also gave Earl Oslac the nickname of 'Beorn' to make the passages where he and Oswald appear together easier on the eye, and I simplified the spelling of Wulfthryth to Wulfreda. Oslac was known as an earl, and so again, for simplification, and consistency, I have referred to all the leading nobles as earls, rather than ealdormen, and their territories as earldoms instead of ealdordoms. This was a period of transition and Danish-style titles were being adopted, but only the Northumbrians are addressed as 'Earl', rather than 'Lord'. I have used the title of prince to describe heirs to the throne. The word was not used by the Anglo-Saxons, but again, it is included here for ease. I chose not to name some characters: the bishop of Winchester who died on his way to Rome was called Ælfsige, and the Red Lord whose lands were so coveted, was Athelstan Rota (the Red). Two others who remain unnamed are Edwy Fairchild's wife and her mother – Ælfgifu and Æthelgifu!

The successor to Mercia, Ælfric Cild, was in all likelihood, married to Alvar's sister, Æthelflæd. I have not included these two in my tale for two reasons: firstly, that almost nothing is known of them before 983 and secondly, they are yet two more characters whose names begin with the Old English diphthong Æ known as 'Æsc'.

I should also add that both Alvar and Brandon were members of families with four sons, almost all beginning with Æsc.

The Mercians: Ælfhere (Alvar) and Ælfheah (Brock) also had brothers named Eadric and Ælfwine. Tantalisingly, their father was Ealhhelm, an unusual name, and the same OE name as the character Alhelm of Shrewsbury, whom readers of To Be A Queen will remember as being an ealdorman of Mercia. Was Alhelm Alvar's father? Try as I might, I cannot quite make the dates fit, and better historians than I have tried. There has also been some suggestion that Alvar and Brock were somehow related to the royal family, but this link is difficult to identify, and so for ease I decided not to include it as a detail. (It is true that Brock adopted the bishop of Winchester's son, and that he was also godfather to Æthelred.) They had at least one sister, mentioned above.

The East Anglians: Those readers of To Be A Queen will also recall the character I called Frith. He was the father of the man known as the Half-king, who makes a brief appearance in 'Queen' as a baby named Athelstan. He had four sons, not three: along with Æthelwold (Elwood) Æthelwine (Brandon) and Ælfwold (Thetford) there was another son, Æthelsige. His career, despite being illustrious, did not have an impact on my story and so, again for ease, I omitted him.

The central love story in this book grew from a footnote in an academic paper written by Ann Williams. Alvar left no children but his successor in Mercia was castigated some years after Alvar's death for depriving a widow of her lands at Wormleighton, Warwickshire. These lands had at one time belonged to Alvar; the widow was a lady named Eadflæd. This is the only known reference to Eadflæd, and I wove their love story around the distinct possibility that she was Alvar's widow, and invented a reason why they might not have had any children together. I also changed her name, because Eadflæd is a particularly difficult name to pronounce.

Most of the rest of my story is true and I have only twice knowingly played with the chronology: Edwy Fairchild succeeded in 955, but I delayed his coronation to coincide with Alvar's investiture the following year. It was not uncommon for coronations to occur some lengthy time after succession. It seems likely that Æthelmund (Edelman

'Greybeard') of Cheshire died in 965, but it suited my story to have him die in the previous year.

There is some doubt as to the order of events following Edward's murder. I chose to have Alvar rebury Edward's body before Æthelred's coronation, but it might well have happened the other way round; no-one is absolutely sure. I strongly believe that Edgar would have been crowned long before 973, even though the chroniclers do not mention such an event, and it seems to make sense that his first coronation would have been a muted affair. No reason is given anywhere in the sources for the banishment of Earl Oslac (Beorn). His Bernician counterpart, whose son was taken hostage by Kenneth, was called Eadulf Evilcild, but I simplified his name and called him Wulf. Evidence points to Oslac's having been an ally of Alvar and Æthelred and there is no reason why his loathing for Oswald would not have matched Alvar's. There was indeed a fire in London around the time of Elwood's death, but I'm afraid I put the two events together. A later medieval story accused Edgar of having murdered Elwood, but has been discredited. The circumstances of Elwood's and the Fairchild's death described here are my own suggestions of what could have happened – their timings were, at the least, convenient for those who benefited from them.

All the domestic events in the book are well documented. Edgar's was a strong and stable kingship; he built up a powerful navy, reformed the coinage, and was an astute diplomat. Under his rule, the machinery of local and central government turned smoothly and efficiently. He was always at pains to recognise the Danelaw and his fourth law code did indeed go out with an instruction to Alvar, Æthelwine (Brandon) and Oslac (Beorn) to let its contents be known throughout the land. He was recorded as having been an unusually short man, and Kenneth really did taunt him about his diminutive stature. For details of Edgar's spectacular coronation at Bath and the submission of the kings at Chester, the collapse at Calne (where Dunstan "alone remained standing on a beam") and the murder at Corfe, one need look no further than the pages of the Anglo-Saxon Chronicle. The bedroom antics of both Edwy Fairchild and Edgar are also well documented. There is some confusion and debate over the exact number and status of Edgar's wives and women; for simplicity, I have gone with the theory expounded by Ann Williams that he only had two, rather than three, 'wives'. The land disputes mentioned in the chapters 976-977 are all based on real cases and all the land charters mentioned in the witan scenes are quoted from the original documents. The oaths sworn at the hundred courts and during the hold-oath ceremony are authentic and as close to the vernacular as I could get without losing the meaning. Alfreda's testimony regarding the conditions of the gift of land at Taunton, mentioned in the meeting at Calne, is a rare, early example of a letter written by a queen. The description of the town layout of Winchester is taken from archaeological evidence and it is documented that Dunstan wrote the oath which Edgar swore at Bath.

I have charted Alvar's rise to power as faithfully as I can, relying on the few known facts. He was indeed a benefactor of Glastonbury and it is true that he only attacked Oswald's monasteries. It is frustrating that Alvar's will is not extant and that we do not know how he died. He was, however, campaigning in Wales in the year of his death, so again I have drawn my own conclusions. I prefer to think that such an energetic man would not have been withered by old age, but stopped only by a spear or arrow.

Byrhtferth of Ramsey, writing his near-contemporary Life of Oswald, called Alvar "The blast of the mad wind from the western territories," but when referring to his role in the reburial of Edward the Martyr, he called him, "The glorious ealdorman." I think that he was both these things.

Lightning Source UK Ltd.
Milton Keynes UK
UKHW011811191119
353829UK00002B/732/P